Ronald Knox and The Murder Room

》》》 This title is part of The Murder Room, our series dedicated to making available out-of-print or hard-to-find titles by classic crime writers.

Crime fiction has always held up a mirror to society. The Victorians were fascinated by sensational murder and the emerging science of detection; now we are obsessed with the forensic detail of violent death. And no other genre has so captivated and enthralled readers.

Vast troves of classic crime writing have for a long time been unavailable to all but the most dedicated frequenters of second-hand bookshops. The advent of digital publishing means that we are now able to bring you the backlists of a huge range of titles by classic and contemporary crime writers, some of which have been out of print for decades.

From the genteel amateur private eyes of the Golden Age and the femmes fatales of pulp fiction, to the morally ambiguous hard-boiled detectives of mid twentieth-century America and their descendants who walk our twenty-first century streets, The Murder Room has it all. **》》》**

The Murder Room
Where Criminal Minds Meet

themurderroom.com

Ronald Arbuthnott Knox (1888–1957)

It was Ronald Knox, who, as a pioneer of Golden Age detective fiction, codified the rules of the genre in his 'Ten Commandments of Detection', which stipulated, among other rules, that 'No Chinaman must figure in the story', and 'Not more than one secret room or passage is allowable'. He was a Sherlock Holmes aficionado, writing a satirical essay that was read by Arthur Conan Doyle himself, and is credited with creating the notion of 'Sherlockian studies', which treats Sherlock Holmes as a real-life character. Educated at Eton and Oxford, Knox was ordained as priest in the Church of England but later entered the Roman Catholic Church. He completed the first Roman Catholic translation of the Bible into English for more than 350 years, and wrote detective stories in order to supplement the modest stipend of his Oxford Chaplaincy.

The Viaduct Murder
The Three Taps
The Footsteps at the Lock
The Body in the Silo
Still Dead
Double Cross Purposes

Double Cross Purposes

Ronald Knox

An Orion book

Copyright © Lady Magdalen Asquith 1937

The right of Ronald Knox to be identified as the author of this work
has been asserted in accordance with the Copyright, Designs and
Patents Act 1988.

This edition published by
The Orion Publishing Group Ltd
Orion House
5 Upper St Martin's Lane
London WC2H 9EA

An Hachette UK company
A CIP catalogue record for this book is available from the British Library

ISBN 978 1 4719 0047 1

www.orionbooks.co.uk

Printed and bound by CPI Group (UK) Ltd, Croydon, CR0 4YY

Note to Readers

In keeping with the spirit of 'fair play' apparent in his Decalogue, or Ten Commandments of Detective Fiction, the author includes a series of footnotes towards the end of this book – as the solution to the mystery unfolds – that point the reader back to a breadcrumb trail of clues.

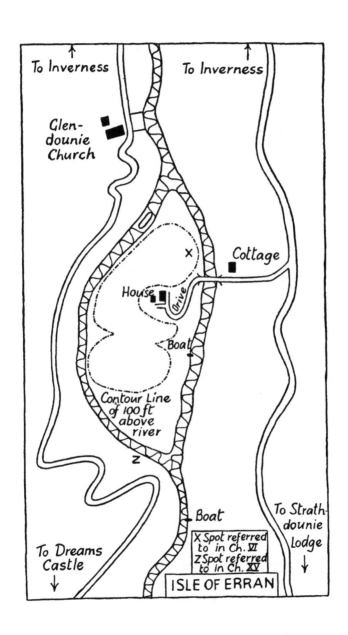

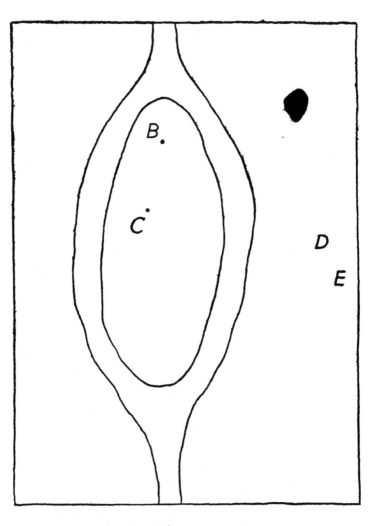

HENDERSON'S PHOTOGRAPH
OF THE CHART.

CONTENTS

CHAPTER I: THE CHURCHYARD OF GLENDOUNIE

" THAT'S THE ISLAND."

It seemed an eternity since they had left the main road. Main roads, in whatever part of the world you follow them, are much of a muchness, and carry with them at least the illusion of speed. Your landmarks are far apart – hills, rivers, towns, signposts, petrol stations, and the beastlier kind of hotels. The scenery is for your subconsciousness ; all that immediately concerns you is the white ribbon of the road itself, and the milestones clicking past. But these lesser tracks, in the Highlands of Scotland especially, were too full of incident, for all their loneliness, to lull you with the opiate of monotony. Now you would be perched over the steep side of a loch, now buried in a gloom of trees, now diving under unexpected railway-bridges ; droves of sheep interfered with you, and droves of school-children, hardly less inextricable, and still more inex-plicable in this lonely country-side. There seemed to be a kirk for every mile, a school for every three miles ; nor did the estate of any landed gentleman let you off without at least three inconspicuous lodges, at each of which a trim notice warned you to make allowances for the owner's habit of sudden egress. The low stone wall which seemed, on either side, to be their unremitting companion gave them glimpses, now of standing crops achieving a late maturity, now of sheep browsing on

1

heathery braes, now of fir-copses unprotected against marauding picnickers, now of stagnant estuaries. The last ten miles had felt like a full half of their journey.

At last it was becoming clear that they were leaving the low ground. Nature does not waste on the High-lands the lush fertility of our English hedgerows ; it would be out of keeping (she seems to feel) with the standards of a more frugal race. But there had been bluebells and scabious by the roadside, yellow clusters of stinking willie in the fields, and fountain-like glimpses of foxgloves by the fallen logs in the woodland. Now, even these became rarer : heather and bog-myrtle overflowed into the ditches ; gorse and broom took the place of brambles. They were coasting along the high-water-mark of that brave flood of cultivation which washes up so far, but no further, on the hill-side ; only the rare crofts, with their defiant patches of head-long tillage, interrupted its native barrenness ; and the woods grew thicker, their gloom more profound, to show that they were cultivated not for amenity or for sport, but as marketable timber. Sudden bridges, with crazy parapets, spanned innumerable burns, and little freshets of hill-water spattered down, from their right, on to the roadway. The air, that had never been stagnant with the summer warmth, grew keener as they approached the heights.

Why there should have been a kirk in that lonely corner of civilisation, it taxed the wit of the Southerner to imagine. Only four or five crofts were in sight, widely scattered ; at least two of these, by the law of averages, must contain inmates who disapproved, for obscure reasons, of the particular doctrines which it preached. Yet here it was, with its doors of glossy pitch-pine shut to the visitor, its glazed windows in an approach to the Gothic manner, its trim manse and glebe behind it. Older, apparently, than the road itself ; or why did the road run between church and churchyard ? The churchyard of Glendounie (for by that name the neglected hamlet is called) has perhaps the finest natural situation of any burial-place in Christendom. Away from the road, it comes to an abrupt end at the top of a steep, steep cliff, that over-hangs the Dounie a hundred and fifty feet below. The road runs at a tangent to a sharp bend in the river's course, so that nothing has prepared the traveller for this revelation. And, just at the extreme edge of the curve, just where the place of graves overhangs it, the river descends by a steep fall, of no great height, yet famous as a haunt of beauty from the gnarled and hollowed rocks which surround it. As you stand on that brink, with the river before you laying bare the recesses of earth, with the incessant thunder of the falls in your ears, the tombs behind you take their place in the scheme of things, and the old text about the dead being caught up into the air seems, for once, more than a distant imagination.

Above the falls, about a quarter of a mile distant, the river flowed in two branches, separated by a wooded island that narrowed to a rocky point as it looked down-stream. The highest part of it, and the furthest that could now be seen, rose to some two hundred feet ; the slope towards the left was rapid, towards the right almost precipitous, the whole breadth being only some few hundred yards. How it came to be there, was a conjecture for the geologist ; the true course of the stream lay evidently to the left, coming round in a slight curve ; on the right it was almost straight, as if the bed of it were a gap that had parted in a huge land-slip, or as if the river, impatient of its *détour,* had found some natural fault and dug itself a canal through the living rock. You could see from the ripples that there were shallows both to left and right of the cape, where the river swirled over rock barriers and held up the heavy boats they use for fishing. From this angle, the island looked altogether deserted ; you could not see the one house there is on it, or the bridge across the further stream that connects it with the mainland. It lay in a cup formed by the steep cliffs which rose on either side, a hundred feet or more high, from the trench of Dounie to the heather and the hills.

" That's the island." The man who had spoken was a young man of thirty or so, healthy in complexion and handsome, if a trifle effeminate, in looks. He stood out on the hill-crest like a monument to the skill of the English tailor who had dressed him so exactly right for a holiday in Scotland. His companion, a man much nearer middle age, could boast rather of dogged and hard-bitten features ; the eyes were too small, and apt to register suspicion. As for his dress, it was much like the other's, but gave itself away by over-doing the thing at almost every point. The plus-fours were a little too baggy, the coat too obtrusively home-spun, the tweed just too violent. They stood together on the very edge of the platform, hard by where a monument, newly erected in hideous pink granite, recorded the decease, at the age of fifty-one, of Angus McAlister, deeply respected by all who knew him. (It is the ambition of the Scot to be respected in death, as it is the illusion of the Englishman that he is loved.)

" It's a tidy bit of an island," said this older man, " and I've seen some. But you said there's a bridge on to it ; where does that come in ? "

" Round the curve, to our left ; you can't see it from here. It used to be a crazy wooden affair, but now it's a sound piece of building in concrete, and the floods don't sweep it away any more. The house is about a quarter of the way up the hill ; just behind one of those big larches, so you can't see that either. It's a lonely sort of place still."

" That won't do any harm. You know, you seem to like all this publicity, newspaper men hanging round in the lounge of the hotel and kissing you good-bye at the station. If it affords you any pleasure, go ahead with it, but don't expect me to be matey with your journalist friends. And the less you ask them to stay week-ends up in these parts, the more I'll like it. When I'm doing a job, I like to stick hard at it, not having to pass the time of day with interviewers and tell 'em what my reactions are. Specially a job of this sort, where you're never certain that things'll work out according to schedule. No, the great lonely forests are good enough for me ; and thank God this is beginning to look more like it. What's that smoke yonder, though, to the right, see ? "

" You mean on this bank of the river ? Not on the island ? Yes, I see ; that'll be tinkers, I expect ; there's no house near. Dreams Castle's further on, where we're going now ; you can't see it yet."

" Nothing on the other side of the river – where the bridge is ? "

" Only just the gardener's place ; if you mean at the bridge itself. Beyond that, but about two miles beyond, is Strathdounie Lodge ; that'll be let for the shooting : fishing too probably. Strathdounie village is beyond that again, a mile or more, if I remember right. God, how this place seems asleep, compared with little old London ; I can't see a shack that wasn't here fifteen years ago."

" Fishing, you say ? I don't like that so much. How do they do it in these parts ; net the river, I suppose ? "

" Good God, no ; not this time of the year. All you'll get on this beat is a couple of rods, and just a fisherman to mind the boat. I don't say that you won't get them coming up and down a good bit ; but think what it would be like on an English river, with a great blasted angling club holding competitions all along the bank, Saturday afternoons."

" Still, it means a man can't go out to do a bit of gardening, as you might say, without having a boating party cruising past and taking a kindly interest in him. That's not my money. Tell you what it is, Lethaby, I wish to God you'd have done this thing on the quiet, instead of having us put it in all the newspapers. Seems to me they'll be running pleasure-cruises before we know where we are."

" Trouble is, Henderson, you haven't got a blameless conscience, like me. As for the boating facilities, look at that line of rapids across the end of the island, and tell me who's going to navigate one of these old fishing-tubs down it – let alone up it ? No, there'll be one beat above the island, and another below it ; and there's too much broken water about to make the fishing good round the island itself. All we'll have to do is to keep our eyes skinned if we're operating at either end. And that, after all, remains to be seen."

" You bet it does. And I'll tell you another thing ; I don't see myself spending the rest of my life grubbing up pig-nuts on a God-forsaken island like this unless I've got clear sailing orders. I know something about soils, and I don't mind telling you that it doesn't take long, in a landscape like this, to get down to rock ; so it's not such a hopeless position as it looks. All the same there are few worse jobs than looking for some-thing that isn't there when you don't quite know where it is. We've got to see that chart, Lethaby, and get a shot or two on the quiet, if we're going to make anything of this proposition ; that is, if we're going to do it on the square. Tell me about that chart ; where's it kept ? What sort of light ? "

" How do I know ? I keep on telling you, it's years since I was at Dreams, and the place has changed hands since then. Chances are, the beastly plan's been sold with a lot of other junk, and it would mean hunting through all the second-hand shops of Inverness to find the track of it. If not, who's going to guarantee that old Airdrie will have kept the place just as it was ? The more I think of it, the less hope I see of getting a squint at that plan. All I know is, it must have hung in the front hall or somewhere close by when I knew the place, about the time I left school, because it's mixed up in my mind with a lot of coats and hats and things – brings back a smell of mackintosh, you know, when I try to remember it. The bother is, it may be in some cubby-hole off the main entrance, where there'd be no light at all. Then, bang goes your idea of a photograph, and I don't see how we'd ask to have a look at the thing without making the old boy suspicious."

" Would it be in a frame ? "

" Can't remember. Why ? Were you thinking of lifting it ? I must say, I don't much like the idea of being given in charge for larceny. No, we've got to trust our luck, Henderson, old man ; that's the fun of a show like this. I never could bear a certainty."

" That's all very well for you ; you've got your allowance and your flat in town, and nothing to do but sit pretty and make love to chorus girls. I've got my living to make ; and I didn't cry off that Riga proposition merely to come and help you revisit the scenes of your youth and get the mackintosh smell right. No, sir, this show is going to pay my fare somehow, if it doesn't do anything more. I haven't any great urge to turn this Airdrie man into a millionaire, and it isn't going to be done if I can help it. Let him look out for his own furniture, that's all. I'm going to get a good look at that chart, if it's on the premises ; don't you make any mistake about that."

" You're building too much on it, you know, Henderson. It may be a straightforward honest-to-God map, and those figures on it may mean just anything."

" Well, if we back a loser there, we've got to get busy somehow else. Meantime, we ought to be on the road if we're going to make half-past four at this Dreams place."

" Were you ruminating on the beauties of nature ? " broke in a friendly voice behind them. They turned, to find a cheerful, red-faced man with a grizzled moustache contemplating them with a twinkle of amusement; his clerical collar, tentatively supported by the rest of his costume, proclaimed him the guardian of the enclosure. " I'm sorry to disturb you, gentlemen ; but it's the time I lock up the gate here, to keep ill folk out of the churchyard. It's a fine sight, is it not, the island ? "

Lethaby raised his hat in salutation. " I knew it years ago, sir," he said, " and I just came to have another look at it. Yes, it's not easy to beat that for a view."

" And what's more," proceeded the intruder, " we've woken up to find ourselves become famous in the night, with all this talk in the newspapers. That's the island you'll have read about, where the English gentlemen are coming to dig up the treasure." Then, a light suddenly dawning on him, " You'll excuse me, sir, but I think I have the advantage of you from your photographs. Is it not the Honourable Vernon Lethaby I'm speaking to?"

"I congratulate you, sir," replied the young man; "up to now, I had not known it was possible to trace a resemblance between those photographs and their original. You should have been a detective. Since I am unmasked, may I introduce my accomplice, Mr. Henderson?" Mr. Henderson's pleasure in meeting the stranger was duly affirmed, with little corroboration from his appearance.

"It's a queer thing," said the minister, "that I should have met you just now; for I was thinking about you only a minute ago, when I crossed the road and saw your car. So you're a believer in the story of Prince Charlie's treasure, are you, Mr. Lethaby?" Nor did the reverend gentleman give him an interval for reply, well knowing that in conversation it is the initiative that counts. He was something of a learned man, and had written, of course, a history of the district. On the period of the '45, especially, he was an expert; and he would not lightly dismiss his audience – audiences, it must be supposed, being somewhat rare in Glendounie. "Mind you," he went on, "there's not a shadow of doubt that Prince Charlie did come this way. Not a shadow of doubt about that. But the question is, do you see, did he leave anything behind him? That's the question. Now, you'll say it's likely enough that there was money and may be jewellery sent over to him from France; mind you, I'm not denying that. And you'll say he was in a hurry to leave these parts, and not much time to pack up his luggage before he started; that's true enough. But you've got to set against that first of all, the fact that the red-coats never found it; and they didn't leave treasure lying about if they could help it, I can tell you. And then there's the Strathspiel family, that had Dreams Castle all those years. Let's see, you'll be a relative of theirs, Mr. Lethaby, and I'm not saying a word against them, but " – and here he grasped the young man confidentially by the lapel of his coat – " the Strathspiel family knew the value of money as well as other folk, and they wouldn't have left money lying in Erran Island if it was to be had for the digging. Now, I'm not grudging you a holiday on the island ; but I'm not very confident that you'll pay the expenses of the let out of what you find there. Perhaps it'll be all for the best, because you won't bring down the curse on you either."

" A curse, is there ? " asked Lethaby.

" Deary me, didn't you know that ? Yes, that's the legend hereabouts, that the treasure's there still, but the man who finds it will bring bad luck on himself and wish he'd left it be. Yes, Mr. Lethaby, great riches can be a curse to any of us, but – well, I see you're wearying to be away ; don't let me keep you here chattering."

" We can't take you anywhere ? " suggested Lethaby as he climbed into the car. " We're going to call at Dreams."

" No, thank you, I'm not going that way myself. If you're a wee bit late for your tea, just tell Sir Charles you've been having a crack with the minister of Glendounie ; he'll know what that means. Good day, sir, good day to you both." They parted with a waving of hands ; but the violence with which Henderson started the car had almost the force of an expletive.

It is but just that the reader should be formally introduced to the two principal characters already mentioned ; the more so, because one of them, Vernon Lethaby, was the sort of person it is quite impossible to hush up. You might as well try to hush up the Test Match, or the Albert Memorial. Everybody who read the cheap papers – and most people do – was familiar with his name. If you had asked people why it was so familiar, they would perhaps have found some difficulty in assigning an adequate reason for the circumstance. He was not, he had never been, an athlete ; he did not fly the Atlantic, or race at Brooklands. He hadn't stood for Parliament ; he hadn't written a book ; he didn't paint, even badly. He was a golfer with an in-different handicap, he danced and played bridge adequately ; in politics, he was just an ordinary Com-munist, of the type fashionable in Chelsea. He had never saved anybody from drowning, or won the Irish sweepstake, or seen a ghost, or performed any other feat which would have legitimately distinguished him from his fellows. A good many of his contemporaries were better looking, a good many were worse living. It was doubtful whether he would get half a column of obituary in *The Times*.

For all that, he was news. That strange, crooked mirror which distorts the world for our entertainment, the cheap Press, had discovered that he possessed, or perhaps decreed that he should possess, publicity value. Nor was this, I am sorry to say, altogether un-connected with the fact that he was the son, although he was only the youngest son, of a peer. We have long ceased to be an aristocratic nation, settling down into a *régime* of avowed plutocracy. Let the scion of a noble house pursue any of those honourable callings which were open to his ancestors – we take no notice of him. In the House of Commons, he will be lucky if he struggles through to an under-secretaryship ; in the Army, he is put down as a good-natured fellow who, of course, does not mean to treat the Army as a career ;

11

in the Church, he is ignored, because nobody can remember whether he is the Rev. the Hon., or the Hon. the Rev. It is the same with his pastimes ; that he should hunt and shoot and go to race-meetings we expect as a matter of course, and if he excels in any of these departments he gets little credit for it. But once you get into the news, the ordinary rough-and-tumble of news, your title becomes an added aureole to the performance. " Countess Robbed " makes a better headline than " £5,000 Jewel Haul " ; you will be a " Peer in Motor Mishap " if you so much as graze the other man's bonnet ; " Earl's Son in Court " and " Titled Shoplifter " will refresh the palate of the most jaded reader, and even " Decree for Baronet," while losing its rarity value, has not altogether lost its appeal. To be born the son of a Duke is, in itself, nothing ; you would have done far better to be born a quadruplet. But, having been born the son of a Duke, to get into any kind of trouble or indulge in any kind of notorious eccentricity is to be in the public eye at once.

What then had Vernon Lethaby done, that the public should delight him, not to honour, but to a kind of good-humoured contempt? He had lived among people richer than himself, and got more than he gave in the way of entertainment ; he had mixed with people cleverer than himself, and borrowed their epigrams, or dined out on their anecdotes. You found his portrait in the illustrated papers, now looking like a Polar bear at St. Moritz, now like a plucked chicken at Cap d'Antibes ; dancing in aid of the Distressed Governesses, dining for the Earthquake Victims, sometimes even going to a party just for the fun of the thing. But the illustrated papers are not real publicity ; they are only a step towards it. He had danced and dined, to be sure ; but what had he done ?

The gossip-writers, if you came to look into it, were responsible. Vernon Lethaby, as the reader will have gathered by now, was not the sort of man to do anything violently sensational. But he was always ready to do something mildly sensational – ready to do it, if it were only to oblige a gossip-writing friend who was hard up for material. He would keep a leopard cub as a pet, or row on the Serpentine in a grey top-hat, or allow a rumour to be put about that he was engaged to a well-known film-actress, or give a cocktail party to two dozen pavement artists – things like that, they would tell you in Fleet Street, he did better than anybody else in London. Sometimes he would branch out further, and almost succeed in being amusing – as when he rode a camel to his club for a bet, or when he sent out invitations for a party on April the first, in the name of a well-known hostess, to the two hundred worst answerers in London ; or when he travelled a hundred miles in a Bath chair along one of the most crowded arterial roads out of London, holding up the cars or waving them leave to pass, as the mood took him.

The adventure upon which he was at present engaged was not, his friends said, just one of his follies. He was genuinely in want of money, for the allowance referred to above did not do much more than cover his racing debts ; nor could he bring himself to leave the flat in London, and bury himself in a remote Perthshire country house, which his aunt lent him on the strict condition that he might not let or lend it. This aunt on his mother's side belonged to the Strathspiel family, as the minister, with the genealogical *flair* of his countrymen, had realised ; and the house, now shut up, was little better than a repository of Jacobite relics, handed down as heirlooms. These, too, were unsaleable, and indeed of little intrinsic value ; so it is perhaps hardly surprising that his thoughts should have turned to those more negotiable relics which, tradition said, lay interred in the Isle of Erran. Sir Charles Airdrie, its present owner, was a Glasgow man who had done well in shipping ; if arrangements could be made with him, it was evidently more appropriate that Prince Charlie's treasure should come back to an heir, albeit by law Salic, of the Strathspiel race. There was, however, nothing furtive or underhand about Lethaby's way of going to work. On the contrary, he had given exclusive interviews to the Sunday papers about it ; the Isle of Erran was on all men's lips ; and if the expense had not been too considerable, he would have had a cinema operator on the spot to record the progress of his expedition.

Such publicity was, as we have seen, little to the mind of his partner in the enterprise, a Colonial by the name of Henderson whom he had picked up at a boxing-match, and treated, for a month or so past, with that extreme familiarity which decadent members of an aristocracy will always show to their undesirable friends. Joe Henderson, called " Digger " Henderson by his intimates, made no secret of the fact that his career had been an adventurous one ; its most respectable phase, to judge by the readiness with which he talked about it, was when he acted as a wholesale importer of whisky into the United States of America at a time when such goods were contraband. His residence in Canada during this time had infected his speech with an intonation, and with a set of locutions, for which northern America must be held responsible ; but the basis of his utterance suggested earlier contact with the Antipodes ; and in the absence of more precise details, he would describe himself as having been born all over the British Empire. He came to London as the representative of a Mexican oil concern which did not encourage questions as to its whereabouts or antecedents, and he can hardly have expected to move, as he did, almost from the first, in the best society of Chelsea. In our patriotic determination to take the Dominions to our bosom, we are apt to do so without references ; finding that the man does not speak like ourselves, we forget to ask whether he speaks as an educated man would in the part of the world he comes from ; we do not expect him to have been at any particular school, or to show any interest in the tastes, the sports of our own leisured classes ; if he boasts of having shot a fox, we tell each other that it is the kind of thing they do out there. In a word, we give him *entrée* everywhere as an interesting kind of barbarian ; it does not occur to us to ask whether he has ever seen the inside of a gaol.

Mr. Henderson had not, as a matter of fact, encountered that experience among the varied experiences of his life ; but his own reminiscences, especially when he was somewhat in liquor, left it to be supposed that his friends had been less lucky. These frank airs of the adventurer gave him additional value, it need hardly be said, in the eyes of Vernon Lethaby, who had a passion for playing with fire ; a Canadian who could be introduced *sotto voce* as " a bit of a crook, you know," was almost as good as the leopard cub. Newspaper interviewers found Mr. Henderson more reticent about his past, and indeed disinclined for their company altogether. They fell back, unanimously, on the expedient prescribed in such cases, and labelled him a " mystery-man," which did no harm to anybody.

It was characteristic of Vernon Lethaby that he should have allowed his newspaper friends to write up the story of his forthcoming treasure-hunt before he had had time to ensure that it would actually come off. The visit to Dreams Castle was to be – among other things – a business interview, in which they were to discuss the terms of the lease. Unless Sir Charles Airdrie proved singularly accommodating – and that was not his habit in money affairs – it was very difficult to see how these initial expenses could be met. Neither of the partners was much better than solvent ; and Henderson would have none of the suggestion that they should form a syndicate. " When you've got a good thing," he explained, " it's a waste to let your own brother in on it." Somebody, he said, would have to underwrite the scheme, and insure them against the possibility of failure ; that there should be any difficulty in finding somebody who would underwrite a pure gamble, was unthinkable to a mind accustomed, as his was, to the broad open spaces of the New World. Vernon Lethaby, quite indifferent to the business aspect of the undertaking, doubted but did not contradict him.

CHAPTER II : DREAMS CASTLE

DREAMS CASTLE, like so many Highland residences, is a mixture. It began life some six hundred years ago – to judge by what remains – as a kind of medieval sky-scraper, a huge tower not much above forty feet square, reaching up through storey after storey, with interminable windings of the corkscrew staircase, to the traditional set of crow's-foot gables which were its battlements. The guide-book is better inspired than usual when it refers to " this historic pile," for pile it certainly is ; you can only surmise that the Highlanders of a past age were so acclimatised to uphill journeys as to make light of seventy or eighty steps when they came back from a hard day's hunting. How they got to bed after dinner, is a speculation still more tantalising. Or was a castle in those days (one is inclined to ask) not a place in which you lived, which you defended against your enemies, but merely a place in which you locked your enemies up to save the necessity of defending yourself against them ? There, in any case, it stands, delightful to the eye, with its soaring lines and its narrow windows ; the thick stone wall through which their embrasures are cut is faced with time-defying plaster, to keep out the agues which must have been the worst enemy of all.

In that short-lived period of prosperity which seems to have visited the North in the time of our grand-fathers and great-grandfathers, this primitive nucleus had, of course, to be expanded. Equally it goes without saying that it was expanded in the baronial Gothic manner, by an architect who seems to have supposed, in perfectly good faith, that he was carrying out the style of his original. Unfortunately, whether from native incapacity, or because his clients altered the design in pursuit of material comfort, the additions had only that measure of resemblance which served to draw attention to their own shortcomings. Enormous square windows with latticed panes defeated the medieval illusion ; useless turrets in unexpected places, and gargoyles at the head of the drainpipes, overdid it. The walls were pointed with badly dressed stone, to conceal the fact that their underlying structure was brick. The very stucco had changed from dead white to a suburban pink, as if in embarrassment at its intrusion.

The policies through which they drove up were, however, after the manner of the country, unpretentious. You could not be certain what was the exact point at which you had left the public highway and entered on the drive. The road lay between sunny banks of heather, carpeted with needles from the overarching pines ; you were free to regard this as a park if you would, but it disclaimed all airs of feudalism. Only the garden, shut away behind grey stone walls on their left, seemed to claim the right of seclusion. This absence of pomp revived the spirits of the adventurers. If Sir Charles Airdrie did so little to shut himself off from the world, he must either be poor enough to accept almost any terms for the letting of an unprofitable island, or conservative enough to have kept the house as it was, with that old plan of the island somewhere in the neighbourhood of the front door. . . .

Sir Charles Airdrie was a man of common sense ; he

made no attempt to sink the Glasgow merchant prince in the synthetic chieftain. He did not wear the kilt, or have his meals piped in, or study Gaelic. He shot badly, and knew it ; fished rather better, and was fond of it ; treated his tenants with just a shade less of consideration than was customary in the district, and sat unobtrusively on the county council. He was a little wizened man, bowed (for he was not much above sixty) a little more than his years warranted ; and he regarded his two guests beneath his bushy eyebrows with a look half of shrewdness and half of amusement, which Lethaby read, and resented, as suspicious. For all that, he was hospitable enough, and affected to feel honoured by a visit which was so plainly not one of ceremony. " Come away now and have some tea," he said ; " you've a long drive behind you. You've got a fine day for it, but these aren't the kind of roads you'll be accustomed to in the South. Mind your heads under that doorway ; this is a terrible old house, bits of it. I'll show you round before you go. But, of course, you know your way about, Mr. Lethaby." In a dining-room of hideous proportions, panelled from floor to ceiling with pitch-pine, they were introduced to a widowed daughter-in-law who kept house for Sir Charles. She was English, and shy ; in her determination not to talk business over meals, she rigorously kept clear of the island, of the local history, of the neighbours, talking of rural depopulation and the Northern meetings until her guests were ready to scream with impatience. Lethaby had already warned his companion, by a quick shake of the head, that the map was no longer to be seen in the entrance hall.

Nor was this to be the full extent of their Purgatory. Before tea was over, there was an invasion of grand-children – a small boy who hung about on one leg and dissociated himself, in an agony of embarrassment, from the conversation, and a still smaller girl who stood in front of you expectantly and looked up in your face as if she was convinced that you were going to say something funny. Lethaby ingratiated himself at once, with the easy camaraderie of the ne'er-do-weel ; Henderson was plainly disgusted by their presence. It appeared, after a certain amount of whispering, that " the two young folks " had " moved with the spirit of the times ; Alan's always such a boy for picking up the latest thing from the newspapers – would you believe it, Mr. Lethaby, they've been burying a treasure in the grounds here, and want us to go out and look for it. You chose the wrong day, Jeannie, for you've got a couple of experts here ; they'll make short work of finding it, I can tell you." A procession was formed, and in spite of the broadest possible hints from the children, it was not till half an hour later that they unearthed the " treasure " – an old packing-case – from the depths of the farm midden. Throughout the proceedings, Sir Charles was at his most facetious, rallying his visitors whenever they seemed to be at fault, and protesting that their present embarrassments were nothing to what they would encounter on the island. It was well after five when they found themselves closeted with their host ; their time was growing short, and the light fading – a bad look-out for the use of the camera.

" See here now," began Sir Charles, " I'm in a very extraordinary position. Most times, when I'm letting property, I'm crying up the place, and advertising how many grouse were shot on it last year, or how many salmon caught. Or if last year wasn't a very good one, we just strike an average ; Mackinnon's a grand man for that – that's my factor's name, Mackinnon. And if he was here, I expect he'd be telling you that the island was simply bursting with treasure, every nook and cranny of it, to make sure that you'd take it. It's a queer thing, but I'm not telling you anything of the kind this afternoon. My plain word is, gentlemen, that you're out on a wild-goose chase."

Henderson looked up quickly, with an air of relief. " I like to hear a man talk business," he said. " What you mean is, what we're buying off you is one chance in a thousand of coming across the treasure. The island may be a beauty spot all right, but we aren't going there to sketch ; and by the same way of reasoning I guess it ain't much good to you when the letting season comes around. Well, that's where cold common sense comes in. If we find anything, you stake out a big claim on it. If we find nothing, you let us down easy with the rent. That's how we hoped you'd see it."

" I see what you mean," returned their host impassively, " but then, I don't think you've quite taken my point. You see, it isn't as if I was particularly anxious to let the property at all ; and the question is, what inducement I've got to let it. If you should find any treasure there, and I was saying I don't think that's very probable, that treasure belongs to me, apart from what the Government claims ; and it's for you to safeguard yourselves in the lease so as to get any rights in it. If you find what I expect you to find, which is nothing, it's not for me to offer you consolation by letting you off part of the rent ; it's not as if I wanted to encourage you. See here, if you *were* wanting to sketch, you might have had the island cheap ; I've a kind of weakness for artists myself. Or again, if you were a couple of young fellows studying for the ministry, and wanted a quiet place by yourselves, I'm not saying but what I might let you down gently. But this is

21

rank foolishness, sirs, by my way of it, and I'll not take a hand in it more than I can help."

There was a slight pause ; and then Lethaby, who never had control of his tongue, added, " Until it comes to sharing out, apparently."

" I don't think that's a very justifiable observation, Mr. Lethaby. Whatever's on that island's mine, and you've no more right to take away thirteen and fourpence, if you find it buried there, than to cut the timber. And that's another question that arises : How are you going to look for the treasure, you that know no more than I do where they put it ? Will you be ploughing the land up, and rooting out the trees as you go ? And is that to go down as tenants' improvements ? "

For just a second the eyes of the two confederates consulted one another. Then, " We shall be guided by probabilities, naturally," said Lethaby ; " but of course we don't expect to find the stuff lying in a neat parcel on the front door step. We shall want your leave to dig, and it's only fair that you should make what terms you like about the damage we may do in that way. As for the timber, it's not likely we shall want to interfere with that ; and my suggestion would be that we shall come to you for your permission when and as we think there's any good to be done by clearing it. But that's a question of extras, and we could arrange it at leisure. What we really wanted to find out – and I'm afraid our time is wearing on rather – is whether you can't see your way to meeting us on easier terms, since it's you who are the gainer, as much as anybody else, if we do strike oil."

" Well then, Mr. Lethaby, I'll be perfectly plain with you. The rent'll be just what Mackinnon told you when you wrote to him, no more and no less. I'd a good mind to put it up on you, seeing that you're making the Isle of Erran a by-word in the cheap papers, and bringing a whole crowd of sightseers, newspaper men too as like as not, who'll give the place a bad name and disturb the fishing. But I'll be perfectly fair with you ; you shall take the place as a holiday place between you, and I hope you'll enjoy your holiday. And until I hear from you, I'll take it that the estate is not going to be the gainer or the loser beyond just so much. Turn it over in your mind, Mr. Lethaby ; and if I hear that you've decided not to take it, why, I'll think the better of your perspicacity."

For a moment it looked as if the young man were going to speak, produce some final appeal to reason or to sentiment. If so, he must have thought better of it ; all he said, as he straightened himself out of his chair, was, " You were asking, Sir Charles, if we would like to see round the house a bit before we left. Henderson here has never seen it before ; and I confess I'd like to refresh my memories of it. I'm afraid we've taken up a lot of your time already, but . . . "

" Nonsense, man ; you're welcome to have a look round while you're here. Mind you," he added, pinching his guest's arm with an appearance of real kindliness, " it's not that you're not welcome in these parts. Your family is still highly respected here. But you must come here on another errand." And he showed them, courteously enough, round the older parts of the house; now pointing out how some narrow window, by accident or design, lent a perfect framework to a long vista of the glen, now explaining to Lethaby where he had made alterations. " You will remember when the turrets had bedrooms in them ; believe me, servants wouldn't stand that now."

The room which had, perhaps, the best outlook of all was quite a small turret room, about half-way up. From the awkwardness of its size and shape, it could not really be made comfortable to live in, and was used, it seemed, as a kind of muniment room ; there were several chests of papers, each with the name of the business it referred to marked in white paint on a shiny black surface ; there was a glass case, containing some incunabula of moderate interest, and on the walls one or two genealogies, as well as a series of coloured maps which showed the boundaries of the estate. Lethaby's heart beat quicker as he noticed among these one which was plainly of older date than the rest ; one which represented in crude outline an island standing in the middle of the river ; one which was marked not (he now saw) with figures, but with capital letters, faintly traced in old ink. It was the plan they were looking for ; by ill luck, it hung close to the only practicable window, so that hardly any light fell on it. Still, it hung on a hook, and if Henderson could be left alone with it for a minute or two there was nothing to prevent his taking it down and photographing it with his diminutive camera before he was interrupted.

A question about the identity of the hill which bounded the view to the extreme left was a good excuse for getting Sir Charles' head poked out of the window, while he drew Henderson's attention, with a rapid gesture, to the object of their search. Then he strolled up to one of the genealogies, and, as if reminded by reading a name on it, said in as casual a voice as he could assume, " By the way, Sir Charles, I wonder if I might have another look at that print of Flora Mac-donald which hangs in the passage upstairs ? I have one at home which is very like it, but I'd like to get it clearer in my mind's eye so that I can compare it when I get home. Would it be an awful bore if we went and looked at it again ? " His host could hardly refuse the

request ; and Lethaby was sensible enough to forestall
any suspicions about the suddenness of it by pretending, when they got outside, that it was an excuse for
having a word with him about the character of his
companion.

" I say, you know," he explained, " I didn't really
want to look at that print. But I wanted to get you
away for a moment, if you don't mind, just to talk to
you about old Digger Henderson. I could see you
didn't cotton to him a bit ; lots of people don't. He
amuses me quite a lot ; but then I'm rather omnivorous,
I've been told before now, about my taste in friends.
Well, what I wanted to say was, he isn't half a bad sort.
Actually, of course, he's self-educated, and what the
Edwardians used to call a bit of a bounder. Not
everybody's money, I grant you ; but he really is a
white man, that's my point. At least, it isn't my
point exactly, because I can't very well expect you to
see eye to eye with me about it, can I ? My point is,
I don't want you to be put off this speculation altogether just because you don't like the look of Digger.
It did just occur to me, when we were talking over
terms, that perhaps you weren't too happy about ever
seeing the colour of your money, and that was why
you weren't exactly keen on it. Look here, would it
make things any better if I signed the contract alone,
and we left Digger out of it altogether ? Because I
shall have to find the money anyhow, if we manage to
find it at all. What I mean is, don't let me make you
feel you're letting yourself in for business dealings
with a crook ; that's the long and short of it."

Sir Charles' eyebrows, which had registered a kind of
nascent surprise at the beginning of this speech, had by
now resumed their customary angle of ironical shrewdness. " There's no reason why you and me should

quarrel over that," he said. " You can trust Mackinnon to see that my interests are safeguarded ; and if your friend Henderson is a man of no fixed address, why, Mackinnon'll see to it that you're responsible for the rent. I'd only say this, Mr. Lethaby ; take care what you're at. I've done business for many years with all sorts of people, and in Glasgow ; I think I ought to know a doubtful character when I see one. He comes round you, does Henderson, because he's been knocking about the world doing things, while you were lounging about London looking for something to do. But he has a bad forehead, and he puts his face too close to you when he talks. If you'll take my advice, Mr. Lethaby, you won't trust him further than you can see him. And if you find me hard to deal with about the rent, perhaps it's partly because I'm not too keen to see you living alone with your friend Henderson in a desolate sort of place like the island yonder. Now we'll be getting back, if you don't mind, or he'll be wearying for us."

This last estimate, at any rate, was far from the truth. Mr. Henderson was fully occupied by himself in the room downstairs, and was not in any kind of hurry to be interrupted. Almost before the door had shut behind the others he had taken the map down from its hook, and studied it intently. The capital letters, which seemed to have been written in with a different kind of ink, some time after the map itself had been drawn, could only be understood as a set of cipher directions for finding your way about the island with some particular purpose in view ; what that purpose was, or how the cipher was to be read, must remain to be considered later. His immediate action, naturally, was to prop up the map, frame and all, on the top of a chest which stood right opposite the window, and secure, in the fading light of the late summer afternoon, a couple of exposures with his camera. Uncertain how long his friend would be able to detain Sir Charles with talk, he did not venture upon any more prolonged inspection ; and by the time the door opened again he was apparently absorbed in the contemplation of a family tree which traced the descent of the Strathspiels, through a putative cadet branch of the Jewish royal family, from Adam.

Even when thus occupied, he found himself a trifle disconcerted by the narrow look which Sir Charles Airdrie gave him on his return. Here was a man, you felt, trained to suspicion. It seemed the moment for a pleasantry in the Colonial manner. " We don't take much stock in those things where I come from," he said. " Stands to reason we shouldn't have been here if the little god Cupid hadn't got busy among the old folks, and we leave it at that." A sentiment with which Sir Charles, shuddering slightly, felt bound to agree. He took his guests down to the main door, gave them directions about a short cut which would save them a little distance on their way home, and stood waving them good-bye, as polite, as unrelenting, as inscrutable as ever.

" What's his game ? What does he want to stick on the price like that for ? " complained Henderson, as they drove out of earshot. " Talks as if his God-darned island was a perishing bird-sanctuary or something on those lines – what the hell's the use of it to him, anyway ? No good telling me that land's any value up here, except according as you can pick up so many brace of uneatable little birds when you've shot over it. The fishing's let, the shooting's let, and that there island is eating its head off. And Airdrie, he's not a blooming caretaker put in by the League of Nations ; he's a business man, and knows the value of his money.

27

You can see that by every inch of him. And can you beat him down? No, sir, a hundred pounds down for the month – and if he charged fifty for it in the ordinary market, he'd have to whistle for it! He's putting up the price on us, just because he knows we're out for big money; and he tells us in the same breath that there's no treasure there. How do you figure out that? Why's he trying to warn us off? That's what I want to know."

Lethaby, at the wheel, did not appear to be in the least affected by his companion's excitement. " The worst of you, Digger, is that you've no imagination. You think, because the man's a Scot, he's out to make money all the time. Human nature isn't as simple as that; much easier to do business if it was. When Charles Airdrie says he doesn't want us to take the island because he believes it's a waste of money looking for treasure there, he isn't bluffing, he's just telling the cold truth. Your real Scot can't bear to see money wasted; other people's money any more than his. Don't you know the story of the man who'd made good getting out of the train at Edinburgh, and wanting to take a taxi to the Caledonian Hotel? Porter says, ' Yon's the Caledonian Hotel – you and your taxis!' Don't you mistake it, that's the sort of man who's made England, and Scotland too; always letting sentiment interfere with business. Of course, it don't work now. But you Dominions people never seem to realise that the thing's still there. What's fifty pounds to Sir Charles? Nothing at all, compared with his pedantic urge to prevent a couple of foreigners *making fools of themselves*. Blast him! "

" That sort of talk is all very well for your London cocktail-parties; it doesn't nearly go down with me. Mean to tell me I don't know when a man's bluffing?

I'll tell you what it is ; old Airdrie has lived in that place for years, with the Isle of Erran just under his nose, and he's never bothered to enquire into that story of the treasure. Then you come along, with your write-ups in the newspapers and your cameramen and God knows what all, and the silly old fool begins to sit up and take notice. Must be something in this, he says to himself – you know the way everybody gets more hotted up about a story once it's in print. He means to get that stuff for himself, and if he don't head us off by putting up the rent on us, he means to head us off some other way – that's my reading of him."

" I never knew a man who had so much knowledge of the world and so little of the people who live in it. Confound it all, he's only charging us a hundred, instead of fifty, which he'd charge anybody else, or thirty, which it's worth. What's to prevent him refusing to let altogether, if he wants to keep us out of it ? And I'm tired of telling you that the only way to persuade people not to take you seriously is to make yourself into a Press stunt. If we'd have gone to Sir Charles with some story about wanting to make a geological survey of the island or dig for fossils or some bunk of that kind, he'd have been fussing round wanting to see our vaccination certificates and putting plain-clothes bobbies on to watch us. As it is, he just roars with laughter at the idea of anybody expecting to collect treasure there, and probably thinks it's all just one of my publicity stunts and we aren't really out for treasure at all. Another thing is, he daren't go and grub up that treasure just when it's been advertised all over London that we're going to look for it. Make him look ridiculously unoriginal, not to say a bit of a skinflint. Not that he could very well, without that chart, eh ? "

" I'm not going to make any song and dance about

29

that chart till I see whether there's any reading the directions. Mark you, I don't have any doubts that there are directions on it – about something. I hope to God the old wowzer didn't see we'd been at it. He's as sharp as a weasel."

" Bet you anything you like he didn't spot anything. I double-bluffed him, you see – pretended I'd got him out of the room so as to tell him you weren't such a plug-ugly as you looked. Did you manage to make sure of the picture ? It would be the devil and all if nothing came out except a portrait of a door-handle in a fog."

" No, I didn't make any mistake about that. As a matter of fact, I took a pretty good look at it, and I wouldn't say but what it might be better to make a sketch of it from memory, to avoid accidents. The photo will be more use, though ; you sometimes get things coming out you'd hardly spot with the naked eye. How'd you be placed if you were asked to make a copy ? "

" My dear old man, it's past me. Only had the vaguest squint at the thing, unless you count happy childhood's days and all that. I'd even forgotten they were letters, you see – thought they were figures. I'd know the look of the thing again, actually, wherever I met it ; it would leap out at me if I came across it suddenly in an advertisement of shaving-soap. But I couldn't have got the details of it fixed in my mind without having a real good lingering gaze at it, and that *would* have put Sir Charles wise, obviously. I hope it's going to make sense, I say, now that we've got it."

" Ten to one it'll be merely notes some fool made about planting trees on the island. Looks to me as if it had been planted for lumber about the year dot,

though it's been allowed to go back most abominably."
Henderson was taking a look at the scene as he spoke ;
for they were now climbing the hill that rises on the
mainland just opposite the Isle of Erran, which appeared at intervals through the trees. There was a
dark and uncanny look about it in the early sunset ;
for the rays which still lit up the hillside on the opposite
bank could no longer penetrate into the river trough
itself, and the *cache* of their treasure, if treasure it was,
lay wrapped in a conspiracy of shadows. The subdued
thunder of the falls reached them, as they breasted the
slope, and came into view of Glendounie.

CHAPTER III : THE MAN WHO WANTED TO BE WATCHED

" Aren't you going to go on weeding ? " asked Angela.

" Certainly not," replied her husband. " When we have a distinguished guest in our midst, like Sholto, I have to drop all lesser occupations, and devote myself to entertaining him. I don't see why you don't stop, too ; it makes me hot looking at you."

" It's an extraordinary thing," said Angela, still thoughtfully pulling out groundsel, " that you always pretend you can listen to my conversation when you're playing that footling patience of yours, although it must occupy most of what for want of a better word we will call your mind ; and yet whenever the temperature's above sixty you complain that you can't think while you're weeding."

" Can't I help ? " suggested their visitor treacherously, with the unconvincing gesture of a man who is prepared, if the worst comes to the worst, to get up out of his deck-chair.

" Sit where you are, and get on with your gin-and-ginger. The canary's a bit off his feed, so it doesn't matter. Besides, we don't let strangers weed in this garden ; because we're never certain what we planted last year, so we have to decide which are flowers and which are weeds as we go along. Angela, do come to roost ; you're making Sholto feel damnably embarrassed ; remember he's been to a public school and all that."

Angela stood up defiantly, and cast an appraising eye over the ramshackle, go-as-you-please acre of garden which they had taken over from the previous owners of the house, and never quite had the heart to tidy up properly. " Have it your own silly way," she said. " I can see by the look in Mr. Sholto's eye that he's come here with a job for you to do ; and if that means getting rid of you for a fortnight, I may have time to do some intensive weeding. No thanks, not before dinner. Let's hear the best, Mr. Sholto," she added, sitting down and swinging herself gingerly on the edge of a hammock.

Sholto looked at his glass, rolling the ice round its surface with a pleasant tinkling noise, with the silence of a man who is not quite certain whether he brings good news or bad. " I'm afraid it isn't a question of a fortnight," he said at last. " It's a waiting job, you see ; no corpses have been scattered round, no jewellery has been stolen, no premises have been burned – yet. It's just that the Company doesn't feel quite happy about the intentions of one of its clients, and – well, it wants to have somebody on the spot to see that there's no dirty work done. Romantic scenery, invigorating climate," he added hopefully.

Once more, I feel that introductions are necessary. Not that the Indescribable Insurance Company should need any more introduction than the Honourable Vernon Lethaby. It shared his taste for headlines and for gossip-column value. It had introduced into the insurance business the methods of up-to-date mass-production, and was proud of boasting that it was prepared to cover anything, from a pair of spectacles to the life of a South American dictator. Film-stars insured their front teeth individually ; fathers safe-guarded themselves (at an absurdly low figure) against

33

the possibility of quintuplets, husbands (at a somewhat stiffer rate) against the loss of their wives' affections. Of this singular institution Sholto was an official – what precise rank he held in its complicated hierarchy I have no means of deciding. Bredon, his host on this occasion, was something much more special ; he was the one and only detective regularly employed by the one and only insurance company which regularly employed a detective.

It was either his nature or his affectation to hate a job of work ; more especially if, as usually happened, that work involved making impertinent enquiries in an assumed character, hanging about where he was not wanted, and spying on people generally. The trouble was that he did all this remarkably well, with that occasional touch of the unexpected which heralds the presence of genius – as on the occasion when it was necessary for him to shadow some people who were frequenting a night-club, and he elected to do so disguised as a plain-clothes detective. There was only one person who really knew how to manage him ; and she, most fortunately, had married him. All he asked of Providence, beyond this happy arrangement, was to be left in his country cottage to play patience and solve an occasional cross-word. His wife saw to it that he was nevertheless uprootable when the Company wanted to uproot him. This did not prevent him from registering, now as always, his official protest.

" I know what that means," he complained. " The Company, blast them, want to park me at some hole of a place like Bognor-on-Sea, and tell me that it's really more like a holiday than a job of work, and I ought to be glad to get my expenses paid. The sea air will ruin my liver – it always does – and the band will be playing "Little man, you've had a busy day." Oh, why didn't I adopt one of the gentlemanly professions?"

"A bit further afield, I'm afraid," said Sholto, still pursuing his musical investigations. "The Highlands of Scotland, to be accurate. Company, on the other hand, more select. If you ever read the newspapers, you might possibly have come across the name of Vernon Lethaby."

"That man? The intolerable exhibitionist who wants to dig up some fabulous deposit of hidden treasure? This is worse than anything I expected. Look here, I draw the line at watching him. It will simply feed his vanity ; he asks nothing better than to be watched. And I suppose your insane directors have agreed to insure his beastly treasure without even waiting for him to find it?"

"It's odd that you should say that. Not because it's what the directors have done, but it's what he wanted 'em to do. Came round with a friend of his – man called Henderson ; queer fish, who looks as if he'd done time somewhere – and asked as innocently as dammit what terms we would charge for insuring them against the disappointment of finding there wasn't any treasure there. Or alternatively, finding that it wasn't worth as much as country-side legends represented. I ask you!"

"Well, why didn't the directors click? I should have thought it was just the kind of thing that was in their line."

"My good man, there is such a thing as legislation about insurance. This would be rank gambling."

"Looks to me as if the directors must have begun to think about their last end ; first time I ever heard of 'em being so particular. So they turned him down?"

"You bet they did. Said the best they could do

was to cover him for the loss of the rent, which wasn't exactly what he wanted. Unless, of course, he was prepared to bring some decent proof that the treasure was really there, and give an approximate estimate of its value. Oh, we were quite nice to them. Pointed out that all they needed to do was to form a syndicate which would share the risks and the profits ; only that wasn't our line of business exactly. Then they went away, and we never expected to hear from them again."

" But you did ? "

" We saw no more of the crook man, Henderson. But Lethaby, the Hon. V., turned up as fresh as paint next morning, with a quite new proposition which seemed more reasonable. Said he'd picked up this partner of his God knows where, and didn't really know a thing about him. He was useful for a curious reason – he seems to be an expert in digging – I mean the actual process. You ought to get him down here, Mrs. Bredon, when you want your beds dug over ; he'd polish off the lot in half an hour by all accounts. Just a knack, apparently ; found that he possessed it during the War, of course ; and has gone round since then like a sort of human truffle-hound, grubbing for gold or Minoan pottery or anything that wanted to be grubbed for. So Lethaby says he's worth while ; useful to have a partner who does all the spade-work. The trouble is, his testimonials only say he can dig ; they don't say he's ashamed to beg, or to steal if there is any urgent need for it. So Lethaby says to himself, Why not insure myself against fraud on Henderson's part ? That's the situation."

" And is that legitimate business ? "

" Perfectly. No reason why a man shouldn't protect himself against dishonesty on the part of a man in his employ, as much as carelessness. The only bother about this case is, Henderson's not going to turn thief till there's something to steal. Lethaby's badly off, he says, and doesn't want to go on for weeks, perhaps months, insuring himself against Henderson running off with a nine-and-sixpenny spade. Could he have a policy which would only come into force if and when the treasure is discovered? That was his proposition; and one sees the point of it."

"Mmm, yes – what about the value of the haul, though? If Henderson finds the stuff and levants with it straight away, how's the Indescribable going to assess the value of the loss? You'll have to make it a fixed sum; and that's asking for fraud. What's to prevent Henderson making tracks for the coast with an empty hat-box, and Lethaby lodging a claim with the Company and divvying up afterwards? I don't like it. What's his figure?"

"He wants ten thousand. The story, for what it's worth, is that Charles Edward carried about with him a sort of nest-egg, jewels and things given him by important ladies in France. Not easily convertible, one would think, but that's the story. And if it's true, the odds are that the treasure would be worth a lot more than ten thousand, because there's the museum interest as well as the intrinsic value. On the other hand, if it's just a stray sum, representing the pay-master-general's arrears after the battle of Culloden, we might be badly let down over it. We haven't given any definite answer yet, but I think we are going to take the thing on. If we do, that's where you come in."

"Meaning that I've got to be on the spot, and make sure that there isn't any funny business?"

"That's about the size of it. A kilt of the old

Bredon tartan, and a tam-o'-shanter, and you will be wholly invisible, lurking in the undergrowth. Won't he, Mrs. Bredon ? "

" As long as he doesn't give himself away by snoring. Miles, this is going to be rather fun. I've been getting rather out of practice with my broad Scots, since Blairwhinnie days."

" Lord have mercy on us, don't start that business. Positively, when you try to talk Scots you make me blush all over. No, but look here, Sholto, how do I stand ? Does this Henderson fellow know that I'm watching him ? I suppose not. But then, does Lethaby ? Am I to be a friend of the family, or just a stranger, comes in R., Lethaby does not notice him ? I don't fish, I don't shoot ; the bagpipes have no message for me. How the devil am I to account for my presence on a Scottish salmon-river ? Monster-hunting, or what ? On the other hand, if this is not to be the kind of expedition on which I take my false nose with me, isn't it going to be just the least bit awkward ? Particularly as Lethaby is just the sort of man I can't stick at any price. Angela would probably like him ; she has a notoriously bad taste in males. But I'm hanged if I'm going to be an elder brother to him. What's the idea ? "

" We thought of that. One way and another, we thought it would be better if you weren't on visiting terms – to start with, anyhow. You see, if we were certain we were merely protecting Lethaby against Henderson, that would be the natural course. But, as you say, we can't be quite certain that it isn't going to be a put-up job, with the two of them divvying up fifty-fifty afterwards. In that case, it would obviously be better for you to appear suddenly from behind the arras, saying, ' Rash and inconsiderate men, your machinations have not passed unobserved by those whom you labour to deceive ' – or any other words that might seem suitable to the occasion. It's the devil and all that you don't fish ; we hadn't thought of that. You'd look rather a fool playing patience on a flat stone."

" Less of this funny business about me playing patience. Do you mean to say the Directors were prepared to take a month's salmon-fishing for me ? That's a bore. I hate wasting good money."

" Money doesn't arise, apparently. There's an old boy who owns most of the surrounding landscape, name of Sir Charles Airdrie, who knows one of the Directors, and is prepared to let our Mr. Bredon have a month's fishing for nothing, as long as he is prepared to keep an eye on the treasure-hunters. You see, it's his land ; so he's interested."

" Which of 'em is it he doesn't like the looks of ? "

" Henderson chiefly. At least, he says if Lethaby's as big a fool as he sounds, and Henderson as big a knave as he looks, there's going to be trouble ; and he'd feel more comfortable if somebody was to keep an eye on them."

" Mmm, yes – he doesn't seem to be a very popular person, this Mr. Henderson. Did you try to find anything out about him ? The police, for instance ? "

" Yes, we got at the police through the usual channels ; and I must say they were more informative than they generally are. Henderson's the sort of man they know all about, I mean all there is to be known, because he's the sort of man they can never quite get tabs on. Born somewhere in Australia ; had a University education of sorts, scientific apparently. Came down in the world, not quite known how ; was a well-known figure at fairs, as the man who pulled your tooth out

39

for sixpence, or sold you dud watches and fountain-pens. Came over to Europe in the War, and discovered this facility for digging ; worked for some excavators in the East for a bit, then was attracted to Canada by the news of a Klondyke boom which never came off. Was more or less on his beam-ends when the Volstead Act came along ; then joined the rum-runners and made good money for a time, but appears to have become poor again since – gambling, the police think. He's been tried before now for holding up a train, but they couldn't fix it on him. The company he " represents " over here is an entirely bogus affair, and he's obviously living by his wits. So, you see, our Highland chieftain isn't badly out in his reckoning ; and Lethaby shows more sense in wanting to take out an insurance policy than the Directors, as far as I can see, in letting him do it. I don't know whether you'll have fun up in the North, but it certainly looks as if your man wanted watching."

" The bother is that by the same token he must be accustomed, by now, to being watched. In lonely parts of the world like that, every man is counted ; you've got to have some excuse for your existence, or the whole neighbourhood talks about you. Camping might do, but I doubt if campers go so far North ; besides, it's a filthy uncomfortable sort of life. No, if salmon-fishing were the kind of thing one could learn in a week-end, so as not to be visibly despised by the local population, I'd have a stab at it."

Angela, still on the hammock, suddenly swung herself up into the air with a whoop of triumph. " Miles ! " she cried. " I've got it ! Edward ! "

" Edward ? " repeated her husband, with furrowed brow. " I have heard that name before ; but taken by itself it means nothing to me."

" Oo, but don't you remember – Edward Pulteney ! "

" Woman, if this is some sinister figure you met in your past life, before you crossed my path, we will talk over him later. Spare the feelings of our guest."

" But, Miles, you must remember that old darling at Pullford, when you took such a long time to find out what had happened to poor Mottram. The schoolmaster who used to fish in the river there. Couldn't we take the fishing at this Scotch place, and he could do it all, while you were the other man who sits at the end of the boat and always looks as if he were just going to fish, but never does ? "

" It does come back to me now that there was an aged gentleman at Chilthorpe – not actually at Pullford – with whom you attempted a flirtation. Am I to understand that you have kept up a clandestine correspondence with him ? "

" He sent me a Christmas card, if you remember ; and you can't call it exactly clandestine, because you kept it on the mantelpiece, and have been tearing little bits off ever since, to stick in your pipe and prevent the mouth-piece wobbling. Not a tidy habit, Miles dear."

" To be sure, it was the very card for a smoker. An admirable consistency. But surely he was too much of a gentleman to put his address on a Christmas card ? A cad's trick."

" No, but it was a picture of the school he teaches in, with the name written underneath. Sent out to parents as an advertisement, I should think ; though it wasn't a very good one, because you could see nothing except the infirmary. Extraordinary how schools will put all their money into building infirmaries, as if no boy ever had a day's health. Anyhow, there it is, and we've got the address. It's no good telling me Edward has made up his holiday plans already, because he nearly always goes and stays with a widowed sister – probably at Bognor-on-Sea. A really appealing little note from me would fetch him, I'm certain ; more especially if it offered him free salmon-fishing on one of the crack rivers of Scotland. Do let's ask him."

" I hate causing agreement between a man and his wife," said Sholto, " but I believe Mrs. Bredon's right, you know. I don't see why it shouldn't work."

" The only objection is, that whereas I can just be prevailed upon, at a pinch, to camp out, and Angela professes to like it, I don't see Pulteney being happy under canvas, as I remember him. I suppose this local magnate doesn't go so far as offering us the loan of a smallish castle ? "

" We thought of that," said Sholto. (The Indescribable thinks of everything.) " We thought you'd want to live somewhere. The joke is, that the fishing tenants, if they're not local people, regularly stay at the gardener's cottage, just opposite the island where Lethaby and Co. will be operating. There's quite an habitable house on the island itself, you see ; but the garden belonging to it is on the mainland, just across the bridge ; the Scots always like to keep their gardens at arm's length, for some reason. On the well-known principle of *Ubi hortus ibi hortator*, the gardener lives on the mainland too, with a couple of rooms to spare and a wife who is said to be the best plain cook for miles round. Sir Charles' idea was that you two should live at the cottage, after the manner of fishing tenants ; and though he didn't budget for your friend Mr. Pulteney, it sounds as if there ought to be room. This means, you see, that you'll be next door to the island – as a matter of fact, it's the only human habitation within a mile of it."

" It doesn't sound too bad," admitted Bredon grudgingly. " What would the nearest links be, by the way ? "

" Good Lord, how should I know ? Nairn, probably. You couldn't expect the unfortunate Charles Edward to park his spare cash under the eighteenth at St. Andrews. This is business, man, business."

They were sitting at dinner – Sholto was staying over the week-end when a fresh problem was suggested. Angela, who had been showing a spirit of regrettable frivolity over the expedition – as when she suggested that her husband, if he would only put himself in the position of Charles Edward, ought to be able to carry off the treasure before anyone else got it – suddenly grew serious. " There's one point I don't quite see, though I don't know that it's got much to do with us. You say the Company is liable to pay out ten thousand if Henderson finds the treasure and decamps with it before Lethaby can stop him. Obviously it has to be a round sum, because in that case there's no saying how much the treasure really *was* worth. But supposing it doesn't work out quite like that – supposing they find the treasure one day, and Henderson makes off with it the next. Is anybody going to give the treasure a glance in the meantime, and settle how much it was really worth ? And if it only tots up to £66 6s. 8d., is the company still going to be liable for ten thousand when it vanishes ? "

" Quite right, Mrs. Bredon ; I forgot to mention that. The Company are going to give general instructions to a curiosity dealer in Inverness, who knows his period all right ; and it'll be part of your husband's job to ring up the moment anything is found, and get this man, Dobbie, to come over. He'll give us a rough estimate ; and, of course, you'd let us know at the same time, so that by next day we can send up an official valuer. All that's agreed upon with Lethaby, as part of the arrangement. He's promised to ring up Dobbie himself, I mean, if he finds anything ; but, of course, he might – well, he might forget, you know."

" It'll be awkward for him, poor dear, when he has to explain all these visitors to the other fellow. *I say, old man, there's an old clo' merchant coming round after lunch to value the stuff, in case you should run off with it –* that kind of thing ? "

" He says that'll be all right ; and, mind you, I believe him. If you knew Lethaby, you'd give him credit for being able to invent any kind of lie on the spur of any moment."

" He sounds as if I should like him. The Imperial Conference person seems rather a tougher proposition, but I dare say we shall get accustomed to his ways."

And she went off to say good night to the children. Her husband, making patterns on his plate with cherry-stones, gave the subject a more serious twist when he found himself alone with his guest. " It's all very well, Sholto," he protested ; " but the question is, Have I the right to take Angela with me on this job ? It's all very well to talk about keeping a watch on this treasure-hunt business, and reporting if there's anything that looks fishy about it. But obviously, if I spot that there's any dirty work going on, the Company doesn't expect me to sit round with a pair of field-glasses putting through trunk-calls. They'll want me to chip in and interfere – stop the man getting away with it. Only an off chance that it'll come to that, you say ; but, hang it all, it is on the cards all right. From your account of his *dossier*, I shouldn't wonder if our Mr.

Henderson is fairly handy with a gun. If Henderson –
or Lethaby, for that matter – starts anything of that
sort, do you see Angela making a graceful bee-line for
the bomb-proof shelter ? Because I don't."

" I know. I was a fool to mention the whole thing
while she was about. Didn't mean to when I came
down here ; but she asked me about it, you remember,
and she isn't the sort of person one can put off with
subterfuges much, is she ? No, I don't deny that the
thing may turn out dangerous. Of course, the Company'd let you have some men, but . . . "

" Impossible. Give the whole show away. No, if
I can't get one of the children to go sick, it looks as if I
shall have to take her. Look here, though, I'm
going to put in all the subterfuge-work I can. I'm going
to let her go on thinking it's a sort of picnic as long as
possible. For instance, I might not want to let her
know that the treasure had been found, if there's any
reasonable chance of keeping it from her. But I've got
to let you know ; and the odds are I shall have to send
the message through by 'phone. Do you mind if we
have a plain cipher meaning *Treasure found* ? Then
you could ring up the Inverness man, Dobbie – it's no
loss of time, really – and I might be able to slink off and
mount guard, leaving Angela to go on fishing with
Pulteney."

" Yes, I think that's rather a sound scheme. Useful
to have a cipher in any case. In the form of a racing
tip ? That looks most natural – if you're wiring to
me, anyhow."

" All right. Only let it be an imaginary horse. We
don't want the post-office people to drop money over
it. What does one call horses nowadays ? "

" Doesn't matter much ; let's see. . . . What about
Ambleside ? Plausible on the whole ; and as far as

I know no animal of that name is fancied. *Put shirt on Ambleside*, how about that ? "

" Good enough. If you get a message to that effect, you'll know that the treasure has been found, but that somebody on the spot – probably Angela – either doesn't know, or doesn't know that I know. I get it at fifty-six shillings the dozen," he added, as his wife entered the room.

CHAPTER IV: HOW THE BOAT WAS
MOORED

THE BREDONS travelled up North rather before the end
of July. The part of the river with which they were
concerned was let, at that time, to local people, so that
the gardener's cottage was already available. The loss
of the fishing did not diminish their pleasure, for they
had not yet been joined by Mr. Pulteney. Mr. Pulteney
was still striding up and down a class-room, invigilating
over candidates for the School Certificate. He was
moved to fierce explosions of wrath whenever, from the
corner of his eye, he saw his own form laboriously
writing down the blunders he had attempted for a
whole year to eliminate ; but these feelings he honourably bottled up until he was in a different part of the
room. He suffered, as all school-masters suffer when
July comes round ; but this year he was buoyed up by
the unwonted vision of himself waist-deep in a Highland
torrent, making that perfect cast which comes to fishermen only in their dreams. To the Bredons, already in
fruition of this imagined paradise, the brawling river
with its alternation of deep pools and treacherous
rapids presented itself as something to be walked along
rather than stood in ; and they had eyes, not for the
silent fish-life that expressed itself in sudden explosions
on the calm surface, but for the mysterious island that
lay, still untenanted, on the further shore.

Lethaby and Henderson were not expected till the

beginning of August, and Miles had insisted on the advantages of being beforehand with them. "For one thing," he explained, " a man who is afraid of being watched is always more suspicious of the stranger who comes along than of the stranger who was there before him. Also, local people always gossip about you for the first day or two after your arrival ; it dies down later on. And then, of course, the sooner you spy out the land the better." So they had motored up through long miles of desolate hill-country ; under frowning ridges of heather, bracken, and jutting rock ; over tumbling burns that seemed to mock, in that dry season, the span of the concrete bridges which bestrode them ; through narrow defiles, where the road zig-zagged in and out among pine-forests mounting above it in tiers and falling in tiers beneath it ; beside long, silent pools, reflecting the early sunset double-dyed in their peaty waters ; past low, white-washed cabins, desolate byres and ruinous distilleries, till the terraced streets of Inverness received them, and sent them forth on further adventures. It was quite dark by the time they reached the broken-down signpost which pointed them to " Isle of Erran," and descended precipitously upon a trim cottage by the river bank ; where, in soft lamplight, a red-cheeked old lady welcomed them without surprise, and ministered to them like an angel.

The word " cottage " is perhaps a misnomer. When they woke from the deep sleep into which the friendly drone of falling water had lulled them, they found themselves quartered in decent comfort (as comfort goes when you are living mainly out of doors) ; two cottages had evidently been knocked into one, so that two low bedrooms and an airy sitting-room were at the disposal of the visitor. One window of the sitting-room opened on to the garden which was the province

of their host ; its material products were, of course,
for the house on the island ; but as a feast to the eye
it was wholly made over to the gardener's tenants.
Being quite modern, it was not protected by walls after
the fashion of the country ; and indeed had no need
of such protection, in that sheltered angle of the valley.
Instead, it was cut out of the hillside, its gay borders
and rose-arbours terminating in a cascade of Alpine
rock-plants. From the other window you looked right
on to the bank of the river, just below where it was
spanned by a leggy concrete bridge. Here the Dounie,
as if protesting, like Araxes in the old Virgilian tag,
against such an indignity, intermitted its smooth flow
and swirled over smooth green boulders, then flung
itself angrily into the bubbling pool beneath ; by its
thunder the banks, with their fringe of rowans and
drooping silver birch, seemed reduced to an embarrassed
silence, just as men are by the presence of some violent
outburst of ill-temper. The stream was now at its
lowest ; but a register of flood-levels marked on one
pier of the bridge showed how treacherously it could
rise, and why the road was carried across it at a height
of twenty feet.

There is that about running water which makes us
all want to stop and waste time. Why this should be
so, it is for the psychologists to determine ; you would
have thought that a river, reminding us by its steady
flow of the remorseless passage of time, might have
spurred us to action, encouraged us to strike one blow
before we too are carried away, like the people in the
hymn. But wherever humanity has built a bridge over
a river, there, unless you are traversing a wilderness,
you will find people leaning over the bridge, absorbed
in the spectacle of running water. Small boys, with
all the opportunities of life opening before them, fritter

49

them away the moment they come to a stream ; a kind
of ritual sense bids them halt, sail paper boats, throw
stones at a bottle, or paddle. Bathing itself, the adult's
compensation for not being allowed to paddle, would
lose half its seductive charm if it were not so evidently
a pure waste of time. And there are those fearless
enquirers into the nature of things who would maintain
that the joys of the fisherman – most solid of all joys,
and most incommunicable – are really determined by
the prodigious waste of time which occurs between
one rise and the next. . . . But I will not argue the
matter.

Anyhow, it is certain that Miles Bredon, who had
set out after breakfast to explore the scenes which were
to be the setting for one of his most bewildering professional exploits, no sooner reached the bridge than
he began throwing sticks into the river to watch them
travel over the falls ; and his wife (who really, like
most women, hated wasting time) humoured him to the
extent of throwing in sticks from a little distance away.
Whereupon the competitive spirit, which is for ever
overlooking and degrading our pastimes, entered the
field ; and the racing of sticks over Glendounie Falls
began to be a game, with its own rules, system of scor-
ing, and technique. The morning might easily have
passed amid such dissipations, if their hostess, Mrs.
McBrayne, had not come out to them in the middle of
it, bearing a telegram with all the circumstance which
attends, in those parts, any such manifestation from
the outer world. It proved to be only a telegram from
Mr. Pulteney, announcing the train by which he was
arriving (the only train, for that matter, in the day).
But it put an end to the game ; they had stopped,
shamefacedly, as we all do stop when we are caught
making fools of ourselves ; and by the time the

message had been read the spell was broken. " Mrs. McBrayne," said Angela, " we were wondering whether it's possible to get leave to go round the island, while the house is empty ? It looks rather fascinating."

Mrs. McBrayne replied in that musical, rather painstaking English which belongs to the Gaelic-bred – so utterly unlike anything which the Southerner describes as " a Scotch accent." She also replied with the perfect courtesy of the Highlander, anxious, without servility, to make the incalculable visitor feel at home. " Oh, I'm sure there wouldn't be any objection, madam ; you see, the gentlemen that come here for the fishing are allowed to go where they like when there's no one in the house. The notice there is only put up to prevent people coming and picnicking, madam, because Sir Charles is afraid they might burn the wood. (Only last week, or it might be a little earlier, there was a fire on the brae at night ; and it must have been picnickers, for it had been put out before Mr. McBrayne reached it.) But the gentlemen that take places on the estate always come and go where they like, madam, except just when the house itself is let. And the gentlemen won't be coming till Saturday first ; so I'm sure that'll be quite all right, madam." And you felt she would have stood holding the gate open at the end of the bridge, had the gate been shut, in those hospitable regions, to discourage the stranger from entering.

They did not, however, follow the drive right up to the front door, as if they were callers. A path on their left, cut through an encroaching thicket of rhododendrons, was plainly the beginning of a walk round the island ; and you cannot know an island, they agreed, without walking round it. Their way was roofed with toppling branches of the shrub, carpeted with the long, creeping shoots that had escaped the attention of the plasher ; then, after a few minutes, they came out upon a grassy lane fringed with bracken, with a steep bank falling away on their left so as to give them glimpses, between oak branches, of the river gliding past in diminished stream. To their right was a slope of some two hundred feet up to the summit of the island, a rude tableland crowned with oak and larch and pine ; it was intersected by deep gullies, whose ferns and moss and rotting trunks testified to the presence of streams in winter.

It was an island fertile in decay. Overwooded, and visited by more than its share of Highland rain, its airs were continually dank, its soil spongy. By the fallen trees which lay there undisturbed, with their fantastic roots turned heavenwards as if in appeal against human neglect, grew toadstools, vividly coloured, mocking the forms of artificial things. Among the strange fungus growths you found, in springtime, that reputed delicacy the morel, an unshapely mass of edible corruption. The ferns which abounded in the rock crevices were, for the most part, of the simplest geometrical pattern, as if survivals from some primitive period when forms were still undifferentiated, old days of nature's apprenticeship. This was in the woods ; in the clearings, rare by comparison, heather and bracken and bog-myrtle delimited their own spheres, invaded continually by the vigorous burgeoning of rhododendrons and azaleas, man's importation. So rapid was their growth that every path, except the main drive, had to be cut afresh almost yearly lest it should relapse into jungle.

Amidst all this foison of vegetable life, there was an uncanny absence of moving things. Flies indeed abounded, and wild bees ; and spiders covered whole tracts of the ground with nets of gossamer that sparkled in the dew of early morning. But birds shunned it for the most part, as if it had been Avernus lake ; song was so rare in the bushes that you turned to hear it with a start. The rabbits which abounded on the mainland seldom scurried across your path here, and no squirrels played hide-and-seek among the branches. All the more startling were your occasional encounters with wild life, when a caper rocketed noisily out of the trees above you, or the herons visited their sanctuary, or a stray roe plunged away in alarm at your footsteps, a brown patch among the undergrowth. The animal kingdom, instead of being a friendly neighbour which surrounded your walks with familiar companionship, alternately awed you by its silence, or startled you by its emergence.

Even the wind, on the surrounding moors a constant and often a boisterous playmate, seldom did more than stir the very tops of the trees, so sheltered was the island in that river-chiselled cup of the hills. As for human companionship, you could not suspect that there was any other representative of your own species this side of the concrete bridge. A stillness of complete isolation made you feel as if you had wandered into fairyland, utterly satisfying to the eye, yet vaguely menacing, uncanny ; you could not but think of yourself as an intruder. To right and to left of you, just beyond the river, were frequented roads, and you heard the crunch of gears changing on the unexpected rise before Glendounie churchyard ; but you felt insulated, cut adrift from your kind, on these few, unserviceable acres of haunted ground.

The path which fringed the island, almost at river level towards the south, but skirting, at the north end, the edges of a precipitous cliff, gave them glimpses of exquisite beauty, but little to feed their curiosity in

the way of human interference. The wooden seats
which had been put up at one or two points, where
the view gave excuse for lingering, had fallen into
advanced decay ; the low bridges over the stream-beds
were moss-hidden and rotten with damp ; a stretch of
wire designed, long since, to mark off the beginnings of
a garden, sagged and gaped ruinously. It was the more
surprising when, after walking perhaps a quarter of a
mile southwards and upstream, they came across a boat,
of the sort anglers use, marooned on a little slope of
sand that traversed, unexpectedly, the screen of shrubs
and high bracken between them and the river. This,
plainly, was still in use ; its timbers were sound, its
paint decently fresh ; the oars, too, had been left lying
in it, with that complete trust in the honesty of the
passer-by which the Scottish Highlands seem to culti-
vate. A four-fluked anchor, grotesquely large to be
carried in so small a boat, moored it firmly to the sand ;
firmly, and it seemed unnecessarily, for it was high and
dry, nearly two feet away from the swirling river, and
a foot at least above it.

"That," said Bredon, "is odd. That is very odd."
He talked in the low voice most of us use in church ;
the uncanny solitude of their surroundings seemed to
impose the tone on him.

"Meaning why do they keep a boat here at all ?
The fishing, I suppose. You can't expect Edward to
stand about all day in his waterproof crawlers, and
besides, it's awfully deep. I expect this is what he
fishes from."

"I know ; the only crab about that idea is that the
boat's the wrong side of the river. The fishing tenants
don't, normally at least, live on the island ; and I
expect you'll find Pulteney has a boat all of his own
rather higher up, on the mainland. No, I should say

this is probably a relic of the days when there was no concrete bridge there, and the wooden one which went before it was apt to get washed away in floods. Tiresome, you see, not to be able to fetch the groceries. But I wasn't thinking so much of why the boat is kept here, really."

" Well, there's no need to be intolerable about it. What's your trouble ? I say, Miles, I know one thing – it's going to be a tiny bit of a nuisance, this boat. Because it means Lethaby and Co. can slink across the river with their oars muffled, however one does that, while you and I are sitting watching the end of the bridge."

" That's true, and pretty damnable. You could land on the other side without being visible from the bridge. However, Pulteney will have to fish off the south end of the island as much as possible. I gather the other side of the island, and the shore opposite, are both too sheer to be much good for boating, except again just at the south end. He can manage, only I suppose he'll look rather a fool always fishing at the same place. Meanwhile, I repeat that this boat is odd – you don't seem to share the feeling ? "

" I know perfectly well that if I show the smallest sign of curiosity you'll start being mysterious. However, come on ; I can see you're dying to tell me all about it. I hope you're going to be a bit more communicative on this trip than you generally are ; I hate guessing."

" It's odd that you should say that, because as a matter of fact it's quite likely that I shall be rather mysterious. I'm not ragging when I say that, Angela ; you'll have to try not to mind. But this little problem won't do either of us any harm. The point being, how long ago was there any water to speak of in this river ?

Didn't Mrs. McBrayne say they'd been having un-usually dry weather for the time of year this month past ? "

" She did, I think ; and she said the river had been low for a long time. What's your objection ? "

" Why, the way the boat's sitting there just a foot or two out of the water. No, don't say somebody hauled it up out of the water. It would be an infernal sweat – look at the steepness of this bank ; and besides, you'd see the marks of the keel where it had been drawn up, and there aren't any. Therefore the boat has been left high and dry because the river gradually shrunk ; it was afloat or nearly afloat when it was last brought to land, when the river was a good deal fuller. Any objection to that ? "

" Something in what you say ; but I don't see why it's specially exciting, do I ? "

" Exciting, you poor mutt, for this reason – that if it was moored when the water was already very low, and since it was moored the water has shrunk even lower, that means, almost certainly, that it was only moored about a week ago. Of course, it might have been moored there as long ago as last summer ; but if it had, the winter floods would have swamped it, and there'd be water in it. The obvious conclusion, any-how, is that it was moored last at some time during the present drought. And we know that nobody's been living on the island for more than a month past. The odd point is, who moored it ? "

" McBrayne, probably. Dash it all, he can trot about the island as much as he wants to. Why shouldn't he have been using it ? "

" Putting on his Leander tie and going out for a nice quiet scull ? You don't seem to me to have got the Highland mentality, quite. If McBrayne wants to wander about the island for any reason, he goes over by the bridge and comes back by the bridge ; there's no temptation to do anything else. No, it's natural enough for people living on the island to use that boat now and again ; when they are taking a walk, for example, in the direction of Strathdounie, right up-stream, it's a short cut to take the boat across from here instead of going all the way round by the bridge. But if a casual day-visitor to the island uses that boat, it looks to me as if he must be up to something funny. That's what's odd."

Though Angela continued to profess a languid interest in these speculations, it was her task, as usual, to " pump " Mrs. McBrayne ; and it certainly did seem that the intending treasure-hunters had paid a visit to the island only a week or so before, " just to look round and see that everything was how they wanted it." They had come by car, soon after luncheon-time, and Mr. McBrayne had, of course, gone up to the house with them ; but they had sent him back to the cottage, professing an anxiety to see how the land lay, and had spent the rest of the afternoon there, only returning the keys at about seven o'clock. Questioned – in quite another context, of course – about the use of the boat on the island, Mrs. McBrayne bore out the truth of Miles Bredon's speculations. There was another boat, higher up stream, which was used for the fishing ; the one on the island was not used much, but was always at the disposal of the tenants. It would be handy for a picnic, now and again, when there were children there. And perhaps the gentlemen would want it, looking for the treasure ; for there were parts of the island where the cliff came down so sheer you couldn't climb down to them.

From this interview, Angela was called away by the

necessity of meeting Mr. Pulteney at Inverness. She found him looking rather lost at the end of a long and melancholy platform, but quite unruffled by his journey. Of the five hours from Perth, he had nothing to say except " I should suppose that they have very few accidents on this line." He was as excited as a schoolboy at getting away from school, and at the unwonted prospect of salmon-fishing. " But I am terrified," he added, " by the thought of fishing in the presence of another human being. In my lonely vigils by trout streams, I have developed habits of soliloquy which might easily lend themselves to misconstruction. And then, the whole technique is so strange to me. I have consulted a large quantity of books, and amassed a considerable amount of theoretical knowledge about the habits of the fish. Or rather, ignorance ; for it appears that nobody knows why the brute behaves as it does ; why it swims up rivers, for example, when apparently it would be much happier in the sea ; why it grows to such enormous dimensions ; or why it insists on taking flies, occasionally, although it has no intention of eating them. It seems as if it were more like a schoolboy than a fish. Tell me, have the treasure-hunters arrived ? It will be something to have neighbours who are engaged on a more sleeveless errand, as they say, than myself."

" They're supposed to be coming to-morrow. Mr. Lethaby is, anyhow ; I suppose one calls him Mister even if one suspects that he's a crook ? He's motoring over from wherever it is he has a house in Scotland ; the other man comes from London. Wonderful what a lot one can pick up in the way of gossip, isn't it, in country places ? I suppose we shall all be peeping through the blinds to see what he looks like. I rather enjoy peeping through blinds, don't you ? "

" My profession precludes me. There seems to be a sort of understanding that schoolmasters should observe a code of honour which never yet existed among their pupils. There is perpetual war between us, with Queensberry rules on one side and all-in wrestling on the other. It will be all the more refreshing, to be thoroughly unscrupulous for once. If there is any particularly low-down job to be executed, I hope I may be chosen for it, rather than Mr. Bredon or yourself. I hope he is well, by the way ? God bless my soul ! Is that an inn we just passed ? I had supposed there were no places of refreshment in Scotland except hotels and public-houses."

" There's nothing with a licence within half-a-dozen miles of where we're going ; so you'll have to be content with what we've laid in. But that's plenty ; Miles always does himself well when the Company is paying his expenses. Tell me, do you ever go back to Chilthorpe ? "

" I was there last summer. They have put in electric light, now, at the Load of Mischief, but Mrs. Davis' cuisine remains unaltered. She speaks of you most kindly, in accents of gentle regret, as if she lamented the passing of those golden days in which it was possible for millionaires to asphyxiate themselves by mismanaging the gas-plant. That is, really, a most satisfying piece of landscape ! It would be impossible to mark it less than eighty-five per cent."
And so the old gentleman rambled on, until they left the sunlight behind, and plunged into those dark shadows of the hills which cool, for the Isle of Erran, the hottest of summer evenings.

Miles Bredon was discovered wandering about the garden and the woods which surrounded it, in the vain hope of finding a vantage-point from which it was possible to see the house on the island from the other side of the water. He took Mr. Pulteney with him, while Angela went to put away the car. " I wanted just to explain something," he began at once. " I'm afraid you may find me rather uncommunicative about this business as it goes on. It isn't just mystery-making for the love of the thing, though I suppose I have a silly fondness for that, like most people. But this time I am really a bit anxious about the job ; one at least of the two people who are after this treasure is an obvious wrong 'un, and that means there may be a spot of danger in it. So the less I explain things to Angela, the less chance there is of her worrying, or possibly even getting herself into danger by putting her nose into it too much. So my idea is to keep the whole thing under my hat, as far as possible, till we're well out of it. I shall be awfully grateful for anything you can do in the way of keeping an eye on the gentlemen opposite. But I shall be still more grateful if you can manage to keep Angela amused, and take her mind off business ; because, as I say, I'm a bit nervous about her butting in. You don't think me frightfully rude, I hope."

" Mr. Bredon," replied the old gentleman, " you may count on my discretion. You are providing me with a mile or two of the best salmon-fishing in Scot-land, and it would be a poor return for your generosity if I repaid it by fishing for information. My curiosity – an odious vice – shall be mortified. As for the danger, I hope you exaggerate it. I will not be insincere enough to wish, with Nestor, that I was young and active enough to help you. Nestor's reminiscences of his early exploits are never, as far as I know, borne out by any independent testimony. And for myself, I feel perfectly certain that I should lose my head in a crisis.

I am more fitted, I think, to be a squire of dames. Ha ! I see Mrs. Bredon waving to us. Unless she is practising a heartless deception on us, dinner waits. It is never too early to dine."

CHAPTER V: THE RETURN OF THE NATIVE

THEY FOUND IT DIFFICULT to understand why, on the Saturday morning, they were all three keyed up to such a pitch of excitement. It would not be Bredon's first sight of Lethaby, or of Henderson either. He had, without difficulty, secured an invitation to a party in London earlier in the month, where Lethaby was as usual both blatant and voluble; and he had plenty of opportunity for studying the habits of that public character – or at least those habits which he allowed to appear in public. Henderson was more difficult to track down; but there are few things which cannot be managed if you have the Indescribable behind you, and Bredon was privileged to stand, in the disguise of a supernumerary waiter, at the doorway of an eating-house which the Digger frequented, so that the look of the man at least was familiar to him. Yet the prospect of " peeping through the blind " seemed irresistible, and the exact manner of doing it occupied most of their discussion during the morning – it was clear that Lethaby, if he had an eighty-mile drive from Perthshire to negotiate, could not be expected before the afternoon.

In the end, it was decided that Bredon, who had the best reasons for keeping himself in the background, should watch from inside the house ; that is, if at the last moment he was able to tear himself away from a

game of patience in order to do it. Angela could have
a deck-chair on the little lawn by the side of the cottage ;
and she posted herself there with a book. Pulteney
was on the other side of the road in a paddock, practising, willingly enough, the art of casting flies. So
they passed a quarter of an hour, perhaps, till the
profound peace of the valley was disturbed by a distant
skirl of bagpipes. This was nothing, in itself, to rouse
interest ; you would naturally take it to be an itinerant
musician soliciting half-crowns. But a remarkable
insufficiency in the performance itself discounted this
view ; and it was observable that the pipes, as they
drew nearer, were sometimes interrupted, most un-
musically, by the blare of a motor-horn. At about two
o'clock, a powerful car was seen approaching, in which
Lethaby, somewhat cramped for room, was occupied
in piping himself home. He was in full Highland costume, and his method of progress had obviously been
designed to impress whatever reporters – and you may
be sure there were not a few of them – might be awaiting
him in the streets of Inverness. But he was a dogged
humorist, and would keep his joke going as long as he
had any fraction of an audience. The grace with
which he bowed and waved his bonnet, first to Angela
and then to Mr. Pulteney, was carefully studied ;
though there may have been some ground for the
interpretation put upon his behaviour by the outraged
countryside, which was that " the gentleman was sadly
in liquor."

If it had been possible to drive a car while playing
the bagpipes, it may be assumed that Vernon Lethaby
would have done so. But he remained in the comparative spaciousness of a back seat ; his charioteer
was designed to attract hardly less attention than
himself. He wore a plain chauffeur's livery, but was

unmistakably part of the pageant – his very red face and very bushy beard suggested the typical Highlander as portrayed in a late Victorian comic paper. The windows on either side of him were shut, in defiance of the weather, and did not look as if they had been cleaned at all recently ; so that it was difficult to determine, with a rapid glance, how much of his appearance was genuine. He seemed to be entirely concentrated on his duties as a chauffeur, not entering into the spirit of the thing, but rather, if you could judge from his general attitude, a trifle ashamed of it.

The luggage conveyed on this curious equipage – it was Angela who reported on this – was quite unobtrusive ; it consisted only of a couple of suit-cases. It was difficult to believe that Lethaby meant business at all, until a lorry drove up about half an hour later, well stocked with ropes, spades, picks, and other implements proper to the sport of treasure-hunting ; among other contrivances, there was an unmistakable rope-ladder. Two men sat in front, and drove away again in the empty lorry ; their identity could be in no doubt, since they stopped and chatted with Mrs. McBrayne for nearly half an hour on their homeward journey ; they were, she reported, men from a neighbouring township, and the goods they delivered had all been hired locally. They had unpacked these, at Lethaby's directions, outside the front door of the house, and left them there covered with a tarpaulin.

The chauffeur's appearance was, naturally, the main topic of conversation between the three watchers over the tea-table. That the man was heavily disguised, Bredon affirmed with more than his usual positiveness. " Of course, the usual tests didn't apply. In the

ordinary way, a man who disguises his face is bound
to give himself away, unless he is a real actor. He
knows that he looks odd, and the effect of that is to
make all his gestures and (as far as you can see them)
the movements of his features unnatural. But a
chauffeur is almost the only person in the world who
has a good excuse for sitting quite motionless and
looking inscrutable ; it is the badge of his tribe. So
I've nothing positive against our friend with the sandy
whiskers, except perhaps that his face looked a bit too
shiny. But if you work the thing out as a problem in
probabilities, the chances are too strong against a real
chauffeur turning out in face-fittings like that. It
simply isn't done."

"It is very singular," mused Mr. Pulteney, "that
the professions people adopt should have such a direct
influence on their tendency to hirsuteness. How seldom
we meet a bearded railway-porter, for example ! The
coachmen of our youth affected whiskers, long after
they had ceased to be fashionable ; but the tending
and driving of motor-cars seems to produce, almost
everywhere, a clean-shaven type. Yes, Mr. Lethaby
is an eccentric ; but I doubt if he could bring himself
to employ, permanently at least, a chauffeur of such
nihilistic appearance."

"There's no proof that he does employ him
regularly," Angela pointed out. "He may have been
hired for the afternoon, just because he looked the
part. I should hate to think that beard wasn't real ;
he looked so touching in it."

"But he knows how to drive," objected Miles, "so
he can't have been just picked up at the street-corner ;
and he knows his way to the Isle of Erran, so he must
either be local, in which case Mrs. McBrayne would recognise him, or else a man who can use maps. His driving

is much more certainly genuine than his face. No, the betting is so heavily on the side of its being make-up that you've got to proceed on the assumption that it was. And, if you make that assumption, the obvious question is, What the devil did he do it for ? "

" What does he do anything for ? " retorted Angela. " Dash it all, you can't treat a man like that as if he were a sort of super-criminal, with a diabolical ingenuity in covering his tracks, and all that sort of thing. The plain fact about Vernon Lethaby is that he's got an awfully bad sense of humour. He thinks it will amuse the comic papers, and annoy all these nice Highland people, if he carries off this absurd expedition of his with a lot of music-hall jokes about kilts and haggis and things. He's quite unlike anybody you've met so far – professionally, I mean ; and it'll lead you right up the garden if you try to give any rational account of the way he does things. He's a bad joke, but don't let's get wrong from the start by taking him seriously."

" Oh, I know all that," admitted her husband. " The only real trouble about Lethaby is that he wasn't drowned at birth. But he's not a lunatic ; he jolly well knows which side his bread's buttered, and he isn't insuring himself with the Indescribable just for fun. Therefore it's always possible that the maddest-looking things he does are really done with a design ; and all the more difficult to see through because they're so mad-looking. He may have dressed his man up like a Guy Fawkes merely for a rag. But it's also possible that he dressed up the man he took in the car with him because he was somebody who would be recognised, and Lethaby didn't want him to be recognised."

" You don't suggest he's trying to hush up this

man Henderson ? His picture's been in all the papers weeks ago. There couldn't be any point, could there, in smuggling Henderson on to the island, and at the same time kidding us that he was still in London ? "

" Dash it all, you're assuming too much. You're assuming he knows we're watching him, which pray heaven he doesn't. But if he does know, he might just find it convenient to do just the opposite – to pretend that Henderson is here when he's really somewhere else. He may be counting on our getting exactly the impression you suggest – that the red-faced Aunt Sally on the box must have been Henderson in disguise. And meanwhile Henderson is up to dirty work somewhere else."

" Sounds pretty thin to me. Anyhow, it's not much good worrying about that till we see whether Henderson does turn up, all present and correct, on the evening train. I wonder whether I could find out, tactfully, from Mrs. McBrayne, whether they were expecting a chauffeur on the island or not ? He'd have to doss somewhere."

" I don't think that's altogether a bad idea. Meanwhile, there is my patience to finish ; so I think I'll sit on guard and see whether anybody goes to meet the evening train or not. Best, I think, if you and Pulteney don't show up this time."

It looked, certainly, as if Henderson were expected according to programme. At a suitable hour, the discreet sound of a motor-horn on the circuitous drive which led down from the house to the bridge attracted Bredon to the window. This time, it was only the comic chauffeur who made his appearance, and no effort was being made to turn the occasion into a triumphal progress. The windows were still up, and it was still impossible to get a good look at him. Bredon stood looking after him, his brow furrowed with thought, and was rewarded by a fresh opportunity of spying. Lethaby himself came down to the bridge ; his head was bare, and it seemed that he must be merely taking an evening stroll. He hung over the balustrade for a minute or two, then followed the course of the drive, and was lost to sight among the trees. Was he conscious that he was being watched, or liable to be watched, from the gardener's cottage ? If so, his movements were admirably disciplined to conceal his thoughts ; he neither looked round nor avoided looking round too much, neither hurried on his way nor ostentatiously lingered. If it was a performance, it was a perfect performance.

Angela had taken Pulteney out for a walk ; the return of the car from Inverness, whither it was presumably bound, could not be expected for over an hour. With the air of a man brushing aside some petty distraction that has interrupted the tenor of his life's work, Bredon went back to his patience. It was fortunate, he reflected, that on these remote Highland lanes there were always sheep or children straying about, to necessitate the sounding of a horn ; he would be disturbed all right when anything fresh turned up. The seven ? No, the eight ; he could have done without that eight. Oh, well, it might have been worse. . . . The next sound which awoke him from his busy trance was that of gears changing, to meet the slope on the further side of the bridge. He leapt to the window, only in time to see the back of the car disappearing, without a glimpse at its occupants. Oh, Lord ! That was a bad bit of staff-work. He would have to admit his dereliction of duty to Angela, and he hated admitting things to Angela. Like most happily married couples, they lived in a state of perpetual propaganda at each other's expense.

She greeted him, however, with words that immediately restored his self-confidence. " Oo, did you see them ? We did ; we couldn't help it, you know, Miles, because we were coming back down the lane, and we only just managed to avoid the car by crushing in against the wall ; came upon us round a corner all sudden-like."

" As a matter of fact, I was rather busy with my patience, and I let it go ; well knowing that as you'd been sent out on purpose to avoid the Isle of Erran party you'd be sure to go snooping at them out of hedgerows. *Was* it Henderson ? "

" What a filthy liar you are. I'm not sure we ought to tell you. Shall we, Mr. Pulteney ? "

" I have contrived to live sixty years in comparative peace, by a strict observance of the rule that you should never interfere in an argument between man and wife. But, if I am called upon to express an opinion, I would suggest that there can be no harm in gratifying Mr. Bredon's curiosity. After all, it will not be long before he finds out for himself."

" That's true. But you do admit, don't you, that you've been caught napping this time over your repulsive patience ? "

" For the sake of peace, I do. Now that I know it *was* Henderson, perhaps you would let me know about any further details that struck your attention. Was he driving beside the chauffeur, or behind him ? "

" Beside him. But there were a lot of odds and ends in the car, more spades and things, so it would have been rather uncomfy to sit behind. I shouldn't start detecting about that, if I were you. Henderson was quite simply dressed, in a Lowland, not to say English costume. He may have had a mouth organ, but he was not playing it as he passed. He was smoking a cigarette ; brand unknown. Anything else ? "

" The chauffeur, ass. Did you get a better look at him ? "

" Well, you know, that's rather odd. We were on the right-hand side of the road, because I always think it's so much nicer to see the cars before they run you over. So we ought to have got a close-up ; but I'm dashed if he didn't lift up his arm just as he passed us, and scratch his head. I've often thought what a bore it must be scratching your head and taking off your cap with the same hand, which is what chauffeurs always do. That just prevented us seeing his face ; and it might, of course, have been done a-purpose. All we could see was his hair, rather matted and untidy, as if to match his beard. Chauffeurs are generally so sleek, aren't they ? "

" Yes, that's well noticed. Now, why can't I take my eyes off these people for one moment without things starting to happen ? He lifted his cap, as if to make an excuse for hiding his face with his arm ; and in doing so he let you have a sight of his hair, which was matted and untidy. What did you make of it, Pulteney ? Did you think the chauffeur was having genuine scalp-trouble, or did you too get the impression that he wanted to hide his rather unmistakable features ? "

" My own impressions were, I am sorry to say, even more fanciful. Just as they came in sight round the corner, the passenger, this Henderson, turned and said something to the driver ; and I got the idea that it was in obedience to a suggestion from him that the driver lifted his arm. But, of course, we are all apt to

be guilty of *post hoc ergo propter hoc*, when an unexpected movement follows on an inaudible remark."

" That would be worse than ever. Henderson had
never seen either of you two before, as far as we know ;
and you weren't near enough to the house, I should
have thought, to be suspicious in any way. No, I'm
hanged if I see it. Unless, of course – but that seems
too fantastic. You didn't know what Henderson
looked like before, I suppose ? "

" No, but I did," put in Angela. " You remember,
you showed me his portrait in one of the papers, and
made me learn it by heart. And there really wasn't
any doubt about it. Those rather pouting lips of his
would give him away a mile off. By the way, I saw
Mrs. McBrayne just now, and she says the gentlemen
did say they would probably be bringing a chauffeur.
There's a garage on the island, only a wooden affair,
but elaborate enough to have a sort of cock-loft fitted
up as a living-room, and she made a bed for the
chauffeur up there, and all the rest of it."

" Yes, it all seems to need a bit of thinking over.
I think I'll take a bit of a stroll for a quarter of an hour
or so – no, I won't be late for dinner. If you want to
shout for me, I shall be along the river bank ; upstream, I mean." And upstream he went, not entirely
to be alone with his thoughts, but with some idea of
verifying an insane suspicion. The soft cushion of moss
and pine-needles buoyed up his feet, the gathering
darkness of the trees enveloped him in a friendly
silence. Smoke rose from the house on the island,
showing that there, too, dinner was being cooked for
its mysterious inhabitants. Who cooked it ? The
chauffeur, perhaps ; or possibly Henderson ; no doubt
a man who had knocked about the world so much had
picked up something of the domestic arts. The path

71

drew nearer to the river, and came out, as he expected, close to the bank just opposite where the boat was moored on the island shore. He tantalised himself for a moment or two by keeping his eyes fixed on the ground, then resolutely looked across to the sandy patch where the boat should be.

There was no mistake about it. Only her bows rested on the sand ; a swirling eddy of water at her stern showed that it was riding full on the river's surface. Bredon whistled slightly. "And that," he said, "is one of the things we do *not* talk about at dinner."

And indeed, there were other matters to discuss. "Mr. Pulteney," said Angela over the soup, "we've got a treat for you to-morrow."

"And to-morrow is Sunday ! I had no idea that Scotland provided any treats on the day of rest, except a sufficient distance from all representatives of one's own persuasion to make church-going optional. But perhaps that is what you referred to ? "

"No ; guess again. You see, the day before yesterday, I think it was, Sir Charles Airdrie called ; that's our landlord. I suppose he really came to see that we weren't poaching rabbits or cutting our names on the windowsill, or whatever it is undesirable tenants do. But it was quite a polite call, and he asked us to go over to lunch at Dreams Castle to-morrow. Local by-laws make it impossible to shoot or fish on a Sunday, but there's nothing against eating, and walking down to the farm afterwards to have a look at the cattle. Are you good at prodding bulls, Mr. Pulteney ? "

"I should hesitate before taking the initiative in that way. It would be putting ideas into their heads. Do I understand that I am included in the invitation ? "

"Of course you are. Dash it all, you're doing all

the fishing, so you're our only excuse for being here. No motive is accepted as an explanation for visiting these parts except wanting to kill things. If I were you, I should cram up one or two more of your salmon books ; they're sure to put you through it, up at Dreams Castle."

The luncheon-party on the following day was much as Angela had pictured it. They were not the only guests ; a complete party of tenants had driven over from Strathdounie Lodge, where they were fishing till the shooting started. They were a syndicate, and neither Sir Charles nor his daughter seemed to be very successful in distinguishing them from one another. All of them seemed to be rich ; all owed their prosperity to mysterious operations in the City ; you had never heard of any of them, yet you felt that with all that money they must be tremendously important. The men gave you the impression of having red faces, puffy necks, indifferent manners, and a rather possessive, back-slapping attitude towards their women-folk. These were a varied but not interesting assortment ; the only one among them who seemed to possess any marked individuality was Lady Hermia Jennings, a mature beauty who had fallen back on a rich marriage and a rather indiscriminate patronage of the arts. It appeared that her husband was among those present ; but nothing short of a fatiguing scrutiny could possibly enlighten the stranger as to whose husband was which.

Mr. Pulteney was much in the hands of the ladies ; his old-fashioned courtesy was an interesting novelty to them, and they were untiring in drawing out his polysyllables. Angela was singled out for the un-remitted attentions of her host ; there was a freshness about her which became the more marked by contrast with the bridge-and-cocktails atmosphere of her rivals, and Sir Charles fell an easy victim to it. As for her husband, he did not get much out of Mrs. Cayle, Sir Charles' widowed daughter, for she spent most of her time bestowing frowns and rebukes on the two children, who were eagerly letting themselves be spoiled by all this grown-up company. He was the more thrown upon the society of Lady Hermia, who sat on his other side at the luncheon-table. She was (as he said afterwards) one of those damnable women who will always look at you soulfully as if you had said something interesting.

She proved, however, unexpectedly well informed on the subject of Vernon Lethaby. Naturally, the general conversation had turned a good deal on the prospects and personality of the two treasure-hunters; on Lethaby especially, whose triumphal progress to the Isle of Erran was already common talk in the country-side, and had not lost in the telling. Sir Charles kept his own counsel, merely shrugging his shoulders when he was asked whether he really believed in the existence of the treasure. But from the other men at the table there was a chorus of gruff reprobation. Feller was clean off his chump – feller ought to have been locked up long ago, everybody knew that; nobody minded his wasting his money on a wild-goose chase, but nobody, dammit, asked him to make a confounded music-hall turn of the whole show; one thing to amuse yourself with these bright-young-thing stunts in Chelsea, but in the Highlands, one meant to say, it was going a good deal over the edge – fact of the matter was, Lethaby was a scug; one had known him at school, and he always was a scug, till the day he was super'd; anyone'd tell you that – what? Good Lord, yes, rolling drunk, and the chauffeur not much better – no, by gad, he did *not* look like a chauffeur;

a Russian or something, people were saying – anyhow, he mustn't be allowed to get away with that sort of thing ; he wasn't going to get asked over to Strathdounie, if he found all the Queen of Sheba's diamonds – rotten exhibitionist, that was the word, yes, that was just about what the feller was.

Fragments of criticism to this effect reached Bredon's ears as he wrestled with Lady Hermia's conversation. From talking about the two children who were present she had passed on to Bredon's own children, their names, their ages, their habits, and so on – a topic on which few fathers like to dilate, Miles Bredon least of all men. He noticed that Lady Hermia was, like himself, overhearing snatches of the general talk, and did not look as if she were in agreement with it. She had a reputation, he remembered, for acting as a kind of fairy godmother to penniless and commonly worthless young men whom she thought clever. It was quite probable that Vernon Lethaby would be one of her cavaliers. On the whole, Bredon decided, it would be better not to commit himself on the subject of the island and its tenants until she had shown her hand.

" They're all wrong," she said suddenly, " about Vernon Lethaby. I've known him for years ; in fact, he's one of my *great* friends. Of course, perhaps he may be just a teeny bit of an exhibitionist, but then I think it's so dull to be quite normal, don't you ? All this song and dance he's making about his treasure-hunt – it's really just excitement, don't you know, like a schoolboy's. And of course, you've got to remember that he's a Strathspiel ; that silly old aunt of his won't let him forget it, lending him a house which is no better than a mausoleum of Jacobite relics. You see, he feels rather like a disinherited prince himself ; he's told me that, often. It isn't just one of his publicity stunts, this ; he really means business. I sometimes think it's quite awful that so few of our generation are trying to understand the young people. They've no morals, of course, most of them, but they *are* honest about it, and I do think that's the most important thing, don't you ? "

Bredon was at that perilous stage in which the soul is besieged in a fortress of boredom, and untimely laughter threatens to come to its relief. He made a kind of swallowing noise, which was fortunately interpreted as assent.

" I knew you'd feel that. Of course, you really belong to the younger generation yourself. I do wish you knew Vernon Lethaby ; I feel you'd get on so well together, somehow. And I'm sure Mrs. Bredon would love him. He does want good influences – he's had such a difficult life ; and to tell the truth, I'm just the tiniest bit scared about him being shut up all alone on that rather spooky island with this Henderson person. Vernon says he's all right ; but then, Vernon's so good-natured *au fond* that he always sees the best in everybody. I suppose you couldn't bear it if I came over one day and introduced you ? I can't very well ask him over to Strathdounie, because it's not his world at all. But of course I shall be going over to see him ; I was wondering if I might pick you up at the cottage one morning, and take you over to see how he's getting on with his treasure-grubbing ? "

This time, it was evident that something must be said. There was a moment's delay, while Bredon considered whether it was possible to get out of such an invitation, and if so, whether he wanted to get out of it. Then – for he was something of a fatalist – he decided to welcome this tiresome woman's offer as a golden opportunity for getting closer to the scene of action. " Of course," he said, " I should love to meet him. You could ring up any time, so as to make sure I'm in when you come round. I don't promise to see eye to eye with him, because I suppose I'm really a bit of an old fogey myself. But if there's any chance of being useful, I'm fond enough of poking my nose into other people's business to see it through."

" That's too divine of you. Oh, Lord, now we've got to go round that beastly farm ; I detest going for walks on Sunday afternoons, don't you ? It all belongs to the Church epoch, and that's so depressing. Well, don't forget ; I'll call round the day after to-morrow, probably, but I can't be quite certain of the day. One's life isn't one's own, even up here."

The pilgrimage to the byres took place with all the solemnity Angela had predicted. Mr. Pulteney confessed to her, as their orbits crossed for a moment, that he had no objection to the breezy call of incense-breathing morn, but towards the middle of the afternoon the agricultural atmosphere became, for his taste, rather pronounced. He was, however, unflagging in his expressions of admiration, though he was generally to be found in the rear of the procession when a door opened on one of the bulls. He would content himself, on such occasions, by describing what he could see of the animal inside as " upon my soul, a formidably developed specimen."

" Well," said Angela, as she took the wheel on their way home, " you didn't half get off with the Jennings woman. What were you being so matey about ? "

" Apart from a strong wish that she was dead," replied her husband, " I have no feelings about her which I should care to utter in mixed company. She is going to be useful, though ; I bet you couldn't have persuaded her to take us over to the island on a morning visit, and introduce us to the principals in the affair."

" Is she really going to do that ?   Miles, dear, do tell me how you managed it."

" I have my methods," replied Bredon.

CHAPTER VI: RELICS OF THE 'FORTY-FIVE

IT WAS NOT TILL the Wednesday that Lady Hermia re-
deemed her promise. All Monday and Tuesday there
was a bustle of activity on the island, though Lethaby
and Henderson seemed to be doing all the work themselves, and no more was seen of the enigmatic chauffeur.
It was surprising that no journalists called at the
island, unless you knew that Lethaby had accepted a
contract to write full and exclusive news of the expedition for one very low Sunday paper, and it had become
a point of honour with the remainder of the Press to
treat the subject with coldness. Mr. Pulteney fished
off the southern end of the island, and got a rise or two,
even hooked one fish, but saw nothing of any activity
in those parts. It was nearly at the northern end, on
the eastern side, and at no great distance from the cottage, that the search was proceeding. First there were
some digging operations near the edge of the cliff;
then these were suspended, and a rope-ladder was let
down over the face of the cliff itself, and there was
coming and going, with much comparing of notes, on
the narrow strip of rocky foreshore. This was child's
play for the watchers; the shore opposite was thickly
wooded, and could be picketed continually without
arousing suspicion, as long as you were careful not to
go home to meals while there was anybody in view.
Bredon even ventured to take some photographs of

the explorers, on the chance that they might come in useful, and forwarded them in a registered envelope to the Indescribable office, to show that he was earning his keep.

Lady Hermia arrived after tea-time on Wednesday afternoon, duly announced by telephone. Her manner was admirably gracious. "Calculated," as Angela said afterwards, " to give the impression that you'd married beneath you, Miles darling, without being the least nasty about it." Angela herself refused a rather tepid invitation to join the expedition to the island. She was expecting a message, she said, by telephone, and it was really rather important, or she'd have loved to come. This was by arrangement ; as Miles Bredon pointed out, it was just conceivable that something might be going on which would make it advisable for somebody to be keeping watch in the woods.

The house on the Isle of Erran is not unattractive on the first view. It is bogus antique, but of that romantic period, in the height of the Walter Scott influence, which is almost beginning to acquire an antiquity value of its own. The stone is of a soft red colour, the roofs steeply pitched, as befits the climate ; crow's-foot gables, queer little turret-windows, and a mass of ivy suggests to the eye, rather than to the mind, that you are in the presence of something venerable. No lawns or gardens surround it, though there are evidences that at some time attempts have been made at such culti-vation, only to be defeated by the island's irresistible fertility of the unwanted ; the old lawns are spongy with deep moss, the paths are almost obliterated by the shrubs which were meant to screen them, and a forlorn sundial opposite the front door suggests rather the primitive struggle against natural conditions than idle hours wasted on sunny afternoons. As they approached, the door stood open, but there was no sign of life in the front rooms, nor did a peal at the bell produce any other answer than its own echoes in the cavernous silence of the house.

" Well, we shall have to explore, that's all," said Lady Hermia. " Come inside the house for a moment ; it's rather quaint, you know." She led the way, as if she knew it, into one or two of the ground-floor living-rooms ; only one of which seemed to be in actual use, while the others contained piles of furniture swathed in dust-sheets, chairs that kicked out mysterious legs as they rested on sofas, and pictures left on the ground with their backs to the wall. Some of the rooms were elaborately panelled in pitch-pine, ruddy and un-varnished, others papered in dark, obsolete patterns. The one which seemed to be in use had already become a wilderness for untidiness ; so soon does the presence of two bachelors induce chaos. Unwashed coffee-cups, a suit of oilskins, a pack of cards scattered loosely over a table, beer-bottles, and an old-fashioned lantern with the candle burnt low in its socket, were among the exhibits which leapt to the eye. Besides these, there was a profusion of books and papers ; maps of the island and of the surrounding district, calculations (it seemed) of heights and distances, and a carefully kept set of accounts.

It was a piece of quite undeserved luck, Bredon said afterwards, that he should have turned over a book and lighted on a photograph, the photograph of a chart. We know, as Bredon did not then know, its history ; it was a print of the snapshot which Henderson had taken when he was left alone in the muniment-room at Dreams Castle. A representation of it is to be found elsewhere on these pages, so that a short description will suffice here. The lines, throughout, were somewhat blurred ; it might be that the camera had been slightly out of focus when the picture had been taken in the first instance, or the print might have slipped in its frame, or possibly it was an enlargement, and the enlarging process had been unskilfully carried out. That the photograph was, from first to last, an amateur's production, did not admit of doubt. At one point a blot appeared, presumably due to the spilling of some chemical while the film was being developed. The chart itself, too, had been very much of a home-made affair ; the island was represented quite roughly almost in an oval shape, although in real life it juts out rather towards the east as it approaches the north, towards the west as it approaches the south. The house was not marked, nor the bridge – possibly because there was no bridge at the time when the chart was made, nor were there any markings of heights or of woodland. The whole design of the artist had been, evidently, to establish the position of certain fixed points, represented by capital letters ; of these, B and C appeared on the island, D and E on the opposite shore, not far from the gardener's cottage.

All this Bredon took in with as rapid a survey as possible. He had, fortunately, the knack of photographing things on the brain by the eye ; a knack which only belongs to the potentially artistic section of mankind. Lady Hermia, with an equal lack of respect for the privacy of her hosts, was examining the list of accounts ; it was not difficult, therefore, to fix his attention on the chart for a minute or two, and order his brain to preserve the image intact. Then, rather clumsily and with a hand which felt as if it were shaking, he took up a cheap novel which was lying on the same table, glanced at its pages, and set it down again so that it covered the photograph. If it was important to have had a glimpse at the chart, it would be almost equally important to make sure that nobody knew he had done so.

" Come on, Mr. Bredon, don't spend all the evening over that shocker," said Lady Hermia, fixing the delay, woman-like, on him. " Of course, they may be any-where ; but the island, as you can see for yourself, isn't inconveniently large, and if we wander round a bit we're pretty certain to hear the pick and shovel busi-ness." She led the way once more ; this time down a narrow path, barely showing at intervals amid a tangle of bracken, rough grass and bog-myrtle, towards the northern point of the island. It was no business of Bredon's to let her know that they had reconnoitred the ground before ; still less, to explain that he knew exactly where the treasure-seekers were at work. He followed docilely, only noting out of the corner of his eye a spot, at some distance to their right, where a deep gash in the screen of rhododendrons showed that Lethaby and his partner had been hacking their way to the edge of the cliff.

The path ended in a little plateau, set about with firs, where a wooden seat, still in tolerable repair, in-dicated that here the traveller would do well to pause, and enjoy the view. And no wonder ; for here the island fell away steeply, down a precipitous slope to which a few rowans and silver birches clung at fantastic angles, towards the falls at its northern and western end. Opposite them, the mainland fell with equal abruptness ; ledges showed here and there, of grass or of heather, but so perched beneath overhanging rocks that you might be sure they were inaccessible ; on the brow of the slope, a covert of firs masked the road to Dreams. A little to the right, the churchyard of Glendounie was in plain view, its tombstones interrupting that prospect of savage scenery with the reminder that man inhabits these remote vicinities only to disappear from them ; river and rock and forest are more enduring than he.

And below ran the river, just issuing from a gloomy defile to which a sheer cliff stood guardian on either hand, deep, swirling, an enemy to navigation ; then brawled in glittering eddies over a terrace of half-submerged rocks, with a murmur hardly audible from above.   Just in the middle of these falls, by some dainty freak of geology, stood another and a smaller island, a mere outcrop of rock running up to a height of perhaps twenty or thirty feet, and ministering soil to the roots of three lonely fir-trees.   It looked like a piece of stage property, so cardboard-like did its jagged edges appear, so flat was the silhouette of the trees against the face of the cliff behind them.   This infinitesimal plot of earth's surface was divided from the land on either side of it only by a few yards of shallow water ; and yet it was easy to conjecture that no human creature had ever set foot on it, remote as it was from all human needs and errands.   It satisfied the eye like a master-piece ; such a wizard is Nature when she presents to us unrehearsed effects of art.

" There is a path down the cliff just here," explained Lady Hermia, " with steps cut and all that.   But it's rather rough going, down below, so I think it'll be better to stay up at the top and keep our ears open. The only thing is, which way shall we try ?   Back on our tracks towards the bridge, or along here on the further side ? "

Bredon considered a minute ; then he said, " Better try along towards the bridge.   You see, if they were this other side, the odds are we should be able to hear them from here ; it's straighter on the whole, and more shut in. Whereas, between here and the bridge, the cliff curves so you'd hardly be able to catch any sounds."

They began skirting the island, accordingly, towards the east and south, Bredon keeping up a decent pretence of peering over the brink occasionally, though he knew they were not yet far enough round to overlook the scene of operations. Once within sight of the break in the rhododendron bushes, he allowed himself an inspiration. " Looks as if there'd been somebody leaving his mark here," he said ; and, in a moment, they came to the clearing, which showed them a grassy slope, terminating in an abrupt drop. At the edge of this stood Lethaby, one hand clasped round a tree's branch for safety, looking over with the air of one prepared to shout directions. As they hesitated to call out, he turned and saw them.

" Hermia, how marvellous of you to come over," he said. " I shouldn't wonder, either, if you're in at the death. How d'you do, sir ? "

" Oh, do you know Mr. Bredon ? He's living just across the bridge, you know. What do you mean about in at the death ? You haven't really found anything, have you ? "

" Not a trouser-button, so far. But I believe we're on the move. You see, we were pretty certain from stable information – I can't tell you how we got that – that it must be about here, and right on the cliff. Anybody can see that a party of gentlemen who are in a hurry to leave are not going to waste their time blasting rock to make a hole for their treasure to lie snug in. So, we argued, we'd got to look out for these little gullies where there's some turf running out close to the cliff's edge, and for cracks in the rock some way down, in case they'd managed to stow it away over the side.

They must have had pretty good climbing heads, if we're right, these fellows. Henderson's an absolute wizard ; call him the Digger, they ought to call him a blasted chamois. Steps quite calmly over the edge of things I can't bring myself to look at."

" Yes, but what makes you think you're on the right track now ? "

" Well, Henderson figured it out this way. If they shoved it in any crack of the rock that showed up from the other side, ten to one somebody would spot it, somebody who hadn't any right to the dibs, and clean out the nest. The only thing to do was to get hold of some crack which was hidden from sight behind a bit of a tree or bush or what not ; if it was a decent-sized tree, it would help the fellow who was putting the loot away to hold on while he did it. And we've just found a daisy of a place ; the tree's come down, of course, long ago, but the roots are there all right, and Henderson's grubbing at them now with a hand-saw. Says he can't start digging till he's got the place clear a bit ; of course, when they put the stuff away, the tree was probably quite young still, and the roots didn't amount to much. Excuse me, I just want to see how he's getting on. Or would you like to look, sir ? I'd hang on to that fir-trunk, if I were you, it's a nasty sort of place to look over."

The invitation was not exactly a welcome one ; but Bredon had not the moral courage to refuse it. Craning his neck over the side, he found himself looking down into a steeply sloping gully, carpeted with heather, over which ran a rope ladder, its top secured by heavy stanchions driven into the ground. On this, his feet and legs below the skyline, stood Digger Henderson, sawing away at the exposed roots of a weather-beaten trunk. A glimpse was quite enough for Bredon, and he made way for Lethaby, who shouted down to his partner to know if he wanted anything.

" May as well sling down that pick, while you're waiting. There's a lot of stones about under this root that'll want dislodging. There ain't much depth of earth here ; we'll soon have it clear."

Some twenty minutes followed of excitement which was, for Bredon and Lady Hermia, all the more intense because of their enforced inaction. At intervals Lethaby, who was either at his post of outlook, or else busied with lowering ropes and carrying out instructions shouted to him from below, would report on Henderson's progress – the stones were cleared, now ; he was getting to work with his spade ; Jerusalem, how that man could dig ! he'd struck up against something hard – something square, apparently, looked like the corner of a box – confound it all, it was all being child's play now, simply shovelling away loose earth with his hands – that's the stuff, he wants the rope let down – gad ! If those knots aren't true ; we should look pretty good fools if the whole show started slipping over the side – now we're to haul ; d'you mind lending a hand, sir ? It's the devil of a weight, thank God – easy now, easy up over the rough ground – there, Hermia, how's that for an afternoon's fishing ?

What they had dragged up with such care was a trunk of very old, thick leather ; it was at least six feet in length, though the other dimensions were less considerable. The leather, which had been of a natural colour, was much stained and darkened, except where stones had scraped against it on its upward journey ; there had, probably, been gilt tooling at certain points, but the gilt had naturally come away, and only the grooves that were made to receive it had survived. It

87

was clearly locked, and Henderson was the man qualified by practical gifts – by experience, perhaps – to deal with the lock. During his leisurely return by the rope ladder, they found sufficient occupation in contemplating the sealed casket in which so many hopes reposed ; the baggage of a prince, dead this century and a half, whose career, now romantic, now sordid, seems to make him a bridge between the old world that lies dead in the pages of history-books, and the new world to which we belong.

What was to be done next ? Curiosity urged clamantly the alternative of forcing the lock there and then ; prudence insisted that a shut box is easier to carry than an opened one, and that a house, be it never so untidy, is a better place for displaying newly found treasures than the edge of a cliff. To the house, accordingly, the chest was carried, on a tray with handles at either end, such as workmen use ; and no attempt was made to pry into its secret till they were back in the room they had left, it seemed ages ago, the room of the coffee-cups and of the chart. Bredon thought – but perhaps it was only because he had a guilty conscience – that Lethaby stole a glance at the place where the chart lay, one tell-tale corner of it peeping out from the shelter of the novel ; a glance which seemed, if anything, to betoken satisfaction.

The forcing of the lock, strong though it was, did not occupy much time. What lay within had been folded in a cloth, of which nothing was left but rags ; through the rents in it showed a glitter of gold, a gleam of silver, here and there a deeper flash of colour. One by one the contents were unloaded, and spread out, with no comment, on a side table hastily cleared for the purpose. One disappointment had plainly overtaken the treasure-hunters – there were no coins. These were

not, after all, the paymaster's arrears after Culloden ;
it looked as if the official legend was more in the right
of it. Some of the objects laid bare had clearly had a
practical use ; silver-mounted pistols, a gold drinking-
cup, a seal, a snuff-box or two. But for the most part
these were spoils of the ladies, rings and lockets and
bracelets and boxes of the toilet-table. You thought
of the little sighs that must have accompanied the
surrender of this or that trinket, the sentimental
associations they must have possessed for those who
surrendered them, the stories of romance and of
adventure that must be their background.

> *Dear, dead women, with such hair, too ! What's become*
> *of all the gold*
> *Used to hang and brush their bosoms ? I feel chilly and*
> *grown old.*

All these sacrifices of memory and of pride had been
made, long ago, for the Prince who never failed to
capture a woman's heart ; they had been thrust away,
in an hour of supreme crisis, into that lonely crevice on
an unfrequented island, to fall at last into the hands of
two vulgar adventurers, who had no thought but for the
exact price they would fetch at the jeweller's.

" Looks as if Charles Edward had been a bit of a
klep," observed Lady Hermia, breaking the spell.

" He knew what he was about, anyway," suggested
Henderson. " I wish he'd kept the stuff in more
negotiable form. I've met dealers before now, and
thought myself lucky if I could get fifty-fifty out of
them."

" Talking of dealers, Digger old man," said Lethaby,
" I know what I'm going to do straight away. I'm
going to ring up a man in Inverness who knows about

these things and get him to come and value the lot, first thing to-morrow. No harm in getting a rough estimate of where we stand. Now, where did I put that confounded card of his? Can't remember his name even." And he fell to hunting amongst the litter on the mantelpiece. Bredon had a shrewd idea of what the name was. But he was not anxious to show any knowledge of Mr. Dobbie, since he too was acting in the interests of the Indescribable. He did not even wait to make sure that Lethaby carried out his honourable intention of ringing up the valuer. It would be easy to verify that by putting a call through himself. Instead, he escorted Lady Hermia, who had suddenly discovered with consternation that she was overdue for an appointment at Glendounie, as far as the bridge, and thanked her with something like genuine warmth for the excitements of the evening.

In the cottage, his first care was to despatch a telegram to Mr. Dobbie, who was not available by telephone after all. Then he reported to his wife, who had watched the proceedings from the opposite bank, and had seen the casket hauled up from its hiding-place on to safe ground. " It was rather amusing," she said, " watching the whole thing in dumb show ; people's attitudes always look so silly when you can't hear what they're saying. You and the Jennings woman, for example – naturally I kept an eye on you – were both dancing with excitement the whole time ; whereas Henderson, who was actually doing the work, went about it as calmly as if he dug up buried treasure every other day. He does dig well, too – I simply longed to applaud."

" Well, it is all a great relief," observed Mr. Pulteney. " I shall shortly be in a position to bestow upon salmon-fishing that undivided attention which it seems to claim. I confess I have been haunted by the fear that our friends opposite would come across their treasure suddenly, and would hasten to remove it from view before Sir Charles Airdrie or the other people concerned were any the wiser. I pictured them trying to escape by river, and myself reviving distant memories of my youth by rowing after them, armed with nothing better than a gaff. Fortunately, whatever may have been their intentions, the remarkable publicity which attended their find has made it impossible for them to practise any concealment. Indeed, they could hardly have chosen a better moment for the *dénouement* if they had been actually wanting to have an audience."

" Oh, it's all right so far," admitted Angela, " but, you see, we weren't really concerned, except as ordinary honest citizens who happened to be living in the neighbourhood, with any funny business about not declaring the treasure when found. If they had managed to do it darkly at dead of night, and both made off together into the great open spaces, the Company would not have been liable to anyone for a penny."

" You're wrong there, though," said her husband ; " your information isn't quite up to date. After the Company had fixed up its deal with Lethaby, Sir Charles came along and had a flutter on his own. He didn't really believe the treasure was there, but there was just an off chance of it ; and of course if those two crooks found it, there was more than an off chance they would try to do the dirty. So he insured himself against fraud on the part of the syndicate working as a syndicate, just as Lethaby insured himself against fraud on the part of Henderson, working on his own. As a matter of fact, it would have been very difficult for him to recover ; because naturally Henderson and

Lethaby would have done their damnedest to conceal every trace of their find. But there was no harm in taking out the policy. I'm ringing him up after dinner, so now he'll be able to take his own measures to secure his property. But for the moment we're still on guard ; and, what's more unfortunate, we've got to reckon with the possibility of a midnight flitting. I'm rather afraid I shall have to be up all night myself ; luckily there'll be just a bit of a moon. I was wondering, Pulteney, whether you would mind strolling out afterwards along the bank, and stowing yourself away in the wood just opposite where the boat is on the island ? You see, they can't get across the bridge without being seen, and they might just try the boat. I'll come out and relieve you about eleven, if that would be all right, and hang round till it gets too light for any funny business. Would it be an awful bore ? I'd take it on at once myself, only there's a little problem I want to work out here which calls for pens, ink, and paper."

" My dear Mr. Bredon, I should be delighted. You do not understand, I imagine, the absorbing interest we poor fishermen derive from watching the fish rise late in the evening, although we can't take a rod to them. If anyone tampers with the moorings of the boat, I expect you would like me to come and report to that effect ? Or should I swim across with a knife between my teeth ? I am no adept, but it seems to be done in books."

" Oh, Mr. Pulteney, don't," cried Angela. " I should never forgive myself if you swallowed it. Besides, you've no idea how cold the water is in this river ; you've only tried it in your crawlers."

Miles Bredon naturally assented : " Once they're in the boat, we shall be able to get their movements taped, and we can always head them off in the car if they try to make a bolt for it. At least, there's just the danger that they might make for the opposite bank of the river, not this ; but obviously Sir Charles must have keepers who are accustomed to late nights, and I was thinking of asking him, when I ring up, to picket the other side of the river and have a car ready for action on the Glendounie–Dreams road. So that we won't be responsible unless they land on this side. That seems to cover the possibilities."

" I will confine myself, then," said Mr. Pulteney, " to keeping watch and making a report if necessary. It is a pity that I have never learned to imitate the cry of, say, the night-jar, so that I might have arranged a code of signals with you. There is so much that we schoolmasters still have to learn."

" You'd better practise it to-morrow," suggested Angela. " You never know when that sort of thing will come in useful."

CHAPTER VII : AT THE POINT INDICATED

" Of course, I suppose it's tremendously important," said Angela, knitting her brows over the sheet of paper Miles had just handed to her. " I'm not a collector myself, but I should think it was a reed-warbler's, or possibly a guillemot's."

" Cut out the funny business. What you've got there is a rough draft of a bad photograph of a rough draft ; so it wouldn't be surprising if it were rather unrecognisable. As a matter of fact, I've made it a fat sight more recognisable than the original. What it is, as you know perfectly well, is a plan of the island, marked, as even your intelligence must have observed, with capital letters. Or rather, two of the letters are on the island, and two on the mainland."

" You haven't got the original about you by any chance ? "

" I have not. The original from which I took it is in the possession of the Honourable Vernon Lethaby, Isle of Erran, who very kindly didn't give me leave to make a copy of it, because why ? Because I didn't ask him. Where the original of that original (which was a photograph) is to be found, I don't know ; I wish I did, because it would have saved me a lot of trouble. As it is, having just given this photograph the once-over – it was lying on the table, over at the house there – I carried it about in my memory,

94

and this is the best I can do in the way of recon-
structing it. Now, let us hear what strikes you
about it ; and do try not to be more facetious than
you can help."

" I'm glad you're picking up the language. Facetious
is an entirely Scots word, you know. Well, my first
impression is a pretty obvious one – that it seems a very
curious instinct in anybody to use the letters B C D E,
when it's perfectly open to him to use the letters
A B C D."

" Good. Might be just an accident, as you say, but
it looks as if there ought to be something behind it.
Now for the next point ; why are there four letters,
no more and no less ? "

" Dunno. Unless of course there are four different
bits of treasure, in which case for heaven's sake let's
have a go at some of the reserve deposits. I could do
with a little jewellery."

" Now you're not being intelligent. Surely it's
obvious that if you want to mark a single spot, without
letting every fool who looks at your document realise
that it is an important spot, the best way is to make
it the intersecting point of two imaginary lines, calling
one A B and the other C D. That means you've got
to take four points, one at either end of either line ;
and that means numbering them with four letters. To
have more letters would be merely confusing ; to have
less would make it impossible to get your bearings."

" Yes. Dash, I wish I'd thought of that. In this
case, however, having a slight down on the first letter
of the alphabet, the man who is drawing the chart uses
the lines B E and C D. They meet a very little way
from the bridge, almost opposite where we are sitting
at the moment, and their point of intersection marks,
no doubt, the place where the treasure was not hidden.

Miles, are you sure you remembered the position of the points right ? "

" Well, they'll do, anyhow ; because I've taken care to make them accurate by reference to the point at which the treasure *was* found. Of course, there's one thing which doesn't come out in this draft of mine, namely that the photographer made a bit of a boss shot, and evidently pointed his camera too much to the right of the picture. Does that suggest anything ? "

" Too much to the right. Missed out, you mean, something on the left ? Oo, I've got it ; you mean E isn't one of the four points at all ? E just stood for East, and if the camera had happened to point too much to the left we should have got a W instead ? Miles, I am being a tiny bit less stupid, aren't I ? And we can find the missing point A by working back from the spot at which the treasure *was* found. What's this great blob, Miles ? "

" The great blob is a fault in the photograph ; one can't tell whether it was a fault in the negative, or only in the print. But obviously it covers, by accident or by design, the letter A which must have stood there in the original from which the photograph was taken."

" When you used to develop your own films, there wasn't any question of accident or design, was there ? I don't really see why it shouldn't be accident, you know. If the developer, I mean the developing person, had got to spill stuff about, it would be quite likely to hit one of the four letters, wouldn't it ? I mean, there's nothing against the law of averages in that. But you mean somebody may have done it a-purpose, so that the casual passer-by, if he was the sort of person who cribbed other people's photographs, should make the mistake of thinking that E was the fourth letter, and so get his measurements wrong ? "

" Yes, that would be just possible. But it seems a bit elementary. If Lethaby and Henderson did it, they failed to take me in. And if somebody else did it, they failed to take Lethaby and Henderson in. They were right on the spot from the start. And there's this to consider – if you were going to obliterate one of the four letters, why obliterate the A ? Why not make it the D, and then there would be just a hope that the inquisitive stranger would try to work with an A B C triangle, not realising that there ever *was* a fourth letter ? That E business couldn't worry anybody for long ; I'm not even sure that in the original the E wasn't a size larger than the other letters ; I certainly read it as meaning East, first go off."

" Pity you didn't look more carefully. You see, it is a teeny bit like a coincidence, that the A should have been washed out *and* the camera held sideways, so as to get in the E and miss out the W."

" Yes, there's just that element of coincidence. . . . Come to think of it, it's not really very likely that Lethaby and Henderson can have got that photograph from anybody who was meaning to do them down over it. Such a person would either know what the chart was about, in which case he'd obviously try and mop up the treasure for himself, rather than let them loose after it, or else he wouldn't know, and, if he didn't know, what would be the point of misleading them ? "

" Ye-es. It doesn't seem very natural. So that if it was design, not accident, it looks as if Lethaby and Henderson were trying to mislead somebody else who poked his nose into the chart. You, as it proved. Did they mean it to be you ? "

" If they did, there are a lot of inferences to be drawn, mostly uncomfortable. It means, for one thing, that they know what we are here for. It also means that they expected Lady Hermia to bring me round on a visit yesterday; which is as much as to say that they arranged with her to bring me round. And then they left the photograph lying around on the table to kid me. What on earth was the sense of that? If they knew they were going to find the treasure where they did find it, what conceivable sense was there in misleading me about the point at which it ought to be looked for? Angela, it's got to be accident, not design. The whole notion of design breaks down the moment you try to work out a motive."

"What you mean is, you don't like to feel that you've had your leg pulled. Or even that anybody tried to pull it. I bet I can put up a plausible set of motives, if you want one. Let's see, how would this do? They didn't mean it for you at all; they wanted to persuade Sir Charles Airdrie that they weren't just setting out on a wild-goose chase, that they had something more than mere guess-work to go upon, and that it wouldn't be necessary to turn the whole island upside down in their search. But they didn't know Sir Charles well, and were afraid he might double-cross them. So they very ingeniously showed him the genuine chart, but showed it him in a doctored form, so that if he started excavations before they could get going themselves, he would look a fool."

" Oh, one can invent explanations like that. But if they had a plan, and showed it to Sir Charles, why did he never tell us about it? It was obviously up to him to give us all the pointers he could. Besides, how did it come to be lying on the table, just when I came into their sitting-room? One doesn't keep a very important document like that lying about in a house with an open front door, and no gate at the end of the drive."

" Oh, but that part *might* be coincidence. They felt

sure they'd got on the track of the stuff, and they got careless about their ordinary precautions ; anyone would."

" I wish I could believe that. But I got such a strong impression that Lethaby looked at that photograph, when we went back to the house together, and was satisfied to see it lying hidden under a shocker. Was that because he thought I hadn't seen it after all ? Or because he realised I *had* seen it, and had stowed it away like that, rather clumsily ? "

" You're always fancying things. Besides, he may quite easily have wanted you not to know *how* they found the treasure, even when you knew they had found it. Or he may just have been smiling at the reflection that, even if you did give it the once-over, it could mean nothing to you, because of the way it had been doctored. What about Henderson ? Was he registering at all ? "

" Henderson didn't seem to take any notice of me. But then, he's got a poker face ; he wouldn't give himself away as easily as Lethaby. The only thing I did notice about him was that he looked shockingly ill, or tired, anyhow, as if he'd got something on his mind and wasn't getting anything like his eight hours. Eyes all bloodshot, and lines under them – funny, that, because he's obviously a hard-bitten specimen. He may be on the drink, of course, but he didn't strike me as sodden, only dead beat."

" Curiouser and curiouser. Do you know, Miles, I rather think I'm going to bed. Because you're certain to wake me up when you come clumping back from your lonely vigil, and I shall probably be too excited to get to sleep again. When do you relieve poor dear Edward ? "

" Not till eleven. I've got an hour or so yet. But

leave me, woman, leave me by all means. I am going to tie a wet towel round my head and think this chart business over, neither once nor twice."

Bredon's ideas of thinking a thing over had, as a matter of fact, nothing to do with wet towels. He always held that if you were really up against a problem, of the kind that seemed to make no sense, it was useless to go on trying to force your imagination over the fence ; the more you gave it the whip, the more it shied. The only chance of seeing the whole question in an entirely new light was to do something quite different ; and to hope that in the course of that other occupation a light would dawn on you from nowhere in particular. Doing something else had, on such occasions, only one meaning for him. He went back to his patience.

There was only about a quarter of an hour left before he was due at his post, when he suddenly sat upright in his chair, with a card poised in his hand. " It couldn't possibly be *that* ? " he said to himself. " B, yes, C, yes, D, yes, E, yes – but not A. Where's that chart again ? Yes, it works. What a nuisance not to be able to get at the bedroom ; never mind, here goes." And as he studied the chart afresh, a curious humming sound came from his lips, bearing some relation to the tune of " There was I, waiting at the church." These half-remembered snatches of music did duty, with him, for a war song.

He found Mr. Pulteney seated on a tree-stump at the post of outlook assigned to him, smoking a pipe with an air of extreme contentment. " You will notice, Bredon," he said, " that somebody has moved the boat. If it had disappeared altogether, I would have put a generous interpretation on my orders, and come to tell you about it. But I observed that it had not been moved very far ; it is only two or three hundred yards further along the bank, towards the south. The visibility, of course, has become poor since I took my observations, but if you look here, along the line of my stick, you will just see the stern of her showing in the moonlight ; the rest is hidden under the tree there."

There was only a slip of a moon, but the sky was cloudless, and the river shone with a faint gleam of silver, contrasting mysteriously with the dark shadow of the boughs that overhung it. The pale strip of sand just opposite was plainly empty ; but a little further to the south, away from the direction of the bridge, there was a silhouette at the river's edge whose lines were too regular to be those of tree or fern. Had it not been for the old gentleman's watchfulness, he reflected, it would have been impossible to identify it as the hull of the boat.

" It does rather look as if the theatre of operations was going to be naval," he admitted. " I wonder if it would be a good idea to have that other boat handy – the one you fish from. Where's it moored ? "

" Further downstream than usual ; in fact, almost opposite the end of the island. I fancy that if you were to walk along to the place, you would find it as convenient a look-out post as this is. Or should I go along and get it for you ? "

" No, rather not, thanks ; you've done your bit for to-night. And I'd like you to be back at the cottage, in case anything breaks loose there. Angela went to bed some time ago, so there's nobody on guard there. Don't sit up, though ; the night's so still that, with water in between, I should hear them starting up the car from here, and could double back if necessary. Not that it's very easy to stop a car in any case, when you aren't a policeman. Well, good night, Pulteney ;

and thank you enormously for letting yourself be bored all this long time."

" I have enjoyed, I assure you, a feast of contemplation. Good night." And the old gentleman receded into the shadows, making passes with his stick at imaginary enemies in the undergrowth, as if he had not a care in the world. Bredon walked briskly upstream, till he got a better view of the island boat moored just opposite him ; then, covering about the same distance again, he made out the shadow of the fisherman's boat on his own bank, and climbed very quietly into it. The trees here overhung the stream so generously that, by keeping close to the bank, he hardly found it necessary to show up at all on the moonlit surface. But he was not content to follow this policy of safety altogether. He rested on his oars for a moment, listening intently for the slightest whisper of a noise from the island. Then he struck boldly across the stream, dipping his oars gently but with a strong pull, and ran his own boat to shore just alongside of the island boat at its new mooring-place.

" Yes, this would be just about right," he said to himself. The spot was convenient enough for mooring ; it was overshadowed by an oak-tree which had contrived to grow, at a crazy angle, on the very brink of the river ; but there was no brushwood to impede a landing, or make the process unnecessarily noisy. Satisfying himself once more that no breath was stirring, Bredon switched on his electric torch, revealing a depth of tangled branches and shadows. Then he turned the light on to the other boat, and made a careful examination of its contents. Before long, he scrambled up on to the bank, and extinguished his torch again. The moon showed him a path at his feet, the path, already familiar to him, which went round the island. Beyond it, a steep but not inaccessible slope led up to its higher levels, deeply sunk in bracken, almost of a man's height. In one or two places, he noticed, the stalks of it had been trampled, as if some human being had made his way through it – or could it be a roe? Or one of those sheep which occasionally strayed over the bridge and got lost on the island? Anyhow, even if these were human paths, it would be a wild-goose chase to follow any one of them under the uncertain light; nothing loses itself so easily as a path through bracken. Further, if he indulged in any exploration, he might be interrupted, and his position then would be equivocal, possibly dangerous. Evidently, it was best to postpone investigation till such time as daylight was available, and the coast was clear. The circumstances gave him every reason to believe that the boat played a part in the next move of the treasure-hunters (or, as he was now more inclined to call them, the conspirators); it was almost certain, then, that they contemplated making that move under cover of darkness. It was now past midnight, and they might appear at any moment. He made his way back to the waterside and the boats. Very carefully he selected the wrong one – they were almost exactly alike, as such boats are – and rowed softly back to the mainland.

Half an hour or so later, he was back at the cottage, where he opened the door with vain precaution, and crept up the stairs as if he were a truant pupil of Mr. Pulteney's. There was, there always is, what we called in our extreme youth a " cavé-board "; it creaked, and the sound of a light being switched on informed him that Angela, after all, had not gone to sleep.

" Miles," she said softly, appearing in a kimono at

the doorway of their room, " is something happening ?
You didn't mean to come back so early."

" Nothing's happening, and I've a sort of instinct
that nothing's going to happen ; so, feeling tired of
hanging about on the bank, I came home. Meanwhile,
it was my impression that you were going to sleep."

" I did sleep for a little, but I woke up again and
couldn't doze off again, honest to God I couldn't.
You see, I knew you'd make a noise when you came in,
and I kept waiting for the other boot to drop, so to
speak. Miles, your hair's all wet ; have you been falling
into the river ? "

" Oh, I had a bathe ; always was fond of moonlight
bathing. I haven't been getting my clothes wet, if
that's what's worrying you."

" But, you fool, it must have been filthily cold."

" It was a bit ; in fact, since you are awake, I'm not
sure we mightn't make a hot whisky, to avoid accidents.
But it was quite a good bathe, and quite deliberate,
I assure you. Now, don't start nagging at me, or you'll
wake Pulteney ; he's deserved his sleep."

" Edward has a good conscience, so I expect he's
sleeping like a lamb. Half a minute while I get that
Ultimus stove. . . . I wish you'd tell me why you
bathed," she insisted, as they reached the dining-
room. " You haven't been over to the island, have
you ? "

" I did, as a matter of fact, go over to the island to
reconnoitre a bit. But I went in a boat and I came
back in a boat. You've forgotten the one Pulteney
uses. The bathe was just an idea that occurred to me
afterwards ; not in the least necessary, I assure you."

" All right, I know what you're like when you insist
on being tiresome. Let's talk about something else.
Why do you think nothing's going to happen ? "

" I only said I had an instinct. But in any case, if the boat is used, it won't be brought over to this bank ; I feel certain of that. You see, if any person or persons on the island want to make a private get-away, they won't land on this side, where you and I and the McBraynes and everybody else knows them by sight. They'll cross to the further side, round the south point of the island, and make for the high road between Glendounie and Dreams, where every passer-by may be expected to be a stranger. As a matter of fact, Sir Charles has done me proud ; he's got two keepers out on the road, one of them with a motor-cycle, so as to be prepared for a chase."

" What a good moon," said Angela, curling herself up in the window-seat. " I suppose, Miles, you aren't being rather fanciful about all this ? You have a bit of a weakness, you know, for the sensational. Having found their treasure all right, why shouldn't Lethaby and Henderson show it to kind Mr. Dobbie, like good little boys, take their rake-off, and live happily ever afterwards ? Why should they *want* to play a crook game, exactly ? "

" I should know more about that if I had devoted my life to the study of second-hand jewellery. But my own perfectly amateur impression was that the stuff they dug up to-day didn't amount to a hill of beans, and if that is all the treasure Prince Charlie left about, they won't be very grateful to him. You see, if Henderson goes off with the swag, they stand to clear ten thousand off the Indescribable, and that's always something. But this loot they've just unearthed – remember, the Government has got a claim on it, at least I suppose it has, and that will take some settling. What is left will have to be divided up with Sir Charles on a fifty-fifty basis, and is that going to leave them ten thousand to play with? I should say they'd be very lucky to get five thousand out of it. Putting yourself in their place, and assuming that you'd got an even more elastic conscience than you actually have, wouldn't you feel some temptation to try and bleed the Company? Everybody thinks an insurance company fair game; I'd lose my job if they didn't."

" All right; we'll pass that. Only I'm not going to put myself in their place, I'm too sleepy. You put yourself in their place, Miles, and tell me what you'd do, there's a dear. Henderson's got to bolt for it, and take the swag with him – how's he going to manage? It isn't too easy."

" Well, I suppose I'm expecting some rather obvious sort of frame-up. The trouble is that these things don't work out according to schedule. They aren't as clever as one thinks, or they're cleverer, or their plans blow out a fuse somewhere, and what happens is never the thing you were all gingered up for. Anyhow, I should imagine Lethaby would take some sort of drug and lay himself out for the night, to give Henderson a free hand. He might arrange to be locked in or tied up somehow, to account for his letting Henderson get away, but a drug is simplest; nobody can prove that a fairly powerful drug wasn't administered without the knowledge of the man who took it. That would get him out of the way. Then Henderson has got to clear off; possibly in disguise; possibly disguised as the chauffeur – I confess I can't understand about the chauffeur yet. I dare say he'd try and make for Glasgow, down the west coast, in a car. But I think he'd be better advised to go by train from Inverness; he's not known much locally, and there's such a packet of visitors going through about now that it would be pretty easy to get lost in the crowd."

106

" His luggage would be rather easily remembered, wouldn't it ? "

" You're assuming Lethaby is going to let him skip with the treasure, are you ? He may be that sort of fool ; but if I were having any dealings like that with our friend Mr. Henderson, I wouldn't trust him any further than I could see him. No, I'd insist that we should hide the treasure in some new place, not on the island itself, of course, and then I'd take dashed good care to hang about, to see that Henderson didn't come back for it."

" But Lethaby would get the insurance money."

" If all went well, he would. But if the Company fought the case, and proved negligence or something against him, he'd look rather a fool. However, if Henderson did take the stuff with him, I grant he'd be more likely to go in a car. Porters remember heavy luggage better than they remember passengers. You know, Angela, all this is the wildest guesswork ; it assumes that the whole situation is very simple. I'm not at all sure that it is very simple."

" It's funny, you know, about your instinct that nothing much is going to happen to-night."

" Why particularly ? "

" Only that it looks to me very much as if the house on the Isle of Erran had caught fire."

CHAPTER VIII : THE MAN IN THE GARAGE

FIRE IS ALWAYS BEAUTIFUL, even when it escapes our control and appears once more in its natural character as the enemy of man. As Bredon ran up the drive, a medley of suspicions and alarms racing through his brain, he was nevertheless struck by the rich glow of the flames, and of their reflection above him and in front of him, strangely contrasted with the darkness and the pale moonlight behind him and beneath. The echoes of the absurd tune which memory had evoked a few hours before thundered irrelevantly in his brain :

> *When I found he'd left me in the lurch,*
> *Lor' ! how it did upset me !*
> *All at once he sent me round a note . . .*

in token that the need for sudden muscular activity had paralysed the processes of his thought. Not that he had lost his head ; Mrs. McBrayne was by now telephoning to the fire station, her husband and Pulteney would follow him in a moment ; Angela was making a slightly more elaborate toilet.

There was nobody in the drive, there was no sign of activity about the house itself as he approached it. He was conscious, by now, that their first impressions had been misleading ; the blaze came, not from the house but from some building at the back of it ;

dangerously near, though, and dangerously near the branches of a neighbouring larch, which might easily spread conflagration and turn the whole over-wooded island into a roaring bonfire. Bredon ran round at once to the back, and saw that the fire had broken out in the garage ; that same wooden garage over which the mysterious chauffeur was supposed to sleep. He could only hope that the arrangement was not still in force ; a mere glance told him that the wooden structure was beyond all aid ; the door ' /as locked, and there was no hope of rescuing any inmate who might have failed to make good his escape. The house itself was clearly in danger of being involved ; and into the house he ran, shouting " Fire ! " in a voice whose echoes he himself could scarcely recognise.

He threw open door after door, first on the ground-floor and then upstairs – how these passages wound to and fro ! – but the house seemed, at first, as empty as the drive. Then, switching on a light in one of the larger bedrooms, he found Lethaby fallen fast asleep on his bed, fully clothed. The effort it took to wake him, combined with the dazed way in which he looked round and answered questions, convinced Bredon that he had not been far out in one point. Lethaby was drugged.

The garage ? No, nobody slept in the garage. The chauffeur – oh, he wasn't on the island at present. Henderson ought to be asleep next door ; they had sat up rather late and Lethaby had gone to bed first ; they must go and find Henderson ; it would be awful if anything had happened to him. He must just get some water ; his mouth was all dry. God ! he hadn't had such a hang-over for years. Henderson – they must find Henderson ; look, he hadn't gone to bed after all. Perhaps he'd been doing something in the

garage ; wasn't there any sign of anybody about ?
They went round the house together, Lethaby still
shouting out " Henderson ! " in something of a feeble
voice.

By this time, not only had the party from the
cottage arrived, but rescuers were beginning to swarm
in from all sides. It was difficult to believe that so
desolate a neighbourhood could muster, and at dead of
night, such an army of visitants. Strathdounie Lodge
had come over in force in two cars, and muscular men
in sweaters were shouting efficient directions to one
another. Later arrivals included Sir Charles Airdrie
and the minister of Glendounie. In fact, as Angela
said afterwards, it would have been difficult to meet so
many influential people without going to a bazaar.
Intentness on a common task served, as always, to
make perfect strangers treat one another as if they
were lifelong friends. But this representative and
harmonious gathering could make no impression on the
fire which was now consuming the garage. The door,
which had been locked, was broken in, but flames and
fumes made it impossible to salvage anything ; it
appeared that there were no tins of petrol inside ;
they were all in a shed at some little distance. When
it was further known that the garage was, or should
have been, unoccupied at the time when it was set
alight, even the most energetic members of the shoot-
ing-party desisted from their attempts to force an
entrance ; and contented themselves with spraying
chemicals on the matchboarding of the house roof,
which had caught in places, or climbing ladders to lop
off branches from the threatened larch-tree.

The fire-brigade arrived at last, as fire-brigades
must ; their hose was not long enough to connect
with the river, which was the nearest piece of water

available, but they chopped away a prodigious amount of the house roof, while they allowed the garage to burn itself out. As soon as it was possible, and rather before it was safe, one or two of them began to investigate the ruin ; and it was one of these who came up to Sir Charles, who had been helping to direct operations, and said in a low voice, but within Bredon's hearing :

" You'll excuse me, Sir Charles, but there's a body yon."

" What, there was someone in there ? Eh, poor fellow, poor fellow. Is the Sergeant there ? He'll look to it. Have it covered up, the way the women-folk won't see it. Is there any recognising it ? "

" Not that you can see, Sir Charles ; it was in the very hottest of the fire, and there's nothing left but just the bones of it. Had I better tell the gentleman ? "

" Ask him to come here ; I'll notify him. Mr. Bredon," he added, as the fireman went off to execute his instructions, " this is a very unfortunate business altogether. You see, there was only just the two of them on the island, and it's not impossible, is it, there was foul play ? With all the publicity the newspapers have given to the thing already, the Fiscal will hardly like to dispense with an enquiry. Do you think we ought to warn young Lethaby to keep his mouth shut, and to stay on in the neighbourhood here for a bit ? I've no great love, myself, for his sort ; but I'd be sorry to see any of his family get into difficulties if it can be avoided."

" Much the best thing, Sir Charles. Here he is. I think, with your permission, I'll go round and suggest to some of these people they might go home. I can stand a few drinks at the cottage ; this has been thirsty work."

The barrel of Senior's ale which the Bredons had

laid in was already sounding hollow, the guests had departed, Angela had gone off, rather unwillingly, to bed, and Mr. Pulteney, with a curious cold-bloodedness of which he had already given evidence at Chilthorpe, was back on the river for an early spell of salmon-fishing, when Sir Charles presented himself at the door of the cottage, and announced his intention of having a crack with Bredon ; " for " said he, " there's a lot you and I know which the general public doesn't know, and we've got to try and put two and two together. Here's an extraordinary thing to start off with : you'd have thought, wouldn't you, that young Lethaby would have wanted to get away from the island as soon as possible, rather than be left alone there ? Would you believe it, I pressed him to come over to Dreams and make it his headquarters for a bit, and he thanked me very much, but said he thought he'd rather stay on the island just for the present, and fend for himself till this business is cleared up. Now, that he's a heartless sort of fellow I can well believe ; and I wouldn't say there was much love lost between him and Henderson at the best of times. But you'd have thought that any man would have just that decent amount of superstition left in him which would make him want to clear out for a bit after all that's happened."

" Well, there's the treasure, you know," Bredon pointed out. " I should imagine, though of course I speak with a rather limited experience, that a man who has just found a treasure has the instincts of a dog with a bone ; he must mount guard over it himself and snarl at everybody who comes near him, to make them keep their distance. I suppose you didn't ask to see the treasure, by any chance ? "

" I didn't. Of course, I naturally felt a certain

curiosity about it, but it hardly seemed decent to show any interest in it just at that particular moment. However, as we've hit upon the mention of the subject, Mr. Bredon, perhaps you won't mind my asking – did it look to you as if it were of any considerable value ? "

" I'm hopeless at that sort of thing. There must have been thirty or forty trinkets, if not more, which looked as if the jewellery was perfectly genuine ; and of course some of the settings would be very rare, but I don't know what price they'd fetch on the market. If you melted the whole thing down, I can't imagine that it would add up to very much. But I suppose its antiquity value would be much bigger."

" Well, Dobbie'll be coming round this morning, I hear ; so we'll know about that soon enough. A very careful man, is Dobbie, and very knowledgeable. But now, Mr. Bredon, let's hear what you think yourself : is there any connection, by your way of it, between the find they made yesterday and what happened last night ? Of course, Maclean's been at me – that's the minister at Glendounie. You'll know him, per- haps ? A man that has a good deal of education, but a terrible talker. He's been at me telling me that there was a curse laid on anyone who should move the treasure ; and he says he met Lethaby and Henderson, some days back, and warned them about it. It's a very singular thing, the way beliefs of that kind linger on in these parts. Well, I just put him off ; but what I want to know is, was there perhaps a closer connection, in the ordinary way of physical cause and effect, between the finding of the treasure and Henderson's disappearance ? "

" Why, Sir Charles, if Henderson had simply dis- appeared, I should have had very little doubt about my answer – that is, if the treasure had disappeared

113

along with him. I should have said there was a very obvious and almost certain connection, in that case."

" Meaning that the two of them had entered into a conspiracy against the Company, and Lethaby had allowed Henderson to run off, so as to be able to claim his insurance money ? "

" Possibly that ; but you must remember, we know very little to Henderson's credit, and it wouldn't have been altogether surprising if he had bolted with the treasure, quite genuinely, leaving Lethaby to settle matters with you and the Company as best he could. The only thing against that is the difficulty he'd have had in negotiating the sale of the stuff ; the ordinary fence wouldn't know anything about collector's prices."

" Still, one way or the other it would be suspicious. But now Henderson's dead, or so we fear, and young Lethaby's no nearer and no further off than he was, as far as getting his money's concerned."

" Yes, that's the puzzle. You see, assuming that Henderson is dead – by the way, is there any likelihood of proving that ? "

" None whatever. You see, it's not thought that Henderson had any kith or kin in these parts, and even if you could find someone who knew him well out in the Dominions, it would be a very expensive proceeding to bring him all the way back to identify the remains. The body's clean burnt out, and nothing left of the clothes except a few buttons ; buttons don't prove much. The doctor says it's a man's body, and would answer the description of Henderson in general, but that's all there is to it."

" Well, let's assume anyhow that Henderson is dead. That cuts off at once all hopes of Lethaby's claiming any payment from the Indescribable. Dead men don't steal; and he's insured against fraud on the part of Henderson, not against any other kind of fraud. Consequently, if the treasure disappears or has disappeared, Lethaby can make no claim without bringing Henderson to life again. That hardly looks as if Lethaby had killed him. Besides, it would be insanely rash to make the murder follow so soon on the finding of the treasure; that's bound to make people connect the two things. And how careless he was, if so, about the staging of the murder; two men on an island, one burnt to death in a garage, with the door locked, and the key nowhere to be found afterwards."

"That's true; there's been no trace of the key. Lethaby says he didn't even know there was a lock to it. I suppose there's no doubt the door *was* locked; it couldn't be that it was just jammed with the heat?"

"No, I can swear to its being locked; I flashed a light on the chink in the door myself, as soon as I got there, and I could see the lock was turned all right. I've never met a Procurator Fiscal, but I don't see how this one can doubt that there was foul play, if only on the strength of the key. Whether the dead man is Henderson or not, it can't be he who turned the key in the lock; somebody must have done that from the outside, and it's a little too much to believe that somebody did it accidentally. By the way, could you tell me how the body was found; in what position, I mean? Did it look as if the unfortunate man had tried to force his way out?"

"It was not very far from the door, but lying at full length on its face. What the doctor thought was, the place may have been so full of smoke that the poor fellow thought it was his best chance to get close to the door with his face to the ground, so as to be able to get air."

115

" And I suppose the doctor didn't find any marks of injury, as if the man might have been killed first and burned afterwards? That's generally the safest way of getting rid of your man."

" There was no injury to be seen. But of course, if it had been poison or strangling, that would have left no mark on a body burned the way this one was. One thing the doctor said – he's a callous sort of fellow, is Moffatt – was that he wouldn't be surprised if the body and the boards round it were soaked in petrol. That would mean foul play for certain; there was no petrol kept in the garage at all; and the car, as you know, was outside."

" And the chauffeur, it seems, away from the island altogether. Did you ask about the chauffeur? It looks extra bad, you see, all this happening on a night when the only available witness happens to be absent."

" I asked him, of course; because there seemed to be some question whether the body that was found might not prove to be the chauffeur's body after all. But he said they had sent the man home almost as soon as they got here; their idea was that they didn't want to have anybody on the island, for fear he might prove dishonest."

" So he went home – one would like his address. You didn't ask about that, of course; no, but I will. Almost the first question I asked Lethaby when I woke him up was about the chauffeur; naturally, because I understood he was to sleep over the garage. And I thought Lethaby was rather confused in his answer, though of course that might have been the effect of a drug; he seemed all anyhow. But if Lethaby is lying, it does seem possible, doesn't it, that it's the chauffeur who was killed in the garage, and that Henderson has made off – with or without the treasure? "

116

" Heavens, man, do you mean we've taken no precautions to see it's still on the island ? "

" I'm afraid not. I haven't the proper instincts
for the servant of a company ; it ought to have been
the first thing I thought of when I went up to the house
last night. But I'm obsessed with these odd, civilised
conventions which make it seem more important to
find out whether somebody is or isn't being burned to
death. Afterwards it did occur to me to worry about it ;
but by that time Lethaby was in full view of everybody,
so it would have been impossible for him to do anything
about the treasure then ; and obviously if the treasure
had been carried off before, it was too late to go hunting after it. I think, you know, it wouldn't do any
harm for the police to circulate Henderson's description,
just in case he should turn up anywhere."

" He was a smart fellow, though, if he did get away.
I had my two men, you remember, posted along the
road to Glendounie, and they were both there when the
fire broke out. One of them stayed to watch, and the
other got on the motor-cycle and came along to help
with the fire. I saw him, and they report that nobody
crossed the river, or even showed up on the island,
on their side. Now, with the disturbed sort of night
you've had, it looks as if you or your good lady or Mr.
Pumphrey – Pulteney, to be sure, I should have said
Pulteney – would have been aware of it if there'd been
anything doing this side. Well, we can soon find out
whether the treasure's there ; Dobbie'll be here before
long, and it's not worth making any enquiries before
that."

Angela came into the sitting-room, looking as if
she had had eight hours of unruffled sleep instead of
being up most of the night. " Good morning, Sir
Charles," she said ; " Mrs. McBrayne and I have got

117

some breakfast for you. At least, I'm afraid the cooking's mine, and you aren't to ask whether it's buttered eggs or omelette ; it couldn't make up its mind somehow. Mrs. McBrayne's gone across to the island, determined to organise Mr. Lethaby's life for him a bit ; she says it's dreadful to think of the poor gentleman all alone over there, and nobody to look after him. She's an angel, that woman."

Conversation at breakfast – Pulteney had not yet joined them – was naturally occupied for the most part with reminiscences of the night's adventures. " I give full marks to Strathdounie Lodge for energy," remarked Angela. " They kept on climbing up trees and dropping ten-foot branches on each other's heads and saying ' Sorry, old feller,' as if it were their idea of a large evening. Was Lady Hermia there ? I didn't see her."

" She was there all right," said Miles, " because I saw her get out of the first car, but I don't know what happened to her after that. I only saw her for a moment, and she said she thought this sort of thing brought out what was best in everybody, and then by good luck I caught sight of one of these Maximin extinguishers, and left her."

Angela made a slight face at her husband – she was not quite sure whether Sir Charles would appreciate levity at the expense of his tenants – and turned the conversation. " I wish I'd taken that bet you were offering the other day," she said, " against any treasure being found. You'd never tried to find it yourself, I suppose, since you took over the property ? "

" No, I can't say I ever believed in the thing. From what Mr. Bredon's been telling me, it can only have been just a fraction of what the countryside legends made it out to be. But there's one thing – it's like

118

having a tooth out ; we shan't have any more trouble about treasure in the future. Eh, I shall enjoy sitting under Maclean next Sunday. He's grand when he talks about the curse of riches ; and then he catches sight of me and calls them great riches instead. He'll have a field day on Sunday, will Maclean."

" You go ahead, and I'll follow," said Bredon, as they strolled out afterwards. " I've got to send a telegram. It's all right," he explained to Angela ; " it's only about a horse."

They walked slowly along the river bank, to find Mr. Pulteney and recall him to a sense of hunger. They were only just within sight of him when Angela suddenly exclaimed : " What *is* Edward doing ? He can't be beckoning to us, is he ? "

Sir Charles took in the situation with a better trained eye. " He's got something on. I'd like to see him catch something. The water's been so bad this year, I've hardly had the heart to let any of the fishing. No need to hurry, Mrs. Bredon ; it'll be some time, by the look of it, before he's got anything to show for it."

It is unnecessary to describe the breathless suspense of the next twenty minutes ; how at first they had to strain their eyes to see the full length of the line, exercise their faith, even as they did so, to believe that it was in contact with subaqueous reality ; the occasional flash on the water's surface, still far off, that gave visible proof of the conflict which was proceeding ; the set look of Mr. Pulteney, unconscious of spectators, unconscious of his own grimaces ; how, as the victim fish was brought nearer, the three watchers on the bank could not help moving their bodies this way and that, like the Athenian troops in the Syracusan bay ; the agonising moments when the fisherman swept

119

with his net in vain, and finally the triumphant scoop with which he caught into its meshes the wriggling mass of glittering scales.

" He's a big one," cried Sir Charles. " I could see he was a big one ; thirty pounds, I should say, Angus ? "

" Oh, he'll be just about that, Sir Charles." The " priest " was brought into action as the fish still floundered vainly on the coarse grass of the river bank.

Mr. Pulteney beamed apologetically under the shower of compliments which broke over him " I have lived," he said, landing from the boat. " I should not have supposed it possible to have a fish on for so many minutes without giving way to a single expletive. But the experience, I found, was one which went too deep for cursing, or even for prayer. It is an added pleasure, Mrs. Bredon, to be able to lay the spoils of conquest at your feet."

" Mr. Pulteney," said Angela, " I'm not going to – I say, is that a car ? "

There came, unmistakably, from the island the sound of a car getting into gear. Bredon broke into a futile run ; but long before he had reached the bridge he realised that he was beaten. His face was flushed with shame, as well as running, when Sir Charles came up. " I'm afraid it can't be anybody but Lethaby," he said. " Do you mind, Sir Charles, if we go up to the house ? Mrs. McBrayne will be there still, and she might be able to tell us something. I was a fool not to be looking out for him."

" Tut, don't blame yourself, Mr. Bredon. What could you have done, after all, if you had been there to see him pass ? Yes, we'll go up to the house, you and me, and see what he's been up to, and how much treasure he's left for us."

Mrs. McBrayne met them at the door, beaming with satisfaction as she wiped her hands on her apron. " I cooked him an egg and a rasher," she said, " and got him to eat them ; poor man, he hadn't tasted anything after all that terrible business. Oh, you wished to see him, Sir Charles ? It's very unfortunate, he's away just this moment. No, I couldn't say at all how long he'll be away ; he just said he was going to Moreton, Sir Charles " (Moreton was Lethaby's house in Perthshire). " He didn't take any luggage with him, so I shouldn't think he'd be away very long. Would you come in and see if he's left a note or anything ? I'll be down at the cottage just now, sir," she explained to Bredon ; " I was just washing up the things and making the place a bit tidier."

" It's very good of you, Mrs. McBrayne," said Bredon, " but really I think it would be better if you left things as they are for the moment. Don't you think so, Sir Charles ? The police might be wanting to have a look round, to find out how this unfortunate accident happened." It did not seem possible to suggest, to so good a nature as Mrs. McBrayne's, that foul play could possibly be in question.

" You're right, Mr. Bredon ; I don't think anything ought to be disturbed just yet. Hark, there's a car coming up the drive ; it can't be Lethaby coming back already ? "

It was not Lethaby, nor Lethaby's imposing car ; only a disreputable little run-about, from which a dapper tradesman with a grizzled moustache unpacked himself, and came forward with the air of a man who is expected. " Why, it's Dobbie," said Sir Charles ; " we weren't expecting you to be on the road so early. Come away in, Mr. Dobbie ; we'll have a look at what was found here yesterday, if we can get at it. The gentleman's away, you see ; I dare say you've heard that there's been a dreadful accident during the night, the garage burnt down, and it seems one of the gentlemen was in it. But if the case isn't locked, we ought to be able to show you something that's in your line." And he led the way into the sitting-room.

The leather case still lay where it had been put down the evening before ; the table on which the treasure had been exhibited had, naturally enough, been cleared. Mr. Dobbie, not a man of excitable temperament, cocked his head on one side in admiration of the case itself, and pronounced it to be " a fine piece of work, if only it had been better cared for " ; as it was, it would look a deal better when it was cleaned up a little. Then he stepped forward briskly, and opened it. It was quite empty.

CHAPTER IX: VERNON LETHABY'S CORRESPONDENCE

BREDON WAS ALONE IN THE HOUSE ; alone, it was to be presumed, on the island. Mr. Dobbie had shown himself remarkably patient over being brought out from Inverness on a fool's errand, " Oh, that's nothing at all ; I'm only sorry I couldn't be of use " ; had been oracular, in the manner of his race, about the probable value of the treasure, rather inadequately described to him from memory, " Well, there's a good many of those about, but I wouldn't say it would be altogether without value. . . . Well, that's a thing that should fetch a good deal of money, if times were better ; but there's been remarkably few of them that have changed hands just lately," and so on. Then, for at last even a Highlander remembers that he has business at home, Mr. Dobbie took his leave ; and Sir Charles, complaining that he had been up nearly all night and that he was too old for that kind of thing, announced his intention of returning to Dreams ; he would leave instructions, however, that he was to be summoned at once if Bredon should want him, " if young Lethaby should come back, for example," he said, " and you wished me to be present at any interview you may have with him."

" Yes, I shall want to have an interview with him all right," said Bredon drily. " Meanwhile, it occurred to me that this might be a good opportunity for me to have a look round the house, in case there's anything to be found out about what happened last night – or this morning, for that matter. I suppose you've no objection, Sir Charles ? Though really the objections ought to come from the tenant rather than from the landlord ; but I don't think there's any need for special courtesies in dealing with Mr. Lethaby. I'll leave things as I find them, of course, because the police may want to smell round too."

" By all means do as you like with the place, as far as I'm concerned," said Sir Charles. " Whatever way you look at it, the man's not dealing straight with us, and I don't think there's any call for us to be over-scrupulous with him."

So Bredon was left alone. He thought of going to fetch Angela, who had a woman's eye for the look of a room, for the deficiencies of a wardrobe ; anybody can see what is there (he told himself), but it sometimes takes a woman to see the thing that isn't there when it ought to be. But there was a kind of menace about the atmosphere of the island, especially since what had happened last night, that made him disinclined to invoke her aid. He set to work by himself, resolutely fighting down an uncomfortable feeling that in that haunted silence he was not alone ; almost that he was being watched.

Only one letter of comparatively recent date was to be discovered among the mess which piled the sitting-room table. It was in the neat but sprawling hand-writing which is common to so many old ladies – old, you felt certain, because the curves were tending to be replaced by little hooks, as if the writer held a pen with some difficulty. " My dear Vernon," it ran, " I am just on my way up North ; and as the Logans can't have me I thought I would break the journey at

Moreton, if you haven't any objection. Of course, I know you won't be there, because I read in the paper that you are still making a fool of yourself over that treasure business. But the Thompsons will look after me, and I shall dine on the train, so that I shall only want breakfast. I am writing to Mrs. Thompson by this post to tell her that I shall probably arrive on Thursday night " – that's to-day as ever is, Bredon reflected, after consulting the date at the head of the letter – " and she is to put me in whichever room is easiest to get ready. Thank God I'm not faddy about bedrooms, and don't mind sleeping alone in the house, as long as there's somebody at the lodge to make me my morning tea. I shall be staying at Laggie, so if your precious friend Mr. Henderson gets you into trouble, as I have no doubt he will, I shall be in a good position to come and bail you out. Your painfully long-lived aunt, CORNELIA."

That seemed straight enough ; the authenticity of the document leapt to the eye, and it seemed to have no particular importance – it hardly seemed to explain, for example, Lethaby's sudden disappearance in the car. It was not difficult to guess that this was the old lady to whom Moreton really belonged ; one seemed to get a picture of her even from this brief scrawl of hers – in fact, Bredon had an unaccountable feeling that he must have met her somewhere. It was while he was putting the letter back in the exact place where he had found it that he noticed a writing-pad on the table, with commendably thin sheets of paper, faintly ruled – the kind of writing-pad which you buy at a small stationer's when you are in too much of a hurry to notice what it is like. This was good – did Lethaby keep a pen ? Yes, but it was a fountain-pen, and like most fountain-pens had run dry ; Lethaby was not the

125

sort of man who would remember to buy reserves of ink. There was a pencil close to the pad ; with any luck, therefore, the top sheet would preserve a fairly good impress of whatever might have been written on the sheet torn off immediately above it.

We all give a slight jump when, unexpectedly, we come across the mention of our own names. And whatever message he was expecting to find half-revealed, half-concealed in the grooves left by the pencil's point, he was not expecting it to start " My dear Mr. Bredon." He felt as if he had been caught out in the act of eavesdropping ; was it conceivable that Lethaby had expected him to ransack the empty house, even wanted him to ransack the empty house, and had left this document to accuse him ? Not, at least, on the face of it. It had only occupied a single sheet, and in the few places where it was not legible the gaps could easily be filled in by conjecture. " My dear Mr. Bredon," Lethaby had written, " I am driven to asking a rather singular favour of you. It is this – could you keep an eye on my partner here, Henderson, during the course of the day, and let him know that you are doing it ? I'm afraid I don't like to trust him alone with the treasure. Unfortunately I have to go to Perthshire by the morning train ; and my chauffeur will not be about either, as he is taking the car there, so that I can come back in it. Could you offer him a game of golf, Henderson, I mean ? He'll be all right if he's watched. I would be so grateful. Yours in extreme haste, VERNON LETHABY."

Bredon whistled as he rapidly made a shorthand copy of this curious missive. Or rather, missive seemed the wrong word ; had it ever been sent ? (Yes, better make a transcript ; if one tore off the sheet there was always a chance that it would be missed.)

When had it been written? Last night, apparently; since their introduction, or the opening would hardly have been so abrupt, but before the fire started – that was quite certain. The post was out of the question; it must have been Lethaby's intention to hand it in at the cottage on his way to the station; then he had changed his mind about that and other things – the whereabouts of his chauffeur, for example. In changing his mind, had he preserved appearances by destroying the original document? There *was* a waste-paper basket, and Mrs. Maclean had not laid her tidying hands upon it . . . but there was nothing in it written by Lethaby, or on paper like this. He had destroyed the original, or possibly just stuffed it into his pocket. Yes, it was all very interesting. The journey South seemed to have come off all right; unfortunately it was not clear whether the absconding treasure-hunter had not changed his mind about coming back.

The accounts which had interested Lady Hermia, still scattered all over the table, must have aroused a purely feminine curiosity. They seemed straightforward enough; evidently Lethaby was acting as paymaster for the time being, but the expenses were to be honourably shared out when their ship came in. Hire of ropes, spades, etc. – that was all right; estimates of living expenses; even Henderson's railway-fare had been entered. Hullo, this was more suggestive – hire of car; only for a day or two, to judge by the sum involved. What did they want an extra car for? And here was some mysterious entry which (in Henderson's barely legible writing) looked more like " tweeds." The sum involved was too large to represent merely Henderson's wardrobe. Perhaps it was some other word; " tools " or something of that sort. Otherwise,

there was nothing to be made out of the bills. Somebody – Lethaby, presumably – had gone over them,
putting a tick against the side of each entry, as if to
admit its accuracy.

The chart-photograph, naturally one of the first
things Bredon looked for, had disappeared. If, hitherto,
somebody had been anxious that it should encounter
the eye of the casual visitor, he had changed his mind
about it, or at least decided that there was no need
for a closer inspection. There were various other maps
of the island, some of which had had points marked
on them, or lines drawn across them, in ink. One of
these looked as if it had been actually used for locating
the treasure from the data given by the chart. The
only other exhibit of this kind which seemed to demand
explanation was a map representing the railway
between Inverness and Perth, on which a light pencilled
line had been drawn from Inverness to Aviemore,
another from Aviemore to Blair Atholl, and a third
from Blair Atholl to Pitlochry. This line, very faint
and curving outwards from the railway between the
points named, suggested a quite familiar action. You
saw one of the two treasure-hunters explaining to the
other some considerations about the route, and making
it clearer by letting the pencil rest now here, now
there. " From Inverness to Aviemore," he would be
saying, " you don't stop at the minor stations," or
something of that kind, " but you do between Aviemore
and Pitlochry." Unfortunately, there did not seem to
be any clue to the precise point which had been at
issue.

It was time to pay more attention to the general
aspect of the room, as evidence of last night's proceedings. Of this general aspect, there could be no doubt,
the leading *motif* was drinks. There was a coffee-cup

at the edge of the table, close by one of the comfortable chairs ; not (to judge by its position) one of the cups he had seen lying about on the previous afternoon. The dregs, Bredon thought, had a very faint smell of some foreign substance ; fresh confirmation of the suspicion that Lethaby had been drugged. Was there another cup? Apparently not ; no doubt it was Henderson who made the coffee, and it would be simple for him to drug Lethaby's – with or without Lethaby's knowledge – if he were not taking any himself. It must almost certainly have been Lethaby who sat there ; the book which lay close by on the floor, as if it had dropped there when its reader had grown heavy with sleep, was a highbrow production – Bredon remembered seeing a review of it ; not the sort of stuff Henderson would be likely to go in for. So much for the coffee ; what was this glass close by, with a white sediment in it ? No, nothing exciting, probably ; you could see over there in the corner a bottle of that refreshing temperance drink which is so widely advertised for other purposes, but chiefly patronised by young gentlemen who wake up the next morning with a " head." That looked as if all the whisky which had been drunk – and there was a good deal of it – had been drunk overnight. But not necessarily by Lethaby ; the drug, if he had taken one, would give him that dry feeling about the mouth which would send him off to the familiar restorative. There was a glass at the further end of the table from which whisky had been drunk, apparently neat. On the whole, Henderson was more the kind of man who would take his whisky neat. There was no siphon, and the water in which the cooling drink had been taken that morning had not been drained of more than one glass-ful. It looked as if Henderson had been responsible

129

for all the execution done here. And it was not inconsiderable ; here was the last bottle but one, and
here was the bottle which had only been opened
last night ; the cork had never been taken off the
corkscrew since it was opened, as if there had not been
even a pause between drinks, and this new bottle
was quite empty. Even if you supposed that the
last bottle but one had only had a few drops left in
it, the impression suggested itself that either Henderson
had a very strong head, or Henderson must have been
three parts drunk last night. That was worth thinking
of ; what was the cause, Bredon wondered, of such
deep potations, and what had been their effect ?

So much for what was in the room ; and now, what
wasn't there that ought to have been there ?   He
claimed, afterwards, some credit for having noticed
the important deficiency – that of light. We are all
so accustomed to turning on switches and seeing
bulbs glow with sudden illumination that we do not
ask ourselves in remote places : Have they got electric
light here ? Bredon stood there in full daylight, and it
was only by a kind of inspiration that he noted the
absence of all electric fittings. There were none, to be
sure, at the cottage, where they used a rather danger-
ous-looking kind of petrol lamp. Ten to one it was
the same at the house as at the cottage ; but if so,
where was the lamp ?   It was not likely that Mrs.
McBrayne had cleared it away, since she had hardly
started to tidy up ; that could be verified. Lethaby
might quite possibly have turned in before daylight
gave out, since it lingers in the North ; but Henderson
was not likely to have got through all that whisky
in the daylight ; nor yet, you felt, in the dark. He had
not gone to bed, that he should take the lamp upstairs
with him ; and indeed, an expedition to his bedroom

showed no means of illumination except a couple of bedroom candles. Where, then, was the light which presumably had rested on the table, the silent witness of that solitary orgy?

Neither of the bedrooms yielded anything interesting to a perfunctory search; except that in Henderson's, Bredon found a garish orange-coloured label, crumpled up as if on a casual discovery and thrown away, without any attempt at concealment, in the empty fireplace. It was inscribed in unnaturally large letters, " J. HENDERSON, Passenger from AVIEMORE to KING'S CROSS." It suggested the problem why Henderson should at any moment of his stay on the island have been on the point of departure; and the further problem why he should have intended to board the train at Aviemore, which he could not reach without passing through Inverness, the train's starting point. It was difficult, though, to suppose that any sinister motive underlay this projected move, or why was the label thrown away with such absence of precaution? Unless, indeed, this was part of a plot to deceive; but what earthly inference could you make from it at the best of times? The only thing which worried Bredon was the size of the lettering, obviously inked in with great care. You did not picture Henderson as the nervous kind of traveller who always expects his luggage to go astray.

Meanwhile, there was the garage to be investigated. As he turned the corner from the front to the side of the house, he came across a fresh fact to be jotted down in the memory – the spanner, jack, and other tools of Lethaby's car were lying on the ground close to the house wall; at about the point where (he remembered) the car itself had been put for safety while the fire was raging. If Lethaby had left these behind, that

certainly suggested that he was not expecting to drive
any long distance. . . . But of course, it suggested another
possibility too. Hang it, if one could only see what the
man was up to ! Anyhow, here was the garage. It
could hardly have been gutted more completely ; the
loft above had fallen through, and made a ruin of
whatever might have survived on the ground floor.
There was a chance, though, that the key might be
discoverable ; or some metal object which had been
in the dead man's pockets, to identify him with more
certainty. Henderson was a smoker, for example ; he
might have carried a gun-metal cigarette case. It was
in his search for such minor indications that Bredon
caught sight of a brass stand lying on its side, almost
hidden in ashes and under the ruins of the loft. A
little patience served to bring more of it under view.
Yes, there could be no doubt of it ; it was the brass
stand of an oil lamp, exactly of the same pattern as
those which were in use down at the cottage.

Bredon experienced a momentary lightening of the
heart. His profession brought him much in contact
with the world's crooked dealings ; with people who
regarded the making of a few thousand pounds as
more important than common honesty, and sometimes
than common humanity. But he had never become
hardened by familiarity with fraud ; the discovery of
wickedness, however enthralling, still gave him a nasty
taste in the mouth. For the last eight hours or so he
had been convinced that the island, during the night
just past, had been the scene of a murder, and probably
of devilish cruelty. Now it looked, after all, as if there
was a more charitable explanation to be found ;
Henderson, let his faults be what they might, let his
intentions have been as criminal as you will, had only,
after all, met his death by accident. He was already

in bad nervous case ; the prospect of some daring *coup* had worked him up to a pitch of unwonted excitement, and, with the fatal habit of his kind, he had made drink his counsellor. Unsteadier than he knew, he had gone out to the garage to make some final arrangements, taking with him, to light his steps, a rather dangerous kind of oil lamp. The wooden floor of the garage was already, perhaps, impregnated with spilt petrol, ready to break into a conflagration. Henderson had fallen, in a sudden drunken stupor brought on by contact with the fresh air ; the lamp fell with him, and spread fire around him as it crashed. So deep was his insensibility that he knew nothing of it while the fumes suffocated him ; he lay prone, as he had fallen, and all that inferno of flame only served to cremate his lifeless body. An accident, Bredon reflected ; why not a straightforward accident, amid all this tangle of sinister plots ?

And then he remembered the key. He had searched, as the firemen had searched overnight, for any trace of the key which had made the garage door fast, and there was no trace of it to be found near the dead man, or in any part of the garage. As a matter of fact, it was not likely that the dead man should have locked himself in, and pocketed the key or put it on one side. Why should he ? The only other man on the island was lying drugged upstairs ; what need for him to ensure privacy ? Somebody, and it was not the dead man, had taken the key away after he went into the garage, and before Bredon himself could come to the rescue.

Could the key possibly be lying about in the house somewhere ? Unlikely, perhaps, that anybody would have been so careless ; but it was just worth while making a second search of the rooms with this definite object in view. In this hope, the house was ransacked once more, but quite fruitlessly. Only one fresh puzzle turned up in the course of this second investigation ; it was while he was going through Henderson's bedroom again. In one of the two smaller drawers of the wardrobe, amid a loose pile of socks, collars, ties and handkerchiefs, he came across a thing which seemed altogether out of place – a made-up bow-tie of white and pink satin, with an elastic loop at the back by which you attached it to the collar stud. Bredon eyed it with all the repulsion which such objects evoke in an over-civilised mind. What a beastly little object it was ! But, apart from that, did it fit in properly with the rest of Henderson ? Everything, no doubt, was possible in his Majesty's Dominions overseas. But Henderson, in coming to the Highlands, had dressed the part ; if anything, as we have seen, had rather overdressed the part. His clothes had such a pronounced tang of the moors about them that you felt the birds would be apt to get up at long range in alarm. From what dump of late-Victorian haberdashery had he dug up this horror, to belie, if he ever wore it, all his pretensions to be humanly dressed ?

The solitude of the empty house was beginning to tell on Bredon's nerves ; the acrid smell of burning which still hung about it disposed him to go in search of purer air. The island, after all, remained to be explored in the light of recent events. Not that the day was a suitable one for such exploration ; it had dawned in a thin white mist, of the kind which ordinarily succeeds a hot day, in places where the soil is damp, and presages another. By now – it was the middle of the morning – the sun ought to have dispersed it, and a bright, if hazy, air should have succeeded in its place. But no rules of weather wisdom apply on the Isle of Erran. You were conscious that the sun stood high in heaven, but its light came diffused through what seemed like a lawn veil of mist, which managed to cling in the trees and settle in the hollows ; you could not see more than twenty yards ahead. The bushes and the grass were still covered with intricate patterns of gossamer thread, as if millions of spiders had been at work on them overnight ; the atmosphere still charged with a damp that seemed to exude from the spongy soil. As Bredon took an upward path that climbed into the woods from the level of the front door, he felt that the island had redoubled its air of secrecy. The wood seemed to promise mysterious encounters, " your own footsteps following you, and all things going as they came." More than ever, he needed a companion ; more decisively than ever, he rejected the idea of inviting the obvious companionship.

A casual remark of Sir Charles' recalled itself, un-bidden and unwelcome, to his memory. The minister – Maclean, was his name ? – had repeated some tradition about a curse which was to be incurred by the finder of the treasure. If one were amenable to superstition, the fatality which had followed so soon after the discovery of the *cache* at the cliff's edge would certainly be calculated to reinforce one's beliefs. Was a curse, Bredon wondered, to be conceived as a mere sentence pronounced against a single man, and taking its effect automatically, by some law as abstract as a law of nature, when the offence was committed ? Or was the offence supposed to let loose some mysterious agency, hitherto held in check, which could now wander freely about the scene of its application ? In the latter case, you could almost imagine – if you were superstitious – that some malign influence was lurking about behind this curtain of mist ; in that thick clump of rhododen-drons, that jungle of bracken, in the shade of stunted oaks and overgrown pine-trees. You would begin to hear twigs cracking as if trodden on ; you would not be quite certain whether that sigh of the boggy earth came from your own footfall, or somebody else's.

And if you weren't superstitious ? The trouble was, that these odd noises accompanied you even so, and you felt that they must demand a natural, which could hardly be a comfortable, explanation. Why was it impossible to move about this cursed island, cursed in the profane if not in the literal sense, without feeling as if somebody was watching you all the time ; as if your explorations were being resented by somebody who had a secret to hide from you ? What made it worse was that, if somebody was shadowing you, he was likely to be somebody who knew his way about, and you didn't. The path on which Bredon had set out was recognisable as far as the crest of the hill ; then, coming out into an open clearing, it frankly lost itself. Here and there a couple of logs crossing a tiny stream, or a gap between walls of bracken, suggested a continuation ; but to find a direction would have been difficult even in clear weather ; in the mist, it was impossible. The island was not large enough to go astray in seriously ; if you kept resolutely downhill, you would be certain to arrive at the edge of it before long ; but if you start out with the feeling that you are unwanted, the absence of all landmarks and all guide-posts is an aggravation of your disquiet. A caper rocketed up suddenly a few feet away from him ; and he felt as if the jump his heart gave had been something audible.

Bredon claimed not to be an imaginative man, and certainly not a psychic one. He was accustomed to situations which involved a moderate amount of danger, and took the pride most of us take in not being daunted by visionary terrors. But the combination of silence and secrecy, the conspiracy of loneliness with the fear that he was not alone, undermined the strength of his resolution. First trying to tell himself that he was bored, and then admitting to himself, with indignant honesty, that he was afraid, he turned back down the path he had taken, welcoming the sight of his own footsteps in marshy spots as if they had formed a kind of human companionship. He was too proud to hurry consciously, but it astonished him to find how short a way he had really travelled ; within about ten minutes his feet were ringing on the hard gravel of the drive. Should he go straight back to the cottage ? No, he owed it at least to his injured pride not to be afraid of the house ; though by now he was so demoralised by his fears that the house itself hardly seemed as if it could be untenanted. Fighting down his alarms, he threw open firmly the door that led into the living-room ; to find there, sitting on an easy chair as if the place belonged to him, the minister of Glendounie.

CHAPTER X: THE CURSE OF DAVID
HABINGTON

IF BREDON had had enough for the moment of solitude,
it is to be conjectured that Mr. Maclean was permanently in the same state; for he never failed to improve
the occasion when he found he had an audience.
" Come away in, sir," he said at once, " though I don't
know that either of us has the right to say that to the
other. But open front doors and no servants means
keeping any kind of company that comes along, so Mr.
Lethaby will have to make the best of us when he gets
home. I just came along, you must understand, to
give him what consolation I could about the loss of
this friend of his; not that I know, you see, what
persuasion Mr. Lethaby's is, but there's such a thing,
isn't there, as a word in season to him that is weary,
and I thought it would do no harm coming. You'll
be Mr. Bredon, I think, from the cottage? Yes, we
know all about our neighbours in these lonely parts,
and we don't wait for introductions; anyone'll tell
you that. This is an awful thing, Mr. Bredon, poor
Henderson meeting with such a dreadful fate, and just
when they'd come across the treasure, too. I think I
heard you were there when they looked into it, were
you not ? "
    " Yes, I happened to be paying an afternoon call,
and saw them bring it up."
    " Then perhaps you'd be able to tell me, did it look

138

to you as though it might have been there ever since Prince Charlie's time? Mind you, I've always said there was no difficulty about believing the legend; but to be quite plain with you I didn't very much expect it would be there yet, after all these years. You don't think they may have come across somebody else's little nest-egg, by mistake? There's a lot of folks round here yet, more than you'd think, who don't like to trust their savings to a bank. I suppose it wouldn't be anything of that kind?"

Bredon was vaguely conscious that the minister, however genuine might be his intention of administering consolation, had not come down to the island solely for that purpose. " I wish I could show it you," he said, in answer to the unspoken thought; " but Lethaby's gone off, and I suppose he's put it away somewhere; one can't leave that sort of thing lying about, can one? I'm not in the least an expert; but there wasn't any cash, you know, which hardly looks as if it was a private hoard, and some of the things must certainly have been well over a hundred years old. There was the chest in which the stuff was found, for example; that's here, in the corner; surely that must go back to Charles Edward's time?"

Mr. Maclean had a good look, and was evidently satisfied. " Well," he said, " it's a warning to a man not to be too positive in his opinions. Mind you, I was quite persuaded that if they found anything, it wouldn't be the thing they were looking for; and it seems I was wrong. But I was right in one thing, after all; I warned them there was a curse laid on anyone who should dig up Prince Charlie's treasure, and that was neither more nor less than the truth."

" Was it the Prince's curse, or whose?"

" No, the curse doesn't go back as far as that ; it was an old fellow who lived hereabouts, not so very long afterwards, a fellow called David Habington, who had the reputation of being a prophet. And it was one of his prophecies that if anybody was to disturb Prince Charlie's treasure, it would be the worse for them ; the dead (that was his phrase) wouldn't rest easy in Glendounie churchyard. And now poor Henderson's gone, by the look of it, and Mr. Lethaby has thought prudence the better part of valour, and left the district ; I wouldn't say but he was wise, Mr. Bredon."

" Yes, I think he has more sense than some of his proceedings would suggest," Bredon admitted drily. " It seems odd to me," he added, " that a curse like that should only fall on the man who's *successful* in finding the treasure. You'd have thought that the will would be taken for the deed, and trouble would begin as soon as people started looking for the treasure, not wait till they'd found it."

Mr. Maclean looked slightly shocked. " You're a young man, Mr. Bredon," he said, " and new to these parts, I think ; so it's not surprising you should find things strange here. But let me tell you this – there's people in the glens who haven't liked to pass along the road that goes by my house ever since this talk of treasure-hunting got abroad ; and there's others will tell you they have seen lights on the island, and on the shore opposite the island, late at night when there was nobody had a right to be there : and all that a fortnight or three weeks past. Well, I must be getting along ; will you be coming my way as far as the bridge, or have you business here yet ? "

Bredon was by this time glad enough to leave the island ; without Mr. Maclean, it did not provide enough company, with him, it seemed to provide almost too much. Mr. Maclean (as he said unkindly afterwards) was certainly the man to speak a word to the weary, whether it was in season or not. They did not continue, on their way down to the bridge, any discussion of the preternatural ; the minister seemed to detect in his companion's attitude a trace of that Lowland scepticism which would dispeople the Northern lochs of their indubitable monsters, and to conclude that argument would be wasted on him.

It was refreshing, certainly, to be back at the cottage again ; to be performing the ceremony of shaving, which had somehow mysteriously been neglected, while Angela reclined in the window-seat of the bedroom, throwing out a tennis ball at the McBraynes' dog, which found a perpetual source of entertainment in retrieving it up a very steep flight of stairs. He had told Angela about all the puzzles he had found in the house, for her inspirations were sometimes useful ; about his cowardice in exploring the island, for she had a tiresome habit of over-estimating his rashness in undertaking adventure ; about Mr. Maclean's conversation, because it was of the sort that is best relished in retrospect. Angela declared that, if she were Sir Charles Airdrie, she would ring up the Psychical Research Society and offer them the Isle of Erran as a ghost sanctuary.

" Talking of ringing up," she added, " Sholto was on the telephone just now. I didn't think it worth while fetching you ; he only wanted us to report progress. And he seemed a bit sniffy because you hadn't telegraphed to him when the treasure was found ; said he read it in the morning paper, which was pretty galling."

" Because I hadn't telegraphed to him when the

141

treasure was found ? Well, I did – no, I suppose in a sense I didn't. What did you say ? I trust you put up a sufficiently disingenuous excuse."

" Told him that, at the rate events break loose in this part of the world, a little thing like finding a few thousand pounds' worth of treasure is apt to slip the memory. Then he asked what events, so I told him about the fire – I hope that was all right. Oh, yes, and there was something I was to tell you – apparently the police have been giving them the low-down on Henderson again, and it seems his career was a little more chequered than they made out at first. In fact, the New York police are after him ; and Sholto thought they would bear up all right at hearing the news of his death. I suppose all that will be in the evening papers ; so there didn't seem to be any reason for hushing it up."

" No, rather not ; no harm done. Now you shall tell me exactly what you think about last night and this morning, while I shave. Nothing like having the jaw perfectly relaxed."

" You could get the same effect with a new blade. Still, I like talking to you when you aren't in a position to interrupt too much. Let's see ; what you want me to say is that although D. Habington has some right to be regarded as a prophet, the efforts of M. Bredon in the same direction are not so good. Because you were making out, only last night, that either Lethaby and Henderson would conspire to defraud the Company, Henderson disappearing with the treasure by arrange-ment and divvying up afterwards ; or Henderson would double-cross Lethaby and disappear with the treasure, not leaving any address. Whereas on the contrary Henderson is dead ; or at least he's looking so dead that Lethaby can't lay any claim to his insurance money. And if Lethaby flitted with the treasure when he made his hurried disappearance this morning, it won't do him much good, because everybody knows he found the treasure, and Sir Charles has a claim on him for his share, if he likes to press it."

" Disregarding the offensive nature of certain expressions used, that seems to sum up the situation quite adequately."

" Meanwhile, the chauffeur has also disappeared in suspicious circumstances. Lethaby having, apparently, expected him to parade all right among those present, when he wrote a note to you yesterday evening which was never delivered. But on being rudely woken up this morning, Lethaby explained that the person under discussion had been sent home days ago. It takes no great perspicacity to discover that there is a flaw here somewhere. I say, Miles, do you think the chauffeur was just Henderson dressed up ? Because that might explain why Lethaby was so anxious to get him out of the picture, as soon as Henderson was dead."

" The chauffeur wasn't always Henderson, anyhow. You yourself saw them driving together. And did Lethaby, when I woke him up, *know* that Henderson was dead ? Looks bad, if so."

" Yes, but dash it all, he must have spotted that his plans had blown a fuse out somewhere, with you coming and shouting ' Fire ! ' in his ear at all hours of the morning. However, as you say, Henderson and the chauffeur were seen together by reliable witnesses ; so there must have been somebody else who either grew those superfluous face-fittings, or was in the habit of assuming them on occasion. Talking of superfluous face-fittings, there's a great blodge of soap close to

143

your left ear still ; I don't know if you mean to do anything about it. Yes, that's better. . . . What was I saying ? Miles, you don't think they murdered the chauffeur, do you ? "

" Well, it's not impossible. In that case, Lethaby's note about sending the chauffeur over to Moreton with the car may have been designed to account for the unfortunate man's disappearance. But in that case, what on earth were they up to ? They've destroyed a perfectly good chauffeur and a perfectly good garage ; meanwhile Henderson's gone, and the treasure's gone, but they're no nearer proving that it was Henderson who took the treasure with him. And as if to make that more doubtful than ever, Lethaby does a bolt first thing after breakfast, all alone when nobody's looking ; and who's going to prove that he didn't cart the treasure off with him ? I know the Indescribable pretty well by now, and I can tell you I don't see it paying up any claim as fishy as this one is."

" Especially as the jury, or rather this Procurator chap, will be almost certain, one would think, to say the corpse is Henderson. If they wanted Henderson to do a bolt, or pretend to do a bolt, it was surely rather careless to leave a corpse about which might perfectly well be his ? "

" You're still assuming, of course, that it was a put-up job, and Lethaby was in the plot. If Henderson wanted to clear off with the treasure entirely on his own account, it might be convenient for him to leave a corpse behind, so that we shouldn't be too energetic in trying to trace him. But, as you say, if that was so, why hasn't Lethaby declared the loss ? And why has Lethaby rushed off like this, instead of hanging round to help the police and give interviews to the journalists ?

By the way, why isn't the island running with pressmen by now ? "

" The police are picketing the end of the road here, and not letting anybody past who hasn't any business to be here ; so the McBraynes tell me. They're expecting a high-up policeman to visit the scene of action this afternoon."

" Good thing I gave it the once-over this morning, then. Let's hear more about what I found in that sitting-room, by the way. Or the bedrooms, for that matter."

" I don't see that you can hold a man responsible for his aunt coming to stay. It's an act of God."

" No, I wasn't suggesting there was anything very sinister about that. Though I confess the arrival of the aunt this evening interests me. If she is his aunt, as my old head master used to say. I mean, is it just a fluke that Lethaby has gone to Perthshire ; or is he wanting to meet his aunt, or is he wanting to avoid her ? No, don't say it ; I know perfectly well how unneptile you are about aunts ; but it doesn't follow that Lethaby feels the same. However, let us pass the aunt. Why was Henderson going to use an enormous label for his luggage, with enormous lettering on it ; why had he got it all written out overnight, and why did he then throw it away ? "

" Are you genuinely seeking information, or do you really know and are you asking me these questions just for fun ? "

" Honestly, I want to know how these things strike you, and what you make of them. If I'm not telling you a little of what I know about this business, it's only a little, and I give you my word that I'm still hopelessly in the dark about the questions I'm asking you at the moment. Nothing I know throws light on them. I can guess, of course ; but then, so can you ; and people's guesses are much more useful when they're made independently."

" Oh, yes, I know all about that. Well, if the lettering really was so large as you say, I don't think we ought to regard that label as a blind, deliberately left about to mislead us. Because if one was doing that, one would take care to make the label look as ordinary as possible, wouldn't one ? No sense at all in overdoing it. Therefore I'm for that label being a genuine exhibit ; only for some reason Henderson thought better of it and threw it away. The only explanation I can think of for his wanting the writing to be so legible is that he wanted people in his railway carriage to read it without difficulty. I'm always snooping at other people's labels myself. Long ago, before I met you, I travelled with a man whose name was Blessing. I thought it was such a jolly name that I very nearly tried to make him propose to me. But that is by the way. Henderson, I take it, must have counted on having one or two label-snoopers in his carriage when he went off with the goods – or pretended to – so that when there was a police wireless asking people to give information about somebody of the name of J. Henderson travelling by the Highland line, there'd be a rush of witnesses. Henderson having meanwhile got out somewhere well this side of King's Cross and doubled back on his tracks or what not. Is that any use ? "

" Yes, that's the right suspicion to entertain ; barring accidents. I would suggest further that he wasn't going to put that label on his own luggage, which is contained, as far as I can see, in a rather small and disreputable kit-bag ; but on some more sinister-looking receptacle which would look so large and heavy

that the snoopers would say to one another afterwards :
Of course, that must have been the treasure ! That's
rather a long shot, of course ; but if it should happen
to be true, it almost certainly means that Henderson
wasn't really going to cart the treasure about with
him ; they were probably going to bury it somewhere,
as I told you before."

" Ye-es ; I hope we're not getting just the tiniest
bit fanciful. And then about that railway map ;
does that come into your scheme of guess-work at
all ? "

" Does it into yours ? "

" Confound you, I thought I'd headed you off that
time. Of course, it's true the label did suggest he was
getting in at Aviemore. And he'd have looked rather
a fool getting in at Inverness, wouldn't he ? Because
the label was so obviously new, and meant to be
operative. And Aviemore was one of the points specially
marked on that map, wasn't it ? Well, I suppose it's
just possible he and Lethaby were going to do a Box
and Cox, one getting out where the other got in. . . .
Oo, yes, Miles, that's not as silly as it sounds, because
this is one of the very few railway lines in the world
where you can successfully race the train in a car.
You remember how we kept on passing the train
as we came up. So Henderson might drive as far as
Aviemore, while Lethaby took the train ; and then
Lethaby would drive a bit further, while Henderson
took the train. Why, I've not an earthly. I shall have
to think that out. But it's ingenious as far as it goes,
isn't it ? "

" Yes, I don't think it's quite as idiotic as it sounds.
Because, after all, we're dealing with Lethaby ; and
we agreed, I think, that he's a man with a distorted
sense of humour. So I wouldn't put it past him to

147

think up some damfool scheme of the kind you mention; double bluff (he'd say) is the right way to deal with a situation of this kind, and the result would be thoroughly fantastic. Indeed, if all had gone well, and Lethaby's schemes were all we had to deal with, they'd probably have been so desperately ingenious that a child could have seen through them. But somebody else, it seems quite clear, has thrown a spanner into the works ; either Henderson, or a third party, or possibly just Providence taking a hand. Try to exercise your ingenuity a little further, dear Mrs. Bredon, and tell me how that happened."

" Who's taking things for granted now ? Why shouldn't Henderson have started to throw a spanner, or some blunt instrument or instruments unknown, into Lethaby's works, and *then* Providence decided to take a hand too ? Providence, I mean, considerably aided by the fact that Henderson was probably quite blotto well before midnight, and that the petrol lamps we use in these benighted parts are the sort of things that demand asbestos gloves if you are going to turn up the wick without burning the house down ? "

" I see. Of course, you realise that you are making Henderson out to have been quite incredibly drunk. There was at least one electric torch in the house ; there was also, heaven knows why, an old-fashioned lantern with a candle in it. Why on earth did Henderson need to take an oil lamp out to the garage ; incidentally giving away, to anybody who might be on the watch like ourselves, only from higher up the road here, the fact that things were happening up at the house ? But let that pass ; you still come up against the difficulty that heads us off every time – the difficulty of the key. Henderson, having drugged Lethaby, had no

148

need as far as we can see to lock himself into the garage ; and if he had, the key would have survived the fire and been found lying among the ruins. That means that, on your showing, somebody else must have been hanging around waiting to pocket the key once the garage was nicely alight with Henderson in it ; somebody who wasn't Lethaby, unless of course Lethaby was shamming drugged. You see, your explanation wants rounding off somehow."

" Dash it, yes, that is rather awkward. Miles, I don't *want* to believe that somebody was so utterly loathsome as to lock the door on the outside and let a man burn to death inside. That is what you mean, isn't it ? "

" I don't quite know that I do. If the idea interferes with your sleep, comfort yourself with the thought that I *have* an alternative explanation of how the door came to be locked ; only it means that the whole thing is even more complicated than it looks at first sight. The door-locker has got to be Lethaby – improbable, because he wore every appearance of having been drugged when I found him ; or Henderson, in which case we must find some other identification for the man in the garage ; or a third party, and we don't seem to have got a third party in view who comes anywhere near to filling the bill. But the door-locker isn't necessarily a murderer. The man in the garage may have been dead before the fire started ; and the door may have been locked so as to make it look like a murder when it wasn't one, or at any rate when it didn't look like one. Or, just conceivably, the door-locker didn't know there was anybody inside ; though in that case we should have to find some reason why the door seemed to want locking just then."

" Miles, I don't want to be pig-headed about it,

but it would just be possible, wouldn't it, for the whole thing to be an accident ? Like this, I mean – Henderson has put dope in Lethaby's coffee, but it's a kind that takes its effect rather slowly, and Lethaby isn't as drugged yet as Henderson thinks he is. Henderson takes the lamp and goes out to the garage ; Lethaby suspects that there's dirty work at the cross-roads, and wants to put Henderson out of action without having a row with him. So he goes to the garage very quietly, and turns the key in the lock, meaning only to keep him prisoner for the night. By the time the fire starts, and Henderson, poor man, is beating at the door, the drug has taken its full effect, and Lethaby is past hearing. That's why, when you wake him up, Lethaby goes round shouting ' Henderson ! ' everywhere, as if he didn't know what had happened to him."

" If so, he lost his head rather. Why didn't he tell me that the chauffeur slept in the garage, instead of saying the chauffeur had gone home ? Then we should have assumed that it was the chauffeur whose body had been found. We should have assumed that Henderson had disappeared for reasons best known to himself. . . . It's true, though, that if there's anything fishy about that chauffeur, it might have got Lethaby into worse trouble than ever. No, I don't deny that your explanation is possible. Only I don't see Henderson as the kind of man who would get up to any tricks until he had made sure that he had put his man out. And I don't think it's likely he'd administer a dope which took such a long time to work. Presumably it was just after dinner that Lethaby took his coffee ; and I take it that Henderson didn't get to work on his scheme, whatever it was, till much later."

" Why do you take it? You're always taking things."

" Well . . . at any rate, he seems to have got outside a remarkable succession of drinks before he left for the garage. And after all, what was he up to in the garage – to take all that time over it, I mean? If he was merely getting the car out, it would have been dashed difficult to lock him in all unbeknownst. And what on earth did he take the lamp for? "

" Nobody said all that wasn't odd. All I mean is, that it's an oddity you've got to explain on any other hypothesis quite as much as on mine. You seem so dead keen on bringing an unknown third party into the business. It isn't – what's that word you're always throwing up at me? – it isn't economical."

" The trouble with you is, you won't fix your attention on the lamp. Surely you see that the lamp looks much more like a faked accident than a real one? On the other hand – I know, don't bother to say it – there isn't much sense in faking an accident, and then locking the garage door in such a way that the stupidest coroner in the world couldn't mistake it for an accident. That's really what we're up against – that and the question why Lethaby bolted this morning, and where the treasure is, and one or two little things like that."

" Miles, look me in the face and tell me, do you *know* where the treasure is? "

" I assisted, yesterday evening – it seems much longer ago than that – at the unearthing of a leather case or chest, as you know, a little further along the coast of the island. When we opened it, there was stuff there which would have kept even you in jewellery for a life-time. Not long after breakfast this morning, Sir Charles and I found the same case or chest lying

151

about in the living-room at the island house, but when we opened it there was nothing in it. Now, it's quite conceivable – and if we had any reason to think him an honest man, it would be the natural assumption to make – that Lethaby, being called away in a hurry for some reason this morning, tucked all that stuff away somewhere, so that it shouldn't be at the mercy of the first comer, with the intention of having it valued, and all that, as soon as he comes back. I'm sorry to say I don't think that. I think in that case he would quite certainly have left a note or a message to tell Sir Charles, who after all is the legal owner, that the stuff was all right. I should be more inclined to believe that he took it away with him, or took whatever of it was left away with him, this morning ; and that the reason why he took the tools out of his car and left them behind was because he wanted to have a *cache* for the bulkier exhibits, which he couldn't stow away in his pockets and under the cushions. If I am wronging him in that suspicion, it is probably true that he has not taken any treasure away with him because there was none left to take. It had been removed, I should suppose, in the night, either by Henderson or by some third party, who, if he ever shows up, will labour under considerable suspicion of being Henderson's murderer. On the whole, I incline to this second view, because I can't for the life of me see why Lethaby should have carted his treasure, or rather Sir Charles' treasure, away with him, instead of hiding it away on the island somewhere and pretending that it had disappeared in the night. But then, I can't make head or tail of his bolt this morning in any case. There, does that answer your question ? "

" I should think it did. You mean you don't know.

152

You have used up more breath in conveying that simple piece of information than I should have thought possible."

" There are times," her husband pointed out, " when it is important to get your terms completely accurate."

CHAPTER XI: MR PULTENEY SEEKS REFRESHMENT

IT WAS A DAY OF CATECHISMS. The " high-up police-man " called at the cottage on his way back from the scene of the tragedy, interviewing all three visitors as well as the McBraynes. Fortunately, they found that the easy-going manner of the Highlands infected even the procedure of the local police ; the inquisitor betrayed an anguished delicacy in eliciting information, which made him seem (as Mr. Pulteney said afterwards) less like a human sleuth-hound than a Royal Commission investigating a scandal in the Cabinet. Every answer you gave was welcomed with an eager " Yes, just so, Mr. Bredon ; that would be it ; I understand perfectly. And now perhaps you wouldn't mind if I raise just one further point," and so on. He betrayed no curiosity whatever about the motives of the Bredons in taking the cottage, though it need hardly be said that he had a long conversation with Mr. Pulteney about the fishing, and about the salmon he had caught – this fact, at least, was " known to the police." It did not appear to strike him as in any way surprising that Angela should have been awake, or that Bredon should have been awake and fully dressed, well after midnight ; there was no need, consequently, to bother him with any information about the changed mooring-place of the boat, or the suspicions which it had suggested to Bredon's own mind. Bredon explained, of course, that he had been present when the treasure was found, but not that he had any special interest in the finding of it ; reported that he had seen Lethaby's car disappearing up the road soon after breakfast, but without mentioning that the sight had in any way disconcerted him. In fact, as Angela said, a pleasant time was had by all.

This obliging official had not only, it proved, the Highlander's delicacy about eliciting information from others ; he had the Highlander's fondness for bestowing it on them. Bredon, accustomed to the severe taciturnity of the English police – " they'll never tell you anything except that they've got a clue, and that's a lie " – was refreshed and materially assisted by this outburst of Northern candour. The corpse (he was told) seemed to be that of a man who was fully dressed at the time of the fire ; buttons were present, and the metal parts of a pair of braces, though there was no wrist-watch. (Lethaby deposed that Henderson had lost his wrist-watch during the digging operations.) A pair of shoes, badly damaged, were lying together in a position which suggested that the dead man had been carrying them in his left hand : " And you know, Mr. Bredon, if it was somebody who had no business to be in the garage just then, he might easily have gone bare-foot, for it's close to the windows of the bedrooms." None of these finds held out the least hope of identifying the corpse for legal purposes ; mass-production, as usual, was the enemy of justice.

The return of Lethaby, about six o'clock in the evening, was the signal for more serious interrogations. Not by the police, who had already retired from the scene, but by Sir Charles Airdrie, who had come down to the cottage in the hope of finding such an opportunity.

Bredon was naturally anxious to be present at this interview, but did not relish the idea of explaining to Lethaby who he was, and so putting him on his guard for the future. It was arranged, therefore, that Sir Charles should take him along as " his witness " ; a proposal which sounded reasonable enough, and may perhaps have been considered by Lethaby as a normal demand, for the Englishman is always conscious that Scots law is different, without having any idea what it is. The part of inquisitor would naturally fall to Sir Charles ; but Bredon primed him beforehand with a set of questions which it was, he said, important to ask ; and there was always the chance that he might be able to put his oar in at the interview itself under colour of clearing up ambiguities.

They found Vernon Lethaby a tornado of well-bred apologies, all punctuated with an irritating repetition of the word " actually " – a habit of modern youth, particularly when it is lying. " My dear Sir Charles," he said, " I wouldn't have had this happen for anything. I'd have been round to explain first thing this morning ; only I'd heard from my aunt that she was coming to stay a night on her way North, and I simply had to go over and see that things were got ready for her. Actually, you see, there's only a married couple at the lodge, and they have to do the whole thing. But I'm afraid the *most* awful thing's happened ; all that stuff we dug up yesterday afternoon simply isn't there. Actually I didn't think about it at all while the fire was on, and all that dreadful business about Henderson being found, you know, if it was Henderson, drove it out of my head worse than ever. And I don't see how we're ever to find out how it disappeared, because actually it might have been any of those people who rallied round last night, mightn't

it ? And yet it would be very difficult to accuse anybody, wouldn't it ? "

" So, by your way of it, it will have been some of
my tenants that were round last night, helping to put
out the fire, carried it off with them ? I ought to tell
you, Mr. Lethaby, that we're mostly honest folk in
these parts."

" Oh, don't think *I* want to blame it on them, Sir
Charles. Actually, I'd much rather feel certain it
wasn't any of them ; because that would mean it was
taken away before the fire started ; and if that was so
it would more or less have to be Henderson, wouldn't
it ? You know, I never did trust Henderson very much ;
you were quite right about that ; actually I took out
an insurance policy against fraud in that quarter,
and I suppose I could recover if only we could be certain it was Henderson who took it. Dead or alive, I
mean, it doesn't matter ; if he's hidden it, it's for the
insurance fellows to find out where, or else pay up,
isn't it ? "

" You're going just a wee bit too fast for me, Mr.
Lethaby. Come, now, let's have the whole story, if
you don't mind. When will it have been you last saw
Henderson, and had you any reason then to suspect
him ? Any reason, I mean, beyond the ordinary ;
did he stay up after you'd gone to bed, for example,
or what ? "

" Actually, I went to bed very early last night. I
started dropping off to sleep in my chair, which I
don't usually do. To tell the truth, I rather think
Henderson must have doped my coffee ; he always
made coffee, and he didn't have any himself, last night.
I should think it would be some time between nine
and ten that I turned in. Henderson always sat up
later than that ; he said he was sleeping badly – actually

that's why he didn't have any coffee himself, or so he said."

" And what had you done, if I may ask, with what was in the case there ? Did you just leave all the jewellery lying in the case, or did it occur to you to put it away safely somewhere ? We might have had a deal of trouble saved if you'd done that."

" I'm awfully sorry, you know, but we left it in the case. We didn't expect burglars, you see, because the word could hardly have got round so soon that we'd found anything. And – well, of course I'd have liked to put it away somewhere where Henderson couldn't get at it without my knowing. But how was I to do that, short of sleeping on the bally thing ? And it's rather awkward, you know, telling a man you can't trust him with the stuff after you've gone to bed. Actually we did discuss the idea of putting it in one of the bedrooms ; but it would hardly have been any safer, and it was a filthy weight, you know, to carry. Still, I'd have done anything I could, if I'd known this sort of thing was liable to break loose ; you can be sure of that."

" So you went to bed, and left Henderson in here. Was he taking drink at the time ? "

" He finished up a bottle, and said something about opening another one. Actually I told him to go easy with the whisky, because our stock was running rather low. Between you and me, Henderson put the stuff away rather. He must have opened a new bottle, and there was none left in that when I looked at it in the morning. But there again . . . however, I suppose you'd give your tenants a good character, and say they couldn't possibly have been at it."

" I was there all the time, Mr. Lethaby, and I didn't see any of them go into your house. The only people I saw go into the house were the party from Strathdounie, when they were wanting to get hold of those Maximin extinguishers. Perhaps you're suggesting that they refreshed themselves on the way ? "

" No, honestly, I didn't mean that ; I thought perhaps it was some of the local people. Still, if you didn't see them go in, it can't very well have been them. I'll tell you what it is, I believe old Digger must really have been one over the eight, if it was he who took that lamp into the garage. I mean, that was a fool thing to do, wasn't it ? I'm not complaining of your lamps, Sir Charles ; but they aren't exactly Davy lamps, are they ? "

" Still, we've got to make out what he went to the garage for at all. It would hardly do to put that down as a drunken man's frolic. You've no idea, yourself, what reason Henderson might have had for going into the garage at that time of night, and you upstairs in your bed ? "

" Well, that's almost a leading question, isn't it ? Not that I mind, of course. Actually it was the first thought that came into my mind, I'm afraid, when you told me that a body had been found in the garage, that poor old Digger had been up to some dodge, trying to double-cross me over the treasure. He'd been in Canada a lot, you know, and hadn't quite our Oriental notions about honesty and that sort of thing. If you ask me, I shouldn't think it's at all impossible that Digger first of all doped my coffee a bit – not anything to do a man any harm, you know, but just enough to put me off properly – and then made a bid to get away with the stuff while the going was good. He'd want to take the car, you see, because this isn't much of a country-side for hiking with a trunkful of assorted jewellery under your arm, is it? The car had been put away in the garage when we last used it; you'd remember that it wasn't there in the afternoon, sir," he put in, appealing to Bredon, who nodded. " Very well, then, he's got to take the car out, and like a silly ass he forgets that there's a perfectly good electric torch lying about. Or possibly he tried it, and fumbled over the catch, and thought there was no more juice left in it – I don't know. Anyhow he just took up the lamp, and started fooling round in the garage, putting the lamp up quite insecurely on a shelf or what not, and then, down it comes, and that's where poor Henderson gets his."

" Yes; the only trouble's about the key. You were saying last night, I think, that you didn't know there was a key to the garage? "

" Not that I ever heard of. Actually we didn't ever bother about locking it up, because it seemed so unlikely there would be any car thieves loitering around on the island. I'll tell you what it is, Sir Charles, I believe the lock must have been sort of half-in, half-out all the time, and then Henderson must have slammed the door behind him when he went into the garage, and the lock must have slipped into position of itself. I don't for a moment believe there was anybody else on the island except just him and me, until, of course, the fire started. So the door must have jammed itself somehow, and that's the likeliest way I can think of."

" Then it's your idea that Henderson meant to flit in the middle of the night, taking the treasure with him, and leave you and me and the Insurance people to make the best we could of it? "

" Absolutely. You see, as I was saying just now, old Digger hadn't any morals much. I don't think he'd have let down a pal if it could have been avoided without loss to himself, don't you know – but then, the way he probably figured it out, there wasn't any loss for me, because the Company would have been bound to assume that he had walked out on me, and cough up the insurance money. Actually I still hope they will, of course ; but there's no denying it would have been much plainer sailing if old Digger hadn't started dropping lamps about in the garage."

"You'll excuse me," said Sir Charles, who was obviously repressing his feelings with difficulty, "but I'm not quite sure that I follow your train of reasoning just yet. Henderson, by your way of it, was just taking the car out, and was going to make off with the treasure. He had got the car outside, and then gone back into the garage for something or other, and the door slammed to on him. Where was the treasure all this time ? And why didn't Mr. Bredon here find it lying outside the garage door ? Or why didn't you find it in the car, when you started her up this morning ? That's what I'm finding difficult."

"You can search me," admitted Lethaby with apparent candour. "Actually if it had been me I'd have popped all the valuables into a suitcase, left the pistols and one or two bulky things, that weren't of any great value at the best of times, as a sort of consolation prize to the legitimate owners, and made tracks as quick as I could, not fooling round in the garage once I'd got the car out. But Digger had rather a tortuous sort of mind, and I think it's quite possible he'd have gone about the whole thing in a more constructive sort of way. He'd have said to himself, There are those McBrayne people over at the cottage, and their lodgers sitting up playing bridge as likely as not ; it would be the devil and all if somebody stopped me at the bridge, and asked where I thought I got off exactly, shooting the moon with several thousands' worth of valuables. So I'll tell you what I think he probably did; he probably took that boat – he was a rare hand in a boat, was Digger – and ferried the stuff across to the mainland; and then he'd have come round in the car and picked it up on his way to the great open spaces. The bother is, of course, that if so it's waiting there all ready for us, but we don't know which bank of the river it's on, or how far along. And there's another thing; he could dig like a mole, that chap; that's how he got his nickname. I wouldn't be surprised if that treasure is lying under a couple of feet of earth somewhere, and the top made so smooth you'd never notice the difference. Naturally, I'm going to have a try at getting hold of it, if you'll let me, Sir Charles. As I say, I don't much believe it's on the island; but I don't suppose I'd be much of a nuisance, would I, having a look along the banks to see if I could come across the trail of it?"

" Well, we'll see what the fishermen make of it first of all. There isn't a great deal you could do on the river bank hereabouts without leaving some trace Angus would observe the next time he passed. And I'll tell you another thing, Mr. Lethaby, if you find that you're wearying of living on the island after the unfortunate experience you've had of it, there's no kind of reason why you should be at pains to stop on here. When you came to ask me about the let, I could see you thought I was a man who drives a hard bargain. Well, maybe I am, but I hope I'm not deficient in common humanity. And I'll tell you what I'll do; if you care to give up the rest of your lease of the island – that's only for the month, I think – I'll not charge you a penny for the time you've had on it or for the use you've made of it. We'll just treat the whole thing as if it had never happened – unless, of course, the treasure comes to light again ; and if that happens, you and me'll go half-shares, according to the arrangement we made. You think that over ; and you don't need to thank me for any generosity. I'm a man, you see, that likes things to be quiet about me ; and the publicity we've had here since you came looking for the treasure has been quite enough for me ; I don't want any more of it. That's the meaning of my offer, Mr. Lethaby ; and you must forgive me for plain speaking when I make it to you."

Lethaby hesitated a little, as if he were either taken aback by the liberality of the offer, or uncertain whether to avail himself of it. At last he said, " Please don't think I'm wanting in gratitude, Sir Charles ; your suggestion's a really handsome one, and it's *most* awfully good of you. But I feel as if I simply must stay on here for a bit, if only in justice to the Company I'm insured with. As far as I can see, they'll at least have to consider paying my claim ; and I owe it to them to make sure that the stuff is not to be found. Actually I don't think it would be very advisable for me to leave these parts until the Procurator Fiscal has held his enquiry ; and as I have taken this place it's surely simplest for me to stop here. Only, if that's what you mean, I'm not going to give any more inter-views to journalists or . . . or play the goat in any way – you know what I mean. This thing's been a bit of a shock, naturally, and I shall want to go quiet for a bit. But I am really most awfully grateful for what you've suggested ; and really sorry to have given so much trouble. That's all I can say. Except " – he added, turning to Bredon – " that I don't believe I ever thanked you properly about last night. If it weren't

163

for you I might have burned to death too, I suppose, or at any rate had a bad time of it."

In spite of the more gracious note on which it had ended, neither Bredon nor Sir Charles could regard this interview as particularly satisfactory. Lethaby had not really put forward any very convincing explanation of his absence during the earlier part of the day ; he could have made his arrangements at Moreton, you felt, by telephone. He had offered no sort of proof that the treasure had really vanished between the time when he went to bed and the time when he went to look for it in the early morning. His account of the lock being pushed home automatically by the slamming of a door was hardly credible ; and the behaviour he attributed to Henderson seemed in the highest degree improbable. At the same time, his superficial air of detached candour made it difficult to penetrate his defences, unless you were prepared to browbeat him with all the pitiless logic of an examining counsel. He was too thoroughly artificial to let you see when – if ever – he was speaking the truth.

Further light was thrown on the conversation, from a quite unexpected source. Bredon was summarising it at dinner, with some aspersions on Lethaby's character for veracity, when Mr. Pulteney, looking up from a generous portion of his own salmon, interrupted the recital. " Do I understand you to say," he asked, " that there is some doubt in Mr. Lethaby's mind whether the treasure was not removed from the scene by his lamented partner, before the fire in the garage broke out ? "

" That's what he thinks, or pretends to think – that Henderson had already smuggled the treasure away somewhere and hidden it, with the idea of picking it up later. Sounds thin to me."

" How fortunate that I should be in a position to reassure him ! Really, when this excellent meal has reached its conclusion——"

" Don't you start reassuring people," said Angela. " Just tell Miles and me what you've been up to ; I ought to have known we couldn't take you for a holiday with us without your making discoveries all over the place. Remember what he was like at Chilthorpe, Miles ; you really couldn't trust him out of your sight for five minutes together. What is it this time ? "

" I must have, I am afraid, an unusually large allowance of what is called human curiosity. You can bear me witness, Mrs. Bredon, that when you awoke me this morning I lost no time in attiring myself in a suitable manner, and proceeding to the scene of action. Without being able to boast that I was the first who bent the knee when the standard waved abroad, I can claim to have taken some share in the work of rescue. I carried no less than three Maximin extinguishers for a distance of some thirty or forty yards, having never realised before how considerable is their weight. Then, finding myself something of a supernumerary, I was content to encourage those very energetic gentlemen from Strathdounie by word and gesture – principally the latter. I had an almost Horatian escape from the fall of a branch, which somebody had cut off, without apparent warning, exactly above my head. . . . About this time I became conscious that it was rather hot."

" Yes, I noticed that," said Bredon.

" Also, I have always observed that there is a peculiar dryness about one's throat when one is woken up after the hour of midnight. I used to find it the same during the air raids. What with the heat and the dryness, I was gratified to remember that, in passing the windows of the front room, I had seen a bottle on the table."

" Mr. Pulteney ! " said Angela, deeply moved.

" It occurred to me that I had earned a drink ; as a kind of perquisite. It also occurred to me that it was dangerous to leave a beverage of such inflammable character lying about in a room which might at any moment become the scene of a conflagration. With this double motive in view, I retired to the front of the house and, finding myself alone, proceeded to the sitting-room. Imagine my mortification on discovering that the bottle was empty."

" You're sure about that ? " asked Bredon. " I mean, you're not just sparing Angela's feelings ? Because as a matter of fact it is rather important to know whether the bottle was empty before – well, before you got at it."

" Believe me, that is not the sort of thing I make mistakes about. I inverted both bottles – there were two of them – completely, and without result. You sigh with relief, Mrs. Bredon, but that was not my feeling at the moment. However, as I *was* there——"

" I say, you do seem to have been having a night out," said Angela. " Next time I take you to a fire I shan't let you alone for a moment. What did you go for next ? The larder ? "

" No, I was not hungry. But I was, as I say, inquisitive ; and, seeing an undeniably antique leather chest lying in a corner of the room, I felt a curiosity to know whether it contained the famous deposit of treasure. I opened the lid, and my eyes were gratified by the sight of a most interesting collection of valuable objects."

" What sort of objects ? " Bredon asked.

" Brooches and lockets and old-fashioned jewellery

for the most part ; but there were some pistols, I noticed, and one or two appliances which might be of service to a monarch in exile ; a flask, for example."

" Anything in it ? " asked Angela unkindly.

" Having feasted my eyes with this sight for a minute or two, I thought it more prudent to withdraw, for fear the owner of the house might come along and misinterpret my presence. I don't suppose the whole episode lasted five minutes. But that the treasure was there, I could take my dying oath."

" And you didn't, I suppose," suggested Bredon, " run into anybody as you were coming away ? Because it's dashed important, you see, to know who went in there after you."

" Since both doors were wide open, I take it that the whole party remains under suspicion ; including, of course, myself. If. you were to accuse me of having filled my pockets, I could plead nothing in my defence, except a series of excellent testimonials given me by head masters who were anxious to find me another post and replace me with a cheaper man. Was there anybody near the door as I came out ? Yes, there was one fellow-labourer who looked as if he might be going in the same direction, and I nearly warned him about the state of the bottles. I was glad, afterwards, that I had not done so, for his costume seemed to imply that he was in orders."

" Maclean," said Bredon musingly. " He didn't have a look at the treasure, though, by his own account. It's dashed lucky that you had that inspiration about looking inside the chest, Pulteney. You're the only witness we've got to prove that the treasure was there after the fire started. And if the enquiry reports that the dead man was Henderson, which I should think it's almost bound to, that means that the Company isn't liable. What a game ! Look here, Pulteney, we'd better keep this thing dark for the present. If by any chance Lethaby is lying – and I think it exceedingly probable – it is just as well he shouldn't know we know that he is lying."

" I shouldn't have thought there was any *probable* about it," objected Angela. " You didn't, I suppose, try picking up the chest, Mr. Pulteney, and seeing how easy it was to carry off ? "

" No, I had suffered quite enough from the Maximins. If I went in for robbery on a large scale – extinguishers, for example – I should certainly have a confederate to do the carrying for me."

" Exactly ; and who's going to scoop up all that stuff and carry it away under his arm, even without the chest, on the spur of the moment like that ? "

" A fireman might," suggested her husband. " I can imagine no profession which would give one more opportunities for casual looting. However, the point isn't whether it's likely anyone else took it away ; we've got to be *certain* nobody else took it away – otherwise I don't see how we're going to prove that Lethaby did. And there's another point ; since we can't prove it was Henderson who was burnt in the garage, we can't prove that Henderson wasn't hanging round all the time, ready to scoop up the stuff when nobody was looking, and escape in the general confusion. No, the important thing is having cleared up our own minds about it. Now we can get ahead, and set Lethaby one or two little tests, to see how he reacts."

" What sort of tests ? " asked Angela.

" At the moment, I haven't the faintest idea. If I had, I probably shouldn't tell you. But it must be possible to think up some test to which a man who's pinched a treasure will react differently from a man who's lost a treasure. Thank goodness he's decided to stay on at the island."

" Yes. I wonder why he has."

" I have, personally, a pretty shrewd idea ; but it's not for publication. Gosh, I'm going to bed early to-night ; I feel as if I could sleep the clock round."

CHAPTER XII : THE TREASURE OF THE LATE PRINCE CONSORT

" WHAT'S ALL THIS ABOUT ? " asked Bredon, as he took a stroll after breakfast the following morning. " This," was a formidable-looking gate, at the mainland end of the bridge, standing shut for the first time in their experience of the place. It seemed as if it had sprung into being during the night, so little notice do we take of a gate which is always open.

" That happened while you were asleep," replied Angela. " You must expect things to happen during your sleep if you don't wake up till nearly eleven. Apparently Sir Charles took Mr. Lethaby at his word about not wanting to give any interviews to journalists ; and as the police aren't picketing the road up there any longer, he sent orders that nobody was to be allowed to pass the bridge without being able to show that he was expected up at the house. There have been some angry men round here this morning, I can tell you."

" The beauty of it is," said Bredon, " that the bridge is now the only way of getting across to the island. At least, I don't see anybody making it in a boat, with the water like this. Gosh, how it's come up. I say, I believe I'd have been drowned in my sleep if I'd stayed upstairs much longer. Look how high it comes on the bridge, where the register mark is ! I should think it's risen a full eight feet during the night – and without a spot of rain – yet. But it looks as if we were going to have no end of a downpour after lunch."

It is the habit of Highland rivers to rise thus mysteriously ; and the natives, if you question them about the phenomenon, will tell you that there has been " rain in the West," a not infrequent occurrence. All the dried-up water courses, miles away, that looked like ugly gashes down the hillside, have suddenly turned into spouting torrents, and come foaming down into the main river, whose deeply sunk channel leaves no room, at most points, for a true flood, so that the whole swirling mass of water has to be carried down, at headlong speed, turning the placid stream of yesterday into a mill-race, the gurgling rapids of yesterday into a maelstrom. Branches that had fallen in that country of wooded river-banks were caught and swept away ; you saw them appearing and disappearing in the froth of the falls. The spray rose high, and seemed to hang in the misty air ; standing on the bridge, with your ears deafened by the roar of the stream, and your eyes hypnotised by its ceaseless motion, you felt as if you had become part of a great whirling adventure, as if you were going singing into battle. The whole prospect had exchanged senile languor for a kind of tempestuous youth.

And, as Bredon said, it looked as if this were only the beginning of an inundation. Though there was no rain where they stood, or on the island opposite, the hills beyond were wreathed in a white mantle of cloud with dripping skirts of mist. It seemed incredible that you should remain dry in this precarious belt of no-man's-land between the waters that threatened to overwhelm you from above, and the waters that threatened to engulf you from beneath. The rocks with their clinging satellites of birch and rowan looked as if they were hanging down, ready to fall into the stream, not based on any foundation of their own. There was no wind, and the hush in the tree-tops felt ominous, with all this boisterous activity raging at their feet.

So occupied were their ears and their attention with the scene below them, that it was only the hooting of a horn close by which informed Miles and Angela that a car had driven up at their backs. It stood still just short of the bridge, evidently waiting for somebody to come and give it information ; the old lady who was the only occupant besides the driver did not even put her head out of the window. You felt they were carriage-folk.

" Gosh, if it isn't Mrs. Wauchope ! " cried Angela.

Hotel acquaintanceships do not often ripen into intimacies ; but the few days which Angela and her husband had spent at the Blairwhinnie Hotel, at the time when the Indescribable Insurance Company felt it important to establish the exact date of Colin Reiver's decease, were days so crowded with incident, and Mrs. Wauchope, though a mere fellow-lodger in the hotel, had taken such a motherly interest in the proceedings, that the sight of her was like the sight of an old friend. Angela and she had corresponded slightly, but had never met since the time referred to. All the same, Mrs. Wauchope was not the woman to forget her acquaintances, nor to stand on any ceremony in her manner of greeting them.

" God bless my soul," she began at once, " what on earth are you doing here ? Oh, of course, I ought to have been expecting it ; with a mystery going on the other side of the bridge, I suppose that inquisitive husband of yours is sure to be lurking about ; what a trial, my dear, to be married to a Nosy Parker like that ! I suppose you'll be staying at some frightful hotel at . . ."

" Not a bit of it ; we're on the spot. Our cottage, or rather, we've rented it. I say, do you want to get through the gate ? "

" I did rather ; only it doesn't look as if it would open. Having found you here, I feel more inclined to come in and have a crack. Isn't one allowed to get across to the island if one wants to ? "

" Not if it's just for a gossip-column, I'm afraid. Strict orders that nobody's to get across without a permit signed by Lethaby, the Hon. V. ; but perhaps you know him ? "

" My dear, if a man's own aunt . . ."

" And I never thought of that ! I say, this is terrifically exciting ; we wouldn't have read your letter if we'd known it was yours, would we, Miles ? I am glad you weren't here last night, with the things we were saying about aunts."

" You were," corrected Bredon. " I didn't say a word that was disrespectful about them, as far as I remember. But you know what Angela is, Mrs. Wauchope ; she didn't like her own aunts, and I've never been able to make her take to mine."

" Of course not ; young people don't," admitted Mrs. Wauchope. " I'm an aunt several times over, and not ashamed of it. But I don't expect my nephews and nieces to like me ; especially Vernon Lethaby, because I don't approve of him, and consequently treat him very shabbily. I lend him a house down in Perthshire – I've just come from there – but I don't give him any money, and consequently it's no kind of use to him. Now, look here, my dears, I didn't come from any desire to see him ; he gets on my nerves horribly. I only wanted to hear the news, and

173

obviously you will know much more about it than he does. You're always better posted in what's happened than the criminal himself, ain't you, Mr. Bredon ? "

" Well, I can't be quite sure of that yet. Perhaps I am, in a way. But why do you call your nephew a criminal, Mrs. Wauchope ? "

" Why ? Only because the people I overheard talking about it at luncheon all seemed to take it for granted that he had murdered his partner and collared the whole of the treasure. Knowing him as I do, I found it hard to believe that he had done anything half so sensible. Now, you really must take me inside and let me see your cottage."

It was not exactly an easy task to put Mrs. Wauchope *au fait* with the situation. Instinctively, Bredon attempted to spare an aunt's feelings by putting the most charitable interpretation possible on Lethaby's behaviour and presumed motives ; invariably he found that Mrs. Wauchope gave the story exactly that sinister aspect he had been carefully trying to avoid, by assuming throughout that her nephew was an irreclaimable wastrel. That he was a murderer, however, she refused to believe. " Not that he's any morals," she explained. " He's what these idiotic people nowadays call a-moral ; which is so much worse, I think, than just being immoral, as young men were when I was a girl. I mean, it's the same thing, only it means being irrationally proud of your weaknesses instead of being ashamed of 'em. But I feel perfectly certain that Vernon, if he started out to do a murder, would bungle it hopelessly. He would start out to shoot Henderson and hit a really valuable dog by mistake ; that's the sort of man he is. And, of course, there's this indecent craving for publicity he

174

has ; I don't think he would find any sort of satisfaction in breaking a commandment without being able to tell all Fleet Street about it. What sort of man was this Henderson ? I never met him ; but I understand he was a rum-runner of sorts. If only Vernon had met him a year or two earlier, he might have found a career, which would have been most satisfactory. But what's all this about your reading my letters ? I can't say I approve of that very much ; I'm rather an indiscreet correspondent, you know, Mr. Bredon."

" But I couldn't tell it was yours, could I ? It was while your nephew was away, yesterday morning ; failing to catch him, I thought it would be a good idea if I had a look round at the house, to see if I could find any explanation of the fire, and . . . and all that sort of thing. And seeing a letter from a self-convicted aunt, who didn't sign her surname, I hardly thought it could be indiscreet to take a look at it. And of course it explained why your nephew went away when he did."

" No, you can take off that poker face, Mr. Bredon – I know perfectly well what you're after. What you mean is, Vernon probably told you that he went south to get things ready at Moreton, because I was coming to stay the night. And, knowing what a liar he is, you want to know whether he really went to Moreton after all. Well, as a matter of fact he did ; that is, if you can take the word of a perfectly respectable couple who live at the lodge and do for anyone who's staying in the house if necessary. They tell me he came there in a great hurry, and didn't even want any luncheon ; said he'd get that on the way back. He talked to them about making me comfortable, of course, but it was perfectly unnecessary ; and the idea of Vernon motoring the best part of two hundred miles to make sure that I was

175

made comfortable, of all people, is the sort of story that doesn't take in anybody. I don't in the least know what he was up to; but he did go up to the house for a bit; and he didn't make me an apple-pie bed, because I should have noticed it. I suppose, from what you've been saying, that you suspect him of having come over to Moreton to stow away the Isle of Erran treasure. Well, he may have, but if so he was precious quick about it, and it wasn't a very safe place to choose. Because he knew I was coming; and he knows that I'm an interfering old woman, the sort of person who pokes round to see that everything's as it should be."

" I wonder – do you know anything about that chauffeur of his, Mrs. Wauchope? "

" I don't believe he ever had such a thing as a chauffeur; hasn't got the money to pay one with. Now, I really must be getting on. I'm on my way to Letty Cochrane's. . . . "

" But you're lunching here," explained Angela. " Mrs. McBrayne has been extending herself like anything. Dash it all, they can't expect you till the afternoon."

" My dear, that's wonderful of you. I wasn't going to tell you, but I am simply famished; we started before eight this morning, you know; and if you can really give me a pick here, and perhaps get them to give the man something in the kitchen, I could take in the bazaar at Birniewood on my way back. Letty Cochrane is opening it, I believe, so it will fit in beautifully. I suppose you don't go to bazaars, being English? They're the chief sport, I expect you know, in these parts."

" We hadn't meant to go," admitted Angela, " but I don't see why on earth we shouldn't, unless of course

Miles insists on seeing that Mr. Lethaby doesn't go off on any more expeditions. Oh, this is Mr. Pulteney – Mrs. Wauchope. Do you go to bazaars much, Mr. Pulteney? He's come here for the fishing, Mrs. Wauchope, and he caught a salmon yesterday; so I think he ought to go to the bazaar and be congratulated by all the important people, don't you? "

" If there is hoop-la," said Mr. Pulteney, " you can count on me. I find a strange fascination in the pastime, though as far as I know I have never won so much as a bottle of scent."

" Oh, you won't find that kind of thing," said Mrs. Wauchope; " they take themselves much more seriously up here. People really come to pick up bargains, not just to be fleeced. What an excellent cook you have here, and what a charming view from the window, if only one could see it ! "

The bazaar took place in a big village hall, conventionally festooned, but not, evidently, concerned to overdress the part. The stalls seemed almost equally divided between what Bredon classed as " filthily useless " objects – photograph-frames, knick-knacks, fire-screens, and whatever lasts in a house only from one bazaar to the next – and " produce," which appeared to mean that you could go home with a large cheese or a haunch of venison bought at cut prices. Nobody knew particularly what the bazaar was about ; it was in some good cause, and it was a fresh opportunity for everybody, high and low, to come from miles round and exchange the gossip of the season with a good philanthropic excuse. There was no hoop-la, which was fortunate, since Mr. Pulteney had been left behind to keep an eye, generally, on any vehicle crossing the bridge. As for Bredon, the alacrity with which he volunteered to be of the party was a surprise to his wife, who knew well his intense dislike for social functions of all kinds. But he was there with a purpose ; somebody might be there who knew a little about the comings and goings before his own arrival, or who had a useful theory about, say, the identity of the corpse in the garage.

He had luck almost immediately. Lady Letty Cochrane, having expressed her pleasure at seeing such a large gathering of neighbours, met in such a really deserving cause, and hoped that nobody would go away until they had bought just a little more than they meant to, was touring the room with a large and particularly hideous tartan rug, which she was raffling (Mrs. Wauchope said) as befitted the descendant of a long line of cattle-raiders. Noticing, perhaps, that Bredon shied at the spectacle, she did not attempt to pass it off as a bargain, but cunningly appealed to his better feelings. " Do take a ticket, Mr. Bredon ; I've sold quite a lot, so the odds are fairly heavy against your winning it. I really couldn't bear it in the house any longer ; I bought it the other day from one of those travelling salesmen who was touring about in a small car, and his things were so hideous I didn't see how he was going to sell any of them if one didn't buy them out of charity. He didn't seem to know a thing about his job."

Bredon had one of those rare inspirations which made him (a director of the Indescribable said once) worth a dozen of the men who are prepared to do an honest day's work. " He didn't, by any chance," he asked, " wear a pink-and-white made-up bow tie ? "

" Oh, I do hope he's not a friend of yours ! Have I said anything dreadful ? That's exactly what he was wearing, and it made him look so touching, somehow."

Having ascertained, further, that the salesman wore a lightish moustache, but without inducing Lady Letty to remember exactly when it was that he called – " it might be a fortnight, or it might be three weeks ago, I'm so wretchedly vague about dates " – Bredon courageously took six tickets, in defiance of the wide-eyed stare he saw on Angela's face, only a yard or two away. Angela put it down to pig-headedness, and it is probable that Lady Letty put it down to something more like mental derangement, when he offered to take the execrable object off her hands, and hawk it round himself for the remainder of the afternoon. But he knew what he was about ; here was a passport which would enable him to discuss itinerant tradesmen with all comers, and he contrived to put in a good deal of such discussion without neglecting, unduly, his own duties as a vendor.

" No," said Sir Charles Airdrie, " I don't usually interview these people myself, though my daughter sometimes does. But word's always brought to me when they come round ; because, you see, some of them aren't the best of characters, and it's useful to me to know what fellows there are that are going round on those errands. Indeed, I won't deny but I some-times take a squint at them from behind the curtains of the front window. And I'm quite positive there's been nobody up at Dreams selling tweeds lately. We're rather out of the way there, as you know yourself, so it's not everybody takes the trouble to come round and perhaps find that I'm away south."

Nor had Bredon any better success with the minister of Glendounie. " It's odd you should ask me that, Mr. Bredon, because as a matter of fact it's not more than two months ago, if that, that a fellow came round to the manse selling carpets, and what do you think ?

179

He was as black as your hat ! Now, I dare say you
don't realise at once what an extraordinary thing that
is ; but it isn't so very long ago that the people in these
glens, if they saw a black man, would think it was Auld
Hornie himself ; that's our name for the Prince of
Darkness in Scotland. So that you wouldn't think it
was a very useful kind of salesman to send round ; and
it does give you a queer sort of feeling, on a lonely
road up in these parts, to come across a nigger with
a great load of carpets on his back. Eh, they can carry,
those fellows. But of course, these cheap motor-cars
have made it very much easier for the men that are
on the road. I did hear tell of this tweed-seller not
long since ; I think my wife passed him on the road
once. But he never came to the manse ; I'm quite
positive about that."

One or two strangers – the difficulty was that he did
not like to ask their names or addresses, except when
they were rash enough to risk incurring ownership of
the tartan rug – could testify to having seen the hawker
in the small car. As for Strathdounie, Bredon did not
suppose it would be much use putting any questions
there, since the tenants were scarcely of older date
than himself. But he did not succeed in escaping the
eye of Lady Hermia, who bore down on him from a
distant corner of the room, and chained him to her side
by professing an interest in the rug. (She had not the
face to call it " a very handsome thing, that," as Mr.
Maclean did ; but she took a ticket, as he did not.)
Her real object, evidently, was to discuss Vernon
Lethaby with somebody whom she insisted, for no
obvious reason, on regarding as his soul-mate.

" I think it was so splendid of you, Mr. Bredon, to
go up at once like that and get poor Vernon out of
bed ; it might have been so dreadful if he hadn't

woken, you know. Not that it isn't dreadful enough, as it is ; that poor man Henderson ! But I'm not really sorry for Vernon's sake, because I do think those queer friends of his don't always have a good influence on him. *You*, I'm sure, Mr. Bredon, won't imagine for a moment that Vernon can have had anything to *do* with it. People have been saying the *most* dreadful things, as they always will ; even suggesting that Vernon locked the man up in the garage and set fire to it ; but, as I tell them, even if one didn't know Vernon as one does, what *sense* could there possibly be in doing a thing like that ? Because, of course, there's no doubt Vernon is in need of money ; but there was plenty for everybody, wasn't there ? It really made my mouth water, that collection of jewels and things. But you don't think, do you, that there's likely to be any *legal* bother about it ? Vernon has so many enemies that they'd be prepared, I believe, to make capital out of anything ; and mud always sticks, doesn't it ? But I hope if you have anything to do with it, I mean if you're called as a witness or anything of that sort, you'll let them see how perfectly ridiculous you think those sort of charges are ? "

Bredon was in some difficulty – not made any better by the fact that his wife had caught his eye again, and was trying to make him laugh. But he soothed Lady Hermia as well as he could, insisting (what was no more than the truth) that Lethaby's sleep and awaking had been, to his mind, those of a man drugged, unless they were those of a consummate actor ; and reporting Mrs. Wauchope's opinion of the charge in question, though without giving the grounds for it. " But I must say," he added, with a vague hope that the remark would be passed on to the proper quarters, " I think Lethaby does himself harm by keeping his own counsel so much, and giving the impression, at any rate, that he has something to hide. I wonder, Lady Hermia, if you would mind answering one question which may seem to you impertinent. It's this – do you know anything about the bearded chauffeur who drove Lethaby when he first came to the island ? You'll understand why it's bothering me. Because if he stayed on the island – although you'll remember that when you and I went over to call there, there was nobody to answer the bell and apparently no third person about – but if he *did* stay on the island, obviously the question arises whether it was his body or Henderson's that was found in the garage. When you've settled that, the further question arises whether it was really an accident, or whether Henderson killed the chauffeur, or the chauffeur killed Henderson ? In either case, the Procurator Fiscal will want to know whether there is any sign of Lethaby having been in league with the murderer. That's why I think it's such a pity Lethaby should go on making a mystery over the chauffeur business."

" Oh, but there's no mystery at all ; Vernon told me about it quite definitely. He hasn't got a chauffeur, really ; he's too poor to keep one. Besides, he drives himself quite beautifully. But when he was going to settle in at the island, he made up his mind to stage a sort of triumphal return to the home of his ancestors, in that whimsical way he has. Well, he was in Glasgow for some reason or other, and met a man in a pub who started telling him a long story about the bad luck he'd had. He'd been a lorry-driver, and had some accident which was really, he said, no fault of his own, and then the firm had sacked him, and he was hard-up to find any work. Vernon didn't really believe him ; thought he had probably been mixed up in something criminal, and grown that enormous beard so that he shouldn't be recognised. But evidently he could drive ; because he was licensed and all that, and Vernon took him a mile or two in the car to try him out. Then he offered to pay his expenses and, of course, a bit over, if he would drive him up to the Isle of Erran. He thought it would be rather fun to play those absurd bagpipes in the car, you see. That's how it all happened ; and the idea was that the chauffeur-man should sleep at the island just for the night ; naturally they didn't want him any longer, because it seemed likely he was a bit of a crook, and it might be dangerous to have him round the place if they found the treasure. As a matter of fact, he didn't even stay the night, because he said it gave him the pip, staying on in such a lonely place, and they put him ashore and paid his bus fare to Inverness. The bother is that if he's wanted as a witness it's very unlikely that we shall be able to find him. Vernon doesn't even know his name or address ; and he probably isn't the kind of person who would come forward in answer to an advertisement, because, you see, he might think it was a trap, and the police were on to him over his past record. The whole thing's been *most* unfortunate ; and it all arises, in a way, out of Vernon's kindness of heart. He just hates to see anybody down and out ; he always has done."

" I see. I'm afraid there's one question I still want to ask, and you may think it a brutal one ; but I do want to get this thing clear, you understand. When was it that Lethaby told you all this ? "

Lady Hermia flushed rather, as if it had been her own veracity that had been called in question. Then she said, " Yes, I suppose you'd have to ask that. After all, you don't really know Vernon as I do. I

183

don't think there can be any harm in telling you – it was when I rang him this morning to know if he could give me a lift to the bazaar. I wasn't sure about being able to get the use of my husband's car, so I asked Vernon if he could send the chauffeur for me. Then it all came out ; he has no secrets from me, I believe, really none."

The passing of time, and the necessity for extending the membership of the Suicide Club which was bidding for the tartan horror, made an excuse for Bredon to get away. He did not really believe that Lethaby had no secrets from his self-constituted guardian angel, and he would have felt some delicacy about questioning her further if that had really been the position. The produce stalls were by now swept bare ; occasional tables were going at merely nominal prices, and lavender-bags could be had practically for the asking. There was a general air of departure, in the midst of which the draw was made for the raffles, and Bredon, with the sensations of a man who has just murdered his best friend, heard the rug knocked down to Mrs. Wauchope. Her magnanimity, however, rose to the occasion. " It will come in useful for private theatricals," she suggested ; " or perhaps I shall manage to lose it in the train. Anyhow, I'm not long for this world, and I shall know how to dispose of it in my will. It shall go to Vernon Lethaby."

Bredon, it is to be feared, did not make any great impression on his wife by the excuses he made to her for his singular conduct during the afternoon. His explanation that he did not want to get on visiting terms with the neighbourhood, as she apparently did, and that he hoped to make himself unpopular with the nobility and gentry by his efforts to saddle them with the treasure of the late Prince Consort was happily thought of, but not altogether convincing. "Anyhow," he added, with more appearance of candour, "the idea had one advantage. I got hold of the book, and destroyed the counterfoils of my own tickets."

CHAPTER XIII : THE BAIT

THE DOWNPOUR predicted by weather-prophets, accustomed to the B.B.C.-made weather scheme of the South, never came ; but all that afternoon and evening there was a fine drizzle scarcely less wetting than rain, and a general dampness threatening ague or rheumatism to the susceptible. Angela was not pleased when her husband, soon after dinner was over, announced his intention of going out into the inclement night.

" Dash it all," she protested, " there's nobody left for you to watch now except Lethaby ; and the treasure's gone ; and the night is not the sort of night in which anybody would turn out to look for a treasure that isn't there. The night before last, you said nothing was going to happen, and there was arson and murder and goodness knows what all. And now when there's nobody left to be killed, and it's raining fit to put out a burning petrol-tank, you want to go out and get all wet. Do try and be reasonable."

" Dear Angela – you always had such a nice, unsuspecting nature. I sometimes think it accounts for my marrying you, and I'm quite certain it accounts for your marrying me. Don't you see that it's just because it's such a pig of a night, with the visibility rather like trying to X-ray a rhinoceros which has swallowed a front stud, that I am expecting dirty work about now ? Granted that Lethaby hasn't got anybody left to murder, we don't know he hasn't got any treasure left to hide, or possibly to find. He may have shoved that stuff under the kitchen dresser, and be waiting for such a night as this to go and put it away safely. It may have been, as he suggests, buried somewhere by the lamented Henderson ; and Lethaby may want just such a night as this so that he can escape notice finding it again, and keep it all to himself this time. There may be traces of the tragedy to tidy up or remove, and this may be just the night Lethaby was praying for, to do it when those inquisitive Bredons aren't looking. No, I don't mean that's certain ; but it's dashed probable."

" Miles, I don't like you going on to that island all alone. You can't take the boat, or you'll quite certainly be drowned, in a stream like this. And I don't like to think of you walking over the bridge, straight into a trap as likely as not. Where *are* you going ? "

" Well, I was going to walk downstream a bit at first, anyhow ; just into the wood opposite where they found the treasure ; where we used to watch them from, I mean."

" At first anyhow ? That sounds pretty thin. Miles, promise me you won't set a foot on the bridge without coming back and asking my leave, or – or I'll come with you ; dashed if I don't."

" Not set a foot on the bridge without asking your leave ? All right, I promise. I don't think I shall be long, anyhow. I bet you and Pulteney don't get the *Jupiter* cross-word out while I'm away. And I'll put an aquascutum on, if that's any comfort to you."

" He really is a rather tiresome sort of man to have married," Angela said to Pulteney, as they sat over the fire – Mrs. McBrayne, accustomed to the Highland summer, had lit one without even asking. " He's always trailing crooks like a real, honest-to-God

187

policeman, and although of course he really is rather clever in some of his ideas, he's no more notion of how to protect himself if one of them turned nasty than you or I have. It's all very well Mrs. Wauchope saying that Lethaby couldn't bring off a murder, but I really don't feel at all certain he didn't murder this Henderson person. Of course, he was blind drunk, or so we think – Henderson, I mean – and there can't have been much worry about bumping him off when he was in that state. But I feel sure he's quite, quite unscrupulous, and he may easily be much cleverer than he lets on to his relations. Do say something, Mr. Pulteney. Though I'm hanged if I know whether I want you to agree with me or to contradict me."

" An admirable frame of mind ; it enables me to express my genuine beliefs without considering whether they are what you want to hear or not. My own feeling about Lethaby – remember I only know him from his reputation, and from what little I saw of him at the time of the fire – is that he is incurably a *poseur*. The more I see of the world the more convinced I become that there are two sorts of people, among the people who matter at all – those who do things and those who have ideas. There's a lot, you know, in *Hamlet*, and in that phrase about the native hue of resolution being sicklied o'er with the pale cast of thought. I should not have been in the least surprised to hear that Henderson had murdered somebody ; he was, I take it, a man of his hands, who did not allow any considerations except those of his own personal advantage to influence his conduct. He acted ; he did not stand outside himself and watch himself acting, if you see what I mean by that. Lethaby, though, is of the reflective type ; so self-conscious that he is always, as it were, seeing himself in a mirror and looking at the figure he cuts ; wondering, too, a good deal what other people think of it. Such a man – I may be totally wrong, for my ignorance of life is startling, I should say, even in a schoolmaster – is not the sort of man to deal with a crisis, or to have a good reaction-time in moments of danger. He might, conceivably, plot a murder when he found his victim at his mercy, though I doubt even that ; he would spend so long reflecting on the most artistic way of murdering him that the victim would have come to before he could be victimised. But I cannot, in any case, see him striking a man, let alone killing him, in hot blood. Indeed, I doubt if Mr. Lethaby has any hot blood. If a stranger suddenly pushed him over in the street, he would be so concerned about picking himself up in a manner suitable to the occasion that it would be some time before he even considered the question of retaliating. But I should hesitate very much before trying the same reaction test on, say, an ordinary coal-heaver. I should expect him to push me over without even taking time to consider whether I might have had any justifiable motive to plead for my unusual conduct. I am wandering a good deal, I fear, but you see, don't you, what I mean about young Lethaby ? "

" Yes, I see what you mean, but I'm not sure that it will wash, really. You say you don't think it likely that Lethaby should kill anybody even in cold blood. Well, how did he manage to kill Henderson, then, or if he didn't, who did ? I don't see it's possible to account for Henderson turning up dead in the garage otherwise. Cut out the question of motive, who was even in a position to kill him ? "

" You must excuse me, but I should be tempted to answer, Almost anybody. To take an instance, only an imaginary instance, you will understand, it might have been your husband. Mr. Bredon relieved me at about eleven o'clock that evening. He came back and joined you some time after midnight, admitting that he had been over to the island, but reluctant to tell you what he did when he got there. Before you had had time to make him a hot drink, the garage was in flames. Merely treating the question as a matter of opportunity, who had a better opportunity than Mr. Bredon that night ? Please do not imagine . . . "

" Oh, don't apologise, Mr. Pulteney. After all, Miles could have had plenty of motive ; he's a servant of the Company, and perhaps he took the best way of making sure that Henderson didn't levant with the treasure, and make the Company liable. But let us hear some of your other selections."

" Well, there is Sir Charles Airdrie."

" Oh, but he's such a nice old thing. Besides, what temptation would he have had, exactly ? "

" Well, he might be in financial difficulties we know nothing about. It is important to him, let us say, to get full value for the treasure without dividing it up with the people who have found it. If he murders Henderson, he feels certain that Lethaby will be accused of his murder and hanged ; or, alternatively, will flee the country, as they say – you will have noticed that he does not seem very anxious for the young man to stay on on the island ; perhaps that is the reason."

" But he'd have been afraid that one of us would see him crossing the bridge. After all, he knew we were on the look-out, didn't he ? "

" Oh, no doubt ; but the bridge is not the only way of reaching the island when the water is low, as it was on Wednesday night. I have come to know a good deal about the levels of it, in my study of the fish world, and I assure you that from the other side of the river, the side from which Sir Charles would naturally approach, you could almost wade across to the southern point of the island ; certainly you would only have to swim a stroke or two. However, let us count Sir Charles out, since he is a friend of yours. Let us take the party at Strathdounie House ; that they are men of action, nobody can doubt who has seen the reckless way in which they cut branches off trees, with inoffensive people standing about underneath. How did they know so early that the fire was happening, unless one or more of them stayed up till a late hour that night, and was actually expecting something of the kind to happen ? As to motive, it is obvious that they don't like Lethaby, and they may have killed Henderson by mistake for him. Or Lady Hermia may have seen fit to remove Henderson because he had a bad influence on Lethaby. Anything of that sort."

" Good gracious, Mr. Pulteney, what an imagination you have ! I see what you mean, though – in the ordinary way, when a murder is at all complicated, the bother is to see how anybody could possibly have been on the spot when the thing was done. Here, the difficulty is to see why any one person should have been on the spot more than another. A one-house island, only five minutes' journey in a fishing-boat from either bank, approachable in most parts even to an indifferent swimmer, with only two people living on it, apparently, one of those a mystery-man whom nobody cares about, while the other is a kind of publicity-man whom any ordinary person would feel tempted to shoot at sight – yes, it leaves a good deal of scope to the imagination. The odd thing is, that Miles doesn't really seem much interested about the murder ; he only gets excited about the rotten old treasure, which anybody may have buried anywhere, so I don't see how he's going to find it."

" It is surely a legitimate conjecture that the appearance of the corpse and the disappearance of the treasure are connected."

" Oh, yes, I suppose so. The rum thing really is that they don't connect. Or do they? Look here, if that was a murder, the murderer was Lethaby, who is open to inspection, Henderson, whereabouts unknown, or a third person, X, who is pure guesswork. You say you don't believe Lethaby did it. But do a little exercise of the imagination; if Lethaby did it, what did he do it for? "

" I take it that you are identifying the unfortunate victim of the experiment, at this moment, with Henderson. Why should Lethaby murder Henderson? Well, one is better than two when it comes to sharing out. But it is rather a question of what terms they made with Sir Charles. If he arranged to claim fifty per cent, then fifty per cent was left for the partners, or for the surviving partner. But if he said, I will give you, Lethaby, twenty-five per cent, and you, Henderson, another twenty-five per cent, then the second twenty-five per cent goes to Henderson's heirs and assigns, and the motive for a murder disappears altogether."

" Gosh, yes, that would be worth finding out. I'll put Miles on to that. But supposing Lethaby *does* stand to win an extra share by killing his partner, you think that's a reasonable motive? "

" Frankly, I do not. By Mr. Bredon's reckoning, the total amount realised from the sale of the treasure would not amount to what is, I believe, technically called a hill of beans. I have no notion what can have been the origin of so poetical a figure. Few men, I think, would care to risk the rope, and incur the certainty of the world's black looks, unless they could promise themselves a really handsome indemnity."

" And that's equally an argument against Henderson having murdered a total stranger, isn't it ? "

" Not quite so strong an argument, I should fancy. Henderson is the sort of man who, once acquitted by a jury, could easily disappear from the world's eye, and laugh at its judgments. But it is difficult to conceive why it should have been necessary to eliminate a total stranger from the ranks of society ; if he stood between Henderson and the treasure, there should have been some more humane way of getting rid of him. Unless, of course – the suggestion must already have occurred to you – Henderson wished to disappear completely, and murdered a stranger so that the corpse might be mistaken for his own. But, if so, why did not Henderson remove the treasure at once, while his partner lay drugged upstairs ? That he did not do so, the testimony of my own eyes bears witness. Did he come back again and remove the treasure, when the whole island was full of firemen, landed proprietors, and remarkably muscular shooting-tenants ? I can hardly believe it."

" Yes, that's the snag, isn't it ? Because it would be just the same if a stranger, X, murdered Henderson. He would want to carry off the treasure at once, while the going was good, instead of leaving it lying about for you to have a peep at it."

" Precisely. And there is a further objection, which also applies to the idea that Lethaby murdered Henderson. Surely the natural thing would be to kill, or at least stun your man first, and then leave him in the garage, already insensible, to be destroyed by the flames. But in that case, why lock the door, and make it clear that murder had been done, instead of leaving it open, as if there had been an accident ? "

" Well, you know, he might have done that to prevent Miles, or whoever was the first comer, from breaking into the garage too early."

" But the garage had a window. Surely it would have been possible, somehow, to throw or push the key in, and leave us to assume that Henderson had locked himself in, and been too drunk to let himself out ? "

" Then you think," Angela summed up, her chin pillowed on her fists with an air of dissatisfaction, " that it was just a coincidence, the fire happening and the treasure being lost on the same night ? "

" Oh, hardly that," protested Mr. Pulteney. " I was only suggesting that the murder, if it was a murder, can hardly have been done merely for the sake of the treasure. But, once the fire had happened, that might suddenly create an opportunity for making the treasure disappear. One of the gallant band of helpers, as I understand Lethaby himself suggested, might have been tempted to carry it away with him. Or Lethaby may have thought that he could improve his financial position by hiding the treasure somewhere, and claiming that Henderson, who was no longer there to deny the charge, had run off with it – so as to get the insurance money, I mean."

" Well, we haven't exactly cleared it up, have we ? I wonder what Miles is doing ? He isn't usually a liar, though he sails rather close to the wind sometimes."

.   .   .   .

While this conversation was in progress, things were happening on the island. Miles Bredon, in describing them afterwards to his wife, insisted on doing so in the manner of a sensational novel, retailing the actions which took place very minutely and leaving her to guess the names of the actors. On a very dark night like that, he said, you couldn't be certain who was who. Little apology is needed for handing on his description to the reader as it stood ; for he (the reader) is probably by this time in a position to disentangle the mystery far better than Angela could.

The house on the Isle of Erran stood on a site which was cut out of the side of a hill, or rather a little knoll, crowned with firs and muffled at the edges with a thicket of rhododendron. There is no such thing as a level space on the island, and the house was, at its northern end, one storey higher, so to speak, than at its southern end ; a cellar, more or less disused, made the difference. To connect the window of the main living-room, which was a french window, with the outer world, a flight of stone steps, not ungraceful, climbed down a height of ten feet or so on to the level. At this window, about nine o'clock on that dark evening of Friday, appeared the form of a man ; the lamp was behind him, so that you could not have recognised the features. He stood there for some time, looking out into the darkness, but rather with the casual glance of one who is spending time aimlessly than with the fixed gaze of one who expects to see anything.

A few minutes later, when there was no longer anybody to be seen inside, a man's form passed just outside the penumbra of hazy light which this uncurtained window shed upon the surrounding darkness. He looked back towards the house, as if to verify the fact that the lamp was burning in the living-room. Then he began to make his way noiselessly along the little path which led downhill towards the northern end of the island. If he carried any light, he did not show it, and – for the path was a mere track of no width – he had to pick his way with difficulty over the uncertain ground ; now a long tentacle of bramble would catch at his feet, now they would be caught in bracken fronds, which tore as he extricated himself, now a faint gurgle would warn him that he was treading on marshy ground. So still was the air that it would not have been difficult for anybody to hear, several yards away, these rumours of his passage ; there was no noise to drown them, except the continual roar of the falls, hushed by height and distance. The man himself seemed as if he were fearful of being watched ; for he stopped for a little now and again, waiting as if to make certain that his progress had not awoken any answering sounds in the undergrowth.

He reached the bottom of the slope, and held on his way towards the promontory. Once there was a sharp ring of metal against rock, as if he had dropped something. Then, for the first time, he switched on an electric torch, holding it only a little distance from the ground, so that the circle of light it threw was inconsiderable. There was an outcrop of rock amongst heather just in front of him, and it was here, no doubt, that the object had fallen. It had rolled off to the side, and very little search revealed it lying close to the side of the path. It was a gold coin. He stood there for a moment or two in a crouching position, as if uncertain whether to pick it up again. Then, deliberately, he straightened himself and continued his journey, leaving it where it lay.

A little further on, the louder noise of rushing water warned him that he was approaching the edge of the cliff and the falls. So dark was it that he actually barked his shin against the seat which stood overlooking them. He switched on his torch again, and began to make casts at the edge of the cliff, evidently by way of finding the steps which led down the water's edge. Having identified them, he stood upright for a moment, fumbling with his hands, and once again a gold coin dropped. He verified its position, left it where it lay, and began, very cautiously, to descend the steps. They were not dangerously steep, if a man negotiated them in full daylight, but it was a slow and perilous progress that he made in the darkness, and several times he had to make use of his torch before he ventured down. At last he stood on a rough plateau of rock that stretched out just opposite the little island, with the three fir-trees, that stood in the middle of the falls. There was again an audible ring on the rocks as the third coin dropped from his hand.

He went to the extreme edge of the shore, where it approached nearest to the little island, and threw a gold coin across ; it flashed in the light of the torch, which he held straight in front of him ; and though it shed no practicable light on the foot of the islet, where it jutted out opposite him, perhaps fifteen yards away across the tumbling water, it was just sufficient to make it certain that the throw had not fallen short. And now, with more confidence and more ease, since man is better built for climbing up than for climbing down, he scaled the cliff again by the steps, and set off with the lighter step of one who has entered upon his return journey. He did not, however, retrace his old path, leading directly back to the house ; he struck instead towards the left, along the line of the eastern cliff and past the spot where the treasure had been brought to light, two days before.

.   .   .   .

" It sounds a dashed dull story, told like that," was Angela's comment. " Is it meant to be a fairy-story,

What the Moon Saw, that kind of thing ?   Because it
is ridiculous to suppose you were among those present,
having promised me, like a good little boy, that you
wouldn't cross the bridge.   Why on earth have you been
so long ?   Mr. Pulteney and I had very nearly solved
the whole mystery while you were away."

" I promised you I wouldn't set foot on the bridge,
if you remember.   Fortunately the parapet is in a good
state of repair, and anybody who was taught gym-
nasium at his prep school———"

" Miles !   Of all the insufferable cads !   Mr. Pulteney, I appeal to you, isn't that a particularly
odious kind of lie ?   And the man calls himself my
husband ! "

" I confess," said Mr. Pulteney, " that through long
acquaintance with the habits of the youth my moral
standards have come to suffer from a curious kind of
obliquity.   I always find myself prepared to overlook
the moral turpitude of deceit, if it is accompanied by a
sufficient measure of artistic ingenuity.   Mr. Bredon's
resourcefulness, not to mention his gymnastic agility,
if he really climbed along that balustrade on his hands,
cannot, I think, be too highly commended.   It was, no
doubt, an equivocation that he practised———"

" Oh, you're all hopeless.   Well, look here, Miles, I'll
only forgive you on one condition – that you tell me
what it was all about.   Heaven knows we're poor
enough without you going scattering sovereigns all
over the Isle of Erran ; though how on earth you got
sovereigns, when I have to do all my shopping with
those dirty little pieces of paper———"

" Calm yourself, Angela.   This display of pettish-
ness in the presence of our guest is hardly worthy of the
position we occupy.   Why, I feel quite county since
the bazaar this afternoon.   I was going to tell you in

any case, because, you see, you are going to come in useful."

" I suppose I shall have to. But if you hand me a bag of sovereigns, you needn't think I'm going to use them for paper-chases, because I can find plenty of better uses for them."

" To be accurate, they were not what you mean by sovereigns. They were gold coins of the period of George the Third ; plausibility is everything in these cases. You see, they were to act as a kind of ground-bait."

" You mean, Lethaby is going to find them and think they are bits of the treasure, dropped about careless-like ? But I thought you said there weren't any coins in that collection they dug up, only ear-rings and manicure-sets and what not ? "

" That's true ; and if I had thought it likely that you possessed any manicure-sets of contemporary date with the '45, I should not have hesitated to borrow them. But as I did not remember any such items in your trousseau, I was forced to do the best I could with a substitute. Finding myself in a position to secure a few of these valuable objects, and strong in the confidence that the Directors will reimburse me for any outlay of the kind, I did venture to use four of them, that was all, as ground-bait. Yes, Lethaby is to find them ; and his reactions on finding them will do something to tell us whether he is really a treasure-loser or a treasure-hider."

" How do we study his reactions ? We shan't be there, shall we ? "

" You will ; no later than to-morrow morning. Bright and early, too. Personally, I shall be fishing at the time, with Pulteney."

" Fishing ? Why, you don't know a fly from a worm "

199

" If you prefer it, I will make enquiries about the green fees at Nairn. But I think fishing would be better, because when you are making an excuse of that sort it is just as well to let your man see that it is a true one. I don't suppose it is possible to fish, really, when the water is like this ; but Pulteney is going to take me along the bank and teach me how to cast. So that you and Lethaby, from the other side, will be able to watch us doing it."

" So far, so good. And what are my sailing orders exactly ? "

" Why, you go up to the house to-morrow morning – bright and early, as I say, because we don't want any nonsense about Lethaby coming across those coins when there's nobody to watch him. You say, reasonably enough, that you want his leave to go along to the north end of the island, if you may, and look at the falls in flood. Of course, Lethaby might let you go alone, but I think the odds are enormously in favour of his offering to chaperon you – especially if you work off a little personality stuff on him."

" Oh, I'll do that all right. And I keep a good lookout, I suppose, and spot where those coins are dropped, and if he seems to be in any danger of not seeing them, I hang about a bit to give him a better chance ? "

" That's it. And when you get to the seat, you admire the view for a bit, and say wouldn't it be rather fun to go down and stand right close to the falls ; only of course, he mustn't dream of coming, because he's sure to be busy, and you'll be perfectly all right climbing down the steps, thanks, because you've quite a good head for heights. Whereupon he will naturally insist on going down with you ; and you will lead him in the same sort of absent-minded way to Coin No. 2, which is at the top of the steps, and Coin No. 3, which is at the bottom. As for the one I threw on to the little island, that may or may not be visible. But it seems to me he's bound to see at least one of them, and if he's even relatively an honest man, he'll pick it up, and say, Hullo, what's this ? The coin on the little island ought to excite him still more ; it's meant to look as if Henderson, or somebody else, had hidden the treasure just there, and can't get at it because of the flood."

" You always were rather fantastic in your ideas. All right, I'll see what I can do. And if the coins have gone before I get there ? "

" That will mean, I'm afraid, that Lethaby is not an honest man – and also that he's a much earlier riser than I take him to be."

THE PHRASE " bright and early " proved to be of unexpectedly literal application. The clouds had passed
in the night, and, although a steaming haze drew up
from the damp soil everywhere, the sun early reached
its strength, and promised a day of breathless heat.
The Dounie, however, still came tumbling down in
cataracts ; it would be many hours before he could
carry off the waters that had collected in the hills.

" I wonder how early Lethaby breakfasts," said
Angela, suiting the action to the word. " Most men
lie in a bed a hoggish long time, if they're unmarried.
Except schoolmasters, of course," she added in defer-
ence to Mr. Pulteney ; then, remembering how he had
failed her the night before, " but, of course, they have
to get up early, so it doesn't count."

" Possibly," suggested the old gentleman, " Mrs.
McBrayne would be able to tell us. She has, I understand, been doing for Lethaby ever since Lethaby did
for Henderson – to employ a locution," he explained,
in answer to a pained look on Angela's face, " which
would serve admirably to illustrate for a foreign pupil
the richness of our English idiom."

" I shall take my camera," said Angela ; " thank
goodness I brought it. It sounds much more convincing to say you want to photograph the falls than just
to say you want to have a look at them. Would you
like me to take a close-up of Lethaby's face, Miles,

when he starts finding the island paved with gold ? Or possibly of the soles of his feet, when he's climbing down the cliff, which would be quite an original way of identifying footmarks. I love being bright at breakfast," she explained, " just to see Miles's face ; poor dear, he's a very solemn breakfaster. I think, you know, the bride and bridegroom ought to have to sit down and eat bread and marmalade at the wedding-breakfast, so as to give their friends an idea of what they'll look like, married."

" I suppose," hazarded Bredon, " that you are getting up steam for making bright conversation to the unfortunate Lethaby. I never liked the man, but I confess my heart bleeds for him. Ah, here is Mrs. McBrayne. We were wondering, Mrs. McBrayne, if you could tell us what time Mr. Lethaby generally has his breakfast ? Because Mrs. Bredon wanted to go over to the island and get his leave to take some photographs."

" Oh, I'm sure the gentleman wouldn't mind her taking the photographs, sir, if she wants to. But I think she'd find he'll be up already, sir, because he's always finished when I go up to clear away at half-past ten. He just makes himself a little tea, and I don't think he has anything else much ; you see, he's not a gentleman that's very regular at his meals – I'll sometimes come in and find that he's cut himself a round of bread and a slice off the ham and eaten them in the larder, it might be late at night or it might be in the middle of the afternoon ; you never can tell when it'll be. But I'm sure he'd be glad to see Mrs. Bredon, if she cared to step up now ; he must be wanting for company, all alone there by himself."

" Excellent," said Bredon, when Mrs. McBrayne had bowed herself out. " Zero-hour has arrived ; lose no time, woman, in getting into the antigropelos and setting out on your mission. Pulteney and I will do our best to tolerate your absence. Later on, when you have asked Lethaby to show you round the part of the cliff where the treasure was discovered, you will find us practising casts a little way up the bank. By luncheon-time, I shall perhaps be feeling fit for the strain of your conversation."

The island was a silvery heap of dew in sunshine. Damp sweated from the spongy moss underfoot; damp dripped from the over-arching boughs of the tall beechwood; damp glistened on coarse grass, and bracken, and on the grey bloom of the azalea-leaves. Across the river, up the hill-side, the last veils of mist reluctantly withdrew. For the moment, the island seemed almost friendly, as if the spell under which it lay had been taken off overnight. Angela, at least, was visited by no such forebodings as had assailed her husband two days earlier; she strode up the drive with a light heart, and rattled with the handle of a spade, the nearest weapon available, at the half-open front door.

Lethaby did not look as if he had been expecting company. He was in shirt sleeves and dressing-slippers; he might have shaved the afternoon before, but certainly not that morning. Chelsea, however, does not stand on ceremony, and he was plainly un-abashed. "Step right in, Mrs. Bredon," he said. "Have some breakfast or something? Oh, but I suppose you've had that long ago. Actually I've just finished. Don't say you've come to tell me Mrs. McBrayne is ill or off work or anything. I used to think I could rough it, but I find there's no fun in roughing it without Mrs. McBrayne."

"No, thanks, we're all fine down at the cottage.

Only I was suffering slightly from loneliness, because my husband has taken some insane idea into his head that he wants to learn how to fish. So I thought I'd take some photographs, and I wondered if you'd mind frightfully if I came and asked your leave to take one from the end of the island there – you know, opposite the churchyard. I'm afraid we gate-crashed the place a day or so before you came, and went round by the path ; and that bit struck me as so jolly if one could only get it decently with a camera. Not that a camera " – she stopped short, blushing slightly as she remembered the chart-photograph about which Lethaby must know so much, to which her husband attached such importance.

Lethaby was quite unembarrassed. " Yes, rather," he said, " the camera always lies, doesn't it ? Look here, I'll just go and put some real shoes on, if you don't mind waiting a second, and take you down there. It's a bit damp still for these things. Actually I hadn't thought of the island as a beauty spot much, but I suppose that *is* rather an amusing bit of scenery if you come to think of it. Sure you won't have some sherry or anything ? " Angela was amazed at the man who could so bravely keep up the appearances of civilisation in this pig-sty of a house, when he lay under suspicion of fraud, arson, and perhaps murder ; amazed at herself for falling in so easily with his mood. Could he really have a good conscience, as his cheerful notes seemed to imply ? Or was it a seared conscience, that could jest under the shadow of the rope ?

Her conversation, as they sauntered down the path – for her companion seemed to be in no more hurry than she was – ranged over a variety of topics, but returned constantly to a botanical *motif*, so that she might have an excuse for directing his eyes, as you may be sure she directed hers, towards the ground. Now she would speculate why rhododendrons bothered to put out shoots on a level with the ground, when it was quite certain that people would come and tread on them ; now she would recall the embargo placed by her childhood's nurse on the eating of blaeberries ; now stoop to catch the healing scent of bog-myrtle, now exclaim at the beauty or strangeness of the toadstools, which the late rain had brought forth in grotesque abundance. " That one's exactly like the sort of jam roll they give you in Tigers' restaurants, isn't it ? Oh, and look at that slice of tea-cake ; I bet you could take in a shortsighted visitor with that." So she went on gaily, but with an inward feeling of desperation ; surely they must by now have reached the spot, so carefully described, at which the first of the gold coins had been dropped ? It should be just to the left of the path, close to an outcrop of stone – that one, surely ? But there was no trace of a glint on the short grass which lay this side of it. She actually picked the shiny imitation of teacake, with an absurd feeling that it might have grown up during the night, to play umbrella to the missing coin. No, there was nothing there.

She had to go forward at last, or her lingering would have become remarkable. Was it possible that the man she had surprised in his *négligée*, so obviously enjoying his after-breakfast cigarette, had taken a turn down the path still earlier in the morning, and pocketed the golden bait ? Anyhow, she reflected, he was not likely to have gone as far as the steps down the cliff ; at least not down to the bottom of the steps. There was only one missing link, so far, in the chain of possible evidence. . . . Now they had reached the seat under the firs ; and, to play her part properly, she had to peer over the edge first of all at the fairy islet, looking so unsubstantial that you wondered it was not carried away in that drift of whirling water ; at the rocky bastions, the gnarled trees, the precarious slopes of heather on the further shore ; at the gravestones peeping over the line of cliff in the churchyard of Glendounie.

" Looks as if that would have been the real place for Charles Edward to stow away his extra luggage, doesn't it ? " said Lethaby. " I bet there haven't been many human beings on that rock since his time. And yet a man could get across quite easily if he put down a ladder there ; or you could do it with a pole-jump, almost." Was it possible, Angela asked herself, that the man who indulged so lightly in these speculations was one who, only an hour or two before, had come across the trail of sovereigns leading to the very spot he was talking about, and was now under a full conviction that the treasure had in fact been re-buried there by his missing partner ? If so, his capacity for bluff must be unlimited. He spoke without a quaver in his voice, whereas she had to discipline hers deliberately as she answered :

" Yes, I wonder they didn't think of it. Look here, Mr. Lethaby, I'm quite certain my camera would make nothing at all of a view taken from up here. I'm going down to the water's edge, if you'll just show me where the steps are. And for goodness' sake don't bother to come down yourself ; I shall be perfectly all right, because I've quite a good climber's head. And I expect you ought to be doing lots of things."

" Of course I'll come down. Nothing lends such a zest to life as the thought of the other things one ought to be doing. The steps are just round to the right here." They had to skirt a wide thicket of very deep bracken, masking a quite sheer piece of cliff ; at the further end of it a half-obliterated path led to a drop which looked no less sheer, but proved on closer view to be the beginning of a dizzy sheep-track.   There was no gold coin, she noticed, at or near the opening of it. It led you down twenty feet or so, with good footing among the tufts of heather ; then following a long wooden ladder or stairway, only wide enough for one person to descend at a time.   Beyond this, the slope was gentler and cut steps or natural shelves in the rock made it possible to achieve the remainder of the climb without much difficulty.

Angela went first, and found it a much easier affair than it looked from above.   The only fear you could reasonably entertain was that the ladder itself, rotted away here and there like most of the woodwork on the island, would come away from the stanchions which held it under your weight.   With this in her mind, she shouted up to Lethaby telling him not to start on the ladder until she had finished with it.   Then, resolutely keeping her eyes on the next rung to make sure that her foothold was true, she made short work of the distance. For a moment she stood looking upwards, at Lethaby just making his first cautious essay of the ladder, at the bare scarp immediately behind him, and the thick fringe of bracken at its summit.   Then she turned and faced away from the cliff to negotiate the steps in the rock.   Almost immediately there was a sharp ring of metal on stone just behind and above her, and something slid past, ricocheting from rock to rock till it came to rest on a ledge a few feet below her.   It was a key.

There was no great difficulty in guessing where it had come from.   It must have fallen, she felt certain, from one of the baggy pockets of Lethaby's coat, which had perhaps caught up against some projecting nail in the crazy balustrade which ran beside the ladder, and so been turned inside out. Her first instinct was to call up to him and warn him against shedding any more of his personal belongings when there were people standing about underneath. Then she remembered that she was the representative of a conspiracy ; remembered that there was a puzzle which was crying to be solved, and that a key played a part in it. That this was the key in question, was only the most distant of off-chances. But there could be no harm in trying ; it would be easy, if necessary, to restore the lost property to Lethaby in some roundabout way. She stuck the key firmly into her dress at the waist, and when Lethaby joined her at the foot of the steps, apparently unconscious of his loss, she made no allusion to it. Instead, she directed his attention to a plant growing in some profusion from the base of the rock, and asked whether it could be samphire. What *was* samphire, and why was gathering it a " dreadful trade " in the poem ? Lethaby did not know. Nor did Angela care ; she was looking, as usual, for a gold coin, and there was no gold coin to be found.

The persistent impecuniosity of the island began to weigh on her spirits and distract her attention from the surroundings. Foolish echoes of a game she had played not long since with her children besieged her mind : " Here we go on Tom Tiddler's ground, Picking up gold and silver." You played it breathlessly, with Tom Tiddler shamming asleep on the forbidden territory, and you knew that he was shamming asleep. One could not have played that game on the Isle of Erran ; the whole atmosphere of the place was too uncanny. . . . She recollected herself with an effort, and, unstrapping the camera from her back, approached the falls, which now thundered in their ears. This photographing business gave you a good excuse, anyhow, for looking narrowly at the little island beyond. She looked, and saw immediately opposite her, lying out on a shelf close to the water's edge, a piece of gold.

Again and again, under the pretence of consulting him about the distance, about the height, about the best view to be obtained of that rocky surface, she saw to it that his eye should rest on the shelf where the coin lay. Never did he show any sign of having noticed it ; did not even peer at it for a moment, as if to make certain what it was. Angela, of course, made no allusion to it, and felt completely baffled by his silence. Was he, conceivably, rather short-sighted ? Or did he see it without emotion because he expected it to be there, and, because it must not be known that he expected it to be there, pass it over without comment ? Fortunately it was Miles' job, not hers, to make something out of it all. She decided to give herself up to the genuine experiences of the moment ; that arrangement of rocks and trees really was insufferably beautiful, and she *must* get a decent view of it. With a sort of treacherous kindness, she allowed Lethaby to take a portrait of her standing in front of it.

The arrangement had been that, when they reached the top of the cliff again, she was to take Lethaby along the cliff path towards the bridge, and let him see the casting practice in progress. She now determined to abandon this part of the programme ; she must let Lethaby take her straight back to the house, and there, by some ruse she had not yet perfected in her mind, get him out of the way while she tried the key in the lock of the burnt-out garage. She was almost certain that nothing had been done yet in the way of clearing up the debris ; and the door, she remembered, had fallen forwards and outwards – it would be the work of a moment to try the key in the wards of its lock as it lay there. . . . Yes, that would do. " Mr. Lethaby," she said, " will you let me take one photograph of the house, just to finish the roll ? Just that south side, where the sun is now, looks so attractive, I think." And, when they had arrived at the scene of operations, and she had located out of the corner of her eye the garage door lying in front of the ruins, she had one more inspiration. " I never think a photograph of a house seems right without somebody looking out of the windows. Would you frightfully mind just moistening the lips and putting in an appearance at, say, the second from the left ? It *is* good of you ; I'm afraid I'm being a most frightful nuisance." And at the second window from the left Lethaby was photographed, with the utmost goodwill on his part. He could not be expected to know that, while he was climbing the stairs, Angela had tried the key in the garage door, and found that it fitted.

" Confound you," said Miles Bredon, irritably, as she entered the cottage. " Here have I been playing ducks and drakes half the morning with silly little bits of hair stuck on to hooks, and Pulteney trying to persuade me that it mattered how I did it ; and devil a bit did you and that Lethaby fellow show up opposite. Why can women never meet a member of the opposite sex without forgetting all their previous engagements ? "

" Said he, little realising that he had married the most accomplished female sneak-thief of modern times. Oo, Miles, I've been having such luck ! "

" What about the coins, anyhow ? Let's have that first."

" You mean, how did Lethaby react when he saw them ? "

" That's what you were told to look out for."

" Well, he didn't react at all, because he didn't see them.   At least——"

" Didn't see them ?   He hasn't gone blind in the night, has he ?   I did think you'd be able to do that bit of manœuvring all right.   Did you not get him to go past them, or what ? "

" Oh, I got him to go past them all right ; but they weren't there."

" Weren't there ?   This is worse than anything we've come across yet.   Is it possible that he was watching me after all last night, and went out afterwards to tidy up ?   But, confound it all, why should he ?   It isn't as if anybody was likely to be wandering about the island except just possibly us.   And if it was us, he could always have headed us off.   I suppose that must have been it, though.   And mark you, that proves that Lethaby isn't on the square, or anything like it.   He's swallowed the bait, instead of rising to it as we meant him to ; and we know where we are with him now.   What about the piece I chucked over on to that island place ? "

" That was there all right ; plain as for anyone to see. But if Lethaby saw it, he must have dashed good nerve-control.   He didn't shy at it a bit ; and I can tell you I was watching him."

" Of course, he couldn't very well have pocketed that, with the water as it is.   Curse – I wish I knew whether he'd seen me last night.   You see, he was meant to think that those coins had been dropped days ago, by Henderson ; in fact on the night of the fire.   ' Ha ' (he was to say to himself), ' that's where Henderson stowed the stuff away, was it ? '   And then he would react as an honest or as a dishonest man accordingly. But if he spotted me last night——"

" Would he have seen it was you ? You said it was so dashed dark all the time."

" Well, he might have a guess it was me ; the district isn't so frightfully populous after all. But the point is, if he saw me, he must have realised it was a plant, and his reactions won't be so interesting. Well, we shall have to try something else, that's all. What was that you were saying, by the way, about having a piece of luck ? "

Angela told him. A long whistle was his only immediate comment, and he sat with his head in his hands for some time, considering this new light on the situation. " There doesn't seem to be much getting out of it, does there ? " Angela suggested at last.

" There does not. You see, Sir Charles said Lethaby told him distinctly he didn't know the garage had a key at all. That's not impossible, in this extraordinary country where everybody seems to come and go as he pleases ; and it wouldn't be impossible for the key to be lying about the house in some quite prominent position, without Lethaby knowing what it was for, or bothering to find out. But you don't slip a key, and a rather heavy key like that, into your pocket unless you mean to use it for something, or have used it for something."

" Of course, somebody else might have slipped it into his pocket."

" Yes, in theory, I suppose, on the night of the fire. But the odds are enormously that he'd have found it in his pocket between that and this. In which case he'd only have kept it in his pocket because he knew what it was, and was determined to keep it in his possession. In which case he's certainly been deceiving Sir Charles, and I imagine also the police, even if it did come into his possession innocently. What I really don't see is why he didn't throw the key into the river, instead of keeping it loose in a coat from which, apparently, it was liable to drop the moment he started to take exercise. No, it's all a rum business, this, about the key ; and you can write home to your children and tell them so."

" You couldn't use the key, I suppose, for another reaction-test ? The last one, as you say, seems to have fallen through rather. I mean, if as you say he knows all about the key and is anxious to keep it hushed up, he'll certainly miss it before long, and be average keen to find it again. It would be possible, wouldn't it, for you and me to leave it lying about somewhere where he's pretty certain to look for it – same place where he lost it, if necessary – and watch to see if he comes and scoops it up ? "

" Yes, but after all we're citizens, and it strikes me that we ought to keep the thing and hand it over to the police. They'll obviously want to go over it for finger-prints ; that is, if they suspect Lethaby as much as I suppose they do. I might have a shot at it myself, but it's not likely to be much use – it doesn't go flat at the handle end, so there's no surface to speak of. Still, I think we'd better hang on to it in any case."

" Of course, it wouldn't prove anything much if there were fingerprints – Lethaby's, I mean. He must have touched it since it was put in his pocket, whoever put it there, mustn't he ? "

" Yes, the only thing that would help would be if there were somebody else's finger-marks on it – but then, we shouldn't know whose they were. Oh, Lord, I wish I could get to the bottom of this ! "

" I was hoping it would brace you rather, my finding the key. I'm sorry it hasn't brightened you up more."

" Well, look here, Angela – short of the possibility of somebody having slipped that key into Lethaby's pocket, what does it mean ? It means that Lethaby shut the door on Henderson, or his corpse, or somebody else, or somebody else's corpse, and lit the garage and left it to burn, *turning the key in the lock*. Now, why ? Almost certainly the man inside the garage was dead, or at least stunned, before the fire started."

" Why particularly ? "

" Because the fire must have started from the inside, by the way it burnt ; the walls didn't catch properly till after everything was blazing inside. The point, then, of locking the door was probably not to imprison the man inside, but to prevent rescue, or at any rate discovery of the corpse, from outside, before a good long time had passed. Now, the door was quite roughly made, and there were chinks under it ; I looked through one myself, but, of course, the smoke didn't let one see anything. Do you mean to tell me there's any criminal in the world who wouldn't have the sense to shove the key under the door again, so as to make it look as if the whole thing had been an accident ? "

" Unless he *wanted* to make it look like a murder."

" You mean, A committing a murder and then trying to palm it off on B – B presumably being Lethaby ?

" But what did he do it for ? And why didn't he pinch the treasure while he was about it ? And why did he bother to stage the thing first of all as if it had been an accident – surely that lamp was meant to make us think there had been an accident ; unless, of course, it really *was* one ? I don't really think that explanation fits – it's not a bit tidy, anyhow. That kind of frame-up means, almost certainly, a motive of revenge, and that doesn't fit in with the Lethaby–Henderson crowd –

people like that are out for money, and there ought to be a money-motive behind anything they do. I was, as I told you, expecting a frame-up of some sort from the first, but not *that* kind of frame-up. If it hadn't been for the door being locked, I should have got the whole thing taped by now, or dashed nearly."

" Well, I'm glad the door *was* locked, then ; because I don't understand the thing from start to finish ; and you're so odious when you understand things and I don't. . . . Miles, tell me one thing, anyhow ; do you think Henderson is dead ? "

" Oh, that's just the nub of the whole difficulty ; if I only knew ! If he's alive, and has skipped, leaving a deputy corpse to do duty for him, why did he skip without the treasure ? If he died by accident, who locked the door, and why ? If he was killed, who killed him, and why ? Lethaby seems the only possible answer ; and, you know, he's the wrong answer. I rang up Sir Charles this morning, and asked him, as you suggested, what arrangements had been made about dividing up the treasure. He says that his offer was to give Lethaby twenty-five per cent of the takings, and Henderson another twenty-five. So Lethaby didn't score, on that basis, by eliminating Henderson."

" But if they meant to lose the treasure on purpose, and realise on the insurance instead ? "

" Then it might be convenient to have Henderson eliminated. But then, with Henderson eliminated *before* the treasure was lost, Lethaby has no claim on the Company. The Company won't shell out a penny, if I know them, until Henderson comes to life again."

" It *is* a bit of a tangle, isn't it ? "

" An admirably cautious way of putting it. You know, sometimes in those long winter evenings when my patience has come out, and I courteously devote my

valuable time to taking skeins out of tangle, when
you've managed to get them all tied up——"

" 'Tisn't me, you cad ; it's the people at the shop."

" Well, anyhow, when I'm spending a quiet hour or
two showing you what can be done by a really
dexterous set of fingers, my instinct is always to start
at the end and work back to the beginning. But it's
sometimes a good idea to vary the process, by giving
the end a rest and going back to the beginning instead.
If you have followed my parable——"

" Meaning that you want to start at the beginning of
this puzzle ? Let's see, what was it ? Oo, I remember ; the first thing that started you off worrying was
finding that the boat had been taken out when it didn't
ought to. That made you sphinx-minded at once."

" Why keep a diary, when a wife will do instead ?
Yes, that was it. Now, let's be a bit *a priori*, if you can
stand the strain. It looks as if Lethaby and Henderson
must be the people who moved that boat. If so,
when ? "

" Presumably when they went over to the island,
before their lease started, and spent a happy day there.
Mrs. McBrayne told us about that."

" Not necessarily. In fact, if you come to think of
it, I doubt whether that's very probable. Sir Charles,
I think I'm right in saying, was fishing that beat
of the river himself at the time. So there was every
chance that if those two fellows took the boat out for
a joy-cruise, which they'd no right to do, they'd bump
into their future landlord fishing, and not too pleased
to have his fishing disturbed by gate-crashers. On the
other hand, if they were up to any funny business,
they'd be even less likely to do it under Sir Charles'
nose, in broad daylight."

" Well, they'd only broad daylight to do it in.

They couldn't very well fix up an excuse for spending the night on the island."

" Yes, but you see you aren't carrying your mind back properly. With this absurd spate on, one thinks of the river as an impassable obstacle, which you could just negotiate in a boat, if that. But when we came here, and for a month or so before that, it was as easy as you like for anybody to swim it – probably wade it in some places, if they knew the right places. What's to have prevented Henderson and Lethaby coming here quite honestly for a look round ? And then they would find the boat, and it would suddenly occur to them, Hullo, this looks as if it might come in useful."

" Miles dear, aren't you being just the tiniest bit inconsistent ? Why should a boat come in so handy if, as you say, there's no earthly difficulty about swimming the dashed thing ? "

" Some people like to keep their clothes dry. Also people who are carting about heavy objects – treasure, for example – find it more convenient to take them in a boat than to push them along on the back of an india-rubber horse. No, other things being equal, you should always judge other people's reactions by your own. When I saw that boat, it immediately occurred to me that it might be used——"

" It occurred to *me*, as a matter of fact."

" As you say, it occurred even to you that this was the sort of stroke of luck a criminal might take advantage of. Therefore, it is fairly safe to argue that the criminals who saw it a week or so before us thought just the same. They might not have used it till after their tenancy of the island started. But, as a matter of fact, we know they did. Therefore they probably used it the same night."

" Why ? "

" Because they were in the district. As a matter of fact, I'm beginning to think that Henderson was in the district for some time about then. But if they had any plans in common, I should think even Vernon Lethaby would have had the sense to be on the spot when they were carried out. He must have known that he was dealing with a crook, whatever he says about it. I'm suggesting, then, as a plausible sort of idea – which may, of course, be miles from the truth – that they used the boat for some purpose of their own that night. I wonder what ? "

" Well, I suppose the sort of thing you're thinking of is that they may, by some stroke of luck or through inside information, have lighted on the treasure straight away, on that first visit of theirs ; in which case there'd be a distinct temptation to carry off as much as was handy on the spot, only leaving the dregs, so to speak, to be divided up with Sir Charles and the Government ? Which would rather account, wouldn't it, for there being no coins found the other day ? They may have taken the cash and let the jewellery go."

" Yes, something like that perhaps. But for our present purposes it doesn't matter much ; the use of the boat seems to indicate that there must have been some fetching and carrying to be done. Now, what point would they use for landing ? Near here, on the Strathdounie side ? Or away on the other side, in the direction of the road from Glendounie to Dreams ? "

" This'd be simpler, wouldn't it ? Shorter voyage, I mean."

" Ye-es. But then, the road's some way from the river on this side, and it's no fun tramping aross fields in the dark when you don't know your ground ; whereas on the further side the road comes down quite close to the river. And, of course, it's much more unfrequented. This side, you'd never know when you might not bump into the McBraynes. Ninthly and lastly, what I'm proposing is that we should look for traces of their landing; and it's no good looking for them on this side of the river; we've explored it so thoroughly, one way and another, that we should have been bound to come across anything which looked suspicious."

"What you mean is, you're determined to go and nose round a bit on the further side of the river, because you haven't been there yet. Just opposite the south end of the island, I suppose? Because it would be a foul job landing anywhere north of that; it's all precipices, right along as far as the churchyard."

"Yes, there's a pretty obvious landing-place just there. And it's so obvious that one would almost certainly make for it if one was operating in the dark. I suppose the chances against there being anything to find there are about fifty to one. But, hang it all, let's get the car out after lunch and have a try. I'm sick of waiting for Lethaby to do things; and Pulteney won't mind being on guard, now the fishing's impossible."

" It can't do any harm," admitted Angela.

CHAPTER XV: A FELLOW-COUNTRY-MAN OF KNOX

THEY TOOK THE ROAD up the glen past Strathdounie House, intending to make a round tour of their expedition and come back by a bridge lower down the stream. This would take them, on their way home, past the Glendounie manse, at which Miles, unexpectedly, announced his intention of calling. "It's a time-taking business," he said, "getting anything out of Maclean; but I'm beginning to think he's worth drawing out. You'll have to do it; he thinks me a bit frivolous."

The hill on their left rose higher and fell away more precipitously; the woods gave place to bare scarps and slopes of boulder-strewn heather. The burns, still running at their winter level, caught the eye, far up, with their polished cascades; a friendly silence and stillness, not menacing as on the island, drew and filled the attention, overawing speech. Then, just as they seemed to have left human habitation behind them altogether, a stone bridge suddenly appeared on their right, and a little cluster of houses, just large enough to be called a village in that remote country where no true villages exist, recalled them to a sense of living realities. The bridge once crossed, they must trace a circuitous path half through, half round, the policies of Dreams Castle; not without some fear of encountering its owner and being lured from their

purpose by untimely hospitality. From Dreams on-
wards, their road lay in the woods again ; cooler airs
welcomed them, and their prospect was shut in by a
nearer companionship of fern and stone. But still,
where the road dipped and its screen of trees was
broken, they could hear the tumultuous bustle of the
Dounie as he carried his unaccustomed burden of
waters to the sea.

At the lowest and last of these dips, a half-open gate
on their right issued a sort of tentative invitation ;
this was not actually a road, it seemed to imply, but
if your car was of the kind that did not mind cart-
tracks, you might make the nearer acquaintance of the
river without fear of actual trespassing. Miles rightly
concluded that this was the spot they were making for ;
evidently it was a short cut to the river bank, where
fishermen could be joined by the cars which were to
take them home, or brought reinforcements in the way
of flasks and sandwich-cases. A solitary peasant,
bowed over his potatoes, touched his cap instead of
offering any resistance to their entry. Marks of other
tyres wound in and out of the ruts left by cart-wheels,
but too confusedly to promise any hope of reconstruct-
ing a midnight passage, if there had been one, of three
weeks ago. When they had gone some fifty yards, a
stone wall interrupted their progress ; they climbed
it to find the Dounie at their feet, and the point of
the island, with the sun dazzlingly reflected from its
shingle, almost exactly opposite.

That the stretch of bank which lay immediately
before them was a familiar resort of rowing-boats,
was not to be doubted. It was a natural bay, some
twelve feet across ; a steep slope of very light sand
formed a natural mooring-place, though the flood-tide
in the river made it impossible to discover, by actual

traces of the fact, whether it had been so used recently. A decayed wooden post showed, however, the print of mooring-chains ; anybody crossing the river thereabouts would inevitably have made this his landing-stage. To their left, just above the level of the banks, was a high thicket of gorse, overhung with beech-trees. A few inches of wet sand at their feet proved that the river was going down, but slowly. The only footprints were those of rabbits which came there to drink at evening.

" It beats me," said Angela, " how you ever think you're going to find anything by pottering round on the scene of the crime, if any, like this. In a house, of course, it's different, because the most careless of housemaids will dust now and again, so that if anything's left about you know roughly how long it's been there. But in the open air like this, and in a place like this where there's bound to be a certain amount of coming and going, things just silt up anyhow. Look at those matches, for example ; how on earth is one to know whether they've been there weeks or months ? And that page from a parish magazine, if that's what it is – too pious for Lethaby, anyhow – has been so rained on that I bet you can't tell in the least when it was laid down. That thing hanging on the gorse-bush looks like a piece of umbrella ; it's extraordinary what a lot of pieces of umbrella get left about, though one hardly ever finds the frame of one. Do you regard that as particularly suspicious, Miles ? "

" Oh, go and spread yourself along the bank and be some use looking for things. Of course an open space like this, close to the river, is a regular port of call for tramps and lovers and what not. I say, though, this is more interesting."

" What have you got now ? A 'bus ticket ? "

" As a matter of fact, there is a 'bus ticket. And not a local one, either ; Glasgow, I see – at least, isn't Cowcaddens in Glasgow ? But what I was meaning, more, is this." And he held up for her inspection an undeniable sock-suspender.

" Splendid," cried Angela. " And I suppose you take that to Glasgow, and show it to all the haberdashers one by one, hoping that one of them will remember the gentleman he sold it to, and what he looked like. The only bother is, there must be some millions of sock-suspenders in use ; and unless you advertised it, of course——"

" Don't be a fool. You think that a sock-suspender is just a sock-suspender, and what's one more or less ? Nothing, says you, to the detective. You're quite wrong ; just let me show you how wrong you are. In the first place, I bet a thing like this belongs to one of the quality. Might be a shop-assistant, of course, from Inverness, but that's an off-chance ; I don't see the local youth wearing 'em. They've more sense, I should say ; never could abide the things myself. Then, it hasn't been here very long, because it's not much dis-coloured, in spite of all that rain. Next, how did it come to be dropped ? It goes round your leg, remember, and at the same time it's fixed on to your sock by that little rubber chap. Therefore, it's not likely to fall off in the middle of a walk ; if it fetched loose from your leg, it would still hang on to the sock. Inference, it had been taken off by somebody ; who was presumably preparing either to bathe or to paddle."

" Oh, that sounds all right, of course. But I don't see it gets you much further. Hundreds of people might come and bathe at a place like this."

" How many hundreds have you seen since we came here ? And yet the weather's been grilling, most of the time. The fact is, these Highland rivers are a dashed chilly affair ; and people don't bathe in 'em much, except kids, of course. But kids don't wear sock-suspenders. On the other hand, grown-ups don't often paddle. It looks to me as if a grown-up person had been stripping here to bathe, not very long ago ; and almost certainly at night."

" Why at night ? I shouldn't have thought any-body except you would be mad enough to go in for midnight bathing, hereabouts."

" It's only a guess, of course, but there are two good reasons to back it. The probability is that you drop your clothes where you take off your clothes. And when you have both an island and an opposite bank, on either of which females are liable to appear suddenly, your delicately minded bather doesn't un-dress on an open piece of grass, when he has a perfectly good dressing-room ready to hand behind those gorse-bushes. Another thing is, a man who is accustomed to wearing these silly things would notice at once if one were missing when he came to put his clothes on again ; and he'd almost certainly have found it if there had been light to find it by. So I say the presumption is that he undressed and dressed in the dark."

" Well, what would he do a fool thing like that for, anyhow ? It wasn't you, by any chance, was it ? "

" I've told you already, and a really good wife would know, that I don't wear the darned things. No, don't for the Lord's sake start talking about darning ; this is just where the point begins to become interesting. Since nobody would bathe here at midnight for pleasure, it follows that he was on business. And as we are accounting for the unmooring of a boat, which boat is moored on the bank of an uninhabited island, I think we can give a pretty good guess that the man had to swim over to the island, because he couldn't reach the boat any other way. Similarly, since he'd got to put the boat back where he took it from, he must have swum back after he'd finished with it. How's that for logic ? "

" Anything more, while you're about it ? "

" Only that he was probably in a hurry. Anyhow, that's enough to show you that you oughtn't to despise a sock-suspender. Now, look here, if you think you're so dashed clever, go and routle about in the under-growth, and see if you can find anything more impres-sive. Meanwhile, I am going to devote my giant brain to this sock-suspender question. What were they up to, anyhow ? What were they burying darkly at dead of night, days before they were supposed to be let loose on the island at all ? That's what's worrying me."

Ten minutes later, with a slight start, Miles Bredon woke up to find his wife standing over him. " I hope you've made up your mind whether it was the right or the left leg," she suggested. " Because——"

" Because you haven't managed to find anything ? Well, don't worry ; this'll do to go on with."

" Oh, but I *have* found something. Of course, I realise that you probably put it there, because you seem to spend most of your time now shedding eighteenth-century antiquities about the country-side. All the same, if you'll come and poke the sand here – wasn't it good of me to leave it lying where I found it ? – there's something for you to look at."

The scene of the new discovery was rather lower down the river, under the shade of the beechwood already mentioned. From a mass of loose sand, just underneath the true bank of the river, the edge of a little box was protruding. Miles picked it out carefully, using his handkerchief in case it should be important to avoid finger-prints. It was a snuff-box presumably, not of valuable metal ; on the inside of the lid was a coloured portrait which you instinctively identified, from the periwig and the Garter ribbon, as Prince Charles Edward. There was nothing beside it ; nor did burrowing in the sand disclose any further keepsakes of the same sort.

" Of course, it makes sense in a kind of way," mused Bredon as they got back into the car. " One can see how it might have been there, I mean ; but not exactly how it got there. Or ought one to allow more for accidents ? I hate doing that, somehow."

" It doesn't exactly fit into my suggestion, does it ? " objected Angela. " I mean, I was supposing they might have licked the cream off their find, so to speak, before owning up to Sir Charles about it. Which would be all very well, but surely this snuff-box affair isn't one of the valuable things you'd keep dark ; more one of the interesting things you'd leave over for the official discovery, because it looks so nice and genuine. I suppose it might have rarity value, though."

" Oh, if it comes to that, that might be exactly the reason why it was left behind instead of being carted away ; it wasn't one of the first-class finds, but got mixed up with them by mistake, so they meant to include it with the other lot, only they left it lying about, somehow. It's the carelessness of it beats me. Whether it's valuable or not, they didn't want to leave it in the hedgerow ; it creates such a confounded lot of suspicion. And then, did it fall out of a package ? Odd, if so, that it should have been so badly done up. Or out of somebody's pocket ? But that again argues such beastly carelessness. I wish I knew."

If they were in any doubt whether they meant to call

on Mr. Maclean as they went home, the question was solved for them by finding him at his garden gate, eager, as usual, for an audience. The admiration expressed by Angela for the over-regimented phloxes and tobacco-flowers in his trim border proved unnecessary; the minister was in an expansive mood, and had quite forgotten any pique he might have felt at Miles' recent scepticism. He volunteered at once to take them through the churchyard to see the view; and the sight of the island nestling below in the haze of its falls was sufficient to bring the conversation back to the fire, the tragedy, and the treasure.

Indeed, he introduced the subject himself. " Will Mr. Lethaby be at the island yet ? " he asked. " I'd half thought of going and having another look for him. But they tell me he's a man of no convictions whatever."

" I don't think he can very well leave just yet," said Bredon. " He'd be in considerable danger of one conviction if he did. But he seems cheerful, you know. My wife saw him this morning."

" He didn't seem to have a guilty conscience," agreed Angela. " Or a curse either, I must say. Mr. Maclean, I wish you'd tell me more about that curse. I'm so frightfully interested in these things, you know. My husband, of course, takes a perfectly stupid line of not believing in anything of that kind; but then, he never had any imagination. One comes across such odd cases of houses that can't be lived in, so that nobody has taken them for years, and properties that never go down in direct descent from the father to the eldest son. Do you really think there's anything in it all ? I'd almost like to believe there wasn't; but some of the evidence seems so difficult to get over. What do you really think about it ? "

" Deary me, Mrs. Bredon, you mustn't come appealing to me as a theologian ; I wouldn't like to say that
I've studied the subject. And in the present case, you
see, it's more like a prophecy than a curse, as I was
telling Mr. Bredon the other day. It was a fellow
called Habington, who had the reputation of being a
bit of a prophet in these parts, a long while back. And
what he said, you see, was that if anybody touched
Prince Charlie's treasure, the dead wouldn't lie easy in
Glendounie churchyard. And there's been queer
stories going round in the glen, that's certain, since
there was talk of these fellows coming to dig it up.
But the curious thing is, it wasn't after but before
the treasure was touched people began to see these
things."

" What sort of things, Mr. Maclean ? Do tell me ;
Miles here is such a fool at explaining things."

" Oh, well, I don't think I'd told him much, now I
come to think of it. I've lived a long time now, Mrs.
Bredon, and one of the things I've learnt is that no
harm came yet, or very little, from just holding one's
tongue. But if you're interested, why, that's a different
matter. There's a fellow lives up the river there, you
can't see his croft from here, but it's a matter of a few
hundred yards beyond the further end of the island ;
a fellow of the name of Patterson, not a fool at all, and
a sober man for these parts. Well, his story is that he
slept badly one night in July, the twenty-first it was,
and an easy day for him to remember, you see, because
that's the day Robbie Burns died – well, he slept
badly, as I was saying, and about two o'clock in the
morning he heard the cat at the back door yowling
to be let in. So he went and let her in, for he's a good-
hearted sort of fellow ; and he stood there at the door
just for a moment or two looking about him. There were

clouds in the sky that night, and that meant something
to us up here, I can tell you, for we'd had awfully little
rain a matter of a fortnight past. And as luck would
have it the moon came out from behind a cloud just
for a minute or two, and shone on the river, as you'll
have seen it, and a bonny sight it is, too. Now, I'll
not deny that in a short interval of time like that, and
at dead of night, a man might easily be deceived about
what he thought he saw. But this fellow Patterson
sticks to it that he saw a boat crossing over to the
island, just not very far from his end of it. Not floating
downstream, you'll understand, but travelling straight
across, just as if a man was rowing it. But the queer
thing is, there was no man on board of it at all – or
rather, there was no man rowing it."

" Excuse me," put in Bredon, forgetting his determination to leave all the conversation to Angela, " but
do you mean that he didn't see anybody on board ?
Or that he saw a man, only as far as he could see the
man wasn't rowing ? "

" Well, Mr. Bredon, he did and he didn't ; but as
far as he could see the man couldn't have been rowing.
And the reason of that was a very simple one, because
he was in a coffin."

" In a coffin ! " repeated Angela. " But . . . you
don't mean he was sitting up in the coffin, or anything?
It was just a coffin he saw, on the boat ? "

" And he was sure it was a *coffin* ? " added her
husband.

" Well, Mr. Bredon, he didn't profess to have been
able to read the lettering on the plate, from that
distance. But that was the shape of the thing, anyway ;
and, mind you, he said he'd quite forgotten old Habington's prophecy about the dead not resting easy in
their graves, though to be sure he had heard it when

he was a youngster. Well, Mrs. Bredon, you can easily imagine there are people up and down the glen who are going about saying that the prophecy has come true ; but if you ask whether I believe it myself I'd rather say that I suspend judgment. It isn't as if I'd seen it myself, or anything else of that kind. But I just don't like the Sadducees to have everything their own way."

" I think you said," suggested Bredon, " that there was some talk of lights being seen where there oughtn't to have been any lights, about the same time ? "

" There was, Mr. Bredon, but to tell the truth, I don't attach a great deal of importance to those stories. One reason is, as your friend Mr. Pulteney will tell you, that there's salmon in this river ; and though it's not like a place where there's towns close to and poaching is common, I wouldn't just say that there mightn't be a perfectly natural explanation of a phenomenon like that. And the other reason's this, that there was just a bit of a fire happened about the same time, up on the brae behind there. You could see clearly what it was from here ; and I went up myself to see if I could help put it out, but it had died down before McBrayne or I got there. Now, if you were to see just the reflection of that from the other side of the river, it would be easy enough to say to yourself there were lights in Glendounie churchyard, though as a matter of fact it was the best part of a mile away, out on the braeside."

" I suppose . . . I suppose you don't remember what night exactly that was ? "

" I do, and it was the night of the twentieth, just before Patterson saw whatever it was Patterson saw. I had to make a bit of a speech at a little dinner we have to commemorate Robbie Burns ; and I recollect that I was just turning over the points of it in my mind, the evening before, when I noticed the light up on the brae."

" Do you often get fires like that round here? Mrs. McBrayne, I think, tried to make out that it was picnickers."

" There's always a few forest fires when we have a dry season like the one we've had this year; and there's generally talk of foul play, but no sort of proof. It doesn't take much to start a forest fire, Mr. Bredon. But this wasn't in the woods at all; it was just on the open hillside, and what was burnt was just a few whin-bushes and some logs of wood. They'd been soaked in petrol, and it was a spot close to the road, so what we thought was that some of these motorists who come out and take their tea by the road side had lit the fire for their own convenience, and not put it out properly, so that it blazed up again after night-fall. There's nothing these people wouldn't do – I mean, the folk that come out in *cheap* motor-cars," he added, a trifle lamely.

" It's your fault for living in such lovely country," Angela pointed out. " Fancy having a view like this just opposite one's front windows! Of course you get motor-fiends like us driving past and making a nuisance of ourselves. And what a place to be buried in! "

" Talking of burials," put in Mr. Maclean, with a return to the professional manner, " the Fiscal says poor Henderson's remains can be put away now, so we were having the funeral to-morrow afternoon. I was wondering, if you will be seeing Mr. Lethaby, whether you would let him know the date, and the time – it's three o'clock, if that's convenient to him. He should have been consulted, because I suppose he's the next thing to a mourner poor Henderson will have.

Odd, how little we know of his family and antecedents !
Well, we're all strangers here."

" It's good of you to put yourself to the trouble,"
said Bredon. " I suppose there's no knowing what
denomination the unfortunate man belonged to ; by
the accounts one heard of him, it didn't sound as if he
was much of a church-goer."

" Mr. Bredon," replied the minister solemnly,
" you'll observe that Henderson is a good Scots name.
And where there's reason to think that the deceased
was a fellow-countryman of Knox, it's for the Estab-
lished Church to do what can be done for him."

It was Angela who protested that they ought to be
on the road again, and the minister's suggestion of tea
– diffidently made, since it appeared that Mrs. Maclean
was out – was vetoed on the ground that Mrs. Wauchope had announced an intention of calling. " It's
the first time," remarked Bredon as they drove home,
" that I remember being thankful for the existence of
the poet Burns. By a stroke of luck, Maclean's got all
his dates mapped out properly. Let's see, a fire on the
hillside on the night of the twentieth. Then, on the
twenty-first we think – we can probably verify that,
though – Lethaby and Henderson came over to have
a preliminary look at the island. On the night of the
twenty-first, certainly, there are odd movements of
boats between the island and the further shore. The
whole thing begins to hang together rather better,
doesn't it ? And all this would be just over a week
before the let of the island officially takes effect. It's
all very interesting."

" Yes, but I can't help feeling it's rather odious of
Mr. Patterson, or whatever his name is, to have seen
the ghost-boat going *from* the island *to* the mainland.
If only it had been the other way about, it would have

fitted in beautifully with my idea about the treasure. Because, of course, that long trunk it was found in would have looked exactly like a coffin, wouldn't it? Not that they would have taken that away (now I come to think of it), because, of course, that's what they found the stuff in the other day, wasn't it? Unless they used it for carting the stuff across, and Patterson saw it when they were bringing it back again. By the way, you seem to have come round to the idea that it *was* Henderson in the garage?"

"Well, apparently he's going to be buried under that name; and as I don't suppose Henderson is likely to reappear in these parts, it won't do much harm if it's somebody else. But, you see, it's some time now since the fire, and it doesn't look as if anybody else had disappeared from the ranks of Society; so it's more economical to assume that the corpse is the explanation of the disappearance. The only thing is, as you say – in that case, what about Lethaby?"

Mrs. Wauchope, it seemed, had been paying a surprise visit to her nephew, and reported that he was in a mood of hopeless intransigence, making no effort to clear himself of suspicion, nor (apparently) taking any steps to claim the insurance on his loss. "He might at least pretend to be honest," she complained. "Of course, everybody knows that he isn't, but I do think a certain amount of hypocrisy is demanded if we are to keep Society together. There's no doubt he found the stuff, and there's no doubt it's disappeared; if he's made away with it himself, he ought at least to have the courage of his embezzlement. Everybody's saying, of course, that he murdered Henderson, and then made away with the treasure so as to make it look as if the murderer and thief was a person unknown. I told him that the world expects a decent cupidity from any man whose conduct will bear investigation, but you might as well talk to a mule. However, I suppose the more mystery there is, the more you enjoy it, Mr. Bredon ? Nothing like feeling useful."

" Yes, I'm not really certain I want him to come clean," admitted Bredon. " If he has the explanation of the whole thing under his hat, it would be rather a bore to be told the answer just when I feel as if I was on the track of finding it for myself. And if he's as mystified as we are, which I think is quite possible, it might only set one off on a wrong tack. By the way, if you don't mind being called in as an expert witness against your own flesh and blood, are you good at Jacobite relics ? "

" Next to scandal, they're the only things I care about. Have you been finding any ? "

" What, Miles ? Not he," protested Angela. " The effort of discovering an undoubtedly genuine twentieth-century sock-suspender brought on a profound coma ; in the middle of which I had to go about digging things up for him. It's really rather a pet, you know, Mrs. Wauchope. Where is it, Miles ? "

" Oh, one of those things ? " said the great lady, when it was produced. " Yes, there are a good few of them about ; I've got one at Moreton. The story is, you know, that a whole lot of them were sent round to the heads of the Jacobite families, just before the '45, to give them an idea of what Prince Charlie looked like. Otherwise, I suppose, you'd have had lots of tramps turning up at the front door and saying they were the only genuine article. Though, come to think of it, a chocolate-box picture like that would give one a very feeble idea of him ; it might be almost any young man of the period. However, that's the story, and naturally

there are several of them still left ; so, as they haven't
much intrinsic value, you wouldn't get a great deal for
it.   But no doubt you look upon it as a clue, Mr. Bredon ? I suppose it would be indiscreet to ask where you
found it ? "

" We found it, I mean Angela found it, on the further
side of the river, quite close to the bank.   We were
hoping it might prove, somehow, to be part of the
treasure.   Indeed, if it wasn't, I don't quite see how
it came to be lying about there.   But it isn't very
valuable, you say – and I suppose never was ? "

" It can't have had any value at all in Prince Charlie's
time.   And if you're trying to make out that he left it
behind on the Isle of Erran as part of his personal
luggage, you've got a difficult job in front of you.
Hang it all, he can't have wanted to identify himself.
But of course that part of the story may be a fake."

Any further discussion of the subject was cut short
by a most unexpected interruption.   The door of the
sitting-room opened without any warning, to show,
framed in the opening, the grotesque figure of the
bearded chauffeur who had driven Lethaby at his
first coming to the island.

IT WAS ONE of those breathless moments which stupefy
the mind with conflicting reactions. Your first instinct
was to laugh ; then you remembered that a man stood
before you whom you had thought of before now as
fighting for his life in a burning garage ; then you
reflected that he might, after all, be a criminal disguised, and that his unceremonious visit might threaten
the peace of the household. It was, however, plain
from the first that his attitude was one of embarrassment, rather than of menace. Indeed, the desperate
way in which he fingered the back of his head in the
neighbourhood of his ears strongly suggested a disguise,
and one which it was easier to assume than to lay aside.
Murmured apologies began to be audible, delayed in
transit by uncontrollable laughter. Bredon was the
first who rose to the occasion, with a cry of " Good God,
it's Pulteney ! "

Angela had to go and help him before he could discover the knots by which the mask was tied on ; had
to extract him from the voluminous greatcoat which
concealed the slenderness of his figure. " Really, Mr.
Pulteney," she protested, " you oughtn't to go away
for your holiday without a nurse. I very very nearly
screamed, and as for Mrs. Wauchope, she looks as if
she'd have to be brought round with brandy. What on
earth made you do it ? "

" Mrs. Wauchope," said the old gentleman, " I am

covered with confusion. As for Mrs. Bredon, I know
perfectly well that nothing frightens her ; and it is a
singular fact that when a man goes about disguised he
never *feels* disguised ; he feels as if everybody must see
through it at the first glance. But I need hardly say
that if I had had any idea there was company to
tea——"

" You are forgiven, Mr. Pulteney ; only don't make
a speech about it, because I'm famishing for tea, with
or without brandy. And don't call me *company* ; it
always suggests being in the nursery, don't you know,
and having one's ears washed. Still," she added, as
they went in to tea, " I think you owe us an explanation, if we let you off the apology. What would you
have done if I hadn't been there to bring you to your
senses ? "

" I confess that I had not thought out any scheme of
operations. Certainly my nerve would have failed me
if I had tried to sustain the part, which is not one for
which nature has fitted me. No amount of imagination
would make me feel as if I could drive a motor-car."

" Yes, but don't be so dashed mysterious about it
all," protested Angela. " Where did you get the face-
fittings, anyway ? Have you been buying them in
Inverness ? You know, Miles, that mask's awfully
good."

The old gentleman looked pained. " These, Mrs.
Bredon, are the genuine articles. It was only the
circumstance of coming across them in rather peculiar
surroundings which suggested to me the idea of what
was, perhaps, a not too felicitous impersonation."

" Not a bit, Mr. Pulteney, it was splendid ; anybody
could see you'd been walking on as Father Christmas
for years. But do tell us where you came across them ?
You're as bad as Miles for telling a story back ways

round. We left you on guard, to see what Mr. Lethaby would be up to."

" To be sure you did," agreed Mr. Pulteney ; " and I was prepared to stand there practising casts with all the fidelity of the Pompeii sentinel. But the proceedings of Mr. Lethaby were such as to complicate my situation. I had not been at my post above a quarter of an hour, when I saw him at the end of the island, evidently preparing to go down the cliff by the same path which you and he used this morning. He appeared to be engaged in some sort of business ; at any rate, he was carrying a short ladder under his arm."

" A ladder ! " said Bredon. " That's interesting."

" It seemed clear to me – I am afraid I have a bad habit of jumping to conclusions – that he was going to follow up the trail of those gold coins he found scattered about the place this morning. They must have made him think, as they were meant to make him think, that the treasure had somehow got reburied, presumably by Henderson, on the little island that stands in the middle of the falls. The interval, on this side, is a short one, and the ladder he was carrying looked as if it was just the right length for bridging it."

" That was well argued ; I wish I had your brains, Pulteney. So what did you do ? "

" Well, you see, there wasn't much to be done. Where I was at the time, it was probable that Lethaby couldn't see me, or wouldn't unless he looked rather carefully ; the spot, as you know, is decidedly umbrageous. But I lost sight of him as soon as he began to climb down the cliff ; and I could only keep within view of him by moving further north along the shore till I could see round the corner of the island, as it were. There was a difficulty about doing that, because it meant that I should have to cross a long stretch of ground in which there was no cover, and Lethaby would almost certainly see me. If he saw me, it was likely that he would stop doing whatever he was doing, and pretend to look for pearl-mussels, or something of that kind. So I decided to leave him to it, and occupy the interval, during which I was sure that he was otherwise occupied, in having a bit of a look-round the island for myself. Mr. and Mrs. Bredon will have told you, I expect, Mrs. Wauchope, that I suffer from an incurable vice of inquisitiveness."

" He does, really," assented Angela. " Put his nose to the ground on the scent of a crime, and he's guaranteed to follow a red-herring for miles across open country. What was the good of going and looking round, Mr. Pulteney ? You surely didn't think Miles would have missed anything ? "

" No, indeed, Mrs. Bredon, I felt it would be presumptuous to put myself in competition with him. But there was one thing he had no chance of investigating, because at the time of his visit it was not there to be investigated. I refer to the motor-car, Lethaby's motor-car. I don't know if you will remember, but when we first met, at the time when poor Mottram died in those unnecessarily complicated circumstances, I went and had a good look under the seats of the motor-car, and found a rather interesting mixture of sandwiches and ten-pound notes. Of course, it is always a mistake trying to repeat a success ; above all when you try to repeat it in exactly the same form. But the human mind, I fancy, has a natural craving for routine ; and when I had wandered up the drive, without having formulated any precise scheme of action, the first thing I found myself doing was looking under the cushions in Lethaby's car. I was rewarded at once. The cushions were, I take it, specially made so as to allow of one or two things being packed underneath without crushing them. And what I found there was what you have seen ; the complete chauffeur's uniform, together with that mask whose features, apparently, must be considered even more terrifying than those with which Providence has endowed me."

" So you just pinched them," asked Angela. " You are pretty cool about other people's things, I must say. Remind me to tell you later about the whisky, Mrs. Wauchope."

" Well, you see, I felt that these paraphernalia could not be of any use to Mr. Lethaby at the moment. He could hardly find any excuse for dressing up as a chauffeur, when he has been so careful to explain to us that there is no chauffeur on the island. For the same reason, he is not likely to look and see whether they are there or not. And even if he does, I argued to myself, he would hesitate to complain of the loss, because it would involve him in some decidedly awkward explanations. So my untimely sense of humour – you must make allowances for a schoolmaster on his holiday – got the better of me. At the same time, I thought the things would interest you, Bredon, as a sort of Exhibit A which might contribute to the solution of your little problem."

" Exhibit A ? More like Exhibit Z. All the same, I agree that they are interesting ; and I'm inclined to add that I think they may possibly come in dashed useful. . . . Tell me, Angela, when you saw Pulteney standing in the doorway just now, who did you think it was ? Not your reasoned inferences, I mean, when you had had a moment to think it over, but your first instinctive reactions ? Did you think there was really a chauffeur after all ? Or did you think it was Lethaby dressed up ? Or what ? "

" Oo ; let's see. . . . I think there was a sort of tiny fraction of my brain telegraphing that it might be Lethaby dressed up. But my immediate feeling, I suppose because I'm a coward, is that it was *Henderson* dressed up, and that he'd come here to make a nuisance of himself. Was that what I ought to have said ? "

" Right for once. Now, put yourself in the place of Vernon Lethaby ; suppose you were suddenly confronted with the sight of the non-existent chauffeur. You'd know that he had no real existence ; you'd have no temptation to mix up the apparition with Vernon Lethaby. Wouldn't your immediate instinct be to say to yourself, *Hullo, here's Henderson come back* ? "

" What unscrupulous people you detectives are ! " broke in Mrs. Wauchope. " This is what you call the Third Degree, ain't it ? You confront my unfortunate nephew with what appears to be the ghost of his dead partner, and then if he sags at the knees at all, you say, *Arrest that man, he's a murderer.*"

" Oh, it's not quite as bad as that, Mrs. Wauchope. But you see, our difficulty is we don't know whether your nephew thinks Henderson is dead or not – quite apart from the question of who, if anybody, killed him. Now, if I can confront him suddenly with something that might be Henderson in the flesh, and might be Henderson's ghost, I can watch his reactions without necessarily making him guilty of murder. He may say, *Hullo, old chap, where've you popped up from ?* in which case we shall know that he thinks Henderson is alive. Or he may produce some more interesting reaction of the King Claudius type, and then we shall begin to see daylight a bit."

" I don't think it's fair to confront him with Mr. Pulteney dressed up," protested Angela. " I don't quite know what it is about Mr. Pulteney, but he does really look quite loathsome in side-whiskers."

" No, I wasn't going to let Pulteney in for any more amateur theatricals," Bredon explained. " He doesn't carry it off well enough, for one thing. I was going to do the dressing-up myself this time. The only thing is, how does one stage the apparition, exactly ? "

" You might just look in about tea-time," suggested Mrs. Wauchope, with a severe glance at Mr. Pulteney.

" Miles," said Angela, " I won't have you walking into strange houses in that get-up when you don't even know whether there are fire-arms about. I'm sorry, Mrs. Wauchope, I know it's not nice of me to suggest that your relations are in the habit of firing at sight ; but really, if I'd had a weapon of any sort when Mr. Pulteney came in just now, I'd have let fly at him ; he rattled me so. You'd much better make an assignation with him, without precisely explaining who it is wants to see him – hear of something to his advantage, don't you know, and all that."

" I'm afraid that particular phrase has been used once too often. But in the circumstances I don't know that an assignation would do much harm ; and it's a little less third-degreeish than the King Claudius business. If I send him a message which obviously implies that it comes from Henderson, we ought to be able to see, from the way in which he keeps or doesn't keep the assignation, whether he is expecting a man or a ghost."

" I suppose we are certain," suggested Mrs. Wauchope, " that it *was* Henderson who dressed up as the chauffeur, and not, for example, my ridiculous nephew himself ? "

" It can't have been Lethaby the first time we saw him ; he and the chauffeur were sitting side by side."

" By the same way of reasoning," Angela pointed

out, " it's as well to remember that after that we saw the chauffeur sitting side by side with Henderson."

" Looks as if they took turns with the whiskers," said Mrs. Wauchope.

" No, but that won't do either," complained Angela. " Lethaby was still on the island when the chauffeur went off to meet Henderson ; you saw him yourself, Miles, after the car had left. Surely that means there was a third person in the business, though preferring to remain incognito."

" The hair, the tousled hair – you've forgotten that," retorted her husband.[1] " Evidently the whole thing was a very careful frame-up, and I can't help believing they must have been preparing the ground for some complicated manœuvre which never came off. Somehow, they must have known from the start that we were watching them, and they arranged the whole business of their arrival so as to plant out this idea of the phantom chauffeur on us. They both arrived together, with Lethaby playing the pipes, and Henderson, who didn't care much for that sort of thing, crouching over the wheel in an unhappy sort of way. Then, Henderson himself dresses up as the chauffeur, and drives off by himself to meet the imaginary Henderson at the station. Lethaby hangs about here at the bridge till he is certain that I have noticed him, and then sneaks along the bank and swims across. Henderson, who has just driven round the corner into the main road, meets him on the bank, and hands over the chauffeur's uniform to make good the deficiencies in his wardrobe. They drive round for a bit to waste the requisite amount of time, and then come back on the road from the station. By accident, they meet you and Pulteney at a turn of the road, standing so close that

[1] p. 80.

244

there might be a danger of recognition ; you had seen Lethaby before. So he takes off his cap as an excuse for putting an arm in front of his face ; forgetting that when he does so he will enable you to have a look at his hair. And you, being a married woman in the habit of making rude remarks about the personal appearance of her husband, actually notice that the hair is untidy. So we know he has been for a swim, and all is well."

" Then you think," said Mr. Pulteney, " that on coming across a whiskered chauffeur Lethaby would assume, by force of habit, that it was Henderson, and vice versa ? But surely he would be a little surprised at his friend's wanting to go about in that costume without any sufficient reason ? The disguise is, *experto crede*, none too comfortable on a warm day."

" But isn't there a sufficient reason, in Henderson's case ? " persisted Bredon. " Assuming, of course, that he's still alive. Because there's the awkward fact of the corpse in the garage to get over ; and if he isn't the corpse himself, it rather looks as if he must somehow be responsible for it. Also, we know that the London police are anxious for news of his whereabouts. For an interview in a public place – and as you suggest, Angela, it might be well to choose a fairly public place for an interview with Lethaby – disguise would be natural. The only thing is, how we are going to make Lethaby believe that Henderson is still hanging about the place ? His interest in the neighbourhood was strictly dictated by the fact that there was supposed to be treasure about. Whatever treasure there was, has disappeared ; why hasn't Henderson disappeared too ? We shall have to send Lethaby a note which somehow gives the impression that it must have come from Henderson, and from nobody else."

245

" We might enclose the sock-suspender," suggested Angela.

" You have an odd habit of nearly hitting the mark, but not quite," said Bredon meditatively. " I don't think the sock-suspender would have any particular message for him. But that snuff-box, now ! However it came to lie where it did, it belongs to a part of this story on which Lethaby and Henderson were in – nobody else. If he found the note lying about in the snuff-box——"

" Well," said Angela, " you'd better be getting ahead with your forgery, hadn't you ? "

" Who said I was going to forge anything ? I'm going to leave a note lying about for Lethaby ; and if he likes to think it comes from Henderson——"

" Oh, you're hopeless ! It's awful, Mrs. Wauchope, having married a man who really hasn't got any morals at all. I do hope you will warn your nephew that the famous Pulteney–Bredon knockabout turn is on his track. Really, it does seem monstrous that we should sit here discussing him in your presence, as if he was a criminal, whereas we don't really *know* anything against him."

" Oh, if that's all you want, my dear, I can tell you plenty. No, indeed, it's the last thing I ever expect anybody to apologise for, criticising my relations. I think it was the main thing that served to shake my religious convictions, hearing a sermon in which I was told that I should meet my uncles and aunts in heaven. Only, whatever you do, don't tell Hermia Jennings that you've got your knife into Vernon ; she's all over him. She was telling me only yesterday that she thought he was such a fine type of the new generation ; so honest and all that. I believe she actually had the impertinence to tell me that it is youth's turn to-day."

"Statistics are against her," Mr. Pulteney pointed out, coming in on his favourite opening. "The distribution of age-groups is coming to tell more and more on the side of middle age. At the present moment, even, I think I am justified in saying that three-sevenths of the population are over thirty-five. And, of course, that is a growing tendency ; if I live another ten years, I believe that youth will have lost the last claim it has to consideration – that of numerical superiority."

"You must give me your lecture on population another time," said Mrs. Wauchope indulgently. "At the moment, I must really be getting back, and recovering from the shock you gave me earlier in the evening. Well, Mrs. Bredon, take care of your husband. Though indeed, I don't think he's likely to come to any harm in a turn-up with my nephew, who as I told you before is a perfect fool, and would be certain not to shoot straight even if he screwed up the courage to fire at anybody. I'll look in to-morrow or next day, if I may, to hear how things are going on."

When she had gone, Bredon shut himself up in the bedroom with a large sheet of paper – it had wrapped one of Angela's purchases at the bazaar – and tried various openings for his correspondence with Lethaby, rejecting one after another as either too menacing or too melodramatic. Finally, he had to remain content with the following legend, written in block capitals with an indelible pencil : "Plans changed ; must see you to-night, 11.30, on mainland, Strathdounie side, opposite where boat moored. Fifty-fifty."

"Well, it looks illiterate enough," commented Angela, who had come in just as the final draft was finished. "It would be perfect if you'd said something about the hollow oak. What's the idea of having your assignation at such a filthy hour of the night? Merely to keep me awake, or what? "

" Well, you see, I thought it would be more artistic if I made it sound as if Henderson was lying low rather, and didn't want to be seen about. Nor would he, as we were saying, if he's really alive, because that garage business would take a bit of explaining. Half-past eleven seemed the right sort of time, because respectable people like you and me go to bed at eleven or thereabouts, so the coast is clear. To put it later would have involved the risk of Lethaby going to sleep in his chair and failing to turn up."

" Won't he be a bit suspicious of the *venue*? It's rather bad luck to drag him across the bridge at dead of night, walking all carefully for fear of waking those blasted Bredons."

" Yes, but you won't think yourself into the position of the imaginary Henderson. If he's wandering about the country-side in fear of his life, it's dashed sporting of him to come as near the island as that, especially when it's Lethaby who's got a car. He, Henderson, I mean, might easily let himself in for a trap of some sort if he ventured across the bridge, whereas Lethaby is on neutral ground. Besides, I'm rather tired of scrambling about at night myself, so I thought I wouldn't make it too far from our own front door. Any more complaints? "

" What's all this fifty-fifty business, anyhow? It'd be all right if it were Henderson who had run off with the treasure. But as far as we can see it wasn't Henderson, it was Lethaby ; and if it was, he knows it ; what does he expect to go shares in? Or why should Henderson expect Lethaby to go shares in what he's collared? It doesn't seem to make sense."

" Yes, but we don't *know*. And if it was Lethaby

who took the stuff, he won't be surprised at Henderson suggesting fifty-fifty as a basis of negotiation, though he may be inclined to think it's bluff. You see, there's no doubt Lethaby has been left in the soup, with a murder charge hanging over him ; and Henderson might reasonably be offering to shoulder the murder charge, on condition of being given some of the spoils to clear off with. Whereas, of course, if Lethaby hasn't got the stuff, this message is calculated to make him prick up his ears and come round with a collecting-plate. Meanwhile, did I hear you telephoning ? "

" Yes, a telegram – guess who from. I hate being told to guess things, don't you ? It's from Leyland, no less, to say that he's on his way to these parts and arriving to-night ; he'll look us up to-morrow. I suppose that kind policeman who called the other day has found the strain too much for him, and they've had to get Scotland Yard to help them. Or do you think he's just on a holiday, and coming here because he wants to cadge a bit of fishing ? Sholto told him about you."

" Dunno whether it's in their beat, even. But, of course, Scotland Yard's interested in the thing at the Henderson end, we know that ; so they may want somebody to cover it for them. Gosh, I wish I hadn't made such nonsense of this business ; Leyland will think me a pretty good fool. Unless, of course, to-night's adventure turns up trumps."

" I shall hate him if he finds out something you haven't. Meanwhile, how do you deliver this message exactly ? The general post in these parts would take about three days to do it ; and the date is for to-night. Do we push it through Lethaby's window and run away, or what ? "

" No, I had an idea about that ; but it rather

depends on how well you can make love to Mrs. McBrayne."

" Oh, she eats out of my hand. Do you mean she's got to deliver it when she goes in to tidy up ? It's about her time now."

" That's the idea. You could tell her that it is meant to be a surprise, so she's not to tell Lethaby about it ; that would sound all right, coming from you."

" Better if it came from Edward ; he's getting so skittish. Where's she to leave it ; in the front hall ? "

" No, there's got to be no mistake about Lethaby's finding it. As well as I can understand her methods, she goes and washes up things in the scullery, doesn't she ; and then leaves everything lying about in the kitchen, for Lethaby to come in and have a snack when he feels like it ? Well, if she took the snuff-box along with her, with the letter inside it, and left it looking fairly prominent on the kitchen dresser, he'd be bound to come across it in the course of the evening. He'll wonder how it got there, of course ; but there's nothing to connect us with it. Even if he does, he'll probably turn up out of curiosity ; and then he'll be put off by the disguise, with any luck. It's all an off-chance, anyhow ; but I *must* try and get something done before Leyland comes nosing round. I've never felt such a fraud in my life."

CHAPTER XVII: A NEW WAY OF DEALING WITH GUNMEN

BREDON PLAYED PATIENCE that evening ; he was too pre-occupied, he said, for the strain of conversation. The game did not bring him any sudden enlightenment, such as he was wont to expect ; did not even rest his mind, if you could judge by the furrows on his brow. Had he done right to challenge this interview, always with the risk of putting Lethaby on his guard – warning him that counterplots were at work ? Had he baited the trap sufficiently, or ought he to have made some definite allusion . . . no, that would surely have been premature. Was it safe to assume that Lethaby would come peaceably ? Perhaps best to take a gun in his pocket, in any case ; certainly Lethaby was not the sort of man you would expect to be quick with his hands, so he wouldn't be likely to get his shot in first. A torch he must obviously take ; was he to shine it on Lethaby the moment he turned up, by way of disconcerting him, or should he wait for Lethaby to show a light first, giving him a more sudden and a more definite picture of the false Henderson ? . . . What would Lethaby do next, if he knew (or thought) that Henderson was dead ? Turn and run, or stand there helpless, or throw a faint ? Take the contrary supposition, that Lethaby thought (or knew) Henderson was alive ; what then ? He would open the conversation on that understanding ; was there anything to be gained by playing the false Henderson a little longer? Yes, if he could only keep it up; he had tried his Canadian intonation before dinner, and it seemed to be in fairly good shape. Yes, best keep up the *rôle* of Henderson for a little, and see if Lethaby would not commit himself to some fatal confidence. Let the unmasking come when it liked.

Would Lethaby consent to come clean, when he was confronted with what he would find on the river bank? Or would it be necessary to put further pressure on him; to produce, and to ask questions about, the garage key? If he showed any signs of becoming really confidential, perhaps it would be best to bring him back to the cottage and give him a drink. The only thing was, Lethaby was so thoroughly false, in his way of looking at you and his manner of talking to you, that you suspected him capable of making up a plausible lie at short notice; would it be safe to sacrifice the advantage of the initial shock? . . . Doubts began to arise about the soundness of the whole scheme, as they always do when we give ourselves too long an interval of suspense. What if Lethaby should take alarm at the mysterious summons, and decide to make a bolt for it? It would be easy for him to get away in the car; and there were no signs that the police were picketing the main road any longer; nothing to be seen of them this afternoon, for example. Surely, though, they must be taking *some* precautions; the message from Leyland was proof that they were not satisfied with the theory of accident. What, again, if Lethaby should decide to treat the whole thing as a trap, or a practical joke, and not turn up at all? How long would it be worth waiting for a Lethaby who did not appear? . . . So the echoes of pre-occupation danced through the background of his mind, while that minimum of mental concentration which a familiar patience demands tried to assert its predominance in the foreground.

Both Angela and Mr. Pulteney were sent off to bed before eleven ; it was essential that there should be no lights in the cottage when Lethaby came past. Angela, at the last moment, seemed disposed to turn rebellious, and imagine all sorts of dangers arising out of his midnight expedition. She asked if she couldn't hang about somewhere in the background and enjoy the fun ; but was told sternly that nothing could be more calculated to put a man out of his stride. Before going upstairs, she helped to fix the mask over his face, and pronounced favourably on the result. " You carry it off better than Edward, somehow," she said. " Though I don't think it improves your looks really. Now, don't go bathing ; and if you bring Lethaby back here to have explanations with him, talk quietly, so as not to wake Edward." There was a curious sense of unreality about starting on a perfectly serious errand, as Bredon's was, when you kept forgetting and then remembering at intervals that you were dressed up as a figure of farce – the portrait of a drunken Scot on a comic postcard. The stuffy sensation of wearing a mask brought back to you Christmas Eves, and that stealthy invasion of the nursery which was only breathless in fun. It needed a constant effort to remind yourself that to-night's work was not child's play.

Outside, there was the usual silence ; or rather that steady roar of water over the falls, that gurgling of eddies round the piers of the bridge, which had grown so familiar as to occupy, in his mind, the place of silence. Once or twice a huge white owl brushed past him in the darkness. The sky was clouded over, and only the faintest glimmer of twilight helped him to find his way along the narrow path beside the rhododendrons ; but he was well used to it enough by now to need little aid from his electric torch. Yet darkness and silence did not weigh on his spirits as they would have, he felt, if he had been walking on the other bank of the stream. The atmosphere of uncanny oppression which hung over the island came to an end with the concrete bridge ; the mainland felt no echo of it. *There*, you would have felt all the time that your steps were accompanied, would have shrunk from the touch of a spray against your cheek ; here, there was no sense of mystery beyond what reason brought you, and reason could deal with. Yes, he had had enough of prowling about the island after dark ; this assignation was much better devised. There would be no encounters except with flesh and blood.

His mind travelled back to the discoveries of the afternoon ; what exactly was the meaning of that midnight descent on the island by its prospective tenants ? What exactly were they ferrying across the strait ; and, if it was treasure in any form, how did it come to be so carelessly packed as the loss of the snuff-box indicated ? Curious, how fond Lethaby seemed of swimming the river. . . . Come to think of it, the floods which had been coming down this last day or two were a pure godsend to the conscientious detective. Because, as long as you knew the river was low, you couldn't keep a really effective watch on the island tenants, unless you had a whole staff of day and night watchers. Three days' rain out in the West, and the river became a real barrier, as formidable as the walls of a prison. Nobody in his senses would take a boat out on it, where it passed through these narrow channels, and the attempt to swim it would be death. You would be washed up a mile or two lower down; a handy place for your funeral. . . . The picture of Glendounie churchyard stood out in his mind, and he found himself trying to recapture the bland accents of the minister, as he told his ghost-story, or put on an air of proper concern in discussing how the remains of Henderson were to be disposed of. " A fellow-countryman of Knox " . . . the words became a refrain which echoed in your mind, somehow, as if they were a cross-word clue which was always on the point of yielding its secret. What was that refrain in *Box and Cox* that brought in the name ? Oh, yes, " Three cheers for Knox, that excellent man " – it would sound like a profanity, if sung in the ears of Mr. Maclean. A fellow-countryman of Knox – the indication of strange possibilities for good and evil.

Bredon had now reached his point of assignation ; the well-known clearing in the woods by the river-bank from which, in day time, you saw the island boat moored exactly opposite you. Here a tiny runnel of water discharged itself into the river between deep banks of clay, and a fence dividing two fields leant over crazily at the edge. Bredon flashed his torch just for an instant, and took his bearings without difficulty. One thing remained to do before he was ready for the expected interview, due to happen now in about a quarter of an hour. He stood listening for a minute or two, as if to make certain that Lethaby had not yet come to keep his tryst. Then, leaning right over the bank a few yards below the fence, he began fishing with the crook of his stick under the tumbling waters of the Dounie. Once or twice he drew up the stick, and examined it with disappointment ; this rushing of the water made it difficult to keep the thing at its proper angle. Ah, that was better ! This time he had succeeded in hooking up a piece of stout cord which was clearly either weighted or tied at both ends ; one, you supposed, must be attached to a branch or tree-root several feet below the level of the water, in the bank itself, the other must presumably be weighted, since it was well out in mid-stream. Yes, now he was pulling, and it was this latter end of the string which gave to his efforts ; a yard of it, two yards of it appeared, then still more, and at last a little canvas bag, its mouth securely fastened to the end of the line, came up with it and lay there dripping on the bank. Yes, that would be enough ; indeed, the whole thing might prove to be unnecessary, but it just gave that added touch of plausibility to the assignation which its melodramatic terms needed. He was still bending over the canvas bag when a flood of light suddenly illuminated it and him. He looked up into the full glare of a powerful electric torch, which shone down on him from about the level and direction of the fence he had just quitted. You did not doubt that a man was holding it, perhaps about breast-high ; but it was impossible to identify even the outline of his figure. The suddenness of this intrusion, and the silence maintained by the watcher, unnerved Bredon for a moment. Then he flashed his own torch, which was still in his hand ; and saw, dimly but sufficiently visible above the blazing centre of the light which confronted him, the face of Digger Henderson.

" Hurry up and drop that ; then put your hands up," was the only immediate comment the new-comer could find, as he gazed down at the extraordinary figure that crouched before him. He seemed taken aback ; though whether at the disguise, or at sight of the canvas bag, there was no saying. Bredon dropped the torch into his open pocket ; he could see that there was a quite unmistakable revolver in Henderson's right hand – there was also an unpleasant look on Henderson's face, as if he was too hard pressed now for exchanges of politeness, and was ready to shoot on little provocation. Yet, by some queer psychological trick, fear had as yet found no ingress into Bredon's mind ; his torch dropped and his hands went up as if automatically ; what flooded his consciousness was a mixture of bewilderment and shame. Somehow, he had mismanaged the affair disgracefully. Almost more intolerable than his failure was the wild miscalculation that had inspired it. Why was Henderson alive, and who was dead ? Had he received, and if so how had he received, the note left for Lethaby to find an hour or two before ? Were the two still hand-in-glove ? Or did Henderson intercept all Lethaby's correspondence ? Where had he been all this time ? How had he lain so low, how had he appeared so inopportunely ?

The idea that Lethaby and Henderson were hand-in-glove was immediately put out of court when Henderson found his voice, and began to sum up the situation. It was a long speech, and fluent certainly, though it could hardly be called eloquent if it is the business of eloquence to avoid over-frequent repetition of the same word. " Double-crossing " was the term which seemed to recur most emphatically ; and it was almost the only term which a delicately minded printer could be asked to set up. What emerged from all this rude philippic was that (i) Henderson thought the disguised person before him was Lethaby, (ii) he suspected Lethaby of having sent the note which made the assignation, (iii) he suspected Lethaby, not unnaturally, of having made off with the treasure, (iv) he interpreted the offer of fifty-fifty as an invitation to himself, Henderson, to go shares in that treasure, or some part of it, in return for clearing Lethaby of the suspicions which hung over him, (v) that he had no intention whatever of accepting that offer, (vi) that he proposed, by way of amendment, tying the supposed Lethaby up to a tree and gagging him while he, Henderson, cleared off with everything he could lay hands on. But in Henderson's style, as in that of so many unpractised authors, the adjective was the enemy of the noun ; and to make these comparatively simple points demanded an intolerable deal of verbiage.

Bredon listened, still in a dazed sort of way, so that only the outlines of Henderson's meaning made themselves clear to him, and even these were immediately tucked away into some remote pigeon-hole of consciousness. What was foremost in his mind now was the simple instinct of self-preservation, coupled with a determination, almost equally instinctive, that Henderson should not be allowed to go free. He felt his temper rising, but knew that he must keep it under and act calmly, if he was to have any chance of extricating himself from the mess his unfortunate manœuvres had brought him into. The immediate question was, Should he keep up the pretence of being Lethaby, or should he correct the mistake ? If he claimed his own identity, hostility on the other side might be somewhat disarmed ; yet he could hardly hope, as Bredon, to ingratiate himself with the disappointed treasure-seeker. On the other hand, if he played the part of Lethaby, Henderson might still be daunted by the idea of an imaginary Bredon sallying out from the cottage to dispute the spoils with him. A hundred subsidiary points, of practical importance, flashed through his mind. Had Henderson got a car at his disposal ? And had he any chance, without a car, of getting clear from pursuit in that uninhabited countryside ? Was there any danger that he would think of stealing Bredon's own car from the unlocked garage ? Any hope that Pulteney, or fear that Angela, would try to intercept him if he did so ? Was it really possible to tie a man to a tree when he did not want to be tied to a tree, and your only argument was a revolver which you could hardly continue to point at him while you were working at the knots ? How much allowance was to be made for bluff ; how much for reluctance to kill, reluctance to make a noise ? If he, Bredon, took to his heels suddenly and did his best to get out of that incriminating circle of light, would Henderson really fire, or would he hesitate, and give uncertain pursuit ? If he, Bredon, shouted for help, was anybody likely to hear, and would it mean a spit of fire from the revolver ? How ridiculously uncomfortable it was, keeping your arms lifted for a few minutes even to the height of your shoulders !

The difficulties of tying a man up to a tree while you are covering him with a revolver had, unfortunately, occurred to Henderson ; and he was beginning to discuss them aloud, with pointed references to the more satisfactory results which might be achieved by letting daylight into the body of the unwanted spectator. For a moment, under the influence of these threats, Bredon considered the idea of betraying his own identity. Then he resolutely compressed his lips ; reflecting that Lethaby was no good at dealing with an emergency, and Henderson knew it – was more likely, therefore, to be guilty of a false step if he under-rated the resourcefulness of his victim. How poorly he thought of his late partner, could be inferred from the contemptuous directions he proceeded to give: " On the word Go, you'll march across, slowly, mind, to that fence, and stick your fat head through between

259

the top bar and the second. You'll put your arms over the top bar, and keep them there till I've tied them. And any time I see either hand going to a pocket I'll shoot without asking for explanations. Got that? Now – go ! "

The glare of the torch, the strained position in which he stood, the very urgency of his position, urged Bredon to acquiescence. He could no longer fix his mind clearly on the alternatives which lay before him, of submission or of perilous escape ; he began to feel light-headed, and phrases repeated themselves meaninglessly in his mind, " a fellow-countryman of Knox " recurring at intervals. Like a man half-awake, he moved his left leg forward, to obey his marching orders. His foot had been standing on a patch of clay, made soggy by the late rains ; his shoe, a heavy brogue meant for the golf-links, was caught for a moment and began to drag away from his foot. So loose was it that he had to curl up his toes to prevent it from coming off altogether. The opportunity which this incident offered worked like a charm on him. He was a man whose brain moved slowly at ordinary times, but was liable to accelerate suddenly, out of all proportion, upon the suggestion of the moment. He had seen his chance of getting clear, and acted on the inspiration as if automatically.

If he had been given time to set his thoughts in order, and unfold the full train of his reasoning, he would have pointed out (to Angela, probably) that the human leg is man's best weapon for achieving long-distance results. The arm, to acquire any momentum, must borrow impetus from the body ; and that means a change of attitude which your adversary can see coming, and can dodge. But the leg has its force ready stored up in its own muscles, and the release of that force involves hardly any change of attitude ; none, certainly, which could be noticed by a man who is keeping his eye fixed on your arms, to see that you do not get at your gun. And on the end of either of these two powerful levers, ready to receive the full sweep of its motion, civilised man wears a ready-made weapon ; man attired for country sports wears a very heavy weapon, shod with iron nails. Miles Bredon swayed a little, shuffled a little ; and then his right foot came forward, with the gesture of a man who is kicking mud off his shoes when he has been crossing a ploughed field. But it was not the mud that came off ; it was the shoe.

You cannot miss your direction badly with a straight kick ; it is only the elevation that is uncertain. Bredon took aim at his assailant's face, but kept his shot a little low, conscious that even a blow in the chest, coming apparently from nowhere, would have a disconcerting effect. By a piece of luck he did not deserve, the shoe caught Henderson's left hand, and knocked the torch clean out of it. It was the left shoe, discharged at a venture in the dark as soon as the kicker had changed his stance, which must have found its true objective, as a bleeding cut on Henderson's forehead afterwards testified. The second kick over, Bredon had the good sense to run in his stockinged feet a few yards to the left – away from the river, where the shadows were less deep, and a tussle might have been dangerous. Henderson did not shoot ; either pain had unnerved him, or he realised that he had lost all chance of taking useful aim. Bredon took out his torch from one pocket of the chauffeur's greatcoat, then his revolver from the other. The torch he deliberately held at arm's length, undecided whether to turn it on or let his adversary make the first move. Nothing showed in the darkness

261

except the glow of Henderson's torch, where it had fallen unharmed on the grass.

A minute or two of dead silence followed, in which either man felt as if his breathing must be audible to the other. Then the fallen torch shifted its position, as if it had slipped between Henderson's fingers while he tried to pick it up. It pointed now towards the river ; there was a patch of fantastically brilliant illumination along the grass, and beyond that a faint penumbra which showed a line of bracken fringing the bank of the stream. Just in front of it lay the canvas bag, with the cord attached to it, lying where Bredon had left them. Suddenly, as he waited for the torch to be picked up, a dark figure sprang across the interval of light, bent down, picked up the canvas bag, and started at a run along the path which led back to the cottage. Bredon had understood the manœuvre, just not in time ; hurled himself, just too late, at the intruding figure, reached, just too late, for the stolen booty. He only just pulled up in time to avoid pitching over the bracken curtain into the swirling water beneath. Odd, how easy it was in the darkness to set your foot fatally on the steep slope of the bank, when you had been expecting to find level ground under the bracken !

Henderson had got a clear start ; but he had committed himself to a path on which there was, for a hundred yards or so, no turning aside ; a thick wall of rhododendrons shut him in on the right, as the river did on his left. Forgetting his own fears in the ardour of the chase, Bredon flashed his torch down the path, to see Henderson's figure just disappearing beyond the full reach of its rays. He ran in pursuit, with his torch still alight ; the danger of a Parthian shot from the fugitive's gun seemed less than the danger of making a false step in the dark, and being hurled into the river. As he ran, he forgot, too, his fears for Angela, and woke the echoes of the night with cries for help. It seemed certain that Henderson would make his escape into the open road that ran past the cottage door before any of its inmates had time to question his passage. But he had hardly covered half the distance when a fresh glare of torch-light sprang up, this time in front of him ; and an unmistakable, drawling voice behind it challenged him with, " Stop there, Henderson ; I've got you covered." It was the voice of Vernon Lethaby.

Astonishment, rather than fear, halted the runaway. He had not thought it possible that the chauffeur's mask and cap could be disguising anybody except the man who shared with him the secret of their existence ; he had addressed his curses and threats as if to Lethaby, and as if by Lethaby they had been accepted and defied. How could a new Lethaby be springing up from the opposite direction ? Or was it possible that his pursuer had dodged round the other side of the rhododendron thicket, and was now trying to head him off ? As if with that hope in view, he turned round where he stood, only to see the light behind him still following, then coming to a halt, while the barrel of a revolver just glinted in the light of it. Henderson turned again ; and in that uncertain cross-glare it was impossible for the watchers to see whether he mistook his direction, or deliberately tried a fresh way of escape. At any rate, he fell forward between the bracken-fronds, and a splash showed that he had fallen where the water flowed close in to the path. Bredon, who ran to the spot, got no view of him ; Lethaby, leaning against the trunk of a stunted oak and flashing a light between its branches, saw, for a moment, something dark being tossed up on the crest of the waves

263

which hurried past. As for swimming, the very idea of it was not to be entertained in such a flood ; a sheep was not more helpless in it than a man.

It was already a battered, senseless body that was swept over the greedy falls, rolled over and over in their white surge ; that travelled, face-downwards, past the crevice in the cliff-side where, three days ago, the *cache* of Jacobite finery was brought to light, past the northern promontory, and the toy islet standing out in the middle of the rapids ; past the great slab of rock from the top of which Glendounie churchyard overhangs the river. With fallen branches the mountain burns had at last found strength to carry away, with broken spars washed from the jetty of the sawmill, with hurdles wrenched from the hastily emptied sheep-cotes, that dark body was washed down seawards, as powerless, as unregarding as they. The man who had been mourned for dead on the night of the conflagration had only reappeared for a few crowded, blasphemous minutes, before the flood took what the fire had spared. It was three miles lower down that they found the body, after a night of hopeless search, washed up on a spit of shingle where a tangle of low-growing boughs intercepted it. The clothes, this time, were sufficient to identify the dead man as Henderson ; and in the pocket of the coat was the little canvas bag, whose contents he had found, and lost, and found again, and died to preserve.

As for Bredon, he was supported back to the cottage by Lethaby, almost fainting from the strain of crisis that had followed on the exertion of the last few days. Angela put him sternly to bed, and would not hear of his demanding explanations that night, though Lethaby's excitement, added to the Dutch courage which had fortified him against the expected interview, had made him turn confidential at last. Lethaby promised that his story should be told the next day, and with that Bredon had to be content. Sleep came to him early, but not before one question had answered itself in his exhausted brain. Putting down his hot whisky on a chair by the bed-side, he burst into a sudden shout of laughter, and cried out to his wife, " A fellow-countryman of Knox – ye gods, a fellow-countryman of Knox ! Now, why didn't we think of that earlier ? " But Angela, who thought he was wandering, only turned out the light.

CHAPTER XVIII: ACTUALLY WHAT HAPPENED

" I've been half-meaning to explain the whole business to you for some time," said Lethaby. They were sitting outside the house on the island, where a semicircle of spongy moss and heather, that had perhaps once been a lawn, commanded a prospect of straggling silver birches and azaleas, with the inevitable horizon of rhododendron shrubs and bracken. Lethaby had his feet on a round stone table, curiously inscribed, the relic of former inhabitants; the collapsible-looking chair on which he sat was tilted to its utmost limit; a panama hat drawn well over his eyes shaded him from the sun, that was now glaring down again fiercely – perhaps would serve also to spare his blushes, if he had any capacity left for blushing, in the course of his narrative. Miles and Angela had made a special appointment to come up soon after breakfast and talk over his position unofficially, before the expected crowd of visitors broke loose on them. Miles sat on the grass, apparently intent on catching little spiders; Angela was working (rather unconvincingly) at her embroidery. Lethaby, they felt, had so much to explain that it was common charity to be looking in some other direction.

" Actually," Lethaby went on, " I'd just made up my mind to when the Wauchope came along, and that altered everything. Of course, I know she's a friend of yours, and I'm not going to make any comments.

But you've got to realise that I don't see eye to eye with the old lady much ; which is unfortunate, because I depend on her for most of what I've got to face the world with, and also, I suppose from some odd freak of childhood-memory, I'm rather afraid of her. And, of course, she talks."

" You're sure it's necessary to bring her in ? " asked Angela. She liked Mrs. Wauchope ; she did not approve of Lethaby, and was still faintly angry with him for not having been Henderson the night before, or rather for Henderson not having been him.

" Actually, you may say that she threw the spanner in the works ; but we'll come to that later. The thing all started when I was rather tight one night and was telling Digger all about Prince Charlie's treasure, and how I thought I remembered seeing, when I was quite a kid, a map hanging up somewhere at Dreams which I used to connect with it in my own mind – I suppose I'd been reading *Treasure Island* or some kid's book like that, and localised the story for myself, as one does, don't you know, at that age. Poor Digger seemed to me to be rather impressed with the yarn at the time ; though I've wondered a good deal since whether actually he didn't just think it was a yarn, and only meant to make money out of it by working out an elaborate frame-up, which I'll explain in a minute. All the same, we did pay a visit to Dreams, and Henderson did take a photograph of the map with his pocket-camera. I think you saw that photograph, Mr. Bredon, when you were up at the house the other day."

" Yes ; I was meant to, wasn't I ? Why were you so keen, by the way, that I should see it ? "

" Actually we thought you'd be a bit suspicious about our coming across the lie of the treasure so prompt ; and we thought it would look a little more plausible if you saw we had had something to work on. We didn't think you'd have much difficulty about drawing lines between the letters and seeing where they intersected. But, of course, if we had come up to you and shown you the thing, that again would have looked rather too much like a put-up job. So we just left it about and let you have a look at it for yourself."

" Look here, I don't want to be inquisitorial and all that from the word Go ; but would you mind telling me whether that was the *only* reason you left it lying about for ? "

" I don't think any other crossed my mind. . . . I'm not quite sure what you're getting at."

" Well, put it in this way ; are there any other copies of that photograph in existence, to your knowledge ? "

" No, not to my knowledge. Of course, it's a bit blurred at the edges, and rather suggests the morning after ; but the letters come out all right, except the A, which was under that blot in the film. Surely you spotted that ? "

" Oh, yes, I spotted that all right. But it would have saved me a lot of trouble if I'd felt sure there was no other copy going. However, carry on."

" Well, I think I really looked on the whole thing as rather a spree. I didn't very much think that Charles Edward was the sort of man to leave valuables about, or that the people round here were the sort of people to let them go on lying about for want of a little searching. But we agreed that we'd try the thing out, and if there *was* any treasure where the treasure ought to be, we'd just scoop it out and divvy up, all honest and above-board, with the proprietors. At least, that's what I meant to do, and poor old Digger said the same ; but you couldn't attach any importance to anything he said much. You see, Sir Charles isn't a bad sort of old buffer, though he stung us like hell over the rent, and I wouldn't like to walk away with a hatful of treasure he had first claim on. Don't know why ; but even when you think morality's all rather rot, specially commercial morality, it still gives you a nasty feeling to do a man down when you know him what's called socially."

" But with a stranger," Bredon suggested drily, " it would be different ? Still more with a corporation, an insurance company, for example."

" You take my point exactly. Digger's idea was, for fear there shouldn't happen to be any genuine treasure at the spot indicated, we'd better bring some bogus treasure along with us, ready to be planted out as and where necessary. It would be the simplest thing in the world, he said, to get hold of some company which would underwrite the scheme, and insure us against the loss of the treasure once we'd found it. (He didn't really believe – that was only bluff – that there were mugs who would actually insure us against not finding anything there.) That meant that one or the other of us had to do a bolt. Obviously it had to be Digger, because, of course, it meant disappearing altogether, at least for the time being, and that was easier for him, because he hadn't any origins much. Besides, it looked more plausible somehow, my taking out an insurance policy against him. He said, give him six hours start, and he'd guarantee to show a clean pair of heels to the police any day. He knew something about that, too."

" So I understand," assented Bredon. " What I can't quite make out is how much and how far you trusted him. You talk as if that policy you took out with the Company was only part of a . . . well, a pre-arranged plan to which you and Henderson were both parties. Weren't you genuinely afraid at all that Henderson would walk out on you ? "

" Oh, Lord, yes ; one didn't *trust* Henderson, you know. Actually I was just going to explain about that – we very nearly had a row about him going off with the treasure. He said it would make it much more plausible if he really took the stuff with him when he decamped. I said that was all very well ; but insurance was a tricky business, and I wasn't going to let him take any more valuables in his personal luggage than I could help. We arranged in the end that he should skip without the treasure, and we'd bury it again where both or either of us would be easily able to find it."

" When you talk about the treasure, you mean the bogus treasure ? "

" Yes ; that's the only treasure I've come across in this rotten business. Of course, you'll say a bogus treasure isn't very easy to borrow, when you're as broke as Henderson and I were ; more especially if it's got to date from the middle of the eighteenth century, to come up to specifications. But that, you see, was just my strong suit. My aunt has a house not too far away, a bit north of Perth, which she gives me the use of because she's no sort of use for it herself. And it's chock full of Jacobite relics ; a pretty dud collection, I can tell you, and some of the exhibits are quite too appalling, but it was just what we wanted for a show like this.[1] There's a perfectly genuine legend in the country-side that Charles Edward's treasure consisted of a whole lot of keepsakes which French ladies had given him. So what was to prevent me picking out the most valuable-looking of my assorted horrors down at Moreton, packing them in a saratoga trunk, and letting old Digger bury them, and then grub them

[1] p. 23.

up again ? There was no loss to anybody, and a clear gain at the expense of the insurance company."

" I represent it," said Bredon thoughtfully. " I'm not sure whether you realised that."

" You bet I did, all along. It was at a cocktail-party of Aubrey Wentworth's, I think, that Hermia Jennings came up and told me there was a man who'd been specially asking to have me pointed out to him. Fortunately I happened to be a bit sober at the time ; and I had a good look at you while you weren't looking at me, and found out all about you from somebody ; can't remember who it was. Of course, I quite see your point of view; you're on the side of the Company. But, you see, my morality doesn't run to it ; an insurance company, to me, is fair game. I'm telling you all this because actually the whole thing didn't come off, so you can't very well have the law on me."

" Let's go on with the story," suggested Angela.

" Yes, let's see ; where was I ? Well, the only thing I couldn't produce at Moreton was a Jacobite portmanteau. And yet it wouldn't have looked too good to have the stuff lying about anyhow in damp earth ; besides, it would have been difficult to make the things look mucky enough. As it was, we had a pretty hard time dulling the silver and all that. Anyhow, Henderson said he'd buy something in the nature of a grip to put the stuff in at an old shop he knew somewhere in a back corner of London ; a place where they didn't ask any questions. I can tell you I was pretty annoyed with him when he turned up at Moreton with a great trunk that looked as if it was meant to carry maypoles about in."

" Oh, it was his choice, was it ? " put in Bredon. " That's interesting. When you say he turned up, you mean he had a car of his own ? "

"No, I had to lend him the money to hire one with; and the kind he got was a sort of commercial traveller's affair, which was really something like a young lorry. You see, he said it was very important, if he was to make his get-away later on, that he should be well-known in the district beforehand under an assumed name and character. Then when the hue and cry began, he'd be able to return to this assumed character, and no one would think of suspecting him. Sound argument that, I thought. Actually, he decided to be a man going round from door to door selling tweeds; we bought a beastly great load of those in Glasgow, to make him look more natural. He had a false moustache, and a beast of a little made-up tie[1]; and he called himself Hewison – he could talk quite good Scots, could Digger, in spite of that filthy Canadian accent of his. So there he was, you see, trading these tweeds to anybody in the district who was fool enough to buy them, for a fortnight or so before we actually started work at the island. He'd become quite a local figure, he told me."

Angela could not resist asking, "Mr. Lethaby, why on earth did you let him buy that tartan rug?"

For the first time in their interview, Lethaby seemed a trifle taken aback. "I say," he said, in an aggrieved tone, "you seem to have been finding out things all right. As a matter of fact, I told him to buy that horrible thing, because I thought it would make people remember him. He wanted to be remembered, you see."

"It certainly wasn't easy to forget," admitted Angela. She felt she was being unpleasant, and tried a more conversational tone: "I suppose the car with the tweeds in it was useful for bringing the treasure up here?"

[1] p. 144.

" Later on, yes. We didn't fetch the things from Moreton till a week or so before we moved in, because, of course, there was no point in having them away from their base longer than was necessary. Though actually nobody lives in the house at Moreton when I'm not there,[1] so there wasn't any danger of the exhibits being missed, you see. The real bother was getting them across to the island, especially a thing the size of that old trunk of Henderson's. I know a good many fellows in Fleet Street, and some of the papers had taken up the story ; so it was a little difficult for me to move without attracting the attention of the camera-men. And that trunk stuck out a mile."

" All the same," Bredon pointed out, " it was a mistake to use the boat. Or rather, you ought to have been more careful about mooring it when you took it back ; you should have given it plenty of rope. That was the first thing which made me suspicious that you hadn't been playing the game."[2]

" I love that phrase, don't you, *playing the game* ? The pill of morality coated with sporting metaphor, so that the Englishman can take it without difficulty. It was no great fun, I can assure you, that business with the boat. You see, Henderson let on at the last moment that he couldn't swim – said he couldn't, anyhow. So I had to do all the bathing, and it's dashed chilly work at dead of night, I can tell you."

" My husband doesn't need——" began Angela.

" He doesn't need any back-chat," Miles put in hastily. " We've got Leyland and Sir Charles and the whole country-side turning up by half-past eleven. So let's get through with this, if you don't mind. It was the day you came over to see the island, wasn't it, that you came back here, and shipped your cargo across

[1] p. 135.   [2] p. 66.

from that landing-place close to the Glendounie road ? "

" Yes – how did you know that, by the way ? Well, it doesn't matter ; that's what we did. I had to swim across, taking yards of string with me, and with that I pulled a rope over, and tied it to the boat. We'd brought the boat round to that side of the island in the afternoon ; bit risky, but nobody was likely to notice. I tied a rope to each end of the boat, turning it into a sort of ferry ; Digger pulled her across empty, and loaded up, and then I pulled her across with the cargo on board. Digger had made a shallow pit in the bracken close by – you should go and look at it, it's awfully well done – and we stowed the stage properties away there, ready for use. Then I had to row the confounded boat back to its mooring-place – and all the time I'd nothing on but a wet bathing-dress. It's different on the Lido, of course."

" Why the rope-trick, exactly ? " asked Bredon. " Wouldn't it have been just as simple for you to row the boat, going and coming ? "

" Just what I said. But Digger, you know, was beastly pernickety about some things ; said the plash of oars was a noise that could be heard miles off, and the trunk was so big it would either interfere with the rowing or else be in danger of falling overboard, and all that."

" Oh, that was his idea, too, was it ? And he just waited and cooled his heels on the further bank while you swam across. Did he seem impatient at all ? "

" Not a bit. In fact, when I'd got the boat tied up my side, he wasn't ready for me ; and when he answered my call, he still had to go and fetch the trunk from where we'd left it. No, there was no hurry about

274

Digger. However, we'd all the time there was, and apart from the chilliness of bathing at that hour, the whole thing wasn't bad fun."

" And you had all the stuff packed in the trunk? I suppose there wouldn't be any danger of anything dropping out? "

" Good Lord, was it *you* found that snuff-box? But . . . why, then it was you sent me that message last night? I thought it came from Digger. You meant me to, of course. I like your idea of playing the game. If you found that snuff-box over on the further bank there, it must have dropped out while we were loading the boat up. *How*, God knows, because it was locked all right, and I should have thought it was pretty snuff-box-proof."

" We found a sock-suspender of yours, too," Angela explained. " We've got it down at the cottage."

" Thank you, Mrs. Bredon; I'm glad it fell into good hands. . . . Well, what else is there you want to know? You saw me arrive, of course; that was with Digger dressed up as the chauffeur. Then, when you'd had a good look at me, I swam across by the same old route, and Digger picked me up on the Glendounie road. I took over the face-fittings, and we drove back again; you'll have guessed all that. The next few days, or rather nights mostly, there was the hell of a lot to do; lugging that beastly great trunk up to the house, and then planting it out where it would look natural."

" Did you carry it all the way? " asked Bredon. " Or did the boat come in useful again? "

" No, we were too scared of you to use the boat then."

" But it wasn't necessary, surely, to keep all the exhibits in the trunk all the time? You could have

275

lightened your journeys a lot by taking them separately."

" Yes, I know, Henderson pointed that out. But actually I didn't very much like the idea, because, you see, I felt happier about the things when they were safely locked up in the trunk – I always kept the key on me. Henderson wasn't really a frightfully comfortable person to share an island with. He never seemed to go to bed,[1] whereas this place always makes me feel dropping with sleep by about ten o'clock. I couldn't even be sure that he wasn't doping my whisky ; I'm quite certain he did, that last night. Anyhow, we hauled the trunk up, and left it in that sort of woodshed place there is close to the garage ; we arranged the wood so as to hide it. Well, so far everything seemed to be going all right, and we weren't in any hurry. We'd got the island for a month, and we thought the longer we took over it the more plausible it would look. That's where Aunt Cornelia butted in and, as I say, spoilt everything. I got a letter from her, let's see, when was it ? On the Tuesday – a letter in which she asked herself to stay the night at Moreton on her way North. It wasn't possible to invent an excuse, because she only wanted a bed, and she knew the people at the lodge could look after her. But, you see, that put the lid on the whole affair – or rather, it made us speed up all our plans. Because those Jacobite relics are the apple of Aunt Cornelia's eye, and she was quite certain to go nosing round and seeing they were all present and correct. So the only thing to do was to find the treasure earlier than we meant to, on the Wednesday ; and to stage the disappearance of it on the Thursday, combining that, of course, with the reappearance of the relics at Moreton. By good luck, we'd got all our plans

[1] p. 109.

worked out, so it didn't seem as if anything could go wrong, though it didn't leave us much time. Actually I wanted to stage the finding of the treasure on the Tuesday, but Digger wouldn't hear of that."

" Oh ! Why not ? " asked Bredon.

" Said there wouldn't be time to dig a proper hole on the cliff-side there, *and* bury the stuff, *and* dig it up again. So in the end we arranged that the finding should be on Wednesday."

" And telephoned to Lady Hermia asking her to bring me round ? "

" Looks like it, doesn't it ? Anyhow, there you were ; so you know that part of the story already."

" You'd put it there the night before, Tuesday night ? "

" Wednesday morning, actually, at some ungodly hour. Digger said we might be watched if we did it too early ; so I went to bed, and he woke me in the small hours. As I say, I'm not certain he hadn't given me a bit of dope that night ; I know I had a frightful mouth when I woke up. And it was some job, I can tell you, lowering that beastly trunk over the edge of the cliff, with just the two of us ; felt more of a weight than ever. But we got it done, and Digger stowed it away nicely. So it was all ready for you next day. As I say, I left the map lying about on the table, feeling pretty certain that you'd see the point of it."

" Yes . . . why was it under a book, by the way ? "

" Under a book ? That must have been an accident ; I left it lying right on the surface. Rum, that. Still, it did the trick all right. The next thing was, we'd got to get clear with the stuff before the confounded expert came and had a look at it. He'd have seen there wasn't much value in it ; he might even have recognised some of the pieces as coming from Moreton.

So I arranged for him to come round bright and early, and for Henderson to make his getaway with the stuff brighter and earlier. It's all a bit complicated, I'm afraid, this part. Tell me if you're not following me, won't you? We were playing the comic chauffeur lead, of course. Henderson was to wear the mask and fittings, and drive me to the station; you were meant to think that he was still on the island. In fact, I'd written a letter asking you to keep an eye on him while I was away. I'd have left it at the cottage on my way to the station; but as it proved, the situation never arose, so the letter was destroyed. I suggested you might give Henderson a game of golf, or something. Then, of course, you'd have gone up to the house, and found no Henderson, and no treasure."

" Yes, I see. You were taking the stuff away in the car with you, of course. But wouldn't that have looked rather transparent? "

" Oh, but it was all very carefully thought out. We were to drive to the station, and each of us had return tickets in readiness. I was to go on board the train at Inverness, and Digger would drive the car, disguised, of course, as far as Aviemore.[1] The advantage of this line is, you can race it in a car pretty easily. At Aviemore, having removed the disguise and stowed it under the seat of the car, he was to board the train, with a large suitcase labelled J. HENDERSON in prominent letters, and was to attract all the attention he could.[2] Meanwhile, I was to slip out of the train, leaving my luggage in the carriage, put on the whiskers, and drive the car on as far as Blair Atholl. At Blair Atholl we were to change places again, in the reverse way; I was to come into the station just the same time as the train did, with no hat on and all that, and walk into my carriage again as if I'd been taking exercise on the platform. Digger meanwhile would drive the short distance to Pitlochry, which is the station for Moreton ; and there he'd drive up and meet me in proper style, touching his hat and all the rest of it. The bogus chauffeur was to make his presence felt – which wasn't difficult anyhow – at various stages on the journey ; you see the idea ? "

" Well, it doesn't seem to make Henderson's getaway much easier."

" Not at the time, no ; his luggage was labelled to London, but probably the police would tumble to it he had got out at Blair Atholl. Only, you see, whatever happened, it would be impossible to connect him with the bogus chauffeur. Because the chauffeur could be proved to have made the journey from Inverness to Pitlochry by car, whereas Henderson would be known to have travelled at least one stage of the journey by train."

" I see. Yes, it was certainly ingenious. And was all this his idea, or yours ? "

" Mine, every bit of it. Actually Digger didn't seem to bother much about how he was going to clear out ; he just said he would manage it somehow, and it wasn't really very difficult to disappear if you were accustomed to travelling and to the ways of ocean-going liners. The general idea was that when he left Moreton he should make for Glasgow by the west coast line ; it's not far. As for his share in the insurance money, I was to keep it until it was safe for him to get in touch with me."

" Yes, it all sounds a bit sketchy from his point of view. Well, you were all keyed up, I understand, on the Wednesday evening, ready to carry out this plan of yours. And then you went to bed, feeling rather sleepy, and probably doped ; you went off to sleep and didn't wake till I came in shouting Fire ; is that all right ? "

" Actually I'm not quite sure. You know how it is when you're absolutely dropping with sleep – you can't quite be sure whether you woke up for a moment or two during the night, or whether you just dreamt it. I don't know what I should say in a court of law, but my impression is that I did wake up during the night, and saw old Digger just peeping in at my door, the kind of way one does to find out whether a kid's asleep. Only I must have dropped off again at once, so I can't really swear to it. But I suppose that was why I thought about Henderson immediately when I woke, and was all ready to believe that something dreadful had happened to him."

" I suppose you must have thought it was Henderson who had been burnt in the garage – at first ; we all did. I don't know if you'll think it a fair question, but I've been wondering a good deal whether you've been going on in that belief all the time, till you saw Henderson yesterday by the river ? "

" What else was I to think ? But that's looking ahead rather. At the time, anyhow, it seemed quite clear to me what had happened. Henderson had put dope in my drink, and had been meaning to bolt with the stuff in the night ; but he'd braced himself a trifle too much, and like a silly ass took the oil-lamp with him when he went to get the car out. Then he'd dropped it, and the whole show had caught fire. How the door got locked I couldn't imagine ; I can't imagine now, but of course it looks now as if Henderson had done it. And that, I suppose, looks as if Henderson had had a grudge against somebody – God knows who or why – and had done him in in that rather elaborate way. At the time I thought, as I told you, that the door must have slammed and shifted the lock a bit in doing so ; which it might, I suppose, if it was half-turned. But if you ask me what business any living soul can have had in the garage that night, except, of course, Henderson, I simply can't imagine ; can you ? "

" No ; as you say, it's impossible to see. . . . Had the car been left out the evening before ? Because if not, of course——"

" Actually I'd been into the garage before I went to bed, to see that our arrangements were all right, and I left her in there. So it must have been Henderson, I imagine, who took her out. Just as well he did ; because I jolly well needed her the next day. There was no time to make up any elaborate plans ; I simply shoved away that confounded Jacobite junk in the tool-box or wherever I could,[1] and made tracks for Moreton. I was in a stew, too, about that snuff-box, because it's just the sort of thing Aunt Cornelia might have missed. That was a pretty lousy drive, I can tell you ; I kept on dropping asleep at the wheel and waking up with a start. But I got away with it at the time ; I should certainly have heard of it by now if Aunt Cornelia had missed anything. These last few days haven't been much fun either ; but, you see, I had to stick on here, because it would have created the devil of a lot of suspicion if I had cleared out, when everybody was thinking I'd done poor old Digger in."

" I suppose that *was* the only reason ? " Bredon asked. " I had just been toying with the idea that you might still have been expecting to find the real treasure somewhere. What did you suppose that note meant, last night, when it talked about going fifty-fifty ? "

[1] p. 141.

" Assuming the note was genuine at all, which I wasn't sure of, it seemed to mean that Henderson had been trying out some other plan on his own ; but that it hadn't worked, and he wanted to come back to our old plan of fleecing the Indescribable, on a fifty-fifty basis. The idea that Digger Henderson had got on to a good thing himself, and was offering to share it with *me*, didn't so much as cross my mind. You didn't know him, or you'd understand. Do you think he was hanging round here the whole time, by the way ? I wish I'd had a few minutes' chat with him, before he went over into the river like that. Of course, he let me down badly ; but I'd like to have got things straightened out with him. I wish you'd tell me, Mr. Bredon, what you really think of it all. You must see a lot that I don't see."

Bredon consulted his wrist-watch. " It's time I was back at the cottage," he said. " I've got a party of interested people looking in in about ten minutes' time ; I shall want to tell them all you've just been telling me, if I may, and then I suppose I'll have to try and figure out what Henderson was at all the time. If you would sooner hear that now, by all means come down and meet these people ; if not, you could look in this evening."

" What sort of people actually ? "

" Well, there's a policeman who's a friend of mine – served with him in the War ; he's just come up to these parts because he was officially interested in Henderson's movements. And then there's Sir Charles, of course."

" I've always found policemen rather easy to get on with, considering the trying circumstances in which one usually meets them. But Sir Charles is a crashing old bore . . . anybody else ? "

" Mrs. Wauchope said she might be coming in."

" That settles it. I could listen to anybody else discussing my conduct, but not Aunt Cornelia. She's so dynamic ; especially where furniture is concerned. But I'd be very glad to talk it over this evening, if I might. You're sure there wasn't anything else you wanted to ask ? I haven't felt so candid for months. Oh, by the way, Mrs. Bredon, there's one more problem to be cleared up – that plant wasn't samphire, after all. I found a book here about wild flowers, so I went down and had another look at the thing."

" That was awfully good of you. Mr. Pulteney said he'd seen you wandering about with a ladder ; I'm sorry you should have put yourself to all that trouble."

" A man doesn't get much privacy here. Yes, I did take a ladder, because, to tell the truth, I rather funk climbing down rocks by myself – you remember that stiff bit before you get to the steps. And there's such a crowd of ladders about, I thought I'd save myself the nervous strain. I'll bring down the book this evening. and show you the flower I think it is."

THE SUNSHINE with which the day had started was to
be short-lived after all ; a bank of majestic clouds had
intercepted it, and as Miles and Angela made their way
back to the cottage the island recovered its air of
secrecy and gloom. The curse, it seemed, had not been
lifted altogether now that Henderson had paid the
penalty for violating these sanctities ; you still felt
that every overgrown path might conceal the recent
passage of a hostile presence, that stunted oak and
towering larch were brooding over a mystery which
remained unsolved. The Dounie, which had fallen
several feet since last night, was chuckling to himself as
he sprawled over the boulders near the bridge, as if he
were conscious of having fulfilled his duty of guardian-
ship. The smoke from the chimney of the cottage
lingered in the air, taking on, to Angela's puzzled fancy,
the appearance of a question-mark.

" Was he telling the truth this time, Miles ? " she
asked.

" Almost certainly. For one thing, I mixed up my
questions a good deal, and he wasn't confused by it.
You see, when you're doing this horrible cross-examina-
tion business, anybody can stick to a lie as long as you
go on asking the question that naturally comes next.
But if you dodge about, and suddenly ask the next
question but five, it rattles him, and he gets confused

with his story ; or, anyhow, hesitates. Lethaby didn't ; which makes me think he was speaking the truth. And altogether, this time, he didn't seem to me to be choosing his words in the careful way a liar usually does. Indeed, he said one thing which he almost certainly wouldn't have said, if he had known more about the whole story than he pretended to."

" What was that ? "

" I've forgotten ; it'll come back to me. But what really convinced me he wasn't lying is that all he said fitted in with the true story of what happened, as I've managed to work it out ; and that couldn't be just guessing, because he can't possibly know the *whole* story. So I think we pass Lethaby."

" Why didn't you ask him about the key of the garage ? "

" Curiously, I don't think he knows anything about it. And I wanted to avoid the manners of a prosecuting counsel as much as possible. Angela, do you mind not talking to me for about two minutes, till we get to the cottage ? Because I really believe I *have* got the whole thing taped now ; only I want to go over the heads of it and make sure . . . Mrs. Wauchope always disconcerts me."

Leyland met them at the door of the cottage, the first of their guests to arrive. Bredon asked him whether he had identified the corpse satisfactorily.

" Oh, Lord, yes," he said, " no difficulty about that. Not that his face was particularly recognisable, poor devil, but he was tattooed, and we had a record of his markings ; he belonged to that roving world in which you do get tattooed, for fear of accidents like this. I can tell you it's a weight off my mind ; because we'd piled up a pretty heavy list of charges against this Henderson, and there'd have been a lot more work to

285

do before we proved 'em. I never fancied the idea of his being the dead man in the garage ; seemed too much of an accident that there should be such a total absence of traces ; didn't it strike you that way ? "

" No, as you say, that didn't look right from the start. Now, look here, Leyland, have you got anything on young Lethaby ? Because I've just heard his story, and I'll have to repeat it if I'm going to make this business clear to everybody concerned. According to his story, he's a criminal in intention all right – not a murderer, though – but was saved by a series of accidents from putting himself within the reach of the law. But if my telling it is going to land him in any unexpected kind of trouble——"

" No, I don't think there's any need to worry about that. Of course, when the garage business looked as if he might have murdered Henderson, we had our eye on him. But if there was murder done, it's Henderson that will get the credit of it now. We're only too ready to let the dead bury one another, at the Yard."

Mrs. Wauchope arrived breathless with excitement over the previous night's adventure, stories of which, presumably circulated by the McBraynes, were now floating all over the countryside. " My dear," she said to Angela, " it's the most marvellous thing I ever heard of ! And how nice for you both to reflect that in future gangsters and people of that kind will always have to say *Feet up*, and make people stand on their heads, don't you know, before they feel safe. I shall never have an argument with you, Mr. Bredon, unless you're in dressing-slippers. And now, do for goodness' sake clear my poor head about what's been happening. For, though I knew Vernon was too much of a fool, as I told you, to bring off a murder successfully, I still don't understand in the least who the poor man was who was incinerated in the garage that night; nor why it wasn't Vernon, if it comes to that. It seems to me quite unthinkable that a man should be staying in the same house as Vernon and want to murder anybody else. Oh, we're waiting for somebody, are we? Sir Charles, to be sure; these business men never can manage to keep an appointment punctually. Oh, there you are, Sir Charles! Yes, we've been waiting ages. Now, Mr. Bredon, let's hear what my nephew has to say for himself first of all; and then you shall put the pieces together. I shall be most disappointed if you can't."

The recital of the disclosures recorded in the last chapter was received, as will be imagined, with considerable *empressement* by its new audience; Mrs. Wauchope's "Good gracious!" and Sir Charles' "Well, what next?" registering an almost equal number of occurrences. It was some time before Leyland could persuade both of them that it was impossible for the police to prosecute for a crime which had been contemplated but never committed. When they were at last satisfied – Angela by this time was fairly dancing with impatience – Bredon accepted the invitation to reconstruct the full story, as he saw it.

"The important thing to realise first," he said, "is, I suppose, that Henderson did genuinely believe in the existence of a hidden treasure on the Isle of Erran. Even when Lethaby was taking the whole thing as rather a joke, even when Lethaby and he were conspiring to plant out a bogus treasure on that ledge in the cliff, Henderson was quite convinced that he was out after a genuine *cache*. Further, he was convinced that the proper directions for finding it were preserved on an old map, or rather a very rough chart, which hangs,

Sir Charles, in your muniment room at Dreams. I expect you will recognise it from this very rough sketch I made of it from memory. I don't at all know what its date is or is supposed to be ; but Henderson clearly thought that it was made by somebody who had good information about the lie of the treasure, and that the markings on it would prove to be a sufficient guide. He went over to Dreams with Lethaby, under the pretence of talking over terms, and secured, with a pocket camera, a photograph of the document which he regarded as so important.

" It was his intention to steal the treasure ; he had no liking for the idea of going shares with you, Sir Charles, or with the Crown, or with Lethaby for that matter. But Lethaby was useful to him, if only as a dupe. The best screen (he must have said to himself) under which you can find and steal a real treasure is to hide, near the same spot, a sham treasure, and then pretend you have found it. Whether the imposition is detected or not does not matter, because by that time you are well away with your real treasure, and have left your confederate to hold the baby."

" The origin of that phrase——" began Mr. Pulteney.

" My dear," said Mrs. Wauchope to Angela severely, " do you know him well enough to tell him to shut up ? "

" To face the music, then," suggested Bredon, smiling. " Anyhow, that is the general lay-out of the scene, you must understand. Lethaby is out to look for a treasure which probably won't be there ; if it isn't, he will turn a dishonest penny by pretending there was a treasure there, and pretending to the insuring company that Henderson has stolen it. He thinks that this is Henderson's design too. But, as a matter of fact, Henderson's design is something quite different ; to get hold of a real treasure for his own advantage, while he uses the sham treasure to dupe, not so much the world in general as Lethaby himself. All the silly ass I have made of myself, as you will see, in trying to follow up this business has been due to an absurd miscalculation ; I thought all the time that Henderson and Lethaby were working *together* ; it was only quite at the end I began to see that Henderson was double-crossing his partner. We will discuss the origin of that phrase afterwards if you like, Pulteney ; for the moment you must allow me to talk of people double-crossing one another without protest.

" I ought to have tumbled to it the moment I set eyes on that chart, or rather the photograph of it. It was lying on the table when I went over to the island with Lady Hermia, the afternoon when the bogus treasure was brought to light. Obviously Lady Hermia had arranged to bring me over there at that precise moment. And the fact that at that precise moment this important document was left lying about on the table suggested at once that I was meant to see it. What was curious was that it was half tucked away, to be more accurate, about three-quarters tucked away, under a book. The book, I now see, was put there by Henderson to hide it from me. It was Lethaby, not Henderson, who wanted me to see it ; Henderson would have preferred that I shouldn't. But I supposed, like an ass, that Henderson and Lethaby together were concerned in leaving it about for my inspection – that both of them, therefore, were trying to lead me up the garden. Lead me up the garden, Pulteney.

" No doubt, in order to create the impression that their find was a genuine one, it was a good thing from their point of view to make me think it had been found at the precise spot indicated on the chart. Indeed,

that was all that was in Lethaby's mind, so he tells
me – and I'm sure he is telling the truth. But I have
a tiresome habit of trying to be too clever ; and, as
you know, Angela, I sweated blood over that chart
trying to find out what was the catch about it. I
found it out all right, but drew, like a fool, the wrong
inferences from it.

" There is the chart, or rather a rough copy of it,
in front of you. The original is almost as rough, as
Sir Charles has probably noticed. The island is represented as if it were nearly a complete oval, though with
the ends flattened a bit ; it takes no account of the
eastward bulge towards the north, or of the westward
bulge towards the south. There is a letter E at the
side, which is simply meant to represent a point of the
compass ; the photograph has been taken, or printed,
in such a way that the W on the other side should not
show ; nor the N and S, which were presumably also
present. There are three additional letters, B, C, and
D, which are obviously meant for guide-posts. There
is also a blot, which looks in the photograph as if it
had been made when the thing was developed ; even
my wife realised at once that the blot is meant to
conceal a fourth letter, an A.

" Now, assuming, as I assumed, that this document
was meant to mislead, I felt quite certain that the blot
over the A must have been introduced, not by accident,
but by design. Nobody could have been such a fool
as to think that a stranger, coming across the chart,
would fail to infer the presence of the letter A. He
might, for a time, be confused by the E, but sooner
or later he would tumble to it that an A had been there,
and that the intersection of the two lines A C and B D
was the operative point – the point at which the
treasure was supposed to lie. (As you will all see, the

290

bogus treasure was found at the exact point of intersection between the two lines, as they are given on this
chart.) No, the man who was misleading me could
not be trying to conceal from me the fact that an A
was there, or the reason for its being there. He must
have wanted, somehow, to conceal from me the shape
of the letter A. Now why?

" I'm not going to wait for you to guess, because to
tell the truth I took a pretty long time over it myself,
even when I'd got so far. But you would all reflect,
if I gave you time, that the shapes of the various
letters in the alphabet are of varying usefulness for the
man who wants to fake a document *by turning it upside
down*. The word OHO, for example, can be read
either way up. But there are a good many letters
which give themselves away when you turn the paper
upside down, unless at the same time you read it as
seen in the looking-glass, or by holding it against the
light. Actually (as Lethaby would say) these are the
letters B, C, D, E, and K – I think that's all. If you
write the word BED, and then hold it upside down in
front of a looking-glass, you will read in the looking-
glass the word BED. But if you try the same thing
on with the word BAD, you will be disappointed. The
A, of course, shows upside down.

" Inference – that the person who was trying to
mislead me was trying to make me read the document
upside down and back ways round. He had obliterated
the A, which would have given the show away. He
had left the B, C, and D, which were all right. He had
left the letter E, which was all right, but had deliberately cut out the other points of the compass, which
would have gone wrong. The exhibit in front of me
being a photograph, it was easy to see how all that
could be done. You had only to put the film upside

down and back ways round in the printing frame, and it would come out as you wanted it, only a trifle blurred. But the photograph I saw *was* a trifle blurred ; I forgot to mention that.[1]

" Well, it was a bore not having a looking-glass to work with – you had gone to bed at the time, Angela[2] – but there wasn't much difficulty about it. Evidently the original map, before photography had faked it, represented the operative point as a point still on the east side of the island, but towards the southern, not the northern end. A little south of the place where the island boat is moored – and incidentally the exact point at which you, Pulteney, saw the island boat moored on that same night. Yes, I read the puzzle all right, and I took the obvious precautions.[3] But I stuck to it in my head that this was a dodge by which Henderson and Lethaby were deceiving me ; I never tumbled to it that it was a dodge by which Henderson was deceiving Lethaby. I didn't realise – not that that made much difference – that the treasure I had seen unearthed that afternoon was only a collection of curios from a museum. I'm not much good at these things, I'm afraid, Mrs. Wauchope. I assumed that the real treasure had been found at the point where the treasure was really buried ; that Henderson and Lethaby had selected those bits of it which were least saleable or least portable, and had reburied them in a faked hiding-place, so as to dig them up and declare them, while they meant to remove the more saleable and more portable bits of it darkly at dead of night, not declaring them at all.

" I hadn't much time to think the thing out, because events began to break loose ; there was the fire, and the corpse found in the locked garage. I may as well

[1] p. 92.   [2] p. 110.   [3] p. 113.

go back to Henderson now, and explain what he was up to that night. He had found the treasure where the map, the real map, said it was ; he had dug it up at night and told Lethaby nothing about it. (He used to use a lantern with a candle in it, partly, no doubt, because it showed up less, but partly, I think, so that Lethaby shouldn't notice what a lot of juice was being used up, as it would have been if he'd taken one of the electric torches with him.)[1] At the last moment, he had to hurry over his preparations, because your arrival at Moreton, Mrs. Wauchope, disconcerted his plans even worse than Lethaby's. But he had found the treasure, and he had got everything ready for escaping with it from the island, by boat, of course, at a time when everybody else for miles round would be busy putting out the garage fire. He would have taken his cargo to the further side of the river, and there picked it up, as soon as it was safe to do so, in the commercial car in which he used to sell his tweeds. That must be about the place somewhere ; the police, I suppose, will find it before long. He had drugged his partner, and a cautious look into his bedroom seemed to show that the drug had taken its effect. Nothing remained, except to carry out his arrangements in the garage. He went out there with the oil lamp in his hand ; he had deliberately poured away what little of the whisky he could not personally accommodate, to give the impression afterwards that he had been blind drunk when he went out on this lamp-lit expedition. It would probably be assumed, afterwards, that his intention had been to escape with the bogus treasure while his partner was asleep. But what men would think of this would not matter ; for by that time they would believe that he was dead – the victim

[1] pp. 91, 158.

of a fatal accident when he upset the oil lamp. Nobody would know that the real treasure had ever existed ; as for the bogus treasure, Lethaby would have to deal with it as best he could – certainly there would be no insurance money, for it was Henderson's honesty that was insured, not his life."

Bredon made a slight pause ; and Sir Charles Airdrie, who for some time past had been shifting nervously in his chair as if determined to put a question, now found the opportunity to enunciate it. " You'll excuse me, Mr. Bredon – your account of the matter is admirably lucid, if I may say so, but don't you think it would help us to follow the course of things if you were to tell us, here and now, who the dead man was who was found burned in the garage ? "

" That ? Oh, certainly ; only, of course, I don't really *know* he was, I can only guess. But I'm very much afraid his name was Angus McAlister."

CHAPTER XX: DOUBLE CROSS-PURPOSES

THE EFFECT of this announcement on Bredon's audience was curious to watch. Mrs. Wauchope, Mr. Pulteney and Leyland appeared simply bewildered. Angela knitted her brows ; you could see that she had met the name lately but could not remember where. Sir Charles' jaw dropped, and he sputtered helplessly in attempting comment. " But, man – but, Mr. Bredon ; what's that you're saying ? "[1]

" It's not pleasant, I'm afraid, at all ; but then Henderson was not a pleasant person. Lethaby said just now, Angela, if you remember, that he couldn't imagine what business any living soul could have had in the garage at that time of night.[2] He wouldn't have used those words, if he'd been any party to what happened ; they were too near the truth. There *was* no living soul in the garage that night, except Henderson. What he put there and left there was the cast-off trappings of a soul which had once lived ; a dead body which he had borrowed for the purpose. We ought to have known that all along, in spite of the buttons and the shoes, which it was easy to leave there. The body was too absolutely burnt out, if you see what I mean, to have been the body of a living man. Some accident, surely, even in that conflagration, would have spared a little besides the bones ; but there was

[1] p. 14. [2] p. 291.

295

nothing. As a matter of fact, I never realised this, till something the minister said put me wise to it. He said he was going to bury Henderson in his cemetery because if a man had a Scottish name it was best to assume that he was a Presbyterian – a fellow-country-man, he said, of Knox. That phrase rang a bell some-where at the back of my consciousness, but carried no message at the time. It was only when I was dropping off to sleep that night that the significance of it occurred to me. *Burke is the butcher, Hare's the thief* – isn't that how the lines run ? – *Knox is the boy that buys the beef.* Henderson was a fellow-countryman of that Edinburgh surgeon who won such an ill name for himself, in the days when you got resurrection-men to dig up bodies in churchyards for the dissecting-room.

" Henderson had noticed, from the first, the con-venient proximity of a graveyard to the scene of action. While he was on his rounds with the tweeds, he spent a long night digging up, with that uncanny skill of his, the body of a man who, on the testimony of the head-stone, was lately dead – he would have looked a fool if it had been a one-legged man. His first care was to light a fire, with plenty of petrol, on a deserted and sheltered part of the hillside ; he incinerated the remains, and had carried them off, hidden under his tweeds, before McBrayne or the minister had reached the spot.[1] He took the charred skeleton with him in the car, and buried it in the light sand by the river further along the Dreams road – just opposite the southern end of the island. To that spot he returned the next night with Lethaby, and with the bogus treasure that was contained in a long, unmanageable trunk of his own choosing.

" It was Henderson, you remember, Angela, who got

[1] pp. 61, 241.

hold of the trunk ; he chose its shape for a particular purpose he had in view. It was Henderson who said he couldn't swim, and sent Lethaby over to the island ; it was Henderson who insisted that the boat should be passed from side to side by a tow-rope, not simply rowed, so that he might have an excuse for remaining as long as possible on the mainland while Lethaby was on the island, out of sight. Lethaby stripped for his swim ; and, as he told us, the key of the trunk was kept in one of his pockets.[1] Henderson took it out, emptied the trunk of its contents, dug up the skeleton from the sand in which he had hidden it close by, and put that in the trunk instead. He had only just time to do this, and, indeed, kept Lethaby waiting a little[2] ; he had more time at his disposal for re-burying the bogus treasure in the same place where the skeleton had been. Yet, through haste, he just failed to get that snuff-box hidden away out of sight, and my wife found it there yesterday.

" So, after all, what Patterson said was true – that he saw a coffin being ferried across the river by moonlight. And, for that matter, what Habington said was true – that when the treasure was found the dead wouldn't rest easy in Glendounie churchyard. I can't say how Henderson managed to convey the bogus treasure, bit by bit, over to the island ; I suppose he did it by boat, during one of those sleepless nights after they had come to live on the island. All that remained was to get it back in the trunk again, and the skeleton out. He must have managed that on the night before the bogus treasure was brought to light ; Lethaby, certainly, has the impression that on that night, too, he was drugged. The skeleton remained under a pile of wood in the wood-shed, ready to be carried across

[1] p. 286.   [2] p. 284.

into the garage on the night of the fire and left there –
sure proof to the world that Henderson had met with
a fatal accident through carelessness with a lamp.

" He arranged all that ; leaving the garage door unlocked, so as to exclude the suspicion of foul play – it
was to be understood by the public that Henderson
fell in a drunken stupor, from which he did not awake
in time to save himself from the flames. He started a
fire with petrol, in the immediate neighbourhood of
the skeleton ; he threw the lamp down on the floor,
and hastened from the doomed building ; hastened to
the spot where he had left the island boat moored,
with the real treasure ready piled on board. Only,
of course, when he reached it, the treasure was not
there."

" Not there ! " exclaimed Sir Charles. " Who'd
taken it, then ? "

" Oh, that was me. As soon as I'd read the secret
of the chart, I had to go and relieve Pulteney, who was
keeping a look-out on the island boat. He drew my
attention to the fact that it had been moved, and I
saw that it had been moved to the spot where the real
treasure lay. So, when he'd gone, I rowed over there
in our boat, and found the island boat all cluttered up
with linen bags.[1] There was a small one, containing
unset precious stones ; the others were obviously gold.
They looked heavy to move, and I didn't want to make
a noise. So I rowed back in the island boat, leaving
ours, which is just the same pattern, in exchange.[2]
When I got to this bank, I tied the end of a line of
strong cord to the treasure (I'd brought one with me
in case of need), and sank it, making the other end of
the cord fast to the bank. Then it occurred to me it
would be a good thing to have the jewel-bag on the

[1] p. 112.   [2] p. 113.

end of a separate cord, in case one wanted to fish it up. That meant diving in, which is why my hair was wet, Angela."[1]

" But, you unspeakable cad, I asked you, the day after, point-blank whether you knew where the treasure was ; and you said you thought either Lethaby or Henderson had taken it away ! "

" Pardon me, I was careful to point out that these doubts of mine referred to the valuables which had been dug up in the leather trunk that afternoon.[2] I said nothing about any other treasure. I have been very correct all through ; for instance, I didn't telegraph to Sholto when the false treasure was found – he complained afterwards of the omission ; but I telegraphed to him as soon as the real treasure had been found – by me."[3]

" You'll excuse me," put in Sir Charles, " but there's just one practical question that seems to me pertinent. Does Mr. Bredon mind telling us where the treasure is now ? For I suppose I'm part owner of it."

" The gold is, I suppose, where I left it, at the bottom of the river. The cord will mark where it lies, though you'll need a boat-hook or something to fish it up with. The jewels were snatched up last night by Henderson, just before he fell into the river ; perhaps Leyland here has news of them."

" Yes," said Leyland, " the bag was found with the corpse, and it's at the station now. Congratulate you, Sir Charles."

It was some time before Bredon could resume his exposition. " Henderson was naturally furious when he found the treasure gone, but not altogether sur- prised. He jumped to the conclusion that Lethaby had found out his secret, had shammed asleep, and had

---

[1] p. 114.   [2] p. 161.   [3] p. 129.

carried off the treasure while he, Henderson, was fooling about in the garage. What was he to do ? To reappear meant forgoing all the advantages of a reputed death, meant also that he would come in for some peculiarly awkward explanations. There was only one thing he *could* do – he ran back to the garage, before you, Angela, had noticed the flames, and locked the garage door after all. He was putting a noose round Lethaby's neck, which gratified his angry mood ; he was also ensuring, he thought, that Lethaby would be watched, so that he could not dispose of the treasure, and that he would leave the island before long, perhaps in custody. Then Henderson's turn would have come to regain the treasure.

" As a matter of fact, things didn't go so easily. Scottish law has a verdict of Not proven ; and therefore a Procurator Fiscal distrusts circumstantial evidence even more than an English coroner. Lethaby was immobilised, but not cleared out of the way. During those last three days Henderson has been living on the island, dividing his time, I should suppose, between the woods and the wood-shed, picking up stray meals from Lethaby's pantry, watching every movement of Lethaby's, and going over every inch of ground for signs of the missing treasure. The island has plenty of cover ; and Henderson, I've no doubt, has been accustomed before now to a rather varied life in the great open spaces."[1]

" Yes," admitted Leyland, " there's very little Henderson hasn't done."

" And now," said Bredon, " began a most extraordinary game of cross-purposes, a three-cornered game played by Henderson, Lethaby, and me. Henderson thought Lethaby had got hold of the real

[1] p. 50.

treasure, and was waiting for some false move of his to betray its whereabouts. He alone knew the secret of the corpse, and of the locked garage. Lethaby couldn't understand these, and knew nothing about the existence of the real treasure. He genuinely thought that Henderson was dead. Consequently it was no use my setting traps for Lethaby, because he had, so far as the matter in hand was concerned, a perfectly clear conscience. I, meanwhile, idiotically went on thinking that Lethaby had been in the full plot, and was inclined to believe that he had really murdered Henderson. And what made matters worse was that Henderson, who was lurking about on the island all the time without my knowing it, kept on springing the traps I had laid for Lethaby."

" What sort of traps ? " asked Leyland.

" Well, the other night, Friday night it was, I went round laying a trail of gold pieces on the island, to look as if the treasure had been carted about in a rather leaky bag. This was meant to give Lethaby the impression that Henderson, before he died, had been re-burying the treasure in a new *cache* – probably on the little islet in the middle of the falls. Lethaby, I said to myself, will see those pieces – to make sure, I got Angela to take him for a walk where he was *bound* to see them – and then he'll go treasure-hunting again, and so give himself away. Really, of course, he'd have been utterly mystified if he *had* come across those gold pieces. He didn't, because they'd been removed early that morning. Not , Angela, by Lethaby himself, as we supposed, but by Henderson.

" The joke of that was that, in meaning to make Lethaby think Henderson had stolen the treasure, I made Henderson think Lethaby had stolen the treasure. At least, he already suspected this, but I made him think that the treasure was actually buried on the islet. And it must have given him a nasty shock when he saw you and Lethaby heading that way next morning. In reality, you were leading Lethaby by the nose ; but Henderson must have thought Lethaby was leading you by the nose – that he was going to stage a new discovery, this time of the real treasure. Henderson was hidden in that long bracken just at the top of the ascent, where the steps take you down towards the islet.[1] And he did, in his desperation, a very ingenious thing. When you were both climbing down, Lethaby last, Henderson threw the garage key, which had remained all the time in his pocket, well over the edge of the slope, so that it fell near you. You thought, as he meant you to think, that the key had fallen from Lethaby's pocket. And we both thought, as Henderson meant us to think, that it was Lethaby who locked the garage door, and therefore that Lethaby was a murderer. Whatever became of the treasure, Henderson was determined that Lethaby should hang before he touched a penny of it.

" And last night there was a fresh move in this same game of cross-purposes. To make sure whether Lethaby was a murderer, I wrote a spoof note which looked as if it came from Henderson, suggesting an interview and a fifty-fifty division of the spoils – by which I meant the real treasure. The interview to be held at the spot where the real treasure really was. That note was left in the kitchen over at the island, for Lethaby to find. But Henderson used to take his meals at odd times by raiding Lethaby's kitchen, as I was saying just now ; that is why Mrs. McBrayne was surprised at the spasmodic disappearance of food.[2] And it was Henderson, not Lethaby, who found the note ;

[1] p. 218.   [2] p. 213.

and naturally thought that it came from Lethaby, not from me. He left it where it lay; what reason to remove it, since he thought Lethaby had written it? So Lethaby found it too, and both Henderson and Lethaby kept the appointment. I had thought that I would make Lethaby think he had seen the ghost of Henderson, and I only succeeded in making Henderson think he had seen the ghost of Lethaby. Or at any rate, he found himself surrounded by Lethabys, and plunged into the river, or fell into it, poor devil. I don't know whether he really couldn't swim, but it didn't make any difference, last night.

"Well, that was that. And now Mr. Maclean will have a couple of bodies to bury, though only one tombstone to put up. And you, Sir Charles, will be left to decide the rather ticklish question whether young Lethaby has a right to any share in the real treasure. He didn't find it; or at any rate he didn't find it on the island, and therefore he has no rights in that sense as a tenant. On the other hand, his partner did find it; which gives Lethaby a sort of right to it. On the other hand, Lethaby didn't co-operate in any way in the finding of it; nor was Henderson, when he found it, acting with an eye to the interests of the syndicate. It seems to me that, if you take the thing to law, it will make a very pretty question for a British jury."

"Why, as to that," said Sir Charles, " I'm disposed to let him take his share. You see, it's not as if I was any way financially embarrassed myself. I don't reckon myself a superstitious man, but I'm beginning to think there's a kind of theological moral behind these stories of cursed properties, and whatever comes to me from Prince Charlie's treasure won't go into my own pocket. I've determined to spend it on the good of the district; and the first thing I'll do, after what we've heard, is to build a good, strong, ten-foot wall round the churchyard of Glendounie. But for Lethaby, I dare say he'll be needing money for this and that."

" He'll be wanting a house, for one thing," suggested Mrs. Wauchope. " It's quite certain he's not going to live at Moreton any longer."

THE END

>>> If you've enjoyed this book and would like to discover more great vintage crime and thriller titles, as well as the most exciting crime and thriller authors writing today, visit: >>>

The Murder Room
Where Criminal Minds Meet

themurderroom.com